THE
LINES
WE LEAVE
BEHIND

OTHER TITLES BY ELIZA GRAHAM

THE LINES

WE LEAVE

BEHIND

Eliza Graham

LAKE UNION
PUBLISHING

Text copyright © 2018 by Eliza Graham
All rights reserved.

Published by Lake Union Publishing, Seattle

www.apub.com

Amazon, the Amazon logo, and Lake Union Publishing are trademarks of Amazon.com, Inc., or its affiliates.

ISBN-13: 9781503903838 (hardcover)
ISBN-10: 1503903834 (hardcover)
ISBN-13: 9781477805152 (paperback)
ISBN-10: 147780515X (paperback)

Cover design by Emma Rogers

Cover photography by Gabriel Martinez

Printed in the United States of America

For Brona

PART ONE

1

They don't like me using anything sharp at mealtimes, so someone has given me a blunt, round-tipped knife that looks as though it's come from a child's cutlery set. I attempt to cut a piece of mutton and the blade bounces against its hard surface. The chunk of meat shoots across the table. Jim and I try hard not to laugh.

Lunch is usually a civilised affair. White tablecloth. A vase of daffodils, sweet peas or roses, depending on the season. But the crockery is a clunky set, not porcelain. You notice the difference when someone clinks a fork against a plate: the sound is duller, thicker. Like post-war life itself. The food has a leadenness, too, but it's not bad, especially if there's fruit. A bowl of raspberries with even the very smallest dollop of cream on it makes a meal into a feast, but it's too early in the season for that.

Apart from my mishap with the blunt knife we all get through lunch fairly well, with no disturbances or interventions. Ingrams looks relieved as he takes out a tray laden with bowls. He returns with the coffee, which they prefer to serve at the table. In the old days, they'd probably have taken it to the conservatory. We're lucky to have someone like Ingrams: he's so strong and fit he should probably be in a heavy manufacturing job. I don't know if he served in the war; we tend to skirt that subject. 'Our little family has quite enough to be getting on with,' Jim will say if he feels the conversation is steering in that direction.

It may be different behind the green baize door on the first floor, but on our side we try to be civilised. We dress with care: no floppy, drab dresses for me. I usually put on a dab of lipstick for meals. Once a week a girl comes to the house to do my hair. I wish I could shave my legs so I didn't have to wear the thick stockings more suitable for an elderly woman, hopeless in such warm weather. I'd love to go shopping and buy myself light silk or nylon stockings, if they're available. I'm only twenty-three, for God's sake. I'm not like those others. At least, I hope I'm not. I pray I retain the distinct edges of my personality and am not blurring into a shadow of myself.

After we've drunk the coffee in the clunky cups and saucers that match the lunchtime crockery, we like to go outside, weather permitting. Since 1939 the gardens have largely been given over to growing food, but there are still flowers. The last tulips are putting on a brave show of yellow and white and the wisteria is at its best. A rose bush by the lawn is already covered in early blooms the colour of amber. The colour of me. I am two people, because some days I feel like Amber and sometimes Maud. Sometimes amber contains petrified insects, doesn't it? Something inside me has been frozen, too. I wish I knew what I contained and how to extract it.

I shake myself out of the reverie and notice that Ingrams is setting up a badminton net on the lawn. 'Fancy a game?' Jim brandishes a racket. He's good at encouraging me to try things. Under his tutelage I am now learning bridge in the evenings after dinner. I attack the shuttlecock as though it's an enemy missile, smashing it back with interest.

'A new talent?' Jim asks, retrieving the battered item from the flowerbeds. 'Or did you play in the past?'

Did I play badminton as Maud? Or was it Amber? No, it's definitely Maud who remembers that particular scent of a racket when you take it out of its press after a winter in a cupboard. Tennis, not badminton. I played on damp grass courts at school and then again, somewhere hot, where aromas, good and ill, wafted round us. Where was that place? I know I have already remembered its name, mentioned it to Dr Rosenstein. I lapse into one of my silences. Jim watches me with his sympathetic smile. 'Want a break? There's lemonade.'

Ingrams has laid it out on a little garden table. One of the glasses has a thicker rim than the others, I can't stop noting. *Small details may save your life.*

'Almost like old times.' But Jim's hand shakes when he lifts the glass. He's not much older than I am; I think that's why we struck up our friendship. North Atlantic convoy. U-boat attack. Ships sunk. Men, women and children overboard in freezing conditions; the rest of the convoy forbidden to stop to rescue them.

The lemonade's good, if a little too dilute, but that's to be expected, given rationing. I recall the more intense taste of lemonade in a small café somewhere distant where I once drank it with a Jewish girl whose name I can't pull out of my head. The city where we drank it was the same place where I played tennis.

'*Cairo.*' I say it aloud, with triumph, and pull out the small notepad and pencil I keep in my pocket at all times in case of sudden recollections. Once the place-name is written down it can't disappear again.

I look around to see if my exclamation has startled anyone. Not that people here are over-sensitive to others talking to themselves. Jim has floated off to help the others, who are weeding the rockery. I'd like to help too but Ingrams isn't keen because of the trowels, hoes and forks. My mother used to encourage me to work in the garden. Perhaps she could write and ask if I might help with something that doesn't involve blades or tines. In the meantime, nobody minds me wandering along the old wall, pulling out shoots of sticky willy from the honeysuckle bushes and checking for bindweed. I reach the dovecot on the lawn, at a slight distance from the wall and trees so it is safe from cats. The dovecot belongs to Woodlands, not to me personally, but it's become mine in the last few weeks. A previous patient took the doves through the homing procedure. Now they fly in and out of the dovecot at will, always returning to roost.

I keep a little stepladder propped up against the wall near the dovecot. When I'm on the top step I can look into the doves' living quarters. Two pairs are out of the dovecot, somewhere around in the trees. One pair is inside, bright black eyes peering out at me.

When I've stacked the stepladder away I check the bird bath and table for water and food, even though I have already come out here before breakfast.

Later in the summer we'll have raspberries, strawberries and blackcurrants. I wonder whether the doves will make themselves a nuisance by eating the fruit? We might have to net the bushes. Apples and pears will follow the soft fruits in the autumn. I'm starting to hate the tinned peaches that have featured in so many meals for so long now. Sometimes, if I stack plates and bring them out to the kitchen to help, I see the large catering cans on the shelves, packed by women on a canning line in a faraway Southern US state. Ingrams ushers me out if he sees me looking at the tins.

This stay has gone on for such a long time now. Perhaps they'd let me go to my parents for a short visit. That's sometimes allowed. Thinking about my parents makes me feel as if syrup from the peach cans is oozing through my brain, sticking all the memories and emotions together. I glance over to the others. Jim's stopped gardening and is now juggling three old tennis balls he keeps in a cracked flower pot. He aims to get to five within the next month. His face is tight with concentration. Perhaps I should try to juggle.

I go upstairs to my room for some quiet time before tea.

On the landing a man stands beside the green baize door on the left. They must be coming out for their afternoon walk. I turn right. I'm not like them. I just need to remember.

Nobody follows me as I walk down the corridor to my own room. I can open my own bedroom door but, once I'm in, it closes behind me and can't be opened from the inside. It's too quiet. I open the windows and the voices of the gardening group reach me through the safety bars. Since the war I seem to need sound.

I can feel my monsters stirring, crawling along my blood vessels, flexing their muscles, making my legs and arms restless. I look at my watch. Too early. I pace round and round, picking up books, magazines, my hairbrush. My body still does not feel entirely mine. 'I miss something,' I told Dr Rosenstein at the last session. 'It's making me feel so unsettled.'

'I know,' she said. 'But you need to uncover for yourself what you're missing and why.'

'Can't you just tell me?'

She looked at me with those kind eyes. 'You need to go through the process.'

Perhaps it would be better to ring the bell and ask if I can be let out again and wait in the garden. But that would be showing a weakness.

At times you will find it very hard to stick to your new persona. You will struggle.

I could write in my notebook, but I can't work out what I want to say. I need to do something, though. They've let me bring some of the books from the library up here, mainly old atlases. I open a *Times* atlas from the middle of the last century and turn to the map of the Adriatic and Balkans, just to the east of Italy, across the Adriatic Sea, and to the north of Greece. My finger traces the outline of a country that didn't exist in the nineteenth century, or indeed until after the Great War: Yugoslavia.

Future Yugoslavia's territories are mostly divided between the old empires of the Austro-Hungarians and the Turks, though the Italians and others claimed parts of it too. I close the thick pages, which seem almost heavy with history, taking out a more modern equivalent, published just before the Second World War. It gives the country the name of the Kingdom of Yugoslavia and shows its constituents: Slovenia, Croatia, Bosnia, Serbia, Macedonia, and Montenegro. So many bits and pieces of territory, invaded, occupied, cut up between powers. *Balkanisation*, that's what they call the fragmentation of countries: a pejorative term, implying splitting into competing and opposing pieces. Just like me, really: I have Balkanised my own psyche. Bits of me are at war against each other.

I push the atlases aside, jittery, thoughts pulsing through me like electric shocks.

Somehow the minutes pass and I hear the clink and rattle of the drugs trolley coming down the corridor towards my door.

I can never be sure what Dr Rosenstein will require of me. In our first session she asked me to identify some strange ink blobs. I didn't know her then and so I simply told her what I thought a rational and sane person would say. I didn't tell her that the blob that was probably a butterfly actually reminded me of an aircraft on fire.

The next morning, as always, Dr Rosenstein asks if I have dreamed and I tell her I can't remember any dreams, even though I keep my writing pad and pencil on my bedside table so I can write them down if they occur. She expresses no surprise and suggests we talk about the person I was before Robert found me. We've already talked about my childhood, so this is the next step. 'You told me that the Blitz was the start of what you called grown-up freedom?'

'I was still only sixteen, supposed to be at boarding school, but I somehow managed to persuade my mother to let me go to one of the few remaining girls' schools near our house in West Kensington. Easy to say I was with friends and sneak out with them instead of going down into the shelters.'

'Where did you go?'

'Cinemas. Nightclubs, if we could get hold of make-up and evening dresses—' I pause. 'I wasn't so keen on them later on. I grew out of that scene, I suppose. But I was in a nightclub in London when I met . . . him for the first time.' I can't quite bring myself to say his name. Dr Rosenstein's expression takes on more intensity. 'That was much later on. The Blitz had ended. I'd finished school and was working. My parents had left the city by then.'

'Can you remember when exactly that was?'

It's in my brain, my trained brain. 'It was 1943, the last weeks of summer or perhaps even early autumn.' We knew the war was building up to an invasion at some point. 'He appeared from nowhere.' My life had felt stagnant; I was no longer in such danger at nights and I almost missed that.

'I wonder how he came to know about you? That you spoke Serbo-Croat? That you had the attributes that would make you good at . . . the kind of work he was offering?'

I've wondered all these things myself. 'I don't know.' My head is a tangle of threads. I close my eyes for a second to see if I can disentangle the strand linking me to the person I was when Robert and I first met: that muddled, immature girl I was before I became Amber.

2

Maud drained the glass and replaced it on the smeared table. Her cigarette box was empty. She tried to catch Peter's eye, but he was playing
some game involving flipping playing cards off the edge of the table and
betting on the way they would land on the floor.

Really, all she wanted was to go back to her own flat. And sleep.
She couldn't turn up late to work. Dr Farish was kind but he did need
a receptionist who turned up before the patients and without nursing a
headache. He'd told her today that she had been the most reliable girl
he'd employed and had the most unusual ability to recall details. Or had
that been yesterday? She squinted at her watch.

The doctor had been referring to her strange memory for names
and ailments and insignificant details about patients: the names of their
cats and dogs and distant relatives – details she picked up while not even
meaning to listen in to waiting-room conversations. She was also adept
at mending the surgery's decrepit equipment. 'I've always been good
with machines,' she'd told him. 'Used to fix the wireless set. Sometimes
even my father's car.'

Peter scooped up a card from the sticky dance floor, caught her eye
and beamed at her. Obviously a good night's sleep wasn't what he had
in mind. She should end the relationship, really. He was no longer on

operations, which would have made ditching him bad form; he was training for bombers now. Judging by the attention he was receiving from some of the other women here, Peter wouldn't be alone for long. She could take a short holiday, visit her parents in Shropshire . . .

A hand landed on Peter's elegant shoulder. An older male's hand, weathered, tanned. 'Old man.'

The scraping of Peter's chair was audible above the band, his normal off-duty lethargy swept away by the appearance of this stranger. He was wearing uniform, but she couldn't quite work out his rank. A chair was produced for Robert, for that was the newcomer's name. Unusual for them not to refer to him by surname or some dreadful nickname; it felt in some sense deferential. Robert spoke mainly to Peter at first, before switching to chat with the rest of the group as if he'd known them all for ever. A bottle of champagne and fresh glasses appeared on the table. Maud sat up. Her drowsiness seemed less enveloping. Robert seemed to be one of those people who could draw conversation from a table of tired, inebriated revellers. The other women seemed redder-lipped, brighter-eyed as he talked to them. The men began to tell self-deprecating jokes and sat up straighter.

Robert-whatever-his-name asked her to dance. Her first impression had been correct; he was a little older than the other men at the table. He wasn't matinée handsome like Peter = his eyes were too hooded – but he had a presence and danced well, with a controlled energy and precision, asking her the usual questions about herself and what she did.

These days everyone had to do something. She told him about her job, admitting that it wasn't very interesting. 'The last receptionist left for the Wrens.'

'Why'd you get into it in the first place?'

Maud concentrated on a flaking piece of paintwork on the wall over his shoulder. 'Couldn't think of anything else I wanted to do and thought I'd be good at it.'

Frankly, any woman, even someone older with kids, could do her receptionist job. But perhaps nobody else could do the extras, such as mending the spirometer. Sometimes the only way to get through the day was to play secret little games with the patients, memorising random facts about each one. *Mrs Bates's younger son has a kitten called Heinz, but he's worried it sounds too Kraut so they're changing it to Harry. Mr Kidd's daughter, Janice, wanted her husband to try for the RAF, but he defied her and signed up for the army.*

'Well, tell me what you can do.' Robert swung her gently around a pillar, missing the drunk naval officer and his dance companion who were swaying in front of it.

Maud listed her academic achievements.

'Anything else?'

Her way with mechanical objects. He said nothing.

'I can speak a bit of German,' she said, trying harder now. But so could many people. Robert's smile told her as much.

'Might be useful later on in the war,' he said. 'If we ever get to invade them.' His grip on her tightened. 'But perhaps girls like you are most useful in keeping the men going.' He glanced at Peter. She'd had a lot to drink but not so much that she couldn't flush more deeply. His hands felt too warm on her waist and shoulder.

'I think I'd like to sit down now,' she said. He steered her towards the bar. A glass of brandy appeared.

'No need to feel you're not pulling your weight, Maud,' he said, lighting a cigarette with his left hand.

She put down her brandy. 'Doctors have to see sick people and they need help managing the appointments and—'

'I'm sure you do your bit.'

She'd actually liked this man at first. 'I speak fluent Serbo-Croat as well as German,' she told him. 'I didn't mention it because it's such an obscure language. And a smattering of Hungarian.'

He raised an eyebrow.

'My mother is a Croat. She also taught me the Hungarian.' Mama had grown up in an Austro-Hungarian territory that was now part of Croatian Yugoslavia. Maud felt weary again. She looked around for Peter and spotted him talking intently to an over-made-up woman who'd come to sit beside him at the table. Robert started talking about films. Maud was too tired to keep up the annoyance so she let him go on about cinemas he liked to go to, restaurants that still served decent food. Holidays.

'Not that we'll be having many of those in the foreseeable, but I did love Greece.'

'I've never been.' She hoped he could hear the coolness in her tone.

'There's nothing like the Balkans.'

'Actually, I know the Balkans further north,' she said. 'My father was director of a British mine in Kosovo Province in Serbia. We lived with him there for a few years. In the summer we went to the Dalmatian coast, usually to one of the islands, a very small one near Dubrovnik.'

The fug of the nightclub fell away. Maud could smell the aromatic sharpness of the trees, see the light bouncing off the sea, hear the waves lapping on the shingle. Her father had bought her a canoe and they spent summers on the water, paddling around the shorelines, sometimes fishing and building small fires to cook fish on the beaches. They'd stayed in an old merchant's house set back from the harbour on the island. Mama would be complaining of boredom within a few days, but Maud had relished every hour, from the moment of waking up to see the blue light flitting through the white shutters in the morning, to the starry nights sitting on the harbour trying to make friends with the local cats.

'I can see you loved it there,' he said, seeming softer. She found herself opening up as he asked her more questions. Peter had never seemed that interested in her family. Robert asked her more about her mother and she told him about Mama and how she'd grown up in Croatia and Bosnia, and had actually been in Sarajevo one June morning when a maid had rushed home from an errand to tell the family that Franz Ferdinand had been shot. Robert leaned forward as she spoke, nodding occasionally, those hooded eyes on her face. They were a grey colour, quite unusual, almost hypnotic when they were focused on you. She'd never told this story to anyone else before.

'One day you'll tell your grandchildren about your direct link to the day the world changed forever.' For a moment they sat, eyes locked. Robert became matter-of-fact again, talking to her about Yugoslavia and its struggles even before the Germans and Italians had invaded. 'Croats and Serbs fighting on different sides in the Great War, then shoved together to form a new state that could barely hold itself together and has now been carved up by its invaders.'

'Poor Yugoslavia.' She hoped she didn't sound maudlin. Maudlin Maud. She still missed the country, could close her eyes and remember the little house near the mine where they'd lived. When they'd sent her to boarding school over here, she'd sat on the lawn looking at the flowers and remembering the neat flowerbeds at that house at Trpca mine. Robert seemed to know about the mine, which was rare. Other than the geography teacher, nobody at school really had the faintest idea where Kosovo was or that there were all kinds of mineral deposits there. Nobody cared about the mines or the importance of the lead. And nobody else in the whole of England seemed to speak Serbo-Croat. Sometimes she'd lie under the starched sheets in the dormitory at night and murmur a few words to herself in the language just for the pleasure of hearing them.

'You're looking awfully thoughtful, Maud.' Peter was standing behind her. 'Time for home, I think.'

She stood up. 'I'm tired. Work tomorrow.'

'Don't look so thrilled at the prospect, darling.'

Robert stood up, too. 'Perhaps something better will turn up.' With an almost continental small bow he left them. Strange how he had hardly even said goodnight properly after he'd spent so much time talking to her.

'How did you come to know that man?' she asked Peter.

His smooth, fair features showed a rare consternation. 'It might have been before the war. Newmarket? Cheltenham?' She could see him puzzling over peacetime race meetings. 'Strange,' he said at last. 'Robert's that kind of chap, very easy to talk to. But when you try to work out where and when you first met, it's impossible.'

3

May 1947

'Do you ever speak Serbo-Croat now?' Dr Rosenstein asks when I've finished talking to her about the nightclub where I met Robert. 'To yourself, of course, as nobody here speaks it, I imagine.'

'No. It feels locked up inside me. I know the words are still there, but I can't reach them.'

She consults the watch she keeps out on her desk. 'We will shortly need to bring this session to an end for this week, but we have time for you to tell me about the next occasion you met Robert Havers.'

Hearing his full name has made my heart start pounding. I might ask her if we could stop now, but I won't. I've been trained to press on, even when my nerves are screaming at me to stop. *You have been chosen because you are the kind of person who can carry on when others would give up.*

'Maud?' She peers at me. 'Would you prefer to stop for now? You can write it down first if that's easier for you and tell me next time?'

I want Dr Rosenstein to approve of me. I push my shoulders back. 'I'm fine. Robert just appeared again from nowhere. I don't think I actually told him where the doctor's surgery was, but I suppose it wasn't that hard to track me down.' Not for a man of Robert's capabilities.

'Tell me what you can.' Dr Rosenstein leans back in her chair. 'I don't need details that might compromise security. It's the relationship between the two of you we need to examine next week. It was later on in 1943, wasn't it?'

'Early September.'

Peter was away training somewhere in Lincolnshire. It was almost a relief to have him gone. Quiet nights in felt restorative, despite the cramped conditions in the flat she shared with two other girls. There'd been no raids for a while now and she'd seen all the films at the local Regent, so she spent her evenings doing crosswords and mending a flatmate's broken torch.

Robert approached her one rainy lunchtime, as she stood, ration card in hand, outside a grocer's shop, weighing up the likelihood of finding a filling for a sandwich she could make in the little kitchenette attached to Dr Farish's surgery.

'Do you like Italian food, Maud?' he asked without preamble, his hooded eyes reminding her of a raptor's. 'You probably only have, what, a couple of hours before afternoon surgery starts?'

She blinked. Where had he sprung from?

'An hour and a half.'

'Let's not hang around then.'

All of the reasons why she really didn't want to have lunch with this man came to mind but seemed to trip over one another before she could articulate them.

Robert was brisker today, almost marching her across the road to Holborn Tube station. She didn't like to ask questions while they were sitting in the carriage with other people. It was only when they were in a road off Wardour Street at a table with a Chianti-bottle lamp and he'd ordered them both an off-ration game-and-herb stew and a carafe of house red wine, that he asked more questions. Exactly how much of her Serbo-Croat did she recollect? What had been her favourite lessons at school? How fit was she?

As she ate the stew – thick and aromatic – the questions became more peculiar. Did she enjoy her own company? How did she solve problems, such as, for instance, the telephone line at the doctor's surgery going down? A patient demanding to be seen right away?

Maud sipped her wine and answered, feeling half-embarrassed, half-annoyed. 'Why are you asking me all these things?'

'Let's just say I am talking to you on an official basis.' He topped up her glass. His voice today was more clipped than it had been in the nightclub.

'How do I know who you are?'

The identity card flashed underneath her eyes almost before she'd asked the question. She caught sight of his rank and something to do with intelligence. He removed a silver card case from his inside pocket and passed her a card. It gave his name, but no rank, and a telephone number was engraved on it with a second name added in pencil. 'That's Scotland Yard's switchboard number. Ask to be put through to that inspector. He'll confirm my identity. You're sensible to be cautious.'

'You work for the police?'

He smiled. 'Definitely not. Scotland Yard doesn't always approve of people like me.'

She answered more questions while eating the marinated pears served for pudding. 'Do certain things stay in your memory, do you think, Maud? More than they do in other people's?'

She told him about her strange ability to recollect minor details about Dr Farish's patients.

'That must be very useful.' He topped up her glass again. She hoped she wouldn't feel too sleepy in the surgery that afternoon. 'People like it if they think you take enough of an interest in them to remember bits and pieces like that.'

'Sometimes they find it a bit weird,' she said.

'I imagine they would. But what about other things? Do you notice things on your way to work? A schoolboy wearing a different coloured cap? Milk bottles placed on the other side of a doorway from normal?'

She blinked. *The number of paving stones between the front door and the Tube entrance.* 'What's so weird about that?' She knew she sounded aggressive. How had Robert known?

'I bet you used to win parlour games, didn't you, Maud?'

She scowled at him. 'I'll need to be getting back to the surgery soon.' She looked at her watch. Twenty-five minutes and thirty seconds to get back for afternoon surgery. Robert was watching her.

'There's enough time,' he said. 'Five minutes to the Tube station.'

'There should be a train within eight minutes.' The service didn't run as frequently these days. 'Less than a minute between Covent Garden and Holborn. Then about three minutes to walk to the surgery,' she said. 'And then three minutes to unlock the door and hang up my jacket before the patients start arriving.' It ought to be enough time but she didn't want to risk it. Sometimes people looked at her a bit strangely when she gave detailed answers like this. Since the war had started, precision mattered more though. How long would it take to reach a shelter? How many vouchers would you need to buy the ingredients for a meal? 'I need to go now.' She stood up. 'Thank you for my lunch.'

Robert smiled at her and she almost forgot how rude he had been. 'You see, Maud, I think you're utterly wasted on sore throats and lumbago and mending radios and torches.'

He nodded at the waiter. 'I think your attention to detail and your ability to stick to a task make you someone who might be interested in another line of work altogether.' He stopped talking as the bill was presented and settled. As they headed for the door he continued. 'I must admit your languages interested us originally. We were worried when we heard you were known as a little eccentric.'

'Who said that?' She heard the indignation in her tone. But it was true.

'Can't tell you. I'm afraid.'

Probably Doctor Farish, then. Or one of her flatmates.

'But those we spoke to also said that you were an unusual and striking young woman.'

She knew she wasn't like other girls. As for being pretty, well, sometimes people thought you were being vain if you were honest about knowing you were attractive. Maud didn't think she was vain, though. Her own looks: hazel eyes and dark blond hair, with a skin tone half a shade darker than most English girls, were something to protect and conserve, in the way her mother had taught her: proper cleaning and moisturising at night. But physical attractiveness wasn't commendable in the same way as, say, training in self-mortification like a medieval anchoress. She'd explained all of this to Peter once and he'd burst into laughter. 'Darling, you are simply unlike any other girl. What the hell's an anchoress?'

'I think you could do something very useful for the war effort, Maud,' Robert said in a warmer tone than he'd used during lunch.

'What do you mean?' He escorted her to the station entrance before answering, though what he said wasn't really an answer at all.

'Are you good at getting people to trust you, Maud? Can you persuade them to do things?'

She thought. The old lady who hated the medicine Dr Farish prescribed and usually refused it. Hadn't she been able to get her to keep taking it? Dr Farish had asked how she'd done it. She'd answered that she had told the old lady that she owed it to her poodle to keep well so she could exercise him. She related the story to Robert. He examined her, eyes half-closed as he walked, as though this would bring her more into focus.

'We'll be in touch.' He held out his hand. When she put hers in it, his grip made her blink. She caught the scent of his wool overcoat and the cotton of his shirt and something else, a lower tone beneath them, almost woody. For a moment she felt almost giddy.

When Maud returned to the surgery she couldn't stop thinking about him, puzzling over him, really. Or over her own reaction to him. Meeting good-looking men was a pleasurable enough occurrence, but she didn't usually brood over them like this. Robert wasn't all that handsome. His manners were sometimes questionable; he certainly didn't have Peter's sweetness about him. Robert wasn't sweet at all. And he was old, probably nearly thirty. Strange that he was exciting her attention like this. Perhaps it was because he had the power to offer her the prospect of doing something more interesting than booking in patients and apologising for surgery running late. Maybe this was what was appealing about him.

A new job, a new start to show herself and everyone else what she could do. That was the cause of this flush of excitement. Robert hadn't even told her that she'd see him regularly if they took her on. Perhaps he was just the recruiter. He hadn't really told her much about his role.

This thought was a cold clamp over her excitement. He hadn't actually promised very much and it might all come to nothing.

So be it. Maud went into the consulting room to change over the hand towel before afternoon surgery.

'I don't even like him.' She hadn't meant to say the thought aloud and it sounded unconvincing, even to her. Maud found herself examining her features in the small mirror over the basin. Her face was flushed – probably the wine at lunch. But her eyes had a wide-open, disbelieving expression like that you often saw on people who'd been caught up in bad air raids. 'And if I do like him, so what?'

The black surgery telephone rang in reception. Maud blinked. Time to stop talking to herself, before the doctor came back and caught her babbling away like an idiot.

I'm drained when I finish telling Dr Rosenstein all of this, even though we haven't even got to the meaningful bits. Perhaps it's all meaningful, though, if you know what you're looking for.

Dr Rosenstein stands up. 'You've done well, Maud. Keep writing down what you remember. Rest now.'

Rest. Exercise gently. Eat slowly. Sip a small sherry before lunch. As though I were a convalescent.

Not for the first time the enormity of my situation hits me. 'Why aren't I in prison?'

There wasn't ever a trial, just visits from lawyers and doctors and injections of various kinds. I was in a hospital bed, waking up, feeling as though something momentous had happened, that I had lost part of myself. Then I fell asleep again. I think they gave me another injection. I remember waking up to find myself in a pack, the cold, wet sheet that wraps round you and pins you to a hospital bed, restraining all movement, my breasts sore where they were crushed.

I recall people muttering about the Home Secretary signing something. Bypassing the criminal justice system, perhaps because of my war record?

'There seems to be no interest in bringing you to trial,' Dr Rosenstein says. 'Your solicitor will keep you informed.'

I have a solicitor? I wasn't aware of this. My parents must have found one for me. I imagine poor Mama begging my father to sort this out, assuring him that there must be some mistake, that I couldn't possibly be capable of such an attack. My father will be fretting silently, writing letters to anyone he can think of, perhaps even the doctor who employed me to be a receptionist in the war, before Robert found me. Mama and Dad haven't been to see me here, yet; though I remember them coming when I was first arrested or certified insane or whatever it was happened to me. 'We need to get you to remember the whole series of events,' Dr Rosenstein says. 'We're making good progress.' Her eyes flicker to the photograph of her daughter as a baby that sits on her desk beside the telephone. I like the way that she allows her patients to have this little glimpse of her child, that she lets us see her as a mother as well as a professional.

When I leave Dr Rosenstein, Ingrams is waiting for me and leads me through the garden. It's one of those May mornings that are almost too perfect to be real: fine weather, unusually warm, but the garden full of golden-green light and the colour of the blossom and flowers. I feel a pang as we pass through the side door and through the dining room into the main hall and stairs, but I know it's best to rest and reflect, as they put it at Woodlands, after my session. At the top we turn right, to the south wing of the house. 'This is where the lady of the manor would have her rooms,' I tell Ingrams. 'Though in a very hot summer, she might move to the north wing.'

'You know more than I do about the history of the house.' Ingrams's accent is that of south London.

'I like looking at the old documents in the library.' They let me read the old books and family papers. It's a harmless enough occupation.

'I like hearing you talk about it.' Ingrams is a kindly sort.

'You see the way the floor level rises?' I ask him. 'That's because this part of the house is Queen Anne whereas the original building is older, Elizabethan.'

'So old.' Ingrams looks impressed. 'You told me the house was shelled during the Civil War?'

'That's why this part was rebuilt. It could have been worse. One son was a Roundhead. There's no portrait of him, probably because a lot of the Roundheads were Puritans and disliked vanity. The other was a Cavalier – that's his portrait.' I nod at a young man dripping feathers and velvet, 'The family saved their property by dividing their loyalties.' That's the conclusion I've reached from reading the archive materials.

Ingrams frowns. 'Sounds a bit devious. As though they couldn't make up their mind what they believed in.'

We've reached my door. 'It saved them all ending up on the wrong side, the house completely lost to them.'

'All the same, brother against brother. That's harsh.'

'Very harsh. Especially for the mother.'

'The mother?'

'I'm just imagining how she might have felt,' I say. But it's not just imagination. Why do I know that a mother would feel such a split so intensely?

'You'd be a Cavalier, Maud,' Ingrams says, probably trying to keep my spirits up. 'Fancy clothes. Nice jewellery and ringlets.'

I certainly used to love those things. Evening dresses – where *did* I find them in the war? Nightclubs. An officer or two flirting tenderly with me: Lydia Bennet in the blackout.

We've reached my bedroom. 'Must have been hard for that Civil War family.' Ingrams is still frowning. I like the way he reflects on things I tell him.

'They made a promise to themselves to do what was best for the family.'

'Dangerous things, promises,' Ingrams says as he unlocks the door.

Especially if you break them. All kinds of promises are made in wartime: promises to be true to a man or a woman, to fight for your country, to keep secrets.

I had to sign all kinds of papers in 1943, even before they told me I had been accepted into the service. I can't describe the details of my work to Dr Rosenstein. She will have to inject me or place those cathodes back on me to make me tell her.

Even from the beginning they made it clear it was all hush-hush.

4

'It goes without saying that this is all confidential. You know what you signed,' the man at the interview told Maud. This was the second time she'd come to the almost airless room in a modern office block on Baker Street. On the first occasion she'd had a very general chat with a man and a woman, unsure what it was they were really trying to get out of her. She wondered if she'd ever see Robert again, half-thankful that he wasn't here this afternoon.

'What's in your head could be your contribution to the war effort: small things that come together,' today's interviewer went on. 'Things you knew about particular places in the past, things you know now, your powers of observation, of persuasion. Of being able to melt into the background at some points and then take control at others. It's only been in the last year or so that we've started training women.'

'Oh.' Maud couldn't think of anything more intelligent to say.

'Do you think you'd be interested in work like this?' the man asked in Serbo-Croat.

'I've certainly never done anything like it before.' Her answer came quite naturally in the same language. 'It sounds interesting.'

'We've heard reports that you're good at observation.'

She nodded.

'And you have parents in this country? Including a Croat mother?'

'That's right.'

'And your mother doesn't feel any divided loyalties? With Croatia becoming a puppet state of the Germans?'

'My mother regards Hitler as a huge pain.'

He looked down at the file in front of him, expressionless. She'd probably said the wrong thing, made her mother sound frivolous, herself too by association. She wished she could read what was written about her. 'Not all Croats favoured the unification with the Serbs after the Great War, did they? Some would have preferred to remain with the Austrians or Hungarians. Your mother wasn't one of them?'

Maud noticed that they were continuing in Serbo-Croat. 'She was happy enough when we lived in Kosovo Province in Serbia. I remember her inviting the Serbian engineers' wives to play cards and tennis at the cottage we lived in.' They'd called it a cottage, and with its red roof and white walls it had a homely appearance, but it had actually been a spacious enough house, with a large garden. She felt a pang at the thought of the cottage. Who lived there now? The Italians had invaded Kosovo first, but now they'd gone. Was some Nazi living in their old home, ill-treating the mine workers and standing out on the terrace at night, admiring the stars and smelling the scent of the last roses of the year, roses Maud's father had planted?

He scribbled something down. 'We carried out some research into the mine and those who worked there.'

So that's how they'd traced her? Had he come looking for her in the nightclub? How had he known she'd be there?

He put the cap on his fountain pen. 'You were schooled over here, Miss Knight, once you'd reached twelve?'

'Yes. My father finished at the mine and then took a job in Belgrade until the war started. Then they moved back here.'

'To . . . Shropshire?' He was scanning one of the sheets. Perhaps any doubts about Mama were outweighed by her having roots in such a solidly rural county. Maud's lips gave an involuntary curl. The man in front of her – he hadn't given her a name – looked at her enquiringly. She told him what she was thinking.

He looked at her emotionlessly. 'Do you like country life yourself, Miss Knight?'

She hesitated, reluctant to sound like a slattern. 'It's relaxing to be in the country and just put on some breeches and boots and wear a scarf round my hair.'

'You like the active life?'

'I enjoy walking in the countryside with my parents. Canoeing off the Dalmatian coast. In Shropshire we go out shooting. Sometimes we ride. I like these things, too.' She'd always enjoyed motion, movement. But there were other times she liked being completely still, dead still, Mama called it, apparently in her own world. She told the man this too, for the purposes of honesty.

He moved on to asking her about her friends. This was an area where she felt vulnerable. There weren't many of them, not other women. She told him this quite openly. 'They seemed to move into war work and do useful things. I don't seem to have as much in common with them now.'

'You didn't volunteer for a uniformed job yourself?'

'I couldn't quite think what I could do.'

'Really? A girl as clever and physically fit as yourself?'

How to explain that she'd felt almost nauseous at the prospect of returning to living and working in close proximity to other women again? School had been bad enough. Had this man or others in his team spoken to her old schoolmates and teachers? They seemed very thorough.

'May I ask you something?' she said. He sat a little straighter, eyebrows raised, but nodded at her to continue.

'How did you know to send R—, your colleague to me?'

He was silent for so long she thought he was going to ignore the question. 'When we wanted to recruit French agents we asked people to send in photographs they'd taken of their holidays in France. Some of the terrain they'd caught in their snapshots was useful. We asked several of the women to come in and talk to us. We were particularly interested in females because they can blend more easily into a civilian background. French is a reasonably common language and people of all backgrounds speak it fluently.' He paused.

'But Serbo-Croat isn't usual at all,' she said. She remembered how she'd whispered to herself in the language at school because there was nobody else other than her mother who could speak it.

'No.' He paused as though to let her know that what he was telling her was more than he would ordinarily tell. 'We examined all the families of British expatriates working in Yugoslavia over the last few years in various areas and industries, finding out how old their children were, where they lived and anything else that was of interest.' He looked down at his notepad. 'There weren't that many names to look at. Because of the nature of . . . the work, we were originally thinking of men, not women.' He folded his arms, making it clear that he would tell her no more. 'We'd actually been interested in the Kosovo mines for some years, reckoning that they might be resources that would eventually catch Hitler's eye.'

'Would I be providing information about the mining industry?' She saw herself sitting with an important Yugoslavian delegate, acting as an interpreter or helping with reports on the capacity lost to the Germans. But why all these interviews and strange questions if this were the case?

'If we take this further you'll find out more.' He stood up and the interview was over. She walked out, still wondering what had prompted Robert to hunt her out in that nightclub.

She hadn't heard anything for another week. The next telegram simply told her that she should make her way by train to a small Surrey town. She would be able to claim expenses and her employer had been informed that she would be absent from work.

'We'd parachute you into Yugoslavia.' Robert Havers smiled at her startled expression. 'If we go ahead with this operation, that is.'

This interview was being held in a draughty house on the outskirts of a Surrey market town. She hadn't seen anyone else waiting to be interviewed. Robert was more solicitous towards her on this occasion, insisting on taking her coat for her. As she handed it over she caught the woody scent of him, very faint, but there all the same. For a moment she felt a return of the giddy feeling. It was simply nerves about this interview, she told herself, nothing to do with this man.

'What is the operation?' Maud rubbed her hands together, wishing she'd kept her gloves on but taken her hat off. Its brim cast a shadow over her left eye and Robert had sat himself slightly to that side across the desk, making it hard to read his expression. Perhaps this was what he had intended. She pushed her chair so it was slanted an inch to the left. Surprise passed briefly across his face.

'You'd go into northern Yugoslavia.'

Into a war zone? On active service? 'I . . .' She put a hand to her throat. 'But . . . How?'

His neutral expression warmed. The change made her feel confused. 'Can't really tell you all the details at the moment.'

Questions bubbled in her mind. 'Would I have to pretend to be Yugoslav?' She was clutching the edge of her chair. Robert leaned back in his own seat, seemingly relaxed. Maud herself felt even more nervous; the air in the room seemed somehow denser.

He shook his head. 'You wouldn't be that kind of agent. You'd be too easily caught out. Yugoslavia's not like France, with a huge civilian population trying to live an apparently normal life under occupation into which you could blend. If you were selected, you'd wear uniform and work alongside the Partisan groups who've started gaining large amounts of Croat territory and need our support.'

She wasn't sure whether wearing uniform would make the work more or less dangerous. 'Partisans?' she asked. 'That's Tito's army?'

She'd read a little about the Partisan leader in the newspapers.

'Yes. He's the best opposition to the Germans at the moment. But the Germans wouldn't necessarily be your only enemy in Croatia.' He paused. 'You've heard of the Ustaše?'

She thought. 'Croat fascists?'

'That's right. With their own militias who share some of the views of their German masters, but are apparently so brutal that even the Nazis complain about them. And then there are the other groups: the Chetniks, in particular, the remnants of the pre-invasion Royal Yugoslav officers. They're mainly Serbs, as Serbia dominated pre-war Yugoslavia, and mostly oppose the German invasion, too. Their leader is a man called Mihailović.' He looked at her sharply as he said the name. She didn't recognise it and said nothing. 'We used to favour the Chetniks, supplied them, carried out missions to meet them. Their war aims seemed to fit our own better than the Communists'.' He paused for a moment.

'But as I said, it seems the Partisans are apparently the ones now killing the most Germans.' Again he looked at her, as though to see how she'd responded to the bit about killing. 'The Partisans and Chetniks hate one another – it's pretty much an extension of the old Croat and Serb antipathy. If you work for us you won't necessarily know who your enemy is until he's shooting you. Do you think you could manage that kind of danger and uncertainty, Miss Knight?' The words were formal, but he was leaning forward, looking almost eagerly at her.

She considered her answer. People sometimes accused her of poring over simple questions and being too literal, but she had the feeling this man valued honesty. 'I think so.'

'And do you think you could help the Partisans kill Germans?'

Kill another sentient being? She didn't even like swatting flies, preferring to open windows and bat them out if at all possible.

'You're giving it careful thought. That's good.' Robert leaned back, looking approving. She felt flustered, yet flattered that she seemed to have pleased him.

'You might have to kill people yourself, though that wouldn't be your prime role. We'd be asking you mainly to pass on information between us and the Partisans about parachute drops and landings.'

How was it that she, Maud, who dealt with appointments and prescriptions, was having this conversation about parachute drops and landings?

'We want to provide them with weapons and other supplies, and encourage them to help us pick up downed Allied airmen and POWs who've escaped from camps in Slovenia.'

'Oh.' She scrabbled around for something less inane to say in response but failed.

'You don't need to tell me your answer now,' he said. 'But you should know that if we pursue your application, there'll be training courses at various locations.'

Had she actually applied for this work? Hadn't they, whoever they were exactly, come looking for her?

'At least two or three courses.'

Perhaps he thought her surprise arose from the variety of training.

'Different sites specialise in different kinds of things,' he told her. 'General fitness. Orientation. Survival skills. Wireless. Surveillance. There's so much to learn. We'll tell you more if we proceed.' Robert stood. 'I need to remind you again that you've signed the Official Secrets

Act. Even if we don't take things further, it may be that we have to . . . deposit you somewhere for a few months.'

Deposit her?

'For security. Just until what I've told you becomes a bit out of date.'

'I really hope I'm successful then, and don't have to be deposited.'

He twinkled at her before switching back almost instantly into his more formal manner. 'Thank you for coming in, Miss Knight.' He stood up. 'The driver will drop you back at the railway station.'

5

Late May 1947

In preparation for my next session with Dr Rosenstein I have written notes in the black notebook. I'm trying to remind myself of how it felt to be interviewed by Robert and the others, and selected for the Yugoslavian operation. I still worry about letting out too much information and say as much as I go into her consulting room.

'Don't worry, Maud, it's the people rather than the operational details that we are focusing on for now. Getting back to Robert Havers, the interviews with him pushed you through a range of emotions?' Dr Rosenstein shuffles the papers on her desk. 'But you're not sure how much of that was to do with the nature of the work and how much of it was to do with Robert Havers himself.'

'It was hard to untangle the personal from the professional,' I tell her.

'From what you've told me, it seems the two of you went through a series of pushes and pulls.'

I look puzzled.

'He turned cool and professional, pushing you away, and then became warmer and more personal, pulling you towards him. Keeping you wondering what his next move would be?'

'At first I thought his manner was part of the interview process. You needed to be adaptable, to handle sudden changes and reversals to do our work. But I don't know.' I put a hand to my forehead. 'I couldn't tell what he was feeling.'

She puts down her papers and flattens the insides of her wrists against the desk, looking at me without saying anything. 'And the switches in his manner continued when you went over to Cairo to finish training?'

'Yes. There were more of us by then, so I thought it might be different. But then he brought in the cake.'

'The cake?' Dr Rosenstein doesn't often exhibit surprise. Her patients must unburden themselves of the most remarkable and appalling things. But now puzzlement is spread all over her face. I really must sound completely paranoid, detecting persecution in the appearance of baked goods. I feel myself smile.

'The cake was the reason why we—' I grow sombre again. 'We were talking about knives; blades, really.' The words stick in my gullet. 'He had to cut the cake and . . . then he showed me how to do it . . . that . . . you know.'

She nods. Of course she knows what I'm referring to.

It's overcast today. Outside Dr Rosenstein's window the light is the colour of ashes. It's cool enough for me to have pulled on a cardigan over my frock. But I can feel the warmth of Cairo. It probably wasn't even that hot. February, when we flew out there: daytime temperatures similar to those of an English summer. But the room in which we were briefed was stuffy and Robert usually turned on the ceiling fan.

Cairo, February 1944

Kassim, the manservant at Rustum Buildings, SOE Headquarters in Egypt, pushed in a trolley on which sat a cake platter, cake slice and plates, along with a white cardboard cake box bearing the famous Groppi name on it. Kassim's face was expressionless – this wouldn't have been the strangest thing he'd seen in these offices. Amber and Naomi looked at one another, puzzlement almost chipping away at the ice existing between them.

Robert was training Amber on one particular matter and Naomi on something rather different. He had been vague at first, merely introducing the two women to one another at a preliminary meeting when they'd first arrived in Cairo, saying they'd be on the same parachute drop. He'd already warned Amber to keep to her new name in Egypt, as any interested party could probably uncover Maud Knight's Yugoslavian background, hinting at the operation in which she was involved. Naomi probably wasn't really called Naomi, either.

Robert opened the lid of the Groppi box. 'Not bad.'

Amber felt her mouth give an anticipatory water. Presumptuous. Robert might decide to eat the entire cake himself in front of them, as some kind of psychological test. During training in England and Scotland she'd already been subjected to strange ordeals like that. *We will build up your expectation that event A will happen, and then present you with event B to see how you react and to train you to be flexible.* She sat up straighter, pulling her navel towards her spine to prevent any embarrassing rumbles. Her stomach muscles were firm, the result of all the PT sessions and cross-country runs she'd undergone before coming to Cairo. She'd maintained her fitness here, too, playing tennis at the Gezira Club most nights. Physical training sessions in a local gymnasium would also be arranged for them, Robert had announced.

Robert carefully extracted the cake from the box. It was a most remarkable shape, not at all like the usual architecturally precise produce of Cairo's most famous café.

'The trouble I had to persuade them to do this.' Robert carefully slid the cake onto the platter and tilted it up so they could see. A trapezium, decorated with random lines and dots of coloured icing, with a wavy, irregular band of blue on the left. *Of course.* Amber smiled. She had it now.

'If Signor Groppi only knew what I was going to do to his confection.'

Naomi let out a brief noise that could have indicated either mirth or exasperation.

Robert picked up the knife with his left hand and cut a sliver of cake from the blue side. 'This was— is, Dalmatia. The coastal part of Croatia bordered by the Adriatic, just east of Italy. The Italians, particularly the Venetians, have long had an interest in the area and they annexed the coast in 1941 when they invaded alongside the Germans. As you know, Italy surrendered last year.' He made a complex series of cuts further into the middle of the cake. 'This is the main puppet Croat state, including most of Bosnia and western Serbia. It does pretty well as its German masters tell it.' He pointed to a jagged shape in the middle of the cake. 'The remnants of Serbia and Bosnia.'

He placed each sliver of cake back on the platter very carefully in the right order. 'Bulgaria took this part of Macedonian Yugoslavia.' A small piece of cake flopped onto its side. Robert eyed it with annoyance. 'Oh dear, it's starting to fall apart now. I wanted to show you what's happening in the north, on the Slovenian–Austrian border. The Austrians took back some of the territory into the Reich, of course. And the Hungarians claimed these territories up in the northeast.' He pointed at the cake. 'Top right. They'd held them before the Great War.' A flicker of interest shone in Naomi's eyes as Robert mentioned Hungary.

He stood back, examining the ruined cake. 'I wanted to show you what had happened around Trieste, near the Italian border, but I don't think even a Harley Street surgeon could make those incisions without this poor cake collapsing entirely.'

Naomi let out a sigh, in appreciation of the cake as an extended metaphor for a fractured Yugoslavia, Amber wondered. Or in impatience?

'Waste not.' Robert offered Naomi the cake platter. After a moment's hesitation she took a bit of Adriatic, complete with a Dalmatian island or two. Amber remembered a day spent in a canoe along that very part of the coast, a picnic on a deserted island.

The men eagerly lined up for slices. They were always hungry. They'd come from Palestine looking well enough nourished as a result of their time on kibbutzim, but they still liked to eat and eat whenever they could. Egypt and its plenty suited them well.

'Amber is looking bored with my little display.' Robert ate a bit of Serbia, including the Kosovo Province, where the mine was. He wiped his hands delicately on a handkerchief.

She knew not to admit that she was remembering the roses her father had once grown in the garden of that Kosovan mine cottage. *You have to lose the past. You are no longer Maud Knight, with all Maud's past. You are Amber.*

'You need a longer knife, sir,' she told him. *When you see me during the day or at other times while we're training, ladies and gentlemen, normal rank applies.*

'A longer knife, eh?' He examined her carefully, pulling a tobacco tin from his pocket. God knows why he still insisted on rolling his own when it was so much easier just to buy cigarettes here in Cairo. There were so many things about Robert that she didn't understand. Perhaps she wasn't meant to. She could have watched him all day long, trying to learn more about him.

He dropped the tin, which was empty and stooped in an instant to pull off the lid, folding it and stamping on it, and swooping up the triangular result. In a single leap he stood in front of Amber and the stamped-on lid had become a dagger pointed at her jugular. She felt her heart lurch. 'At any moment,' he whispered. 'While you're sleeping, while you're eating.' He stepped closer and she could smell his pressed cotton shirt and the slightest aroma of clean sweat. 'While you're fuck-ing some handsome young Partisan.'

Amber concentrated on the cool whiteness of the porcelain cake tray.

He laughed and sounded more like a normal man again. 'Dear me, how rude of me. Amber wouldn't do anything like that, would you, my dear?'

'Is it part of the operation, sir?'

There was a brief spark in his eyes, of something that was possibly closer to approval than she had seen for a while.

'In any case, the Partisans are apparently rather prudish about sex,' he said.

'Anyway,' said Naomi, who was probably prudish, too, Amber conjectured. 'Is there more we need to know about Yugoslavian geopolitics, sir?'

She was intense, this Jewish-Hungarian girl who'd come to Cairo with her male associates from Palestine. But intensity was an attribute that would be demanded of them. Since she'd arrived in Cairo, Amber had felt her own purposefulness ebb somewhat. The warmth after the British winter, the food and drink. And him. Robert. The way he was with her, almost teasing her in a brotherly way at times, then growing cold and critical. She'd try harder: answer more questions. He'd approve for a while, joking with her, placing a hand on her shoulder. Then suddenly he'd switch his attention, sometimes slanting his body away from her.

'You need to know more about Hungary, Naomi. Of course.' He always sounded so reasonable when he spoke to Naomi. It was just Amber who seemed to annoy him. She couldn't work out why she found Robert's shifting mood towards her bothersome. Perhaps if she pretended to herself that she wasn't picking up on it, it would help.

Robert returned the knife to the cake platter. 'I'm afraid the baked goods aren't quite clear enough for our purposes here, so I have a map.' He swept it out from under the desk and attached it to the blackboard in a few easy movements.

'You will land where the cross is.' It was drawn on a wide-bottomed valley in northern Croatia. 'Naomi and the rest of her team will then head to point Y.' Robert pointed at the map. 'Naomi, you'll signal to let us know you've met up with the couriers who will take you over to Hungary.'

For the mission that had not been described to Amber.

'When do we fly out?' Amber asked. He looked at her expectantly. 'Sir,' she added. 'Sorry.'

The apology seemed to soften him. 'Probably next week. To Bari, in Italy.'

Bari: now the centre of Allied military activity in the Adriatic following the invasion of Italy. Amber's heart thumped. It was so close, this operation of theirs, this thing she hadn't even been sure she really wanted to do, certainly not at the stage of the long cross-country runs and endless press-ups and sit-ups. Or during the long, wet, dark nights at Arisaig in the Highlands, carrying out exercises in surveillance and making herself invisible. How had she got from sitting at that table in the nightclub in Mayfair with Peter to being here in Cairo? Peter had vanished from her life so quickly once Robert had made contact with her.

One of these days Maud, now Amber, might find a way to ask Robert some of these questions that flickered through her mind in the rare moments when training and partying allowed them time.

'Amber is daydreaming. Again.' Robert folded his arms.

Damn, damn, damn. Just when she'd thought things were going better.

'Perhaps she already knows the agreed signals the Partisans will leave on the landing site if they cannot greet you because of enemy presence in the area? Or she's happy to risk that bayonet in the small of her back. The ride in the back of the van to the interrogation centre?' His voice was icy.

'Sorry, sir,' she mumbled. 'Two branches crossed over, placed on the eastern side of the landing strip.' It was the first thing that came to mind, but she knew it would be correct. She always remembered details like that. She made herself meet Robert's eyes. Impossible to tell what he was thinking.

'You may find it hard to see in the dark. What else?'

'Password, if anyone approaches.'

'The presence of uniformed women would also be a positive sign,' Naomi said. 'There are very few women on the Chetnik side.'

'Good.' He swallowed another mouthful of cake. 'Not all Chetniks are a problem. You may come across some who offer help. Some of them have rescued downed Allied airmen, but for most Chetniks the interests of Serbia come first, second and last. If that means fighting the Germans, they'll do that. If they think that fighting the Partisans is best for them, that's what they'll do. If it means placating the Ustaše fascists, well, they'll do that.'

Naomi drew herself even more upright at the mention of the Ustaše. Robert propelled himself off the desk and drew down the shutters. Amber nibbled a bit of her cake, wishing her stomach wasn't lurching.

'And some of the Chetniks are furious that we have dropped our support for their monarchist cause. That makes them dangerous. Let's look again at those slides of uniforms.' He nodded at Kassim, who plugged in the electric projector and pulled a white screen into position.

Amber knew the uniforms – it hadn't taken her long to learn their differences. Her mind turned to the mission. So complex, as it had been explained to them since they'd arrived in Cairo, with all its different components: Naomi going on to Hungary with some of her men. She staying with the Partisans along with the others.

Robert had stopped talking and was examining Amber coolly. 'Ustaše cap batches too dull for you?'

'Just thinking about the components of the mission, sir,' she said. Lying got you nowhere with Robert: he always saw through you. 'So many different parts to hold together.' In the light of the projector thousands of dust motes spun around. The room was growing hot despite the electric fan. Amber could smell the photographic slides and the baby powder she'd dusted under each arm. 'My role. Naomi's role.'

'My mission in Hungary is discrete,' Naomi said quickly. 'You do not need to bother yourself with it.'

'Amber will assist your team by encouraging Partisans and other helpful civilians to rescue Jews and pass them on down the line,' Robert reminded her.

'True.' Naomi's eyes seemed to lose a little of their flint as she looked at Amber. Perhaps Amber should move out of the large villa on Gezira Island on the Nile, where Robert had suggested she rent a room. Take a bed in the bedbug-ridden hostel in central Cairo in an attempt to show the Jewish group that she was no softer than them.

'I haven't yet told you about what Naomi and her team will do alongside assisting you, Amber . . .' Robert looked at the other girl. 'Now's the time.'

Naomi looked at him steadily. Amber had to give her credit for being this collected.

'She and Samuel will be going to Budapest to set up resistance groups in advance of a German invasion.'

Amber blinked. The possibility of a German invasion of Hungary wasn't such a surprise – it had been likely for months now, ever since the Hungarians had started discussing an amnesty with the Allies. But organising resistance? That was more than dangerous.

'With particular emphasis on warning Jewish communities that they need to be prepared,' Naomi said.

'We will discuss the weight that should be attached to each component of your mission,' Robert said.

'There's nothing to discuss.' Naomi spoke softly. 'When you recruited us, you told us we'd be helping Jews in occupied or soon-to-be occupied Europe.' The men behind Naomi murmured in assent. 'You trained us in parachuting, signals and sabotage and told us we could save Jewish lives.'

'We will continue this conversation later.' Robert's cheeks were white.

Was he rattled by Naomi's firmness? Amber couldn't think of anything to say that wouldn't have been platitudinous. She hoped her face expressed the admiration she felt.

'Uniforms,' Robert said. 'To return to the subject in hand.'

The door opened and a bald man with a thin moustache, wearing a white linen suit that looked as though it was a size too small, stuck his head around. 'Sorry,' he said. 'Thought the room was empty.'

'I believe Kassim told you it was occupied,' Robert said.

The man wiped his brow and squinted at the slide image on the screen. 'Ah, uniforms. So hard to tell who's who, even when they're wearing them, isn't it?'

'My agents don't think so,' Robert told him.

'I wonder if we can really be entirely certain,' the perspiring man said, stroking his moustache, one side after another. His eyes lit up at the sight of the ruined cake. 'Don't suppose any of that's going spare?'

'Help yourself,' Robert said coldly. 'Macedonia's probably your best bet.' The man took a plate and cut himself a large piece of southern Yugoslavia. Cake crumbs settled in the moustache as he ate and he wiped them out carefully. Something about the way he did this made Amber feel faintly nauseous.

'Don't mind him, he's unimportant.' Robert was already flicking onto the next slide.

'You're so unkind to me, Havers.'

'You're wasting valuable teaching time. Finish your cake, not that you need it, and get on your way.'

The interloper licked his fingers, placed his empty cake plate on the tray and left.

'Now then,' Robert said, 'Slovenian militia groups. Some of them just as likely to cut off your limbs as their cousins in the Croatian Ustaše.'

'So there was an element of violence and danger in your relationship with Robert even at that stage?' Dr Rosenstein asks when I've finished. 'The way he placed the knife at your throat, for instance?'

'It was as though he was pushing me.'

'Yet he tolerated questioning, sometimes even challenging, from Naomi?'

'He seemed to.'

'Tell me more about her? There weren't many other women in the service, were there?'

'Not going where we were going.' I choose my words cautiously, having been careful about how I told the story of the Yugoslavian cake. It's fairly well known that British female agents were sent into France; Yugoslavia was a far less common destination. I haven't mentioned where that X on the map was placed. Dr Rosenstein may guess, though.

'Did being the only women bring you closer to Naomi?'

I consider a patch of wall above Dr Rosenstein's right shoulder. 'No. In fact, I think we really disliked each other at first.' I can almost smile at the memory. 'They sent us for an intensive period of PT to boost our fitness. Things between us deteriorated quickly.'

It had admittedly been a mistake to come out here to train while nursing the worst hangover ever. Robert's group of trainees was in the gymnasium of a requisitioned boys' school on the east bank of the Nile. Amber rubbed her bare arms; Cairo was still chilly this time of the morning. The instructor started them off gently enough, telling them to run at a moderate rate around the walls. Amber could manage this if she kept her gait smooth and didn't change direction too suddenly when she came to the corners. Or so she thought. Her stomach lurched. The lavatories were the other side of the school and the single ladies' cubicle always seemed to be locked. She'd noted some empty terracotta plant pots outside the gymnasium. If things became worse she could perhaps dash out there and . . .

She curved around one corner and heard Naomi sigh. 'You're cheating, cutting off huge chunks of the run.'

'Hardly huge.'

Naomi eased up on her inside as they approached the end of the gymnasium, preventing her from cutting the corner. 'You know what I mean.'

'What's it to you?' For a moment, Amber was fourteen again.

'We're supposed to be a team.'

Amber wanted to say something back, but the nausea returned and she needed to concentrate on breathing through it.

'Stop that chatter, number one and number two.' That was Naomi and Amber. 'I'll have you doing twenty-five press-ups.' The PT instructor scowled at them. 'Number two, you look like something a dog has vomited up. Don't let me see you coming here again in that state. Come to think of it, you and number one will do the extras press-ups anyway. You've obviously got surplus energy if you're both gossiping like a pair of old grannies.'

'Thank you very much,' Naomi hissed as they made their way to the centre of the gym. But she performed her press-ups without too much effort.

Amber found herself lying on her stomach after the tenth, the smell of her own sweat bringing back her nausea. 'Rather be back in bed, number two?' The instructor stood over her. 'You can do five extras for that.'

'If you'd kept your mouth shut that wouldn't have happened,' Amber said to Naomi when she'd finished and they were drinking water before preparing for rope climbing.

Naomi put down her water bottle and scowled at her. 'What time did you go to bed last night?'

'What business is it of yours?'

'We're training for a dangerous operation. If you're not fit enough you could put us in danger.'

'Why don't you concentrate on your own physical fitness and leave me to concentrate on mine?' Amber wiped her brow on her sleeve. She was starting to feel a little better now. Perhaps the stale alcohol had now been violently forced through her circulation, no more to trouble her. Another hour in bed would have been good, though.

To spite Naomi she pulled herself hard up the rope, her biceps aching by the time she had reached the top. Gratifyingly, Naomi couldn't climb as fast as she could, even though she'd probably had a wholesome eight hours' sleep. Well, Naomi could sleep all she wanted. Amber had no intention of not enjoying herself in Cairo. The men certainly did. Why should women have to have early nights and avoid parties just because they were women?

They finished by forming two teams, Amber and Naomi co-opted to opposing sides.

'I know you probably all loved relay races at school.' The instructor smiled at them, looking as though he were about to give them a treat. 'But here's one with a twist – the team that loses will have to run the whole course again. Four-a-side. Two lengths of the gymnasium for each runner. Number one and number two, you can run the last lap.'

Naomi and Amber eyed one another. The first two runners on Amber's side provided a comfortable lead. But the third man slipped as he came round the last corner. He managed to regain his balance but seemed to pull a muscle. 'Sorry,' he muttered as he touched Amber on the shoulder. She was still ahead of Naomi, it ought to be all right. She'd seldom lost a race at school against a girl her age. But Naomi had determination, even though she wasn't a natural runner, and it kept her on Amber's shoulder. One last surge and she'd be free of Naomi . . .

They reached the end of the gym. Naomi was smaller and could turn more quickly. Amber crouched as she approached the wall and spun round. As she did, Naomi's plimsolled foot caught her calf. She tripped. Like her team mate, she avoided falling, but by the time she'd regained her balance, Naomi was a yard ahead. This could not be allowed to happen. Amber pushed herself, closing her eyes for the last little bit, her lungs about to explode.

'Interesting,' the instructor said. 'A dead heat. Perhaps I should make both teams run the whole thing again to produce a winner.'

'You kicked me,' Amber muttered at Naomi.

'I didn't mean to.' Naomi turned her back.

'Number one and number two think they're back at school again.' The instructor observed them. 'Perhaps I should make the pair of them run against one another?'

Amber forced herself to stand up straight and look him in the eye.

'Dismissed, all of you, except number one and number two.' He waved his hands at the men, who shuffled off, looking over their shoulders and laughing at the women.

'You two are supposed to learn the principles of teamwork,' he said. A small vein had appeared on the side of his head. 'I should make you run through the streets until you drop to your knees. But I won't. I'll ask you to think about why you're here and I will report back on this.'

He left them standing together. Reporting back presumably meant he'd be talking to Robert. Amber hung her head.

'If you hadn't turned up in that state this wouldn't have happened,' Naomi said.

'If you weren't such a nagging prude.'

'Listen to yourself.' Naomi picked up a towel. 'People are dying in Europe, but for you it's all just a party.'

Amber wanted to throw something back at her, but what was the point? She dreaded seeing Robert this afternoon. With just a week to go until they left, he wouldn't be thrilled that the two women still did not seem able to work well together. 'It's not a party for me,' she said quietly. As she said the words she realised how true they were. Training, the drop into Croatia, fulfilling her mission, it was about the only thing she'd ever done in her life that had any significance at all. 'It matters.'

'Prove it, then.' Naomi walked away.

Robert said nothing to the women that afternoon when they were back indoors for yet another briefing on German positions in Yugoslavia. Amber made a point of studying the maps intently. Apart from anything else, it was satisfying to see the German army pushed northwards.

'But don't run the risk of believing that the territory you see here as Partisan-held means that it's safe,' Robert told them. 'The Partisans don't have air cover, for instance. They may hold ground that the Germans can strafe and bomb without opposition. And positions change all the time. Most of the important cities are still held by the Germans.' He pointed at the capital, Zagreb, and the other main communication centres. 'But the ability of the Partisans to blow up bridges and important railway links is impressive and important. It has convinced Churchill to switch to supporting the Partisans, despite some opposition to their political objectives. You will find that your *odred*, the Partisan group you work with, probably has a commissar in it, or close at hand, to make sure that communist views prevail.'

When they'd finished, Amber stepped out of the building feeling almost light-hearted. Events this morning had reminded her of being back at school, never entirely fitting in. She'd go for a swim this evening. The pool at the Gezira Club would be cool in the winter evening but would ease her sore muscles. Then she'd have an early night. They were due back in the gymnasium the next morning and she would be there first to wipe that sanctimonious look off Naomi's face.

Amber treated herself to a taxi. None of her housemates were home. She found her costume and took herself the few blocks to the club. Most of the civilian members had abandoned the pool as the temperature dropped, but a few over-enthusiastic young officers were dive-bombing one another.

It was only after she'd swum a number of lengths to ease her limbs that she saw them: Naomi and Robert, sitting at a table together. Naomi wore a sleek, long-sleeved dress that showed off her figure. Robert was pouring her a glass of wine and she was looking at him intently. He said something to make her laugh. Neither of them seemed to have noticed Amber. Robert took Naomi's hand in his, speaking to her more seriously. Naomi nodded. Amber threw herself into an energetic crawl, hands slashing the cold water as though it were the enemy.

'Of course he'd probably followed me in a taxi when I left the offices and seen me emerge with my swimming things,' I tell Dr Rosenstein, staring through a clear patch in the smeared glass that is my memory. 'He drove back to collect Naomi and to tell her to get changed quickly. He wanted me to see them together. He wanted to wrong-foot me.' Dr Rosenstein says nothing. Probably thinks this is all paranoia. 'It's the way he works, keeping you off-balance so you can't predict what might happen next.'

'Did his tactics work?'

'They kept me feeling insecure.' I can feel anger sweep through me, three years on. 'It was a dangerous game. Naomi and I were supposed to be team members, to be able to rely on one another, but somehow he seemed able to play on the things that set us against one another. I could never quite work out how Robert managed it, but he did.'

'He wasn't sleeping with Naomi?'

I blink. 'She wasn't that kind of girl.'

'But you . . . ?'

'I probably was that kind of girl.' Dr Rosenstein shows no disapproval. 'But our relationship hadn't become intimate at that point.' Though I do not doubt that Robert was already planning this next stage. I was always a step behind him, never able to predict what he might do. I hadn't realised just how attracted I'd been to Robert until I'd seen him with Naomi that evening. I wasn't used to feeling jealous; I'd never cared enough about any particular man to mind.

'I tried hard to forget it.' I'd swum until I felt dizzy, almost witless, and dragged myself back to the villa, shivering in the cool air.

'You managed to form a better working relationship with Naomi?'

'Yes. Though I don't think she ever really approved of me.'

Amber appeared outside the gymnasium before the caretaker turned up with his key to unlock it. Appearing five minutes later, the instructor gave her an approving but surprised nod. The others arrived, men from their all-male hostel and Naomi from the women's hostel. Naomi didn't seem to notice Amber as she tightened the laces of her plimsolls.

This morning's session concentrated on self-defence. Amber half-hoped the instructor would pit the two women against one another. There'd be some satisfaction in showing Naomi a thing or two, throwing her down on the floor, perhaps, but he set the women against the men. 'It's unlikely that you would be able to overpower a fit young German soldier or a Chetnik, without an element of surprise,' he said. 'But if you're pitted against a middle-aged Home Guard on night duty, some of these tricks will help you.'

Amber managed to twist Samuel's arm behind him and remove a dagger from Daniel, and let herself relish the looks of surprise on their faces. 'Not bad,' the instructor told her. 'But keep your temper, number two. Remember why you're doing it, to fulfil your objectives.'

Naomi, breathing fast after a bout with one of the men, her face pink with exertion, seemed to freeze momentarily in disagreement. For her combat was always personal, Amber guessed. The two women showered next to one another in silence and took a taxi to Rustum Buildings for the day's briefings, which ended at half-past three.

The men walked to their hostel, just a block away. Amber found herself standing with Naomi outside the building, looking in vain for a taxi. Drops of rain began to fall. Egyptian rain always seemed to have a particularly dense and wetting quality to it.

'Look, let's get some lemonade or tea or something,' Naomi said. 'No point getting wet. I know a café. It's clean. We can shelter for a while.'

Amber blinked. Perhaps she should try a few words in Hungarian with Naomi to show willing. She managed to stutter out a few words. *A drink would be just the thing.* She wasn't sure she'd got the sentence exactly right.

Naomi stopped, amazement blazing across her face. *I am parched,* she replied in the same language, and then looked cautious. 'I'm not sure,' she said in English, 'that you should have done that.'

'Why not?'

'Perhaps you were supposed to listen in to my conversations with the men, and report back if you heard me say anything suggesting that I was more interested in the Budapest part of my mission than in finding airmen?'

'Nobody told me to do that,' Amber said.

'Robert Havers,' Naomi said. 'He is a good trainer, but I don't . . .' She looked back over her shoulder at the street. Amber looked too, seeing nobody but the usual beggars sheltering under canopies and people hunting for taxis so they could escape the rain. 'He has a very peculiar way of instructing us.' Speaking her mother tongue she sounded more humorous. 'Last night, when we were at the Gezira Club . . .'

'I saw you,' Amber said. Her voice was neutral. Good.

'He . . .' She looked over her shoulder again. 'He said I should keep an eye on you while we are in Croatia and let him know if you spoke to anyone outside the Partisan group.'

'Why would I do that?'

Naomi shrugged.

'And why are you telling me this now?'

Naomi gave her a long, penetrating stare before stopping and opening the door to a café.

'You can trust me now,' Amber said. 'I understand what you're saying.' Her face was burning under the dusting of Coty face powder she had powdered on this morning as soon as they'd arrived from the gymnasium. 'I don't think he has encouraged us to work together.'

They sat down at a zinc-topped table. The café was deserted. 'HQ has a strange atmosphere,' Naomi said. 'Some of the people in the organisation really dislike one another, don't they?'

'You mean that man who put his head around the door?'

Naomi nodded. 'With the moustache.' She gave a little moue. 'Not the kind of man you'd want to be alone in a lift with.'

'I felt like that too. But there are some strange individuals in that place.'

Sometimes Amber would bump into people on the stairs in Rustum Buildings and they'd look straight through her as though she wasn't there. She had experimented with smiling at them, nodding coolly, or ignoring them herself, and always received the same blank response. Did belonging to Robert's team mean that other people didn't feel they could even acknowledge your existence? There'd been some kind of undercurrent in that exchange between Robert and the moustached man in the too-tight suit that afternoon.

'Do you still have family in the place we are to visit?' Naomi asked in Hungarian, eyes still on Amber's face.

'The odd distant cousin.' She laid the insides of her wrists down on the zinc table surface. It was blissfully cool.

'I wondered . . .' Naomi glanced over her shoulder and lowered her voice. 'Well, about old connections . . .' Naomi smiled for the first time, a rueful grin. She herself probably still had family in Budapest, friends, old schoolmates who might pick her out in the street. 'Whether that was what Robert meant by keeping an eye on you, on who you spoke to.' Naomi sat back in her chair and looked at Amber again in her penetrating manner.

'Robert wouldn't like us talking like this, would he?'

Naomi nodded. 'You could go straight back to him and report on this conversation.'

'I won't.'

'You'd better not.' Naomi's eyes were cold. 'I can't go into this operation not trusting one of the people I'll be working with. The men are fine. We're a team and we have been since the British first selected and trained us in Palestine. But you, you're an enigma. I think we're on the same side now, but I'll be watching you, Amber. And not just because Robert Havers has told me to.'

'I . . .' Amber's face flushed.

'It worries me that you go to those parties. How can you know who's there?'

'I'm careful.' Amber thought about it. Disquiet about her past behaviour built inside her. How could she really have known who the other partygoers were? 'But you're right, it's risky.' Other British people might pick up on areas of her cover story. Other Europeans might not be all they seemed. There were French nationals in Cairo who resented the action the British had taken to destroy the French fleet once the Germans had conquered France. And as for the Egyptians themselves, some of them were said to be plotting to throw the British out of Egypt. Robert himself went out and about, casually referring to nightclubs and cocktails on the most fashionable terraces. But Robert was Robert. 'I wasn't taking things seriously enough before. I was wrong to behave like that. But you can trust me now.'

The other woman's face softened. 'It takes some courage to admit to being wrong. But it may be what saves us.'

'What do you mean?'

Naomi half-closed her eyes. 'We need to acknowledge our weaknesses. Let others tell us when we need telling. It's so dangerous, what we're to do.'

Amber moved closer to the other girl and dropped her own voice. 'Especially for you. Going where you're going. At this particular time.' It was likely she'd still be in Hungary when the Germans arrived.

'Knowing what I know, how could I live with myself if I didn't try to help my people resist? Or at least give them a chance to escape and hide, if it's still possible?'

Chances were that Naomi would end up thrown into some cell, shot in some gloomy courtyard. At the moment, the Hungarians didn't seem to be deporting Jews to camps in the same way as the Germans, but who knew how long that omission would last? 'Of course.' Amber tried to sound conciliatory. 'I understand.'

'No,' Naomi said. 'I don't think you do. Not entirely. Most British people don't. They think we Jews are a bit of a nuisance, whining on about mass executions and atrocities when everyone's trying to get on with winning a war. Especially those of us in Palestine who also annoy the Arabs with our insistence on living there.'

'I'd never really thought about Palestine.'

Naomi gave her a look that was half-contemptuous and half-amused. The lemonade came and they stopped talking to drink appreciatively.

'We should go.' Naomi pushed her glass aside. 'I need to wash some clothes. Hard to imagine it's still February, it's so warm during the day.'

'When it's not raining.' Amber looked out at the street.

'Our holiday destination will be cooler,' Naomi said. It would be very early spring. Still winter up in the hills, though. Amber put coins on the table. 'Let me pay for mine,' Naomi said.

'Buy me a drink when we're back.' Wherever it was they would come back to. Perhaps she and Naomi would not return together to the same place.

They locked eyes.

The rain had stopped but the street was still deserted. 'We're the only women ever sent to . . . where we're going, did you know that?' Naomi said.

'When I was being trained at home I only ever seemed to meet women who were going into France,' Amber said.

'At least the Partisan men will treat us with respect because they're used to working with women who aren't just auxiliaries. One of the advantages of communism.'

'Is it?'

'Working on the kibbutz has changed the way I see things.' They turned a corner and saw a woman sitting against a shop wall, infant in lap. The woman raised crusted eyes towards them, appearing too lethargic even to beg. 'I find this poverty hard. The women and children and old people suffer so much.' Naomi gave the woman coins and received a muttered blessing. 'When we have daughters, we will be able to tell them they can do anything. It is better in Palestine in that respect than it was in Budapest. We have little, but men and women are the same, which is right.'

Could she, Amber, really do anything a man could? *Bright but idle*, the headmistress of her school in Sussex had written in her last report. *Good at languages. Possesses a little-employed, yet remarkable speed and agility on the sports field, but regards most games as beneath her. Shows an interest in mechanical matters that this school cannot accommodate.* Nobody expected middle-class English girls to know how the Upper School wireless set worked, or offer to help tidy up the Physics labs.

'I really don't know why they chose me to do this,' she admitted to Naomi. Probably the wrong thing to say and not what you wanted to hear from someone you were going to rely on in the field.

'They're very particular,' Naomi said. 'They take a lot of time and trouble when they select us. There must be something about you that marks you out, Amber.'

'Can't think what. I didn't exactly distinguish myself earlier in my life.' She would have liked to have told Naomi about her receptionist job, but it was against the rules to talk about life before they'd come here.

'Your particular talent might be something quite hard to discern.'

Amber turned on Naomi, and then saw the smile on her face.

'Whatever it is, it's obviously unusual and valuable.' There was almost warmth in Naomi's voice now. 'Forget what I said to you in the gym. I was trying to provoke you, make you pay attention.'

'I'm paying attention now.' Their eyes met in understanding.

They parted at a junction, Naomi heading for her hostel and Amber walking west through the rain-refreshed streets, crossing the bridge to Gezira Island and her villa. She paused at a fruit stall to buy a pomegranate, a fruit she'd never eaten before. The little pink jewels inside always fascinated her. The rain gone, the late afternoon air felt warm again. From a nearby minaret the muezzin call to prayer began and she stood for a moment to listen, suddenly more aware of the fact that she might never return to Egypt.

She was still thinking about what Naomi had said to her as she walked inside the villa, trying to work out why the words had stirred her up so much. Perhaps because no other woman of her own age had ever challenged her like this, forced her to confront herself, and then accepted her as an ally. Most girls at school had regarded Maud as an outsider, leaving her alone except when they wanted her for a sports team. 'I have actually made a friend,' she told herself. Perhaps this was a dangerous assumption; Naomi would probably tell her they were colleagues or associates, that was all.

One of her housemates had left his tobacco tin on the table next to the gramophone. She put down her pomegranate and picked it up, wondering how quickly she could replicate Robert's turning the lid into a blade. He'd used his left hand. *Small details about people could be important, note them.* Had the teachers at his school punished him for not writing with his right hand?

'You want cigarette papers, miss?' the houseboy asked. 'I buy for you?'

'No.' She replaced the tin, blushing slightly. 'Thank you.' She looked at her pomegranate. 'Could you please bring me a fruit knife and a plate?'

6

I tell Dr Rosenstein about the way Naomi challenged me and how, just before we flew out of Cairo, we started to form a working relationship. Dr Rosenstein looks pleased and writes a brief note.

She moves back to the subject of Robert's tobacco tin.

'Robert himself taught you how to turn a tin lid into a blade and inflict a mortal wound, piercing a lung or the liver.' Dr Rosenstein says it as though summarising a schoolteacher's lesson.

I nod.

'Yet your attack only resulted in a few scars on the torso?'

'There was a lot of blood.' I can see the improvised knife in my hand, the red line spreading across the front of my husband's shirt. I remember the pain in my own pelvis and back. More images of blood on my upper thighs flash through my memory, which I can't account for. Had I been undressed when I attacked him? Had he tried to force himself on me? No. He could be forceful, but I couldn't recall him treating me with such aggression on previous occasions. Not that it would make any difference in proving my culpability or otherwise, as there is no such offence as rape in marriage.

'You couldn't kill him?'

For a moment I feel like I did at school when the domestic science teacher complained about my scones not rising properly.

'Why do you think that was? You were highly trained, after all.' Dr Rosenstein folds her hands in front of her like a small girl who's been well trained at sitting patiently. I think again of my husband. I see our bodies close together and the blade between us. I see him falling. I can almost taste the metallic tang of blood flowing out of him.

'Did you love him too much to want him dead?'

Oh, I loved him. The very scent of him, the way he moved. Acknowledging this at the same time as the fear and hatred I felt – feel – for my husband makes the monsters awaken inside me. They stretch their limbs and flex their muscles. 'Why can't you just give me more drugs?' I ask. 'Or another ECT session?' Just strap me to the bed, place the cathodes on me and shock all the wickedness out of me, make me good again.

'You don't need those things, Maud.'

'They work.' When I came to after the first ECT, I felt as blank and calm as a newborn. The word is that Dr Rosenstein doesn't like ECT, Jim tells me. Regards it as a last resort.

'Answering questions like this is a better way to help you return to the world outside. And reducing your drugs means you can spend more time doing enjoyable things like playing badminton or walking. You might even like to venture farther afield. Into the village, perhaps?'

'By myself?'

'Ingrams would go with you at first.'

In the village there's a shop that sells sweets, writing pads and other odds and ends. I picture myself buying a new writing pad and perhaps a pencil and a bar of chocolate.

'I don't believe in shutting people away from the world any longer than necessary.'

'But I'm dangerous.' *Mad, warped.*

She gives me that little smile of hers and can't seem to resist a peep at her daughter's photograph. 'What you're telling me is helping to untie all the tangles in your past.'

I think again of the Official Secrets Act, of all that information about the mission, no matter how coded, that I must be imparting. My worry must show on my face.

'There are no names or exact wartime locations in my notes. You've never actually given me precise details about your mission or full names of those you worked with.'

I probably didn't know their real names myself. At that stage, could I even be sure that Robert Havers was really called Robert Havers? Could I be sure of that even now?

I must still be looking anxious, though, because she places one of her hands on mine. 'Don't worry, you won't get into trouble. You're doing so well.'

I nod.

'Before our next session I want you to think about the start of your sexual relationship with Robert.'

I will. I'll write notes in my book. I'll do anything she says.

'I'll set up an appointment in a fortnight, so there's time for you to prepare yourself.'

I murmur something in response.

Ingrams takes me back to my room. 'You're quiet,' he tells me.

'So much to think about,' I mutter.

He nods. 'Sit in your room for a while, perhaps. I'll order you up some tea and come back for you later. You can play badminton with Jim if he's not practising his juggling. Or he can perhaps give you another bridge lesson.'

'I must check the doves,' I say. 'See if the eggs have hatched.' Woodlands Asylum provides quite the social whirl. But nothing could compare to Cairo.

The young American, one of Amber's housemates, was bored too and suggested jumping in a taxi and going to a party held by some of his compatriots. 'They have great booze,' he told her. 'C'mon, Amber, you've already read that magazine and we've listened to all the gramophone records at least three times. What's happened to the party girl I used to know and love?'

'We could just go to the club.'

'You're always there.'

An American party would probably be safe as they wouldn't know British people working in the Signals base where Amber was supposedly spending her days filing, and wouldn't ask potentially compromising questions. And the Americans were allies.

But when they arrived Amber could pick out the clipped accents of several of her countrymen on the verandah. She turned to go back inside. Robert stood by the gramophone, cigarette in one hand, whisky in the other. He put out a hand and introduced himself to her. She took it, showing no recognition as she met his eye. She exchanged a few polite words with their hostess and retreated to the opposite side of the room. A cocktail was placed in her hand. It was cool and dry and she drank it quickly before making her excuses. 'Headache, so sorry, lovely party . . .'

When she slipped out to hail a taxi Robert suddenly appeared at her side.

'Sorry, sir,' she said. 'I know I shouldn't really be here.'

'You managed the situation well. And I didn't confine you to barracks.' He seemed more relaxed this evening. Perhaps it was the whisky. 'Just cautioned you to be discreet when you're socialising because there are people in Cairo who could see through your cover story.'

'I should have stayed in.'

'An early night? You?' He looked at her appraisingly. 'Although, the first time I met you in that nightclub with Peter you looked as though you'd rather have been home with some knitting and a decent play on the wireless.'

She blushed.

'Certainly doesn't match the impression I've been given of you since you arrived in Cairo.'

'I'm trying to clean up my act.'

'Good girl. But no need to go too far in the other direction. Mind if I share this with you?' He nodded towards the taxi. When they were seated inside she wondered if they'd sit in silence. People said that Cairo taxi drivers sometimes spied for the Germans. 'Most people find Cairo very tempting,' he said, as he sat down. Perhaps he was still testing her. Wanting to see if she'd be careless, say something she oughtn't about the operation.

'Young Naomi's very austere in her approach,' he went on.

Amber said nothing.

'Her attitude is impressive.'

She nodded.

'But we need to make sure her mission objectives are the same as ours.'

She didn't know how to answer.

'You're very loyal, Amber.' His shoulder touched hers. 'That's good. Don't worry, you've responded exactly as I hoped you would.'

'Have I?' She put a hand to her head. That cocktail had been stronger than she'd imagined. Perhaps it wasn't the alcohol, though.

'Let's get out and walk the last bit,' Robert said. He spoke to the driver in Arabic. How many languages did this man speak? But his Serbo-Croat wasn't as good as hers.

The exercise would help clear her head. Did Robert think she was drunk? Once again she had let herself down in front of him. But he seemed relaxed tonight.

'Beautiful.' He nodded at the lights twinkling on the island. 'Come on. Let's walk across the bridge.' The cool air folded itself around her bare neck and shoulders.

'I love Cairo at night,' she said.

'Me too,' he agreed. 'But I wouldn't swap a day here for London on a foggy winter day, either. The lack of sunlight, the gloom.'

'That's what I missed most when I started boarding school,' she said. 'Sunshine even in the winter. It could be miserable up at . . .' she looked over her shoulder. It had become a habit. Nobody behind them. 'At the mine. But often there'd be brilliantly sunny days.' It had made her feel alive, watching the sunlight glint on the snow.

'Perhaps a lot of the way you lived in England was an attempt to feel alive again,' he said quietly.

'The way I lived?' Her cheeks flushed. She was going to ask him what the hell he meant, but, of course, she knew. And he was right. Damn, his research had been good. What a failure she'd made of her time in London. All those men. The dull job. She'd never be good at relationships or life. Something about her was too intense. She was best off distracting herself with work, with playing a part, like she was here. Or, more truthfully, becoming the part: becoming Amber rather than Maud.

They were halfway across the bridge. The light reflected off the water below. Amber shivered.

'Cold?' he asked.

'No, just had the strangest feeling . . .'

He halted, looked over his shoulder. 'What?'

'Nothing. A sense of something I can't explain.'

He looked suddenly serious. 'You should trust those intuitions. Sometimes they mean that you're picking up on some signal your conscious mind hasn't quite grasped. Remember what Harry said?'

Harry was the man who had trained them in the use of what he called special gadgetry, such as maps printed on silk squares sewn into the linings of coats, and buttons that concealed compasses. Before the war he'd been a conjurer, an illusionist, trained to read the feelings of his audience and exploit them.

'I used to see signs in London.' She flushed again. 'It sounds as if I was mad. Perhaps I was. I'd see omens in the number of pigeons sitting on a telegraph wire or whether the next bus would pass me from the left or the right. Neurosis, I suppose.'

'A lot of people probably did the same thing during the Blitz.'

'But I've always looked for patterns, even before the war.' Why was she confiding in him like this? 'You probably think I'm mad and unsuitable now.'

'We had you thoroughly evaluated,' he told her. 'If there'd been anything that worried us, you wouldn't be here. Let's just say that many of the people who work for us are not entirely . . . orderly in their psychological make-up.'

Well, that was her: not quite orderly in her mind. They'd almost reached the island.

'Is Naomi orderly in her mind?' She couldn't resist asking. Was she still jealous of Naomi?

'Oh Naomi's pretty sane. Obsessed, though.' His pupils were dilated as he mentioned the Jewish girl. 'She'd only be happy if the entire Allied war effort were deployed against the people allegedly running the death camps in Poland.'

'But she'll do what you want in Yugoslavia?'

'Naomi will play along with our objectives for as long as it suits her.' He gave Amber a sidelong look, sounding harsher. 'And I know I can rely on you to warn me in your transmissions if that's not the case.'

Amber nodded. If she hadn't brought the subject of Naomi up now, had he intended asking her to do this later on?

He stopped again. 'Let's just stand here for a moment.'

He gazed intently at the city lights. Beneath them, a felucca turned in front of the bridge, its triangular sail lowered. The reflections of its lanterns shone like small broken coins on the river's surface. Voices reached them. Cairo never seemed to sleep. 'Magical, isn't it?' he said. 'Like a scene from the *Arabian Nights*.' She'd never had Robert down as a romantic. At first she'd regarded him as almost aggressively masculine with his hooded eyes and broad shoulders. 'My wife didn't like the Orient, but it pulls at me in a way I find irresistible.'

'Your wife?' Amber stood up straight.

'She died. Early in the Blitz.'

'I'm sorry.' She had met people who'd lost those close to them, of course – most people had by this stage in the war – but she still felt tongue-tied.

'It was a few years ago now,' he said. He stood looking at the water below.

Amber tried to remember what Mama had taught her about moving a conversation on if it grew too difficult. 'Will you stay in Cairo while we're . . . away?' she asked. 'Or do you fly over, too?' Almost immediately she realised her mistake. 'Oh God, sorry, sir, I know you probably can't say.'

His arms were around her waist before she had finished the sentence. 'You don't have to call me sir now. Let's not talk any more.'

She took a step back, feeling the bridge parapet against her back. Amber still had enough of Maud in her to respond to the old sensations. His mouth felt rough on hers at first. It had been some months since she'd kissed like this. Peter had been a young man, a boy, really. His cheeks had been soft. Robert felt coarser, as though he needed to shave even though no stubble showed, but more exciting because of it. It was always a relief, she remembered, when you stopped talking and started kissing. The tension she'd felt between herself and Robert ever since they'd first met had puzzled her. Why did he sometimes seem to dislike her so much? Had it just been an unacknowledged attraction causing the strain between them? She was almost disappointed. Was it always going to come down to sex? Was any ambiguity between a man and a woman, any unanswered question, always about a physical pull?

But this wasn't just a physical pull. Something more was happening to her. It had been so easy dealing with men in the past. She took her pick and let the chosen boy flatter her. In return, she gave them something back: emotional, if temporary, support, and erotic companionship that hopefully helped them at times of great strain. When they went back to flying operations or embarked on some military venture, Amber knew she'd done her best to distract and relax them. It was a deal. Many of her female friends behaved in a similar way. But with Robert she couldn't make out the nature of the deal, or its price; only that she had signed up for it and every vein in her body now felt as though it were flowing with champagne.

He was stroking the small of her back. She'd never thought of it as being one of those body parts that could feel so delicious. She laughed.

He released her and looked at her enquiringly.

'I feel like a cat.'

'There is something a little feline about you, my dear.'

And possibly about him, too, she thought. Though he would be one of the big cats: mesmerising, powerful. She tilted her mouth towards his.

'You want some more?'

This time the kiss was more powerful, almost violent. Her mouth felt bruised.

'My villa will be unusually quiet tonight – all my housemates have gone out,' Robert said, breaking away. Her legs were actually shaking. 'And it's only five minutes from here.' They walked onto the island, his arm around her back. She passed the turn to her own house. Not too late to change her mind. He wouldn't hold it against her, she knew him well enough to be sure of that. Her mouth opened to tell him she wanted to go home by herself: she was tired. But on she walked. Of all the women in Cairo he'd chosen her. Not perfect, pretty Naomi or any of the impeccably groomed and sophisticated women at the parties. Her.

They reached a wrought iron gate and he led her through the jasmine-scented garden and into the villa. 'My houseboy will be hovering downstairs,' he whispered. 'Let's go straight upstairs quietly.' Halfway up the stairs he stopped. 'There's still time for us to do the sensible thing.' His eyes scrutinised her. She didn't move. He smiled and took her by the hand.

Beside his bed there was a bottle of brandy and two glasses. Had Robert expected to bring someone back with him? He poured her a generous measure. She sat on the edge of the bed sipping it and watching him. Now that they were here the heat between them seemed to have cooled. Wasn't this a bad idea after all? She was probably just flattered by Robert's attentions, erotically charged by his physical presence.

No. Something more was happening. Despite her wariness of him, he'd got under her skin. The tired old cliché was the only one that would do.

He sat next to her, almost companionably, drinking his brandy. 'Some of the people in the same building as us aren't reliable, Amber.'

She nodded, thinking of the plump man with the moustache, trying to think of something she could say to indicate that she understood this, but failing yet again to find the right words. She was never this inarticulate with people other than Robert.

'Those office doors and walls seem to have eyes. People go to parties. They swim at the Gezira Club, and have their hair shampooed and set at the same French hairdresser you probably used. You haven't met them, but they've noted you.'

'I really shouldn't have gone out tonight, should I? You were just being kind before when you told me it didn't matter.' She felt suddenly almost tearful. Maud could never ever get people right and Amber didn't seem to be doing much better. She'd ruined things with Robert. Why the hell were they sending someone like her out to Yugoslavia on such an important mission?

'I'm never kind. I just don't want you bored and lonely. The service asks such a lot of you. And it's hard, isn't it? Coming somewhere like Cairo and not knowing anyone apart from us. Oh, I know it's tremendous fun being out here after living in dark, battered old London. But it can feel overwhelming.' His voice was soft, confiding. 'You want to grab at all it offers because you may never have the chance again, but you want this operation to go well. You've worked so hard, Amber, harder than you ever have before. You've given your heart to our work.'

She stared at him. How had he known this about her? Was it in her notes, or was he just able to read her? Nobody else had ever shown such insight into her. Robert put down his glass and moved towards her, murmuring her name: Amber, her real name, as she thought of it now. There was still time to say no. But she didn't.

Much, much later, lips bruised, the inside of her mouth furred from the brandy, Amber crept out of the villa, scared of meeting one of Robert's housemates. He had offered to go down with her and walk her back to her own villa, but she was wary of them being seen together. It was well and truly light now. She was due to be in the briefing room with the rest of her group and an instructor who was going to refresh their geographical knowledge of northern Yugoslavia. There would be topography, maps, and bearings to memorise. The session was to be followed by a refresher lesson on wireless repairs, run by someone flown over from England. Concentration and focus would be demanded. She groaned. Perhaps a bath and a cold compress for her eyes. This wasn't how it had been supposed to go, her life in Cairo. Amber was slipping back into bad habits. *I must try harder.*

She must have said the words aloud because a boy pushing a cart laden with figs and dates turned his head to stare at her.

7

As I promised myself, I've written down a brief description of how the affair with Robert began. Describing that first night gives me an impression of ordering my past, making sense of it. He was my boss, in the parlance of the modern workplace, and he'd chosen me. Not the efficient Naomi. Me. *I'm still not sure when fascination turned to love*, I write. *I didn't spend many nights with him. He switched to employing an almost avuncular banter with me in the classroom, but the harsh rebuffs didn't completely stop.*

It sounds very clinical. I think I'm afraid to break the carapace I've built around those old feelings for Robert. I close my eyes, willing myself back into Cairo, trying to feel my gym kit sticking to my back, smelling that mixture of aromas, hearing the racket of the streets. And feeling his touch on my skin.

I was disciplined enough to try to detach from the relationship between us when we were training. But in the evenings, if I couldn't see him, I found myself hanging around in the villa, not wanting to go out, but not knowing what to do with myself. I'd go for my swim, looking out for him all the time. Once I spotted him talking to a group of women, all beautiful, all well dressed, placing a hand on a tanned and shapely arm then leaning in to light a cigarette placed between a pair of perfectly reddened lips. I watched the women, sophisticated, worldly females, play with locks of their hair, pout and look up through their lashes at him. I looked down at my own muscular body in its plain swimsuit. I couldn't wear anything more glamorous to swim the vigorous front crawl I needed to do to maintain fitness.

But then when we were together he made me feel as though I filled his world. In bed, when I lay back on the pillows, sated, he'd ask me about my childhood, the time I spent at the mine. I told him about the Serbian cook who let me chop up vegetables and baked pastries for me. About Mama's little dog who once took on a snake he found in the bushes, how the Albanian gardener had rushed out with a fork to slice the snake in two, and how the two parts of its body had twitched as though it had become two snakes. About the first days back at boarding school in England each September, when I would pull the coarse sheet over my face at night and stuff my knuckle into my mouth so they wouldn't know I was weeping. Robert would listen, propped up on one elbow, silent, nodding from time to time, his eyes never leaving mine. And I felt as though I had stripped myself inside out and he knew everything about me. He'd kiss me on my forehead as though I were a small child.

But in the mornings we'd return to the briefing room or head out on training exercises and he would be back to treating me strictly, like the naughty baby of the family who can't be relied on. The others noticed. 'You're the best at a lot of this stuff,' one of the men said. 'But he chews your head off, doesn't he, if you make the slightest slip-up?'

Finally, these recollections flow from my pen. I'm so relieved. I want Dr Rosenstein to be pleased with me, to feel that I'm making a good fist of this. I never cared what teachers at school thought, so this is a new sensation for me.

I am lucky to have Dr Rosenstein as my psychiatrist. Jim sees a Dr Manners.

'Dr Manners is more old school,' Jim says at lunch. 'Not so much talking things through. Electrodes and wrapping if you get too excited. I've heard he likes the old insulin injections, too.'

I haven't ever had one of these, but I've heard about the procedure. They inject you and you fall into a coma, sometimes only after you've had a few seizures. They bring you back from the coma with an injection of glucose and you wake up, often soaking wet because you've been sweating. Or because you've wet yourself. If it works, you feel calmer and less obsessed with whatever it was that brought you to madness.

'You're making progress, aren't you?' I ask Jim.

He shrugs. 'Suppose Dr Manners is right, though? Suppose the time for talking really does have to come to an end?'

'Do you mind talking about . . . what happened to you in the North Atlantic with him?'

'I don't know what I mind or not. It's easier just to do what I'm ordered.'

I've noticed that Jim is happiest when we adhere to a routine. Get up. Have breakfast. Read in one's room or go for a walk. Lunch. Help in the garden. Badminton or bridge, depending on the weather. Practise his juggling – he's up to four balls now. Write letters. Read letters. Supper. More bridge. Or a play on the wireless, if Ingrams deems it suitably unexciting. A perfect life. For someone of eighty. Not for someone Jim's age.

'I'm not sure how much longer my people can afford to keep me here,' Jim says quietly. 'They don't say anything, but I know it's a struggle for them. I have younger brothers and sisters still at home.'

I don't know what to say, how to reassure him. Woodlands costs. I know that my husband probably paid my fees and expenses at first. And now my parents must be footing the bill. I go up to my room to reread the letter my mother has sent me. She cannot keep off the subject of my husband. *He is so vengeful. He loved you and you hadn't been married long. I can't believe he wants to punish you like this and deprive you of what should be yours. There must be a way of ending this. I am coming to see you soon, darling.*

I'm not sure I want Mama to see me here at Woodlands. She might inadvertently drag in too much of the outside world that I am still struggling with. On the other hand, it would be good to talk in that other language of ours, to reconnect with clear skies and the smell of herbs and trees dripping with fruit. I start to write my mother an answer but can't concentrate. So I ring the bell and one of the nurses takes me outside. In the garden they've trimmed the bushes and Ingrams is directing Jim in turning over a large canvas sheet filled with clippings. When it's rolled up it looks like a corpse.

I walk on. The sun has rediscovered some of its warmth, but the heat is still gentle. As I approach the dovecot I see that someone has chucked a rusty old tin over the wall. When I go inside I will throw it away. The lane behind the wall leads down to the village. Sometimes we hear young men, boys really, congregating in the lane. They whistle when they hear us and call us loonies, talk to one another in gobbling, slurring voices. I'm relieved they aren't in the lane this afternoon.

I unfold the stepladder and peer into the dovecot. Three pairs are inside, livelier than they were when it was hot. 'Hello,' I say softly to them. 'It's me again.' They peer back at me with mild curiosity but little surprise. White doves, symbols of innocence. But vulnerable. I fear that my doves – for so I think of them – will become prey to a raptor, one of the buzzards I've sometimes seen in the distance.

I may not have been dove-innocent in the weeks before I left Cairo to carry out my operation. But I did feel vulnerable. I was falling for Robert, for the gentle man I saw when we were alone together. Even if that gentleness wasn't always guaranteed. He could switch into something much colder.

'I rang for a taxi and it will be here soon.' Robert shook Amber gently.

It was 2 a.m. His housemates must be home. This was the third time she'd come back to his villa.

'Thank you, darling,' he added.

'I'm not a geisha, you don't need to thank me.'

'Not at all. You really do like the bedroom side of things, don't you?' She sat up, grimacing.

'Here.' He poured her a glass of water from a jug on the bedside table. 'You look a bit rough, sweetheart.' He leaned over and kissed her breast. 'But you taste of salt and honey. Biblical, really.'

'I'm sure that's blasphemous.'

'You're probably right.' But, as always when he conceded some advantage to her, Robert would do something to show her who was really in charge. They never entirely seemed to escape the roles of master and student. He rolled her over, his movements gentle at first, but becoming more urgent.

'I thought the taxi driver was on his way?'

'He'll wait.'

When they'd finished she reached for her cigarettes. 'I feel awful.' Probably the worst was yet to come. The brandy on top of the whisky . . . Her father had always warned her not to mix drinks.

Robert stroked her forehead and lit her cigarette. He had been the one who'd insisted on that last whisky. 'Hope you can make your supplies last when you're up in the hills.' They were issuing her with a ration of Balkan cigarettes, something she could offer round to the Partisans.

She blew a smoke ring in answer.

'I don't want the Partisans complaining that our agent is moody because she's run out of fags.' He ran a finger down her breast. 'Or because she misses . . . other indulgences.'

'I'm sure I'll survive any shortages.' God, she hoped she wasn't pregnant. Imagine being up a mountain, belly swelling, nauseous.

He smiled but then his features hardened.

'What is it?'

'The Partisans may find you a bit . . . advanced in your morals.'

'Oh?'

'You're a woman who's enjoyed,' he emphasised the word, 'several partners.'

She felt her cheeks warm. The report from the security vetting she'd had to undergo had certainly been thorough. As he liked to remind her from time to time.

He reached towards the pile of coins he kept on his bedside table. 'You'd better get a move on.' He handed her some money. 'For the taxi.'

'I don't need cash, I'm fine.' She nodded at her evening bag.

'Take it for something else, then. Food, books, I don't know. A glass of lemonade on the terrace of Shepheard's Hotel.'

'You pay me a good salary.'

'Women always need extra cash.' He stroked her thigh.

She looked at him. 'Are you paying me?'

Robert reached for the cigarette case. 'No more than you deserve. You're such an incomparably good f—'

'Don't call me that.' A bit of her spittle landed on his cheek. She was glad.

'Sorry.' He dropped his head. 'Don't know what got into me. Unforgivable.'

'I thought . . .' She had misjudged everything. Failed the test Robert had set.

'What did you think, my darling?' He put his arm around her.

'You and me, is it some kind of a test? A psychological exercise?' Anger was sweeping away her dismay.

'You must think I'm very sadistic and very sophisticated.'

'Is sleeping with me part of the training process?' Perhaps he already had the next batch of female agents lined up, and they too would be taken to his bed.

'I can't imagine you being part of any process,' he said quietly. 'I've never met anyone like you before. I think that's why I'm sometimes . . . Well, it takes me by surprise and I don't know how to handle that.' He took her hand, interwove her fingers into his. 'And then, of course, there's the operation. Knowing you'll be off there shortly.' He took their linked hands to his mouth and kissed the back of hers. 'I've trained you, but I won't be able to help you, except by wireless signal, when you're out there alone. Perhaps that thought is making me feel unsettled. Very unprofessional of me when I should be providing constant reassurance. I'm sorry.'

'I hadn't realised you felt like that.' Amber shook her hand free and pulled him to her. The resultant kiss would leave her skin sore but she didn't care.

Eventually he released her. His expression suddenly took on a more casual appearance. She knew by now that this was when he was actually at his most watchful. 'I do need to talk to you about the drop.'

'What's happened?'

He shook his head. 'It needs to be with the others. Later, darling.'

She pulled on her dress, a red silk number with cap sleeves, cut on the bias, very tight and completely inappropriate for daytime. The taxi driver would know she'd stayed out all night. She couldn't face sorting out stockings and suspenders, but forced herself to pull on her silk drawers, newly bought in Cairo, where it still seemed possible to find luxuries. She stuffed her feet into her shoes, which seemed to have shrunk overnight, and picked up the bag she'd discarded on the rug. 'See you later on.'

Five hours' sleep and a bath and she'd be fine for the last training session she'd ever have with Robert. Perhaps he was thinking about this too.

'This time tomorrow you'll be packing up.'

'I won't have much.' Certainly not as far as personal items were concerned. A few clean shirts, underwear and toothbrush. A lipstick and some hair-grips. Good quality, yet light and comfortable boots that Robert himself had selected. At least she wasn't going somewhere like France, where the girls had to look like French women in every single respect. Amber was going to be with Partisans, a fighting force.

She would be a combatant, not passing for a civilian and living under a cover story.

She sat in her taxi feeling the disapproval oozing off the back of the driver. Robert was right. The Partisans would regard behaviour such as hers in an equally unfavourable light. Drinking. Sleeping with a man who wasn't her husband.

'I pick you up later,' the taxi driver told her, pulling up outside her apartment. 'Take you to the secret building.'

So much for the location of SOE HQ being classified information.

Yugoslavia would be a further step away from being Maud, she told herself as she got out of the taxi. She'd be Amber over there, Amber who operated sleekly and efficiently, who evaded the Chetniks and Ustaše militiamen. She was leaving behind Maud with her rackety past. This operation of hers would be a success, her opportunity to show both Robert and the discarded Maud exactly what she could accomplish.

8

June 1947

I'm sitting on the window seat of my room looking out over the drive, it being too wet today for spending time in the garden. May lulled us into thinking that summer was going to be as it is in the books, sunny and bright. This cool and damp spell is not supposed to last, however. I hope the doves are dry in their dovecot.

I get a good view of Dr Manners when he arrives for his next appointment with Jim and his other patients. He wears a smart mackintosh and a hat that seems to intimidate the rain from dampening it. Before he enters the main door Dr Manners pauses and looks up at the first floor. I freeze. Has he seen me?

Stand down, I tell myself. This isn't a surveillance exercise and I'm in my own room, exactly where I'm supposed to be. Indeed, I could push the bell and Ingrams or one of the others would come and let me out. I walk over to the button and place my fingers on the brass to show myself. But I don't press it.

Jim looks brighter this morning when we meet for coffee in the drawing room. 'Dr Manners is a sharp man, Amber. Notices things.' He pauses. 'But every time I see him, there's this cold feeling in the pit of my stomach just before I go inside his room. It's fine as soon as I sit down. I don't know what I'm worried about. It's as though I'm still back in the war, waiting for . . . something to happen.'

I know what he means about that sense of danger in the pit of the stomach, cold, sour tasting, heavy. Before I can stop myself I'm back there at the airfield in Italy, preparing to be flown to Yugoslavia. Young. Scared.

Perspiration beads my brow. Jim's preoccupied himself with a crossword. I mutter an excuse and go up to my room. Once I'm there I pick up my pen. I can control my feelings and update my journal by writing about the parachute drop.

I'd trained for the drop in England and had been an assiduous learner, mastering the steps from jumping off a tower, from a balloon and then from the training plane. I found it easy to understand the physics behind parachuting: the way the chute increased my surface area and thus my air resistance, reducing the gravitational force that would otherwise bring me crashing to the ground.

You can concentrate a lot on the parachuting, but it's what happens when you hit the ground that's the important part. Nothing prepared me for what would happen when I was safely on Yugoslav soil.

The RAF sergeant eased the webbing of the parachute between Amber's legs. 'Just open a little wider . . .' He blushed.

'How indelicate. Lucky she's not a married woman,' Robert said. Everyone laughed in an over-nervous way.

'Still can't get over ladies doing this kind of thing,' the sergeant said, a slight reproach in his voice.

'What makes you think my agent is a lady?' Robert said. Amber made a face at him. 'Just make sure the straps are done up properly on her shoulders.'

'I'd put my mother-in-law in those straps,' the sergeant said, patting Amber's shoulder. 'Without the chute, though.' He caught Robert's expression. 'She's safe, sir.'

But they couldn't be entirely safe, could they? Several Allied liaison officers had already fallen to their deaths during drops onto the unforgiving mountains of Yugoslavia. And Amber and the rest of the team were now going to be descending on a zone they had not had time to research in detail, because of yesterday's change of plan.

She wasn't going to be one of those who died. She would remember everything she'd ever been taught about parachuting. Robert crouched down in front of Amber, his gaze on her serious.

'Remember how you threw up in the Highlands on a night exercise when the temperature was well below freezing? How you blacked out once because your muscles had used up all your oxygen and your brain couldn't cope?'

She shuffled uneasily on the hard floor. He'd obviously read all the notes on her training.

'And how you and Naomi slugged it out in that sweaty gymnasium in Cairo?'

She nodded.

'You did all of that for a purpose. This is it, Amber.'

She bowed her head. When she lifted it again he was still looking at her, intently, warmly. Her heart suddenly skipped a beat as the words *I love him* floated into her head. The realisation came to her at such an inopportune moment, and with what felt like such certainty, that she wanted to laugh. It was just nerves talking, wasn't it?

'This is for you.' He pushed something small and metallic into her hand. A silver cigarette lighter. 'I've had it personalised.'

A small bird engraved on the side carrying a letter A.

'It's lovely. Thank you.' The lighter felt warm where his hand had held it.

'Well, let's not get all sentimental.' Robert took Amber's hand, suddenly formal. 'Best of luck, my dear. We look forward to receiving your first transmission in twenty-four hours' time. Sorry for the last-minute change of arrangements.' The original plan had been to parachute them around fifty miles farther east, much nearer Hungary. Increased German activity in that area had resulted in a revision. Naomi was not happy: it would take her far longer to reach Hungary now. She and Robert had quickly consulted the maps, deciding on a revised route.

Robert moved on to wish the others similar luck. She watched him to see if he was giving Naomi a lighter, too, but he had his back turned, blocking her view. Then he was gone, the doors shut. Amber felt his absence like a change in pressure. She might never see him again; those murmured night-time confidences might have gone for good. She'd miss the talking as much as the physical intimacy. Nobody now knew as much about her as Robert did. Perhaps nobody ever would.

The bomber bumped over the runway. For all its size, the Halifax was quickly airborne, its humming engines rendering conversation impossible. She didn't want to talk, anyway. Closing her eyes, Amber sank back among the bags and cylinders of supplies for themselves and for the Partisans, which were to be dropped with them. *You may find your hosts more enthusiastic about receiving the weapons, especially the Stens and Brens, and medicines than they are about you.*

Amber wore a flying suit, but her teeth chattered. She unrolled her sleeping bag and stuck her legs into it. Naomi sat beside her. Occasionally their eyes met and they exchanged half-smiles, though Naomi's face still wore concern about the change of drop site.

In the floor a hatch had been cut out, and when the light above it changed colour, they would drop out of it. Like bombs, Robert had told them, but hopefully landing with rather less noise.

The despatcher offered round a flask of hot toddy. The lacing of rum made Amber's stomach lurch, but she drank. The toddy was a tradition, to settle your nerves before you plunged. She wondered where they were now. Passing over some of the Dalmatian islands, perhaps? It would have been reassuring to have picked out her childhood holiday spot like a little jewel on an azure velvet background, but the Halifax's windows were blacked out and anyway it would be dark outside.

The despatcher took the empty flask from the last of Naomi's group, looked at his watch and gave them the thumbs-up. Perhaps the Partisans were already in position at the drop site, lighting fires for the pilot. Down below men and women would be anticipating their arrival, hoping that they could help bring about the great aim of ridding the Balkans of Hitler. *I'm only twenty. How can someone like me really help anyone?*

The engine's hum grew less insistent. The pilot would be slowing for the drop. The despatcher opened the circular hatch and flashed a torch signal down towards the ground. He must have been satisfied with the signal he received because he nodded at his passengers. Time to stand, roll up the sleeping bags and strap them onto rucksacks. The despatcher rolled the containers out one by one, reminding Amber of barrels of beer being delivered into a pub cellar.

Amber and Naomi strapped their slip lines onto the hooks on the inside of the fuselage. When they jumped, the lines would unravel until their full length was reached, automatically opening the chutes. A red light flashed on. The despatcher raised and lowered his hand. The light turned to green. Naomi sat down, legs dangling over the hatch before the darkness beneath silently swallowed her up. Aaron jumped after her. Amber now. She sat at the hatch, watching the light and the despatcher's hand, and then found herself in the dark air before she'd even realised she'd left the Halifax. The ground was already coming towards her – they jumped at low height to avoid radar. Below, the landing fires twinkled. *Feet together.* And there she was, on Croatian soil. The chute landed on the ground beside her. She tugged it towards her and released herself from it, then folded it quickly, as she'd been taught. *Patrols of local pro-German Home Guards could be close by. Don't keep your reception group waiting.*

Around her, she heard voices murmuring.

A figure in dark clothing approached her. She saw the red star on his cap. 'Eagle,' she said, giving the password. '*Zdravo.*' Hello.

'Falcon,' came the answer. Correct passwords given, the figure grinned at her. '*Smrt fašizmu, slobada narodu.* Death to fascism, freedom to the people. And welcome to Yugoslavia. Or what passes for it, these days.' He reached out and tugged at her sleeve. Amber ducked the aluminium tube that was floating down to the ground. The wireless. She jumped aside as it thumped to the earth. A pack pony was led towards her. 'We'll load this on here,' her companion said. Around her dark-clothed figures led more ponies onto the field, loading them quickly.

'We should go.' The man nodded at a boy standing next to him, who reached for the parachute in Amber's arms. 'We will take care of this for you.'

Men, women and ponies were moving almost soundlessly off the field towards the cover of the beech and fir trees. The lamps to guide the pilot had already been extinguished. Above them the bomber's engines sounded more distant. The whole operation had only taken minutes. Amber breathed in the cool air. '*Ovdje sam.* I am here.' She spoke her childhood language to herself silently.

'We have a long walk,' her new companion told her. 'Thanks to the Chetniks breaking through.'

Chetniks; interesting. Robert had only mentioned German movements.

'I'm Branko, by the way,' he said, raising his right fist and clenching it in the Partisan salute.

She saw he wore what looked like a former Yugoslav army jacket, but with breeches and boots that might once have belonged to a Wehrmacht soldier. She returned the salute with the traditional British version, palm out. 'Amber.'

'Delighted to make your acquaintance, Comrade Amber,' he said in careful English. He was pulling a tin out of a pocket, offering her a cigarette.

'How long have you been with the Partisans?' she asked in Serbo-Croat, pulling out the lighter Robert had given her to light his cigarette and hers.

'Since the beginning, since 1941,' he told her proudly. 'My mother and I were with Tito himself when he began the defence of our homeland in western Serbia.'

Like coming over to England with the Normans, she thought.

Branko moved forward to direct the man leading the ponies through the trees.

A hand landed on Amber's shoulder. She turned to see Naomi. 'Safe landing?'

'Yes. You, too?'

Naomi nodded at one of her companions. 'Just one slightly twisted ankle between us all, and he's been given a ride on a pack pony.' She grimaced. 'Might be worse than walking on the ankle, given how bony that poor animal's back is.' She became more serious. 'Unfortunately, it's Samuel.'

Samuel, also trained as a wireless operator, would be going on to Hungary with Naomi.

'Shame we now have to move even farther to the south,' Naomi said. 'It'll take us even longer to reach the Hungarian border. Increase the risks.'

Every atom in her being was propelling her forward to Hungary to warn her people, Amber thought.

They were walking between beeches and firs now, the air moist and resinous. Amber couldn't resist drawing a breath, appreciating the difference from the odours, good and ill, of Cairo and the burnt-brick-and-metal reek of London. *Boughs of evergreen or pine of about four foot long can be used to construct a shelter if it is necessary for an agent to live out in the open.*

Branko had returned. 'How far are we marching tonight?' Amber asked.

'Twelve more kilometres.' He grimaced. 'I'm sorry we can't give you hot food and a rest when you've just landed, but it's not safe.'

'What's our bearing?' Naomi asked.

'South, maybe south-southeast.' He opened a map and showed them. 'There's a series of caves we can hide in for a few days until we've treated the wounded and things are quieter.'

'That far south?' Naomi said.

'It's not what I intended, either.'

Naomi frowned. 'I need to talk to my people about this. Can we send an emergency signal now, Amber, asking Cairo for a view on this?'

Amber translated for Branko. 'No time for that,' he said. 'Too dangerous to stop while you set up your wireless. You'll have to wait until tomorrow.'

Naomi said nothing, but Amber could feel doubt radiating from her. 'It's only twelve kilometres,' she told her. 'You're fit. Fast. Remember that race in the gym?'

Naomi gave a little smile.

'In daylight, when we know the situation with the Chetniks, you can easily make up the distance.'

'If Samuel's ankle heals quickly enough. But once we're up on the karst the going is slower.'

The karst was the limestone-dominated landscape, with its thin covering of trees on some slopes, and steep drops to waterfalls and streams. They walked on in silence, Branko ahead of Amber, whistling what sounded like a folk tune, in turn melancholic and upbeat. She recognised it. Mama had sung it to her when she'd been a small child, its lyrics telling of ill-fated love and loss.

As her eyes accustomed themselves to the dark and her ears picked up more of the sounds around her, the sighs and grunts of people carrying heavy loads reached her from behind. She glanced over her shoulder. Stretchers, with wounded people on them. Carried by tired-looking men.

Branko saw what Amber was looking at. 'We tried getting the ponies to pull the stretchers, but the track is too rough and it jolts the wounded.' After an hour, he raised an arm. '*Odmor.*' Rest.

A flask was passed around, containing something burning and strong, making her eyes water but warming the very core of her body. Amber sat on a rock rubbing her hands. She had gloves, but the cold still seemed to seep into her fingers. It was early in the year to be up in the hills of Croatia at night. Her mind switched to Robert. He wouldn't stay long in Bari, she knew. But he'd be there tonight, probably asleep. Or out in some bar. Why was she even thinking about Robert now?

One of the young men standing beside them stiffened, removing his rifle from his shoulder in a single fluid movement, then placing a finger on his lips. Without a word being spoken the Partisans ceased their whisperings. A current of wariness ran through the group. Two men – boys, really – ran silently into the trees. Minutes passed. Nobody spoke. Even the ponies seemed to quieten.

An owl hooted twice.

'Chetniks ahead.' Branko had moved silently back to them. 'We'll wait it out until they move on. They haven't seen us, but they're clustered around a bridge we need to cross.'

Amber felt Daniel stiffen beside her. She knew he was thinking of the weapons they had brought with them. 'We could take them out,' Daniel muttered. 'There're enough of us.'

'If it goes wrong, we'll be left with a slow-moving trail of wounded we can't take across that bridge,' Branko said sharply. 'It's the only crossing. We can't retreat because there's nowhere we can shelter with the casualties. We can't fight tonight.'

Naomi sighed. 'We can never fight our enemy, it seems.' She said the words so softly that only Amber could hear. 'Don't worry, I'm not going to force the point, but it's frustrating.'

'Fighting isn't our objective,' Amber said. 'Settling in with this unit is. We need to wait until we've made the transmission before we do anything else.'

'We've been trained in night combat. We could be down at that bridge before they've heard us, slitting throats,' Daniel said.

'No.' Amber heard the authority in her own voice with surprise. Technically, as liaison officer, she was superior to the others, but Robert had positioned this operation so that they would work in parallel.

'We can defend ourselves,' Naomi said. 'We shouldn't wait for the enemy to make the first move.'

'We're not under attack,' Amber said.

'Yet,' Naomi murmured.

'This unit is not well armed, and we haven't unloaded the cylinders yet.'

'Let's do it then, let's take the guns out,' Daniel said.

'In the dark? Without making a noise? Unpack the guns, assemble and load them?'

'We should do something,' Daniel said sullenly.

'Ah, the newcomers seek to tell the Partisans how to conduct themselves?' Branko had moved silent as a panther to crouch beside them.

'No,' said Amber. 'We're happy to follow your lead.' She glared at Daniel.

Naomi let out a sharp breath.

'You think we like letting our enemy get away?' Branko almost snarled the words. 'But in the meantime, one of the wounded is haemorrhaging. Can you remember which cylinder had the medical supplies in?'

Amber went over to the ponies, shining her torch on the cylinders to read the markings. 'This one.'

Branko ordered the pony to be unloaded. As he unpacked the cylinder a small, dark, middle-aged woman took the bandages and a bottle of antiseptic from him. The medic, Amber guessed. She followed the pair and saw the woman wipe an oozing leg wound with antiseptic and unroll a bandage to dress it, simultaneously hissing quiet but effective instructions at a colleague holding an improvised drip above a patient.

Murmuring behind her made Amber turn. The Partisan boys who'd run ahead were returning. 'The Chetniks have moved on,' the first said.

'A large group,' the second added. 'Mounted on fresh horses and well armed.'

Naomi had approached as the boys returned. 'What are they saying?' she asked Amber. When she'd heard the translation, she looked down at the ground for a moment. 'So you were right,' she told Amber. 'It would have been a mistake to engage them.'

The break was over. Men drew themselves to their feet. The packhorses shuffled in protest as their tethers were undone and their harnesses tightened. Directed by the medic, the stretchers were lifted up. Amber stood back to let them pass ahead of her. The ground was steeper now and it took longer for the column to progress. The carriers must be weary. How long had they travelled before they'd even reached the drop site?

'Should we help carry the stretchers?' Amber asked Naomi, who narrowed her eyes.

'You want us to tire ourselves out helping to carry people in the wrong direction?'

'I think we should show willing.' Amber's tone was sharper than she realised. 'We need to show these people we're on the same side. I'm going to offer myself.'

Naomi blinked and nodded. 'No need. It makes more sense for the men to do it.' She muttered to her team and Daniel and two other men offered their services to the female medic. She waved them towards a man lying with a bandage over his eyes.

'Unconscious,' Branko said. 'Head wound. Chetniks.' He spat the last word out. 'When we've unpacked all the guns you've sent, we'll have a chance to retaliate.'

'You are thinking that this is a perplexing country.' The voice was low, female. The medic. 'My name is Ana,' she said, giving the clenched-fist salute.

'Amber.' Again Amber returned the salute in the conventional manner.

'The bandages and antiseptic were urgently needed. But did your plane drop the other medical supplies for us, Amber?' There was the hint of something in the older woman's voice: a threat? No, more a wary expectation that she might be let down.

'Our controller told us they'd packed anaesthetics and blankets. Syringes and sheets, too. There's another cylinder of medical supplies.'

Ana nodded. 'When we reach our camp, we shall unpack all you have for us. I hope very much it will not be as it has in the past, when we have found such oddities as mis-paired boots.' There was still the hint of a suggestion that she would hold Amber personally responsible if the supplies failed to live up to expectations. How could she have predicted that this Partisan medic would be glaring at her, holding her personally culpable for every missing jar of pills?

'When we move, we take our wounded with us. We don't leave men or women behind.' Ana seemed to stand taller. 'Sometimes it means carrying them for hundreds of kilometres. We have set up field hospitals for them, hidden in the forests.'

'It's impressive.' Amber hoped her words expressed that she was moved by the thought of injured people being borne along by their comrades.

'Sometimes we take civilians with us, too. When the Italians capitulated and the Germans were moving in on the Jewish internment camps on some of the Dalmatian islands, Partisans liberated the Jews. We took old and sick people with us.'

'That must be difficult if you need to be quick and agile to fight the Germans.'

'That's the dilemma.' Ana's voice grew harsher. 'We signalled the British and asked them to pick up the sick Jews from the coast or inland where there were suitable landing strips and take them to Italy. They wouldn't come.'

It was complicated, getting agreement from the RAF and the navy to mount such a rescue effort. Complicated, but perhaps not impossible. Amber translated into English for Naomi.

She said nothing in response, but moments later Amber heard her telling Daniel that she would take over his end of the stretcher.

'It's not far now,' Ana said in English. She gave a half-smile at Amber's surprise. 'My son and I speak your language.'

'Your son?'

'Branko. He is one of the youngest leaders in the whole Partisan movement.' A note of pride entered her voice. It was too dark and too much concentration had to be given to the uneven track to look for family resemblances between the two. Ana strode forward to Branko, asking him what he thought he was doing, setting such a brisk pace that her stretcher bearers would collapse before long. Beside her tall son the medic looked tiny. Ana hadn't seemed so small when she'd interrogated Amber about supplies. 'We have been fighting the Germans all the time you British were waiting to take them on,' she said, falling back to walk with Amber and Naomi again.

'You didn't want to fight just then,' Naomi said. 'You let those Chetniks go.'

'We know when to pounce. You will learn, young woman.'

'I already know that it is necessary to destroy the enemy,' Naomi said matter-of-factly.

'Perhaps you thought you could come out here and teach us unruly Yugoslavs how to do their job?'

'We didn't think that,' Amber said, interjecting before Naomi could answer. 'They told us you were the experts at blowing up railway lines and roads and disrupting supplies. Some of us are trained to do those things, but you have done them for real, in your own country. You have experience and local knowledge, and we will learn from you. Perhaps there are things we can show you, too.'

Ana said nothing, moving forward to the stretchers. Amber hoped the moment had passed.

'That was well handled,' Naomi said softly over her shoulder. 'She's prickly.'

More than prickly. Terrifying.

'Perhaps I would be too, in her position,' Naomi went on. 'As you say, we will learn from these people. Ana's obviously very . . . professional.'

The track wound its way uphill and became looser underfoot. Even the ponies seemed to struggle. A mist had fallen, blanketing the trail so that Amber could barely see the people ahead of her now. She kept her eyes on the rucksack on Naomi's back, trusting that Naomi was paying similar attention to the person in front of her. In Amber's own rucksack she carried only essentials: a change of underwear and socks, spare shirts, a toothbrush, a bar of soap, emergency rations. *Don't flash luxuries in front of the Partisans, some of them have lived rough for more than a year now.* In her jacket pocket she had her torch, code book and compass, and a lipstick, carefully chosen to be a brand available in the Balkans. *You never know when a dab of cosmetics might help morale. Or impress some male who needs buttering up.* Her knife was in her belt and her pistol, a Ballester-Molina specially imported from South America for SOE on grounds of its accuracy and reliability, in her holster. Her rifle was in one of the canisters.

Amber must have fallen into a trance as the group scrabbled along the track. She found herself nearly knocking into Naomi's rucksack when the line came to an abrupt halt. Someone called out a password. An answering call followed softly.

'We're here.' Branko pointed at a dark opening, just visible through the mist, illuminated by a faint and flickering lantern. 'The cave entrance is there. Women sleep inside. Men in the open. The wounded are in a second cave. Put your things inside. We'll heat a pot of food on the fire after we've fetched water from the stream.' Metal pots were unloaded from ponies and men and women disappeared with them down a slope leading, Amber assumed, to a stream.

Naomi and Amber found themselves spaces on the floor of the cave, nodding politely at other women, who ranged in age from schoolgirls to the middle-aged, undoing belts of grenades and pistols as quickly and confidently as any male combatant. It might have been the first day in a new dorm at the beginning of a school term.

'We should help with getting water and firewood,' Amber said.

Naomi nodded, looking approving. Perhaps she really was getting the message that Amber understood the importance of teamwork.

They grabbed cans from the pile beside the ponies and followed the track. As they passed the cave where Ana was organising a field hospital, the medic watched them. Amber thought she detected surprise in the older woman's face. Maybe she thought the newcomers would believe themselves too good to carry water? Mist still obscured the side of the mountain, but the faint clink of metal indicated where the Partisans carried the pots down to the stream. The sound reminded Amber of camping trips with her father: waking to hear him return to their tent with water. The difference then had been that he had not attempted to muffle the sounds he made as he went about this task. Naomi must have been thinking something similar.

'I remember youth camps when I was younger,' she said. 'Back home.' There was a vulnerability in her tone that Amber had never noticed before. She hadn't heard Naomi talk much of her youth, and as Robert had never encouraged too much personal revelation between his operatives, she hadn't liked to ask questions. She didn't even know Naomi's real name. But something about the dark trees around them, the adrenaline still flowing in her veins after the parachute drop, and the trek here made Amber push aside the reticence.

'I liked camping, too. I used to go with my parents. It always seemed an escape from everyday life. Even now . . .' She stopped, feeling foolish. Surely she hadn't been about to say that she was enjoying this first night on enemy territory?

'Our past lives follow us.' Naomi sounded solemn.

'We'll go back to them when we've done our work.'

'I hope so,' Naomi said. 'I'm not really sure where I'm from any more, or where I'll go back to. Hungary? That was a good life, with my parents, lots of comfort, intellectual challenge, music. Or Palestine: in the countryside, doing farm work. Not intellectually challenging, but being with so many other young people, all so optimistic about what we can achieve . . .'

They rounded a boulder and joined the other women standing at the edge of the cold, fast-flowing stream. One of them, an older woman, said something disapproving.

'What was that?' Naomi asked.

'She says we're guests and should not be working.'

Naomi made a tutting noise. 'In the kibbutz if you don't do your fair share, you're in trouble.'

Branko was standing by the fire as they came back into the camp, looking surprised at the full cans of water in their hands. 'I was looking for you,' he told Amber. 'When you've had a chance to . . . freshen up, come and find me here.'

A woman standing by the fire handed Amber a can of warm water. In the cave she switched on her torch and examined her face in her hand mirror. Her hair, which she'd endeavoured to keep tied back, had escaped from its bindings on one side, hanging lankly over a cheek. At some point in the trek she must have put a dirtied finger to her face, which bore a black smear. She tidied up as best she could in the gloomy interior of the cave and went to find Branko. He offered her his flask. She took a sip and wished she hadn't, trying not to gasp as she swallowed the liquid.

The scent of the goat stew warming up in a pot over the fire wafted round the camp, aromatic and rich. Amber's stomach gurgled. For a moment she was back in a childhood kitchen, with a Serbian or Croat cook stirring a pot on the stove. Game, pastries, fruit . . . How she'd missed those dishes in wartime Britain.

He motioned her to a bench constructed from a plank of wood on two upturned buckets. 'We will unload the supplies that arrived with you.'

'I hope it's what you need.'

'So do I.' His tone became sterner and he looked older suddenly. 'It is very important that Cairo supplies us regularly. We cannot keep up this pressure on the Germans without support.'

'I know.'

'And you'll transmit tomorrow and tell them this?'

'Tomorrow night. We have an agreed time for regular signals.'

'If you go up the slope you should find it easier. We will stay here for a day to let the wounded and pack ponies rest. To stay any longer is dangerous.'

'Which way will we go then?' Naomi had approached them silently.

'South for a bit.'

'That's no good for me,' Naomi said. 'It takes me even farther away from the border.'

'It's the same for us.' Branko rose. 'Our objective is to press north. But we cannot get through the Chetnik positions with our wounded and we will not leave them.' He said it with passion. 'You should get some stew now, before it is all eaten.'

They queued for bowls and spoons and ate in silence. When they'd finished, they rinsed out their bowls in the pail of warm water by the fire and retreated to the cave. Naomi sat down on her sleeping bag, pulling objects out of her rucksack: a frock, a powder compact and lipstick, along with a beret.

'Very pretty,' Amber said.

Naomi folded the dress, which was wool, obviously well cut. It would show off her figure.

'Would you wear your boots with it?'

'I brought stockings. A thick pair for the hills and some lighter ones for the city. My boots are a bit clunky, but it's not a bad look.' She removed a cigarette lighter from her rucksack, a different make from Amber's and black in colour, not silver – probably Hungarian to fit in with Naomi's cover story. Amber felt a guilty relief. 'Robert gave me this, but as I don't smoke I'll leave it here.'

'When we move on?'

The other girl looked over her shoulder. The cave was empty apart from the two of them. Everyone else surrounded the fire or was clearing up the supper dishes and making sure the pack ponies were securely tethered.

'When *I* move on. Alone. You're not going to send a signal until tomorrow morning. That's too late.'

'You're leaving us?'

'I've been thinking it over while we ate, making calculations.'

Amber wanted to grab Naomi, to force her to stay, not to leave her. She linked the fingers of her hands together to stop herself from acting on the impulse.

'I can't wait for Daniel's ankle to heal. Anyway, it's probably safer if I'm by myself.'

'But you can't go alone, you—'

'I'm just a love-sick Magyar girl who followed the Hungarian troops over the border when they annexed the northeast provinces.'

'Pretty dangerous. Would a civilian girl really do something like that?'

Naomi gave her a sideways look. 'You know how it is when there's someone you just can't stop thinking about?'

Amber felt her cheeks burn.

'Someone you'd do anything for? Someone you fall for in wartime, when feelings suddenly run hot? You'd do anything, go anywhere, wouldn't you, Amber?'

'You know about him?' She felt shame. This relationship with the officer who had recruited and trained them, who was directing their operation, it had been so wrong. She'd known it at the time if she were truthful. But she'd hoped the others hadn't found out about it.

'About you and Robert? Yes. I guessed.'

'The others?'

Naomi snorted. 'Those boys are about as obtuse about matters romantic as it's possible to be. Don't worry, your secret is safe with me.'

Amber let out a breath.

'Can't say I thought it was the most sensible thing to do, but the man has a certain magnetism about him, I suppose. Just be careful.'

'Careful? You're a fine one to talk.' This conversation had to be turned back to Naomi's dangerous proposal. 'Those territories that the Hungarians occupied are hundreds of miles away. If you're caught, they'll want to know what you're doing over here.'

'Oh, I drifted around looking for work.'

'What happened to soldier boy?'

'He disgraced himself in a brothel. Now I'm out of money so I'm going home to my mother.'

'What's your planned bearing?'

'North for a bit. Then east. I haven't decided yet whether to make for Zagreb. There may be more chance of getting rides from the city to the border.'

'You won't have a wireless operator with you if you go alone.'

'Having a man with me wouldn't exactly fit my lovesick maiden story.'

'Robert thought it all through. There were reasons why you weren't to go into Hungary alone.'

'But the original plan's been thrown out, anyway. We didn't land near either the Slovene or the Hungarian border.' Naomi frowned. 'And I'm still not sure why.'

'Increased German reconnaissance flights,' Robert said. 'You need to wait until we've heard from Cairo.'

'I know what Robert said.' She sounded sharp. 'But I'm hundreds of miles away from where I ought to have been. I can't afford to have my mission derailed like this. I'll be less noticeable alone.'

'You'd never be unnoticeable, Naomi.' She was so pretty, but seemed to have no idea. She hadn't noticed how the RAF sergeant had looked at her when he'd fastened the parachute straps around her, or how the men here seemed to blink when they saw her for the first time. Amber prayed Naomi's looks wouldn't draw attention to her at border crossings.

'I'll scrub off the lipstick if I'm in danger. I also have these.' From a pocket of the rucksack she pulled out a pair of round spectacles.

When she put them on, Amber had to smile. 'You look like a filing clerk. But won't border guards and police wonder why you didn't have your specs on in your identity photo?'

'I'm taking two identities.'

'Two?' Additional identity cards were supposed to be hidden away, only taken out with them in extreme circumstances.

'They won't find the other one.' She looked Amber in the eye.

The additional identity would be in a skirt lining or in the side of the rucksack, undetectable unless you knew where it was. Robert had shown them half a dozen places where they could hide dangerous documents. For a man who was casual enough to smuggle her into the villa, Robert was meticulous when it came to his work. *Those who design your rucksacks and prepare your clothes know that they do so with me standing over them, asking them if they would send their own wife or daughter into enemy territory with the equipment they have provided.*

'I'll find our contacts in Hungary and get a signal to Cairo as quickly as I can, so they can tell you that I'm all right.' She spoke with a quiet confidence.

'What will the others do?' Amber asked.

'Wait for instructions from Cairo. When his ankle's better, Samuel can follow me over the border. The others will continue the objective of aiding Allied airmen, and identifying and clearing possible landing strips.'

'So you're off?'

Amber blinked at the sound of the voice at the cave entrance. Once again, Ana had appeared out of nowhere. 'You think you can navigate in the dark?' she said in English. 'With bands of Chetniks still around?'

'I have no choice. If you were listening in, you will know why.'

Ana nodded. 'I would probably want to do the same thing in your position. But before I did, I would want to be absolutely sure I knew all the risks. You do not know as we do what some of the people, if you can call those animals people, out there are like.'

'We were briefed,' Amber said. 'They told us about the Ustaše militia, they—'

Ana raised a hand. 'Hearing about it and seeing it are two different things. We have seen the bodies of some of those they have tortured and killed. Your friend has not.'

A coldness filled Amber. She wanted to beg Naomi, plead with her not to go when they'd only just arrived among a group of strangers. The fleeting sense of this being just another camp in the hills was a mirage. It was a temporary Partisan base, housing many seriously wounded fighters, and surrounded by people who wished to kill them. She needed Naomi. But this wasn't about her feelings, was it?

Ana shrugged. 'As long as you know. I do not understand all the elements of your operation, but suspect there is another objective that is personal to you. That's fine. This war is personal for me, too, at times.

But I'm a Partisan. I work with my comrades. The collective objective always comes first.' With a curt nod Ana was gone.

Naomi took off the spectacles. Her hand found Amber's. 'I wish I didn't have to leave you so soon, but it was only ever going to be a short time together, you know.'

'I know.'

'I'd have left for Hungary soon anyway. But I'll miss you, Amber.' She grinned. 'Back in the gym in Cairo, I never thought I'd say that.'

'I was a brat at first.'

'And I was a bit of a prig.'

'Just a little, even if you were right. I'll miss you, too. I hope you manage to do, well, what you want to do.'

Naomi's voice dropped to a whisper. 'I've heard stories about what will happen to the Jews of Hungary if the Germans get hold of them. I cannot get these stories out of my head.'

Amber forced herself to take a breath, to try reason. 'But you must be exhausted. Why not wait until morning?'

'I'll sleep when I've regained some of the mileage we lost this evening.' She put a finger to her lips. 'I've left a note for Samuel. He'll find it in the morning. I don't want to tell them or Branko this evening.'

'Ana will tell Branko.'

'Which is why I really do need to slip away now.'

'Good luck.' Amber said it flatly.

Naomi smiled as she swung her rucksack on to her back. 'We've changed roles. You're playing the sensible one now, Amber. You've become a real leader.'

'Have I?'

'Attacking those Chetniks at the bridge on the way here? That could have been a serious misjudgement, if you hadn't stopped us. And you persuaded us to take a turn carrying the stretchers and made the Partisans trust us.' She touched Amber's hand briefly and straightened the beret on her head.

For a second they stood together in the dark cave. Then Naomi vanished into the darkness outside, silent as a cat. Amber sat on her outspread sleeping bag staring at the cave entrance as though she could still make out the girl's slight outline. The cold feeling in the pit of her stomach didn't leave her. Ridiculous to feel alone when Samuel, Daniel and the others were still in the camp. But they weren't women. Strange, she'd never seen herself as a woman's woman before, finding men the easier companions. School had often been miserable. But she and Naomi had found an understanding, a sympathy. A comradeship. Now it was gone.

You will feel isolated at times. It is natural. Find something to do. Amber set her shoulders. Make a start on writing out tomorrow's wireless transmission. She found her notepad and pencil and began to compose the message, which would have to be précised and turned into Morse. Her head began to nod. Time to turn in. She stashed pad and pencil in her rucksack and went out to find water to wash in.

She must have slept almost immediately after climbing into the rucksack because it was light when raised voices woke her. Amber pulled her legs out of the sleeping bag, reached for her pistol and ran to the entrance. Branko stood, taking the Beretta from his holster, calling softly but decisively to his people. The Partisans, employed in everyday, almost domestic duties until a second ago, were suddenly warriors, on guard, alert. Amber cocked her own gun.

Intruders.

9

June 1947

I'd felt exposed as those intruders invaded the Partisan camp. I feel almost as vulnerable this morning, going for my next session with Dr Rosenstein.

There's nothing about Dr Rosenstein's appearance that should make me fearful: her brown hair that is never entirely contained by its bun, her long, slender fingers that surely must have played a violin or piano.

I've watched those hands as she's swept files left and right across the desk, looking for a slip of paper. Jim, who seems to know everything about everyone here, told me Dr Rosenstein escaped from Berlin with her family in 1938. They don't always tell you much about themselves, these psychiatrists, but she has photographs on her desk. Once, she told me about her daughter eating a banana for the first time. She looked a little guilty, as though she weren't really supposed to confide in patients.

But I'm not like all the other patients, not like those ones behind the baize door. I don't insist on eating my food from a bowl on the floor, or wear my dress back to front like that woman who saw her husband and children burn to death in an air raid.

She listens to me recount what I've written in my journal about how it felt to fly away from Robert and nods when I've finished. 'There's obviously much more we need to talk about where he's concerned. But for now, tell me about your arrival in Croatia.'

I tell her about the anxious wait above the bridge while the Chetniks lingered below, about the prickly Partisan medic, Ana. I tell her about Naomi leaving: how lonely that made me feel. And I describe how I'd awoken on the first morning to find the camp in uproar because intruders had come in.

'You'd been training for such an event, but it must have been daunting. However, you didn't panic and start shooting before you ascertained what was going on, did you?' she asks.

Of course not, I want to retort. 'There was discipline on our side, and on the Partisans'.' The previous evening I'd been worried about some of the men who'd come over with us, they'd wanted to rush into things, but they had followed Branko's orders.

'You felt, what? Afraid?'

'There was no time for that. My response was automatic. We'd had so much training on how to respond that I barely had to think.'

'You could control your fears?'

'Yes.'

'What we're planning is for you to show us that we can trust you to leave this . . . institution and live a life that doesn't pose a threat to any other person.'

She means living alongside people without trying to kill them.

'I want you to show yourself and everyone else that you are a measured, reasoning person. That you aren't suffering from some trauma that makes you dangerous to others.'

'Do I have shell shock?' The words burst out of me. I think of young men shaking, hands on ears, because they were in trenches for too long. I have never done that, but perhaps the trembling part of it is not universal. They used to give them tap-dancing lessons. At Woodlands, we play badminton. Jim is teaching me bridge, too. I suppose it helps.

Dr Rosenstein taps her fingers on the black notebook before she answers. 'It's not what I'm thinking, no. You saw awful things, of course, and they may have affected you afterwards. But you were chosen for the work and carefully vetted.' Her gaze lifts from the notebook to me. 'Are you all right, Maud?'

My attention has drifted. 'I was just . . .'

She waits, pen in hand.

'Sorry, my mind has slipped back to something that's just started to puzzle me, something from the beginning.' It's so frustrating, I get so far in remembering my past and then something from earlier on will trip me up and demand that I examine it.

She looks at me encouragingly.

'You said I'd been chosen. Some kind of distant memory has come to me.'

Dr Rosenstein observes me patiently.

'I think they came out to the mine before the war started, just before my father was sent to Belgrade.'

'Who do you mean by "they"?'

'Robert Havers and a colleague.' Something about me had caught their attention. My languages? I'd been packing up Dad's mineral cabinet at the time, but I had probably been as quiet and precise in my movements as I'd been in everything I did as a child. 'Two men came out to talk to Dad about security at the mine; I think I told you about them? I only met one of them. The other one didn't come inside. I wonder if he was Robert.'

'Impossible to know,' Dr Rosenstein says.

'The one who came into the house,' I say. 'Something about him . . .' I shake my head. 'My mother had baked some cakes and he was very keen on them.' I remember him brushing the crumbs off his face.

'You think this man is important to your story?'

'I don't know. It was such a long time ago.' Centuries ago.

'Keep working on it,' Dr Rosenstein tells me. 'Keep writing things down, Maud. You're stimulating your memory in two ways: by talking and by writing. We'll go on with your story in the next session.'

As I leave the office two of the servants are escorting a new guest upstairs. Nobody introduces you, so I can't even greet him properly. When they reach the top of the stairs I turn right towards my bedroom, but the staff take the man by the arm and lead him through the baize door. These are not servants, I remind myself. They are nursing staff. This is a psychiatric hospital. An asylum. Bedlam. A madhouse. Just because it doesn't seem that way in my section, it doesn't diminish that fact. The other wing behind the door houses the lino-floored wards and seclusion units, where disturbed patients are placed in packs: cold, wet sheets, and then layers of blankets and tied down on the beds until they're calm.

I have been packed myself. Not here at Woodlands, some time ago, before Dr Rosenstein started treating me. Jim and I agree it's not the worst thing that can happen to us, almost like being a swaddled infant. I remember my Serbian nanny wrapping a cold wet bandage and then a warm cloth around my sore throat. The pain went. In a pack you can't hurt yourself or anyone else. But if they don't do it properly the circulation in your legs stops and it's agony when they unwrap you and your blood flows into the extremities again. I'm reminded of being in the Halifax on the way to Yugoslavia: we were so cold, even in our flying suits and sleeping bags. I think, too, of a mummy I saw in a Cairo museum: embalmed and wrapped for placing in a tomb.

Instead of resting, as I ordinarily would after a session, I decide to crack on, to write down more of these reflections. I find my notebook and sit in my usual spot on the window seat to write.

We'd been well schooled on ranges, and in gun fights in mocked-up villages in remote parts of southern England. We knew how to defend ourselves. But it was still a shock when the two Chetniks burst in on the Partisan camp just after first light.

They dragged a prisoner with them: a German officer.

My first German. Amber stared at the prisoner like a silly schoolgirl. Branko approached the trio, revolver pointed at them. 'What's this about?' His voice was low but angry.

'You like German officers, and so we bring you one.'

'What do you mean?'

'You say we're too soft on them. Now's your chance to show us how we should treat prisoners. He's for sale.'

Branko's lip curled in contempt. 'We don't trade for prisoners.'

'This isn't just any German officer. He's Intelligence.'

From the cave entrance Amber felt her skin prick.

'We ambushed his car. Before he died, the driver said he was taking this man up through Slovenia and over into Austria.'

'You didn't kill the German, your marksmen need more practice.' Branko was walking away.

'Major Max Stimmer, German Military Intelligence HQ in Belgrade.' The Chetnik paused, looking for a reaction. 'He will know about Nazi plans to attack you.'

'I'll save you a bullet.' Branko aimed the gun at the prisoner.

'Big drop of supplies last night,' the Chetnik said. 'Our boys followed you from the drop zone. Give us what we ask for and then you can make him talk.' The German prisoner must have understood some of the language because his eyes narrowed. The ponies moved on their tethers, some dropping their heads to graze at the thin grass.

Ana moved swiftly and silently to stand next to Amber. 'We should shoot the three of them,' she whispered.

'No.' The inspiration came to Amber. 'Tell Branko we should take the officer.'

'What?'

'Cairo can interrogate him. Find out what the Germans are planning.'

Amber had lost Naomi. The drop zone had been moved south, making it harder for her to carry out her own mission of exflitrating Allies out of Yugoslavia. But the whole business could be turned around, made into even more of a success than they could ever have hoped for during their briefings at Rustum Buildings.

She could make Robert proud of her.

'Keep the German,' she told Ana. 'When I make my transmission, I'll confirm it all with Cairo.'

Branko lent her a pack pony to transport the wireless up the slope. Amber stopped to wipe her brow on her jacket sleeve and the pony took the opportunity to nibble at the meagre vegetation. She spotted a rock that could act as a transmission desk, then unloaded the wireless and laid out the code book and the message she had composed in the relative warmth of the cave. The pack pony lifted his head briefly to eye her apathetically before returning to cropping the sparse grass.

She opened her notebook, put on the headphones, turned the SEND-REC knob and switched on the current. Turning the tuner, she searched for the pre-agreed signal Robert's team had given her, thinking of an unknown girl, probably her own age, hundreds of miles away, pencil in hand, waiting for the transmission. Strange for her, the formerly cold Maud, to feel such emotion at the thought of contact with this other girl. She swallowed. *I chose you because I knew you could do this.* Robert had told her this several times with that slow, almost mocking smile of his. *I knew you could cope with the pressure, Amber. Generally wireless operators are kept away from operations, but we don't have enough people in Yugoslavia at the moment, so you'll have to carry out both functions.*

If Naomi had still been here she'd have come up the hillside with Amber and helped her set up, stood guard as she transmitted. How far had Naomi got now? Was she hungry or cold? It was hard to think of her giving in to such weaknesses. *Get on with the task. Input the password and remember to include the pre-agreed 'mistake': substituting a random letter for each eighth letter of the coded message. Make a mental note to burn the one-use-only code in the book when you've finished.*

Amber looked over her shoulder. If someone came up behind her when she put on the headphones and absorbed herself in the transmission she might not hear them. She resisted a shiver and swept the dial a fraction to the right.

And there it was, the answering return signal. The girl at the other end knew it was her. Amber was no longer alone on the hillside, but part of a web of communication. She answered the personal security questions, the name of the terrier Mama had owned at Trpca and her own favourite brand of chocolate: CADBURY. When these answers were cleared, she tapped in the message she'd encoded. *Clarity, accuracy and brevity.* It was hard to explain the derailment of the mission and the arrival of Stimmer in this way. Was she being too cryptic? She tapped in the last characters, stating that she would tune in for any answer in an hour, took off the headphones and switched off the set. Not enough time to dismantle the aerial. Surely up here in this inhospitable terrain she'd be safe from mobile detection units triangulating her signal.

The breeze blew cold on her neck. The pony lifted his head and let out a high-pitched neigh. The strangled sound seemed to echo something inside Amber. She heard footsteps and swung round. A girl, perhaps a year or so younger than herself, rifle slung over one shoulder, stood staring at her. She carried a basket full of what looked like straggly weeds but were probably herbs. It might have been a scene from any time in the last millennium, when women foraged for something to eat out on the karst at the close of winter. Only the rifle placed the girl in the middle of the twentieth century, in a struggle that was convulsing almost the whole world, not merely a corner of the Balkans. With a nod, the girl walked by. Probably going to boil the herbs for soup. Amber resisted the urge to call her back, to ask her about herself, her family, the home she'd left, anything to make herself feel less alone. She looked at her watch. Perhaps something had gone wrong with the transmission. She'd checked the coded message so carefully, but had she missed something? She walked up and down, waving her arms around in an attempt to keep the blood flowing, peering at rocks and shrubs, reminding herself that she had her pistol.

The hour was almost up. Amber returned to the rock and replaced her headphones and repeated the process of tuning in to the signal. She translated the words as they arrived in Morse and wrote them down.

Want decommissioned Belgrade parcel STOP. You confirm arrangements soonest STOP. Paprika consignment noted STOP.

How quickly they'd forwarded her messages on to Robert and got his approval for the airlift of Stimmer. What about Naomi – the paprika consignment? He'd seemed to accept her absconding alone. Perhaps he thought it made such good sense it barely needed comment. Naomi's mission was always going to be dangerous.

Once again the strange churning in her stomach caught her by surprise. It must be a combination of relief that the transmission was over and loneliness at losing the brief, cryptic contact. She pictured Robert himself standing by the wireless operator in Bari or Cairo, dictating the reply. He knew he could trust her. She closed her eyes briefly, almost smelling his particular scent: wool and cotton and that woody aroma. Did he miss her? Probably not as much as she missed him. He'd enjoyed sleeping with her, that was all. Time to forget all that. Robert was simply her handler, even if she'd felt more for him than she should. Naomi had been right to call the relationship dangerous.

When Amber had stored her equipment, she found the German prisoner and asked him if he needed water.

'Please, I am thirsty,' he replied in fluent Serbo-Croat. His lips curled slightly as he registered her surprise. 'I spent some years in Belgrade before the war. And have had many opportunities in the last eighteen months to practise the language.'

'Doing what?' German military intelligence wasn't supposed to be as evil in its methods as other German security departments, but the bar was not set high. Had this man interrogated prisoners in their own language, resorting to the other language of pain and fear, too?

He narrowed his eyes.

'We both know that it is in your interest to be cooperative.'

He continued his silence.

'I could tell this group that I've changed my mind. They can do what they want to you. I hear Germans aren't well treated when they fall into Partisan hands.' Robert had told them how Partisans would occasionally mutilate prisoners before killing them. *Don't imagine that our allies adhere to normal wartime rules.*

He stiffened.

'Who are you, Fräulein?' he asked. 'You're not a Partisan. Last year there were some Canadian-Croats around these parts.' He looked at Amber inquisitorially, forgetting who was the prisoner and who the interrogator.

She took out her pistol to remind him.

'One of your number has headed north.' He gave her a curt smile. 'I overheard them talking about her. In English.' He nodded towards Samuel and Daniel. She looked at the young men. It was dangerous for them to discuss Naomi anywhere near the German. They'd need speaking to. Strange how it now seemed natural for her to do this.

Someone shouted. '*Avioni!*' She heard the planes overhead, screaming towards them, and grabbed the field glasses she wore around her neck to identify them: German Stukas.

'Get down.' She waved her pistol at the German. The pack ponies screamed, kicking out and pulling at the stakes to which they were tethered. Little puffs of earth flicked up around the clearing. Explosives landed nearby and the ground shook. Amber rolled onto her back. The pistol wasn't going to accomplish much – she needed her rifle, which had been unpacked and stored in the cave. The planes banked for a return.

She ran for the cave, very low, as though starting the sprint at sports day, diving on to her sleeping bag, throwing off the field glasses, and pulling the rifle from its hiding place. As she left the cave, the planes were overhead. Three of Naomi's group ran to the patch of firs on the side of the clearing, rifles in hands. They dropped to their knees, firing up at the formation. From behind them further shots rang out, Branko shouting between rounds. Had he had time to assemble the weapons dropped yesterday night? Amber fell to the ground behind the log, timing her shots. The Stukas flew very low. A tree beside the cave entrance catapulted into the air, roots and all.

A salvo of heavier fire opened up to Amber's right: the Brens, the machine guns dropped last night. With no time to attach them to their tripods, the Partisans were firing them from their shoulders. A Stuka's wings flashed silver and orange. The plane turned away, seeming to have survived with just a flesh wound, before it screamed and spiralled to the ground. Its companions banked sharply and retreated. The men cheered.

Amber stood up. Two of the pack ponies writhed on the ground, one appearing almost untouched, the other spilling intestines onto the ground, a dung-stench already spreading from the animal. Branko pulled out his pistol and shot each between the ears. 'Get them carved up quickly,' he told a man on his right. 'Don't let them spoil.'

The Partisans who'd fired the Brens patted the weapons as though they were pets. At least something from the parachute drop had proved its use.

Ana emerged from the hospital cave. 'We got off lightly,' she said. 'Two ponies killed and some of our comrades with flesh wounds. This will cost us when we travel onward.' She looked past Amber. 'Where's that Nazi of yours?'

Amber looked where she was staring. The stake was still there. Stimmer was gone. The blast must have shaken the post from the ground and he'd released himself, unnoticed in the melee.

'He knows our numbers and how we're armed,' Ana said. 'He's probably overheard us talking about where we're heading.' Her eyes, when she turned to Amber, were cold with anger. 'You insisted that we give up supplies to take him prisoner. We were wrong to listen to you.'

Naomi had been wrong about Amber, too. Some leader she was proving to be. 'I'll find him.'

Ana stared at her, her upper lip curved, 'You'd better hurry.'

Amber ran down towards the stream. The German would be making for the scant protection of the trees, then he would work his way back upstream, where there was most cover. As she ran, her hand went to the small of her back: damn, her rucksack was still in the camp, the map inside it. No time to return for it. She reached the stream and ran uphill, forcing herself to remember the terrain. At the top of the slope Stimmer would need to scrabble around a steep rock face and then walk down to a track leading to the road.

Amber was fit, fresh from training, armed. She patted her jacket pocket. Good, her torch was safely inside it. She could stalk him all day and all night, if necessary.

A fine drizzle fell, almost cold enough to become sleet. Amber pulled her cap down over her eyes and walked on, ears pricked for the slightest sound indicating that Stimmer was on the move again. The slope grew steeper. She climbed the rock face at the top, grateful for the Cairo gymnasium sessions that had strengthened her arms.

She reached the summit. On the other side, somewhere to the north, was the border with Slovenia to which Naomi was heading. Because the drop location had been changed at the last moment, there hadn't been as much time to learn the new locations, but she recalled a German garrison some twelve kilometres to the east, where the landscape sloped into less rocky terrain, with trees and fields. With her field glasses she made out the track leading downhill. Something shadowy jumped out a couple of hundred yards away. A deer startled by something?

He sprang suddenly from behind a rock, just feet ahead of her, pushing her over, his booted foot stamping on her right hand. He stooped and removed her pistol from the ground.

'A reversal of fortunes,' he said in precise, barely accented English. 'Stand up slowly and turn out all your pockets. And take off the field glasses.'

She felt her stomach flip as she stood and placed her things on the ground. He picked up her identity card and examined them. 'So you're claiming military status, Fräulein? Even though we both know you're a spy.'

'I'm in uniform.'

He looked at her cap, flying jacket, breeches and boots. 'They set you loose on the dressing-up box?'

Her head thumped.

'Pick up your possessions. Except for the field glasses.' Feeling nauseous, she obeyed, replacing her few personal items in her jacket. She could smash the mirror and turn it into a blade, but he'd need to be looking away . . .

'Put them back in your pocket. Don't try anything with the comb, or mirror: I know all the tricks. You and I are bound for the nearest garrison, where we will talk in detail.'

He would interrogate her himself, but bring in rougher guards if necessary. Then there would be a cell, perhaps further interrogation. Then a short walk to a wall where she would be shot. They wouldn't believe she was really a combatant. Despite the uniform, they'd say she was a spy.

'You had a map?' he said.

'Left it in the camp.' Amber was surprised at how level her voice sounded. It didn't seem quite real yet, this abrupt end to her operation.

She didn't even feel scared. Yet. Just sad. So much time and trouble bestowed on her for it all to come to nothing. How long would it take word to reach Robert of what had happened, for her parents to be informed? Would they send a telegram to Shropshire or would someone visit the house in person? She swayed, the world spinning in front of her.

'Sit down there.' He pointed to a spot on the ground five metres away, close enough for him to catch her if she ran, but far enough away that she couldn't grab at the pistol. 'Hands on your head.'

The sickness was passing. Apart from a throbbing right temple, she was uninjured. Without moving her head, Amber surveyed the landscape over which she had just come. If she sprinted she could make the dead ground behind her, hide on the far side of a limestone outcrop. She might gain a second or two – she'd always been a fast starter in school sprints.

Stimmer made a faint sound. Surprise? Relief? She strained to hear. Below them a motor engine purred up the track, which must be more navigable in its lower parts than it had seemed. Stimmer said nothing, but even without seeing his face she could feel the satisfaction floating off him. The car braked and the ignition was switched off. Doors opened. Footsteps trudged towards them. She couldn't turn her head to see whom the car had delivered.

'May we help you, sir?' one of the voices said, in Croatian-accented German.

'I have a prisoner.'

They walked around to examine her. Two men in black uniforms. Ustaše militia. *Do all you can to evade capture by the Croat fascists. I could tell you stories of the limbs of murdered women and children floating down rivers and blocking culverts . . .*

'Lucky for you that we were in the area, sir,' the more senior said. Amber was back in the classroom at Rustum Buildings, memorising insignia: this one was a captain, his companion a lieutenant.

Stimmer glanced down towards their black car. 'A relaxing drive?'

The captain glowered. 'Reconnaissance, sir. Fortunately, we are able to help you. One of the Partisan bitches, I see?'

She looked down at her boots. The lieutenant's hand smacked her on the left cheek.

'You going to tell me where your friends are or shall I beat it out of you?'

Calculations ran through Amber's mind. The Partisan group below had already been fired on by the Stukas. They'd be moving out now, not waiting any longer. If she could wait an hour or so longer before giving their location away, it would give them precious time.

'Let's take you back to headquarters, sir, along with your prisoner. We'll send more men back here.' Amber said nothing. The lieutenant slapped her other cheek. Her eyes watered.

'Not bad looking, is she?' the captain said.

'We have a moment, sir.' One hand reached for her jacket, pulling the zip down, fumbling at her jumper, trying to tug it up and expose her breasts. Amber's mouth filled with bile.

The captain's other hand groped between her legs. 'She's attractive enough. Shame these Partisan whores insist on trousers.'

'Shouldn't present much of a problem, sir.' The lieutenant shoved Amber down onto the stony ground beside the track. She winced as stones cut into her. One of his gloved hands held her by the throat, as though she were a dog that needed disciplining. The captain pulled at her breeches. She could feel him hard against her leg, smell the scented oil on his hair. She kicked at him. The gloved hand tightened on her throat. His smell sharpened with the aroma of sweat and metallic excitement. Everything seemed to be happening very slowly. Part of her brain knew what was happening, was going into shock, while the other half insisted on control, on calm, as she had been trained.

'Little she-devil.' The captain was having trouble with the button of her breeches. She squirmed on the ground so that his fingers wouldn't be able to undo it.

She winced as he pressed her down. He undid the button with a grunt of satisfaction and pulled the breeches down, undoing his own clothes to expose himself. She closed her eyes, but could feel him hard, jabbing against her, trying to enter her. She squirmed from side to side to stop him but the other man held her tighter. Perhaps it would be easier to submit, to let him penetrate her, but instinct wouldn't let her stop defending herself, even though she was probably receiving more injuries than she would do if she surrendered. He gave a bigger thrust and this time he succeeded in his attempt. He gave a sigh of satisfaction. His eyes glazing as he looked down at her.

'Stop,' Stimmer said quietly but with an authority that made the two men turn to him.

'Sir?' the lieutenant said.

'This is my prisoner,' Stimmer said.

The captain flinched, his hand loosening on Amber's breeches as he withdrew. She shook him off. 'Of course, Herr Maier, I—'

'You will drive us immediately to the German garrison.'

The captain rose to his feet, brushing down the front of his trousers, breathing heavily.

She pulled her clothing back up and stood up. As she did another mouthful of bile made her cough. *Be aware of the signs of shock in yourself. Account for the way it will affect your reactions.*

She was trembling, cold. To calm herself she forced her mind back into the present. *Look for escape routes.* As they walked towards the road her legs struggled to respond to her brain, wanting to fold beneath her. This side of the mountain was almost treeless. An exposed rock face rose from one side of the track, a steep drop fell from the other. Nowhere to run to. The captain opened the door and motioned her inside with the lieutenant. The car reversed and bumped down the rough track. With each jolt Amber winced. She needed to take her mind off what had happened; she couldn't let the feelings overwhelm her and cost her any chance of escape. Her companion on the back seat would probably shoot her before she'd got the passenger door open, even if it wasn't locked.

They reached the road. Progress would be faster now.

The world fragmented into shards of glass and a series of bright flashes.

Amber's brain synapses registered the attack a whole second after she dropped her head behind the front seat. The car skidded before lurching first to the left and then to the right, hitting a rock on the inside of the track. It came to a halt.

Silence. She raised her eyes, and then her head, inch by inch. Whoever had shot at them would be approaching. Her pistol was still in Stimmer's pocket; if she could reach for it or one of her guards' guns, there might be a chance . . .

The driver seemed motionless. So did his subordinate beside her on the back seat. Stimmer wasn't moving either, slumped over so that she couldn't retrieve her pistol. She pushed herself through the space between the front seats. The driver's forehead had a red hole in it. She wasn't sure about Stimmer. Amber crawled over the driver and reached for the door handle. A voice called out. She fell onto the road on her hands. On all fours she crawled to the back of the vehicle, instinct screaming at her to run.

You will want to run, but before you do, have you left anything behind that might save your life later on? She was unarmed. Amber forced herself to crawl back to the driver's door and removed the Walther P38 from the captain's holster, shoving it into her belt. A woman said something the ringing in her ears made impossible to hear. Amber crouched behind the open door. This time the woman called her by name.

10

Ana called me by name and everything changed. I put the cap on my pen. I can't write any more today, I'm shaking at the memory of what happened to me, of what that Ustaše militiaman did to me. I need to see my doves. Ingrams comes when I push the bell. 'Are you all right, Maud?'

'I think I pushed myself too far.' I put a hand to my temples. I sound flat, worn out. The scene outside revives me a little. Jim is helping the gardener erect a trellis, probably for sweet peas, looking distracted by the work. Ingrams walks with me to the dovecot. He spots a smashed bottle on the path.

'Those boys.' He picks it up carefully.

'I wish they'd leave us alone. They . . .' I'd been going to say they frightened me. It's because I've been writing up the scene with the Ustaše officers and have violent males on my mind.

'You're safe, Maud, they can't get in.' Ingrams puts down the bottle and erects the stepladder for me. 'Look at your doves. They'll make you feel better.'

He's right. The same pairs are inside. Their gentle sounds make the back of my neck feel less tense.

'I'm worried about that buzzard,' I say to Ingrams when I'm down again.

'I've never known him take a bird from here,' Ingrams says. 'Sometimes when I'm cycling here I see him gliding above me on an air current.'

'He's elegant, I'll give him that.'

'It's hard to tell who's an enemy and who's not in nature.' Ingrams stoops to pull up chickweed from the edge of a flowerbed. 'I like these little white flowers, but they're weeds, really.'

There's a sadness to his face when he says it. Jim has finished helping with the trellis and is standing on the terrace with his tennis balls. I see him juggle the four balls with confidence.

When I'm settled in my room, Ingrams appears with tea and a piece of toast for me. 'Don't write any more,' he says. 'Read some more of those history books.'

I try to read about the Civil War. The books normally grab my attention with their historical detail, some of it local to Woodlands. But I still keep seeing different scenes, a remote road in a country a long way from here. A car that's been attacked, uniformed men slumped over. Me in the back. Shots. A woman's voice.

I close my eyes and let the images fill my head.

Ana. It was Ana who'd come to my rescue.

Ana aimed her pistol at Stimmer's temple.

'Wait,' Amber called to her.

'For what? More trouble?'

'These two also knew about your friend, the one who's heading towards Slovenia. Their police must have told them,' Stimmer said in rapid Serbo-Croat, his voice low.

'What do you mean?' Amber asked. 'Give me back my pistol and tell me what you're talking about.'

Slowly he removed the gun from his jacket and handed it to her. 'Look in the front footwell.' He attempted to sit up straighter. Ana waved her gun at him.

Amber saw Naomi's beret.

'And the map there.' He nodded at the space between the two front seats. Amber pulled it out: Naomi's. A cross was marked on a village in a valley about sixteen kilometres to the north. 'The cross probably marks the spot where they found the beret,' Stimmer continued. He'd picked up these details so quickly as they'd driven down the track. Well, he was Intelligence, after all. 'We can assume they know a woman – a stranger – is heading north. Probably alone. She lost her beret and her map, so perhaps she ran into trouble.'

Amber shivered.

'They know she must have come from a base with more people. The police have sent word north to their colleagues to capture her and they came looking for the rest of you in this valley.'

Ana had been listening intently. 'Guesswork,' she said. 'Why were there only two of them?'

Stimmer shrugged. 'Local militiamen who happened to be there when the call came through. Thought they'd have a sniff around and telephone any information to the base from the nearest police station.' His voice was becoming more confident as he pieced it together. 'Their colleagues will pick up your friend before she reaches Slovenia. And if she does cross the border, I can assure you that the Ustaše have Slovene associates who'll act on their intelligence in an equally unpleasant way.'

'That's no concern of yours.' Ana aimed her gun at him.

'Wait.' Amber put out a hand.

'He has caused us enough trouble.'

'I can help you.' Stimmer sounded quietly confident.

Ana let out a harsh laugh.

'I spent some of my childhood in Slovenia,' he said. 'I know the routes across the border. And I know many of the German authorities in Slovenia. I can probably get your friend safely over the border into Hungary.'

'Why the hell would you do that?' Ana asked.

'The Allies are slowly pushing north in Italy. Tito is winning in Yugoslavia.' He looked at them in a more calculating way.

'Your side will put a bullet into you for desertion and aiding the enemy,' Ana said.

'Not if you fly me out to Egypt for questioning, as was the original plan, I gather.'

Ana cocked her gun at him again, glancing sideways at Amber without turning her head. 'We've wasted too much time on him. Our unit is moving out. We should be with them.'

'Naomi—'

'Is just one individual.'

'But—'

'Our cause is bigger than a single person.'

'You agreed you'd help us in all aspects of our work in return for drops of medicine and guns.'

'Many of which we had to give away to the Chetniks. Because of you.'

'There'll be more drops, Ana. But only if you help me find Naomi.' Amber faced the older woman, a head shorter than she was, with eyes that seemed to have been forged in the fieriest depths of a volcano. Ana's mouth tightened. 'Come with me,' Amber said. How strange that the former Maud, the girl who'd never understood female friendships, was once again yearning for the presence of another woman. But reason, not emotion, should be the basis of this argument. She made an effort not to let the longing manifest itself in her voice. 'It's in your interest to help me track her down quickly.'

Ana emitted a long, low sigh and looked down at the ground for a moment. She whistled. A boy hopped out from behind a rock. He must have observed the ambush. Of course, she wouldn't have come here alone. Ana said something rapidly and quietly to him. He ran off in the direction of the summit. She nodded at the car, with its bullet-shattered windscreen. 'We can drive until the petrol runs out. By then the local HQ will be missing these two. We need to put their bodies in the boot.' She waved her gun at Stimmer. 'That's for you to do.'

'Thank you.' Again the women held eye contact.

'You are in our debt,' Ana said. 'Once more. I hope I will not need to remind you of that, Amber, when the time comes for you to repay me for abandoning my unit to go with you.'

The older woman would probably pursue her through hell itself to force her to honour the obligation. 'I won't forget.'

Ana screwed up her eyes and examined her almost forensically. 'The back of your jacket is covered in dirt and you have bruised lips.' She turned so that Stimmer couldn't hear. 'Did they try something?'

Amber nodded. The older woman's expression lost some of its harshness. 'Do you need me to examine you?' It was easy to forget that Ana was a medic, that she had been trained to heal. And yet her black-mittened fingers on Amber's forearm were slender and looked as though they would search gently for any injury. The nails were cut short, remarkably clean.

Amber shook her head. 'It was . . . brief. Just one, briefly . . . He stopped them.' She nodded at Stimmer. Ana followed her gaze, still frowning. 'If I had some water and a cloth, I could . . .'

Ana nodded. With her knife she ripped off the front of the senior officer's shirt. She sniffed it. 'Clean on this morning.' She handed the torn material and her water bottle to Amber and pointed at an outcrop. 'Don't take long. Someone may come looking for those two.'

Behind the limestone rock Amber squatted and pulled down her lower clothes, washing away the blood, hoping the bruises would come out quickly and not affect her ability to do her work. At least she probably didn't have to fear pregnancy. But there was still the chance of disease. *An ability to push unwanted and unnecessary thoughts out of your mind will be of immense help.*

'I had to forget about it,' I tell Dr Rosenstein. 'About what the Ustaše did to me.'

I am telling her what I wrote down. There's a lot to catch up on; my pen flew across the pages of the pad.

'I couldn't brood on it. We had to go on, we had to find Naomi. I thought . . .' That if she had also been captured, what had almost happened to me would have been inflicted on her, and she would have nobody to defend her. 'Nothing had happened as it was supposed to, but there was still a chance to make things right, to save Naomi, guide her . . . where she needed to go safely and return to the group. And my wireless.'

'You wanted to make good. For Robert? Or for yourself?'

'Both. I felt ashamed.' I pause, trying to express why that was exactly. 'Because I'd let him down. Things hadn't gone to plan.'

'So there was still a sense of Robert mattering very much. Not just because of what he was, but because of how you felt about him personally?'

My silence says everything.

'But what happened to you is important, Maud.' She observes me between narrowed eyelids.

'I suppose it made me feel tainted. Even though it didn't really go . . . all the way. And I wasn't exactly unspotted beforehand.'

'It was rape.' There is a hint of emotion in Dr Rosenstein's voice. She is normally so measured.

I have hardly used that word, even to myself.

'It would be useful if you could think of how that rape might have affected you.'

She looks at her watch. 'That's all we have time for now. This part of your story is key, Maud. I'm glad we are unravelling it. Write down more. Don't worry if you have to edit or expunge names and details. It's the themes we're looking at.'

Ingrams is waiting outside her door. He asks if I want to go to my room, but I decide to check on the doves, so we go out towards the dovecot. One of the hen doves looks at me with something in her eyes that is different. There's been a change: I spot two eggs beneath her and my heart gives a small thump. I wonder how long it will take for them to hatch. I'll need to hunt out books on doves or pigeons in the extensive library. I feel like a child, impatient for Father Christmas. No matter how bad things are, there's always the chance that something good will happen.

Jim is watching me as I descend and put away the stepladder. 'You look pleased.' I tell him the news.

'How are things going with you?' I use the guarded code for asking about our sessions that we usually employ.

'Exciting news, I'm apparently to have visitors who for once aren't just members of my sorrowing family.'

'Who are they?'

'Some kind of civil servants, it seems.'

Perhaps some ministry or other wants to talk to Jim about what happened to him in the North Atlantic. Or they're still accounting for everyone lost when the ship was torpedoed, all those children who drowned or froze in lifeboats. How could he possibly remember after such a long time? But I'm the amnesiac, not him. Perhaps he has full recall. Would he want to regain this memory, though?

'It's probably just about my pension,' he says. I hope for his sake that it's something as mundane.

It's nearly lunchtime. I make my excuses so I can wash my hands and comb my hair, still thinking about memory and how we lose it. Dr Rosenstein is stalking mine like a hunter tracking a shy and wary prey, and luring it into the open where we can capture it. Going through all the details leading up to the events precipitating my certification as mad is taking so long. Too long. I need to be out of here. I feel a flash of panic at how much time has passed since they certified me. *Autumn, the leaves were turning.* Why this sudden sense of urgency? The war is long over. Nobody relies on me any longer.

I wish we could fast-forward over the Ustaše assault on me. But I trust her; I trust the process. After lunch I will return to my journal and I will make myself write more, being sure to leave out sensitive details while not omitting any of the truth. I will take myself back to that road leading north to Slovenia where the three of us – a British agent, a female Partisan medic and a German intelligence officer, sounding like the players in a bad joke – found ourselves thrown together.

When Stimmer had deposited the Ustaše officers as instructed they drove north, Amber sitting in the back with the German, his hands and feet bound with twine from Ana's pocket, Amber's field glasses back around her own neck. He sat motionless, studying the landscape. Even if he had managed to jump out of the car, with its locked rear doors, he'd be alone on a road in a part of the country where Partisan raids were frequent. He'd be vulnerable, just as Amber had been.

Then he turned to look at her as though she were still the vulnerable one. To control her shaking she sat back in the seat, wishing she had something alcoholic to drink. *Put it out of your mind. Concentrate.*

Amber's thighs throbbed from being forced open. On her clothes she was sure she could still smell the scent of the man whose body was now bouncing around in the boot. He couldn't hurt her again, but she wondered how long it would take for her to lose that smell. She thought of the carbolic soap in the shower rooms at school, how she'd hated its abrasive pungency. If only she had carbolic soap and water now.

Ana drove silently, letting the car slide down the mountain slopes when she could, glancing at the fuel gauge. The landscape grew more wintry in aspect, taking on a flat, grey light as they neared the higher peaks near the Slovenian border. As they drove through a silent village she slowed the vehicle. 'This is where that cross was on the map,' she said. 'Where your friend there says the Ustaše found Naomi's beret and map.'

Amber peered through the car window. Nobody around. 'Could we ask if anyone's seen her?'

Ana shook her head. 'This village is known for its anti-Partisan sympathies. Our best hope is that they think we're officials and don't look at us too closely.'

Amber turned to look through the opposite window. Not a sign of anyone anywhere.

Ten miles further on, the car spluttered once and slowed. 'That's it,' Ana said. 'We're out of fuel. It's better for us to get off the road now, anyway, they've had plenty of time to come looking for the car.'

'Where are we?'

Ana pointed to a spot on the map. 'We need to take the uniforms off those two and use them to keep warm at night.'

Amber's sheepskin-lined jacket and silk underwear were insulating her. But her gloves and scarf were in her rucksack, left behind in the cave. The temperature was dropping and it would freeze again tonight.

Ana's rucksack sat on the seat beside her. She'd obviously taken the time to grab it. Amber wished she'd shown the same forethought. Hopefully the medic's bag contained food and water.

'Hands on your head,' she told Stimmer as he got out, 'and move slowly.'

In the boot, the two Croat officers lay with their eyes still open. Amber removed the Walther from the lieutenant's holster. She cut the twine from Stimmer's wrists and he removed the men's jackets and shirts and pulled the gloves from their hands, tossing them on to the ground. 'The undershirts might be useful,' he said.

Both men wore vests made of woollen fabric. The thought of wearing something that had been against her attacker's skin made her want to vomit again. 'I can't,' she told Ana. 'You take them if you want them.'

Ana treated her to one of her fierce scowls. 'I hope you don't regret it. Take the gloves.'

Amber stooped, pistol still in one hand, to go through the pockets of their tunic jackets. 'Keys. Cuffs. Cigarette cases, identity cards and wallets. I don't suppose money is very useful any more but I'll take the bank notes.' Amber remembered to retrieve Naomi's map.

Stimmer removed the belts from the men's breeches. 'We can roll up the clothes we can't wear.' He produced two neat bundles. Perhaps he'd once been a Scout. Probably too old to have gone through much Hitler Youth training.

'We should bury their guns,' Ana said. 'I thought behind those rocks.' She pointed to the far side of the road. 'We can come back for them.'

'Take one of the Walthers,' Amber said. Ana nodded.

'Better than this old thing.' She pointed at her scratched-looking pistol. Ana also helped herself to the dead men's cigarette tins and the handcuffs before hiding the surplus firearms in the rocks, marking the side of the road by snapping off two branches of a small shrubby tree to make a cross.

They walked on for three or four hours, the road becoming steeper as they headed north. Ana stopped, indicating that Stimmer could sit on the grass at the edge of the road. She unfolded the map. 'There's a mountain hut up here I remember from before the war,' she said.

Perhaps Ana had taken Branko skiing here as a child.

Amber looked at the map and then lifted the field glasses to her eyes to examine the mountains with the green denoting the covering of birch, fir and small oak trees, and the sharp inclines where rivers turned into waterfalls and plunged underground. Where was Naomi now? Had someone taken her in that silent village, or had she evaded them, losing the map and beret in the process?

If only she still had her wireless: she could have alerted friendly contacts via Cairo to look out for Naomi on her way through.

Behind them in the southwest the sun was dipping down. It had hardly penetrated the smudge-coloured sky during the day. Darkness would make their journey even more unpleasant.

As they walked up into the mountains they met the snowline. Amber looked out for small, female boot prints. Was it possible they'd overtaken Naomi?

They walked for another kilometre. Ana stopped, raising a hand, nodding at the thin clump of trees to the side of the track. The three ducked behind the birches. Horses' hooves crunched on the snow ahead of them.

'Chetniks,' Ana whispered. And indeed they wore the trademark grey caps with the double-headed eagle badge. One of the men sported the bushy beard that the Chetniks were so fond of. Concentration seemed to pulse through Ana. Silently she tapped on Amber's arm and pointed at the field glasses. Amber handed them to her and Ana examined the men. She let out a gasp. The bay mare ridden by the first of the approaching riders shied.

To remind him of his perilous situation, Amber poked Stimmer gently in the ribs with her pistol, causing him to scowl at her.

The bay's rider cursed silently. 'A deer,' said one of his companions, a young man on a grey.

'I can't see anything.' The bay's rider held his horse in check, humming a tune to calm the animal. The cold seeped through the layers of clothing Amber wore, the blood pooling in her legs as they waited for the riders to leave.

Ana watched the young man intently as he rode off.

'Ana?' Amber whispered.

'What?'

'The way you looked at him . . .'

'An interesting reaction,' Stimmer said quietly.

Amber had heard that hummed tune before, but the concentration needed to keep to the steep track drove the memory out of her. Trees were fewer now and those that remained wore patches of snow that spring had not yet melted. Light was fading and birds made roosting sounds. Occasionally bushes and stones moved as small animals came out to hunt. At least, Amber hoped they were all small. Bears, lynxes and wolves were known to inhabit this part of Croatia.

'It's just ahead,' Ana said. 'There might even be wood for the stove if we're lucky.' She stooped at the edge of the track and stuck a hand under a rock. She pulled out a large key. 'Good. I feared we might have to break in.'

Amber made out the outline of a small hut. To one side there was some kind of little outhouse, probably the privy.

'Watch him while I open up.' Ana twisted the key in the lock. A minute later, a glow of light appeared through the open door as she lit a lamp.

The mountain hut was simply set out: two iron-framed bunks on opposite walls each side of a fireplace hung with cooking implements, a table and a pair of chairs. 'I'll handcuff him to a bedhead while we bring logs in from the woodpile outside,' Ana said.

In silence the women walked back into the dark to the lean-to that housed the logs. 'I should have left you inside with the prisoner.' Ana shook her head. 'As I child I was scared of the dark. I think the fear's gone, but sometimes it reappears and I don't like to be alone.'

'*You* are scared of the dark?'

'No need to sound so surprised.' Ana turned the beam of her torch towards the woodpile. 'I'll load you up with logs.'

'You seem so fearless.'

'I've had to pretend since my . . . when Branko was little. If you're a mother you can't show fear in front of a child. Then the pretence became real.' She gave a low laugh. 'These days there are plenty of other things to be scared of, so it's not so bad. But I might as well make use of you to help with the logs.' She put a finger to her lips, frowning. Amber heard a rustle. They stood in silence.

'Just a fox,' Ana said.

Or a wolf?

Ana must have seen something in Amber's expression in the torchlight. 'Wild animals didn't trouble us,' she said. 'When we came here . . . before.'

Amber pictured the three of them heating a simple meal on the fireplace in the evening and drinking slivovitz. Perhaps they sang folk songs; Branko had a fine voice, Amber recalled from their march from the drop zone.

Inside the hut the women stacked the logs by the fireplace and Ana lit a fire, observed by Stimmer.

'There's a spring just up by the pines,' Ana said. 'Fill the pots with water.'

Amber gave her a long look.

'I know you don't mind the dark.' Ana's eyes showed a sly humour.

Amber found the spring and filled the pots, before splashing her face with chilly water. She pulled down her breeches and undergarments, scooping up handfuls of water to apply between her legs. The cold stung but anaesthetised her. She pulled her clothes on quickly, feeling vulnerable, listening out for sounds, but hearing only her own heartbeat.

When she returned to the hut, Ana was sitting at the table, the Walther she'd taken from the Ustaše officer in front of her. 'We are doing all the work while our prisoner rests,' she said. 'Unlike the Nazis, who like their prisoners to work.'

From the bunk came a sigh. 'I'm no Nazi.'

Ana snorted.

'I'd suggest a game of cards while we wait for supper,' he said. 'But it might be difficult in my present position.'

'Hold your tongue,' Ana told him.

Stimmer looked down at her intently. 'Or we could sing. The folk music of this part of the world is rich with meaning and memories, isn't it?'

She pushed her chair back. 'You want to spend the night tied up outside?' He looked away. Ana turned to Amber, her voice low. 'I kept some ointment here for treating injuries, just a simple thing for preventing infection, but the herbs take the edge off the pain.'

It must have been obvious to her medic's eye or by the way Amber walked that she still hurt.

Ana went to a cupboard built into the wall beside the fireplace and took out a small stone jar, along with a clean piece of muslin and some other piece of folded fabric. 'Take these with you into the privy.' Amber remembered similar jars from childhood visits to pharmacies. She went outside again and did what Ana had told her. The second piece of fabric was a pair of women's underpants, presumably a spare pair Ana had kept here at the cabin for her own use. She felt better when she put them on.

Stimmer sat up on the edge of his mattress to eat, managing to handle a bowl and spoon with his left hand, employing a deftness Amber had to admire. The women ate too, and afterwards Amber uncuffed the German and took him out to the privy, wishing she had a toothbrush, left behind in the cave. The women washed in turn by the fire, making Stimmer stand facing the wall, hands cuffed behind him.

'We leave at dawn,' Ana told them. 'I will take first watch, Amber.'

Amber found Stimmer's deep breathing in the bunk above her curiously reassuring. She had spent an entire night in Peter's bed often enough, but never in Robert's, had never listened to his breathing while he slept, never woken up to feel the warmth of his body beside her.

By now, Robert might have found another woman to keep him company during the sultry Cairo nights. He'd never given her any reason to believe the relationship would be long-lasting. Yet she had hoped, without acknowledging it to herself, that he might miss her, might make arrangements to see her when she was back: assuming she did come back? Robert would do what others did: line up the next girl.

Hadn't she behaved a little like that herself in London: not really expecting an RAF boyfriend to return? Keeping half an eye out for the next boy? Reprehensible but understandable, she'd told herself at the time.

Picturing Robert with someone else made her feel nauseous. Would he have the same confiding conversations in the dark with her replacement? Would the next woman feel that Robert was the only person on earth who could understand her?

She was probably just a single piece in the jigsaw of his work. She still had the silver lighter in her breeches pocket; Stimmer had let her replace it when he'd searched her. She wrapped her fingers round it, feeling it warm in her hand, thinking of Robert choosing it for her, having that little bird engraved on the side. He hadn't given a similar lighter to Naomi, though there might be operational reasons for that, she reminded herself. But still, it had to have meant something. Feeling foolish and glad of the darkness Amber pulled the lighter to her lips and kissed it before replacing it in her pocket.

Amber slept, dreams twisting through her sleep, scenes in which one of the limestone rocks out on the karst metamorphosed into Robert and tapped out a rhythm on the window. He walked through the door, dressed as a Ustaše militia officer and told her she'd disgraced herself and would stand trial in a London nightclub, in front of all the pretty women and their officer boyfriends, for sleeping with the enemy. Then he became softer in tone, telling her nothing had changed, it was just war. *Nothing has changed . . .*

Amber awoke properly and sat up. And there he was, sitting at the table with Ana, talking to her in a low, urgent tone. He wore a Yugoslav army greatcoat. On the table in front of him sat a cap with a double-eagle silver badge on it. An enemy, a Chetnik, the young rider she'd heard humming a familiar tune.

The rustling of the straw mattress made the Chetnik turn. His hand went to his holster. 'It's all right,' Ana told him urgently.

Amber pulled her pistol from under the pillow. 'Who's this?'

'My son,' Ana said. 'Branko's younger brother, Miko.'

11

'The boundaries were blurred,' I tell Dr Rosenstein. 'I thought I understood that Yugoslavia wouldn't be entirely black and white, all those competing factions wanting their bit of the country. But I didn't really comprehend it. Not fully.'

'Ana . . . She wasn't who I'd thought she was.' The fierce, patriotic medic who seemed to detest everyone who wasn't a Partisan had vanished. She was just a mother, a parent of a son who'd chosen the wrong side.

'How did that realisation make you feel about yourself?' she asks.

'Confused.' I half-close my eyes and see myself back in that mountain hut, uncertain as to whether I was still dreaming, blinking to see whether the image vanished.

'Put your gun on the table and your hands on your head.' Amber swung her legs out of the bunk. 'Now.'

The young man looked at Ana.

'Tell him to do as I say before I shoot him.'

The Chetnik did as she ordered.

'Stand up. Where's your horse?'

'Tied up in the trees. I came the last bit on foot.'

So he'd be quieter. With her left hand, Amber patted him down quickly. No other weapons.

'How many others did you bring with you?'

'I came alone. To see my mother.'

'Turn round. Walk towards the door.' She'd drive him away. If he resisted, she'd shoot him. Would Ana try and stop her? She'd need something to muffle the shot in case there were others outside. With her left hand, she pulled a pillow off the bunk.

'No.' Ana pushed herself between the gun and her son. 'You're wrong about him.'

'You're the one who was so adamant that the Chetniks were bad news.'

'But not him, not my boy.'

'How can you be certain?'

'He doesn't collaborate with the Germans,' Ana said urgently. 'His unit has rescued Allied servicemen.'

'We're the most successful courier line in Yugoslavia for retrieving your personnel from the interior and escorting them down to the coast,' he said.

'You've had contact with Allied combatants?'

He smiled. 'I have an invitation to spend time on Long Island and a pilot from Michigan is going to give his first son my name.'

'But . . .' She tried to push away her drowsiness and concentrate. Robert had told them that the Chetniks had been the side favoured by the Allies before the switch to the Partisans; had some of the Chetniks failed to understand that they had been abandoned?

'Let's sit,' Ana pleaded. 'Let him explain. Please Amber.'

Her finger tightened on the trigger.

'Please,' Ana said again. Amber felt her head nod. She loosened her grip on her pistol. The three of them sat down.

Miko was pulling a photograph out of his inside coat pocket: a middle-aged man, who must have been Ana's husband and Branko and

Miko's father. Ana, in Croatian national costume: white embroidered linen dress, with a lace panel and a brocaded black waistcoat. Her hair was tied back into a sleek bun, a small red cap on the back of her head. Miko wore what looked like the uniform of the pre-war Yugoslav Royal Guard. Branko and his father were both in neat suits. 'The diplomat, the lady doctor, the lawyer-to-be and the soldier boy,' Miko said.

Ana took the photograph from her son. 'You always gave me trouble, Miko,' she said. 'But even then I was surprised when you joined the Yugoslav army.'

'I thought it would be fun. Before the war, it was. Strange that old Branko turned Communist, though. I remember him as a boy, saving up all his pocket money to launch some chocolate-selling scheme with his school friends. Strange that you took the Marxist route, too, Mama.'

'The Partisans are the only ones who can free this country.'

'Put it in the hands of Stalin's supporters, you mean.'

Ana handed his photograph back to him. 'You should be careful whom you show that picture to.'

'Why is your son here?' Amber asked Ana.

'We saw each other by chance on the mountain track,' Miko said. 'It was hard, not to react. I couldn't let my companions see you.'

'See your Partisan mother?' Amber said. 'Very dangerous for you.'

He gave her a long, silent look.

'I knew it was you, my son, even before you started humming,' Ana said. 'You sit a horse like nobody else. You may put on a different uniform, grow a beard, but I was the one who taught you to ride, when you were four.'

Miko put his hand on hers and turned to Amber. 'The Chetniks are not all as you imagined. But there isn't time to go into all that now. I must return to the others. And it's snowing, which will slow me down.' Amber glanced at the shuttered windows and made out the silvery gleam of snow through the slats.

'I do not know how it has come to this.' Ana no longer spoke like the brusque, efficient Partisan medic, but like the sorrowful mother of a divided family.

Amber closed her eyes. *Always keep your objectives in mind. Find downed airmen in Croatia and Bosnia and get them to the coast for rescue, using the established courier lines. Work closely with the Partisans and identify airstrips. Signal all this to Cairo, arranging air drops of essential supplies at the same time.* And here she was, approaching the Slovenian border. Three valuable days had passed and she had made no progress towards fulfilling her objectives. Everything had started to go wrong as soon as the German had appeared in the Partisan camp.

'To prove my good faith, I can tell you there are escaped British prisoners of war not far from here,' he told his mother. 'A least half a dozen of them who came south from a work camp in Slovenia.'

'Where?' Amber asked.

'Do you have a map?'

Ana pulled Naomi's map out of her rucksack.

'We're here.' Miko turned himself away from the bunk on which Stimmer lay, blocking the German's view of the map. 'They're down in this valley, in a farmhouse.' He pointed at the spot. 'About sixteen kilometres away.'

'Are they secure there?' Could they continue the pursuit of Naomi, see her safely into Hungary and return to retrieve the POWs? Amber tried to calculate distances and time needed.

'For a day or two. The Germans have stepped up their patrols around the valley. We need to move them out soon.'

Amber looked at Ana.

'If you could call off your Partisans so they're not harassing us, it would be easier to devote our resources to protecting the prisoners of war.'

'I don't have the authority to make such a decision,' Ana said.

'You have to do what my brother says, I suppose. Or what the commissar orders.'

Ana flushed.

'How do we know you really have those men?' Amber asked. 'You might just be claiming you do to reduce Partisan activity.' She hadn't let go of her gun and felt her fingers tighten on its barrel.

'You can trust Miko,' Ana said. 'He's made poor choices, but he's never been a good liar.'

'Yes, you can trust me. The farmer who took them in doesn't have any argument with the Partisans. But he's married to a Chetnik's daughter.' The young man paused.

'What?' Amber asked.

Miko steepled his fingers and looked through them at the table. 'I'm not sure. It's just a feeling I have.'

'A feeling?' Ana said.

'Or more of a warning.' He spoke slowly. 'A young woman came through this afternoon. A stranger. She asked for water at a farm we know. She barely knew enough of the language to do so.'

Naomi? Their instinct had been right: they were on her trail.

'Someone was following her.'

Amber sat straighter. 'What do you mean?'

'Our people have noticed signs of someone living rough, using a cave we know of.'

'An escaped POW or downed airman?' Amber asked.

'He's not in uniform, apparently.'

'But you haven't seen him yourself?'

'I know nothing more. There are other Chetnik groups up here. They may know more.' He laid his hand flat on the table. 'I must go.'

'At least you're alive,' Ana said. 'I am grateful for that. We can settle our differences after the war.'

'I hope so,' Miko said.

'Yugoslavia can work,' Ana said fiercely. 'When I was a schoolgirl they sat us down, Serbs and Croats, and showed us how to write one another's alphabets. The words meant the same in both languages, we just couldn't read them.'

'I know, the Partisans are beacons of brotherly love and internationalism,' Miko said. 'Unless you're a devout Catholic or a factory owner who'd like to keep his family business.' Miko stood up. He looked at Stimmer, eyes narrowing, before turning to his mother. 'Let me have a closer look at the map, Mama.'

She pushed it across the table.

'There was a small airfield south of here, before the invasion.' He took a pencil stub from his pocket and marked the map. 'It's not far from the farmhouse.'

He picked his cap up off the table. Ana seemed to forget the presence of Amber and Stimmer for a moment, letting herself be folded up into Miko's embrace. 'Remember,' he whispered, 'the three of us promised Papa we'd look after one another. I swear that I will come to you, if you or Branko need me, Mama. No matter what.'

Ana dropped her head onto his shoulder. 'And I, too. If you send for me,' she whispered. 'I will come, my boy.' Amber turned herself away, allowing the pair a moment to themselves.

She heard the click of the door latch. Then he was gone.

'Thank you,' Ana whispered to Amber. 'For trusting me. And him. I won't forget it.'

'Touching,' Stimmer said. 'Any chance of some sleep now?'

'Keep your mouth shut or I will cut out your tongue,' Ana said. Amber did not doubt that she meant it.

'It's my turn to guard him.' Amber knew she wouldn't sleep now, anyway. Fragments of her so-far neglected objectives mingled with the words Miko had spoken. If they could take the airmen from the farmhouse and find a way of escorting them to the coast or flying them out, Robert might not regard her operation as a disaster.

She watched the embers of the fire glow. Outside, a wolf howled. Amber imagined it prowling around the hut and shuddered. The isolation of this cabin, the feeling that enemies were close at hand, and hiding outside on the karst mingled with Amber's memories of her old nurse's folk stories. The monsters that lurked in darkness . . . Enough. She stood up quietly and poked at the logs on the fire.

Staring at the glowing hearth made her drowsy. Her eyelids felt heavy. She clenched the pistol hard to keep herself awake. An hour before dawn, Ana woke and ordered her to return to the bunk for a last sleep. 'Take my bed, it's still warm.' She could smell the scent of Ana's body on the blanket: clean, or just about, and slightly metallic. Amber scratched a leg. Chances were she already had lice, Cairo had warned they would pick them up quickly.

She slumbered, dreamless this time, like an infant until Ana shook her awake, the first signs of dawn visible through the shutters Ana had opened. 'I've heated up some more soup and there's hot water for washing.'

They let Stimmer down from his bunk and gave him food and drink. He ate in silence, rubbing his right wrist where the cuff had been.

Ana locked the door, replacing the key in its hiding place at the edge of the track and pausing briefly to look at the little hut one last time.

They made brisk progress. 'If we carry on at this rate we should be in Slovenia by noon,' Ana said. Amber peered at the track for Naomi's boot prints. Still no sign.

An hour into the journey they stopped to fill their water bottles at a stream. As they drank, stones downhill to their left scattered onto boulders – something heavy was moving. A sheep?

Ana put out an arm, warning them to be silent. Amber peered across the limestone and shrubs, and saw a dark outline moving away from them. A male figure? She removed her pistol. 'Watch Stimmer,' she whispered to Ana.

She could run almost silently and explosively fast, the PT instructor in the Wiltshire training course had told her. But the man had a good start. From what she could make out, he appeared well built. On the uncertain surface of the slope, she could gain on him. Amber felt her blood roar inside her as she made up the ground. The man tripped on a hidden root or rock and fell to the ground, dropping the pistol he was holding. He scrabbled for it in the dirty snow, his fingerless mittens exposing a shorter bandage-covered finger on the left hand. The tip of his little finger was missing. Something about him made her feel suddenly nauseous . . . The synapses of her brain whirred, but there was no time to process the thought. He grabbed his pistol and pulled himself to his feet, agile for all his heavy build. She fired at him, catching him on the shoulder. He wheeled around, shooting at her, the bullet flying wide. She took another shot, and missed.

Amber replaced the pistol in her belt and crawled forward to the rocks, listening out. She wanted to follow him down, but Ana was waiting up on the track with Stimmer. Naomi was the priority.

Ana frowned, whispering a curse when Amber joined them. 'He wasn't in uniform?'

Stimmer looked down the slope, eyes narrowed. 'Your Chetnik son was right.'

'What do you mean?' Amber said.

'I saw the man, too,' he said. 'My eyesight is good. That was no Slav face.'

'Shut up.' Ana spat the words at him. 'No time for this old racial poison now.'

'No racial poison,' he said. 'That man was American or British, or some other Anglo-Saxon type.' He looked at Amber. 'You'd have caught him easily if you hadn't had the discipline to keep to your mission.' He sounded approving, though. *Other opportunities may present themselves, but remember that you are not intelligence officers. Follow the objectives we set you.*

Even if this pursuit of Naomi could only loosely be classed as following objectives.

They walked on for half an hour, pausing occasionally to listen for pursuers, before stopping at the summit of a hill. 'The village where Miko said Naomi was spotted.' Ana pointed down the slope. From this height it looked like a child's toy, a perfect central European model, with red roofs and pale-coloured walls and a church with an onion dome, hardly touched by war, its telephone lines undamaged, cattle in fields smoother than the rocky landscape they'd come from, fringed with willows. Ana screwed up her eyes, surveying the scene. 'I'll go down alone,' she said at last. 'You and he,' she nodded at Stimmer, 'stay up here, out of sight.' She passed Amber the water bottle. 'If I'm not back by noon, carry on without me.' Ana said the last bit dispassionately, looking every bit one of the firm-chinned Partisan women depicted in the propaganda posters Robert had shown them in Cairo.

Amber wanted to say something to acknowledge that Ana might not return, to thank her for rescuing her from the Ustaše, and for having come this far with her, but the older woman put up a hand, forbidding further conversation, and strode away.

Stimmer and Amber sat on rocks in a patch of furtive spring sun. He dozed for a half-hour or so. Amber yawned but kept her eyes open. When he woke she offered him the water bottle. 'It's a strange place, Yugoslavia,' he said, softly.

Her need to answer was taken away by the sound of boots walking briskly towards them. Ana. Her face bore witness to good news. 'I've tracked Naomi down,' she said. 'They're going to bring her down to meet me.'

'They?' Amber asked.

'A contact of mine. They were helping her. We have to be there in an hour, so we can make our way down slowly. There's a stream halfway there, so we can fill up the water bottles. And a woman selling bread and cheese from a hut.'

'Was Naomi all right?'

'They said she was well.'

'Who exactly is this contact, Ana?'

'The local doctor. An old friend.'

That was good. Naomi must have been tired, hungry and cold. She would be relieved to see friendly faces.

They descended to the hut Ana had earlier identified and stocked up on cheese and bread. Provisions seemed plentiful in this valley. But the woman looked at the trio with unease. 'It's all right,' Ana told her. She tapped Stimmer on the chest. 'He won't do you any harm.'

'Ustaše soldiers in the valley,' the woman said. 'And others. Outsiders.'

Amber's skin pricked. 'A man with a fingertip missing,' she said. 'Do you know who he is?'

The woman turned her back and rearranged some potatoes in a box. 'They do that,' she said. 'Take off fingers. If there is a betrayal.'

'Who does?'

The woman's shoulders were almost rigid.

'We need to move on,' Ana said.

'Who cut off that man's finger?' Amber asked again.

The woman picked up the box without a word and retreated to her hut, bolting the door behind her.

'Partisans cut off fingers of those they regard as traitors,' Stimmer said.

'I know nothing of this,' Ana said. She seemed to slump. 'I don't know the Partisan groups around here; they probably come from over the Slovenian border. Let's go and collect your friend.'

'Stay here,' Amber said. 'You rest here with him. One of us alone will be less noticeable than three.'

Ana looked at her, before nodding. She pointed to a row of pines downhill from the peasant woman's hut. 'We'll wait there. Naomi will be in the school, just beyond the church. There'll be a yellow van parked outside. Come back through the far side of the village, the track loops round and brings you back up here.'

Amber walked down to the village, stopping every hundred metres or so and turning sharply to make sure that nobody was following. Before she reached the first buildings she threw herself behind a clump of trees, barely breathing, watching, listening. Nothing.

Despite the hour, shutters were still drawn in the houses. Nobody on the streets. Although from a distance it had seemed serene, the village gave off an air of watchfulness. Twice she darted into doorways, peering over her shoulder to check she wasn't being followed.

The yellow van was indeed outside the school. Empty. Amber tried the front door of the school building. Locked. She walked around to find a back entrance. She listened. Not a sound. Could Naomi really be here? And yet Ana had been so definite.

She pushed the unlocked door open and walked inside to what looked like the sole classroom, desks pushed to one side, dusty, lids hanging off. Amber blinked. On a chair in front of the blackboard sat a woman with her back to her, staring at the half-rubbed-out chalk words. The woman was concentrating very hard on the faded script; she hadn't even heard Amber come into the classroom.

She recognised the girl's straight back and the colour of her hair. She'd watched Naomi whisk up that hair into a bunch when they were out on exercises. 'Naomi?'

The girl said nothing. 'It's me.' Amber laid a hand on her shoulder. Naomi crumpled over onto herself. A coldness filled Amber. She walked around Naomi. 'What have they done to you?'

She lifted her gently by the shoulders to look and heard her own gasp, harsh in the empty classroom. 'No.' Amber closed her eyes and opened them again. But there it still was: a single bullet wound to Naomi's forehead, blood streaking out of the side of her mouth, her lips bruised and swollen. They must have pulled some of her teeth out. Naomi's eyes were open. Amber laid her on the floor and tried to close them but the eyelids stayed stubbornly up, as though Naomi were insisting that Amber should look into them. Hadn't people once believed that you could see a reflection of a murderer in a dead person's eyes?

Bile filled Amber's mouth. She gave up her attempt to close her friend's eyes. She crossed the girl's hands over her chest. Was that the wrong thing to do for someone who was Jewish? She didn't know, and Naomi's arms were stiffening now; she didn't want to force them into another position. 'I'm so sorry.' Her voice broke on the last word: foolish, inadequate words to say. Amber did her best to tidy the girl's hair, which had fallen out of its usual neat arrangement, thinking of Naomi's mother, who must have done something similar so many times for her daughter in childhood. Stop. *Emotional control is essential at times of stress. It is human to mourn the dead, but your own life depends on rational responses to events.*

She was Naomi's friend and she would mourn her properly later. In the meantime, she was a trained operative in danger herself. Time to reassert her role as Amber: cool and logical.

'I have to leave you now,' she told Naomi, wiping her own eyes on her sleeve. 'If anyone I know is responsible for this, I will kill them myself.' She pictured herself with a knife, deliberately aiming for the murderer's chest. 'I wish I could stay with you for longer. I wish I could say whatever the Jewish prayers are for the dead. But there is no time.' For Naomi, time had run out completely.

She could hear them outside now. Grief turned to fear. Amber wanted very badly to run. Her legs were pulling her towards the door through which she'd just entered. But this is what they would be expecting her to do. They would know that seeing Naomi like that would shock her, and that this was when a mistake might be made. Another mistake. *At times of great strain your training is your only hope. Use it.*

Armed only with a pistol, she would be vulnerable. Amber looked around. *Additional resources are usually not far away.* The teacher's desk had been upended in some kind of skirmish. Perhaps Naomi had still been alive when they'd brought her here and had refused to die easily. A piece of fabric hung out of a drawer. An old Yugoslav flag. Amber had a lighter in her pocket. She crept to the back door where she found a can of paraffin, empty but for a few precious drops, probably once used to light lamps or the stove.

Someone moved in the yard beyond the back door. The key to the front door was still in the lock, Amber noted. They wanted her to come out that way. Amber dragged the teacher's desk towards the window and climbed up. The old iron window frame was hard to open but she forced it. The flame from the matches set the flag alight. She dangled it out of the window and jumped down again to sprinkle half of the paraffin on the floor, then ripped out sheets from an exercise book and stuffed them into the neck of the can.

She couldn't bear Naomi staring up with those unseeing eyes, so she found an exercise book in which a child had copied out the same sentence again and again in Croat script and placed it over the girl's face. She touched Naomi's chest above her heart briefly, as though hoping to feel movement. But her friend's heart would never again skip a beat at the sight of a man she liked or fire rapidly as she sprinted around a gym.

Someone was opening the back door now. Amber upended three of the children's desks and made a barricade.

She took out the first man with a single shot between the eyes, and the second one fell back when her bullet caught him in the shoulder. By now the fire had snaked down from the flag and ignited the paraffin. Amber sprang from her hiding place and jumped over the flames towards the front door, scooping up the paper-stuffed paraffin can, glancing back at Naomi one last time before she unlocked the door.

The yellow van had not moved. Amber lit the paper in the can and threw it through the windscreen. The explosion warmed her back as she ran.

Ana had told her to come back the long route, skirting to the far side of the village, but she retraced her steps, swiftly, silently. Once she heard the rumble of a car engine ahead of her and ducked into a doorway, but it drove past.

She pressed on up the hill despite the pain in her chest telling her to stop, rounding the last bend in the track and reaching the row of pines so silently that Ana gasped with shock. 'Surprised?' Amber grabbed her around the throat and pushed her pistol into her neck. 'Your son Miko,' she said. 'Who did he talk to after he left us last night?'

Stimmer was saying something but she couldn't hear him above the roar of her own anger. 'You have two seconds before I blow your head in.' She half-pulled the trigger.

'You were there, in the hut, Amber, you heard me talking to him.'

'Only when I woke up. What were you saying before that?'

'Nothing, what's wrong? Naomi?'

'Yes, Naomi. Tortured and killed.'

Ana blinked.

'Oh come on, this was your doing. You and your son's.'

'It wasn't her.' Stimmer spoke sharply now, his words reaching Amber. 'I woke up when her son came into the hut. I heard it all. She didn't say anything about the Jewish girl.'

'So it was you?' She released Ana, throwing her to the ground, and approached Stimmer. 'You told Miko about Naomi?' She aimed the gun at him.

He shook his head. 'There are no Germans near this village. And I've never worked with the Chetniks up here.'

'It was the Ustaše,' Ana said in a low voice. 'Torturing her, leaving her like that for you to find. I said nothing about Naomi, not even when Miko told us a young woman had been seen here.'

Amber crumpled forward, coughing up sour liquid. 'Amber,' Ana went on, 'you can see that it doesn't make sense that Miko was involved. He has no problem with the Jews. Nor do my contacts.' She frowned.

'That man you saw earlier on, the one Miko and that woman who sold us the food told us about . . . ?'

'He went in the opposite direction.'

'He might have doubled back. Or killed Naomi earlier on.'

'Who is your contact in the village?'

'The local doctor. He is trustworthy. He hid Naomi in a barn and told me he would bring her down to the schoolhouse.'

'Why couldn't you go straight up there?'

'He said the local farmer would be up by the barn feeding livestock and he didn't want anyone else to see Naomi. The doctor trained me when I was a medical student. I lived with him and his wife in Zagreb. They have hidden people before.'

Stimmer sniffed. 'Anyone would betray their friends if their own family is threatened.'

'Nobody was threatening them. He said he'd walk up to the barn himself and fetch Naomi when he knew the farmer had left.' She frowned. 'Someone must have been watching his house.' Amber thought again of the man she'd chased.

'Bad news for the doctor,' Stimmer said. 'Probably bound for a Ustaše camp now.'

A veil of grey mist fell over the trio as they retraced their steps. At every rustle of the undergrowth, every clink of loose rock, Amber imagined she felt eyes on their backs. Stimmer's presence, unarmed as he was, felt more like that of a comrade, which made no sense because he was still their enemy and would doubtless betray them if he had a chance of freeing himself.

They trudged on. Occasionally, Ana raised a hand and swung her rifle off her shoulder to prod the surface of the path under the snow, ensuring it hadn't eroded or that a sinkhole hadn't opened beneath them.

'Karst country,' Stimmer said quietly. 'Full of hidden caverns, sink-holes and disappearing streams. All kinds of dangers if you don't know where you're stepping.'

'You know this part of the country?'

He nodded. 'Before the war, I hiked here. It looks barren at times, but underground there are pools of water and mineral deposits.'

Amber's father would have found Stimmer's knowledge interesting. She shrugged off the thought. Stimmer was an enemy.

'On occasions our lost soldiers' bodies are mutilated when we find them. But sometimes we don't find their bodies at all. I've heard rumours of each side throwing live prisoners down fissures in the rocks and leaving them to die. Sometimes they send dogs down . . .' He looked at her face and silenced himself.

'She'd had teeth pulled out,' Amber told him, furious that he had managed to make her feel a connection with him. 'I suppose your intelligence colleagues would know all about that kind of work, too?'

He said nothing. Naomi had taken two sets of identities with her, the second securely hidden, she'd promised. But someone had perhaps found it, and then they would have known that Naomi was not who she claimed to be.

Mist seemed not only to obscure the landscape, but also to envelop the very identities of those walking through it.

12

The sunshine ripples in through Dr Rosenstein's consulting-room window, softened by the budding leaves on the chestnuts and oaks outside. I put a hand to my head as I pull myself back into the present. 'Of course I knew how dangerous our work was, that dying was always a strong possibility. We'd been prepared for it. But for it to occur to someone I knew, someone I had become fond of, so soon after we'd landed, that was a shock.'

Dr Rosenstein lets the silence sit for a minute and writes something in her notebook.

'This may seem like a somewhat cold question after all the human cost you've described, but would you say your operation was ultimately successful?' Dr Rosenstein crosses her arms and looks at me. I don't answer immediately. It's a question I've tried to answer many times.

'It was partially successful by the end. We found Allied servicemen,' I tell her. 'They were safe. I started to feel, well, that I might salvage the operation. We had to renovate a landing strip. I did that: organised the labour, told them what needed doing.' Even then I'd felt the strangeness of all these men: prisoners hardened by years in camps or airmen who'd survived exploding planes, doing as I, a girl still shy of twenty-one, instructed.

The landing strip had been neglected since the German invasion, colonised by weeds. Rocks had worked their way onto its surface, but otherwise it was perfect. Whatever else Miko might have done, he had certainly identified a good location for airlifting personnel.

The POWs and airmen she and Ana had found sheltering in the farmhouse agreed to clear the strip even when Amber explained that their labours wouldn't benefit them directly. A plane large enough to lift them all simply couldn't fly into this sector of Yugoslav airspace because of increased Luftwaffe activity. Most of the men would have to continue on foot to the Dalmatian coast, with a courier. From there, a series of boats would take them from island to island, dodging German patrols, until they reached a westerly enough point for the Royal Navy to evacuate them to Italy.

This had all been confirmed by the time Ana sent a courier down to Branko, explaining their circumstances and asking for Amber's wireless set to be transported north so she could send a signal to Cairo. Ana seemed on edge, uncertain how her temporary abandonment of the Partisans would have been viewed by Branko. It was fortunate, the courier explained on his return, that the day after the women's departure, the Partisans had ambushed the same Chetnik group with whom they had reluctantly exchanged weapons and medicines for Stimmer. They had reclaimed their bartered provisions.

'So Branko took possession of an important German prisoner without paying as much as a box of cartridges for him,' the courier said, drawing on his cigarette.

Branko's face had been saved. The family disloyalty could perhaps be overlooked, especially as Ana was now assisting in the airlift of Allied personnel.

Amber sent a signal to Robert, describing the loss of the paprika assignment. Summing it up in the terse Morse of the wireless transmission took her longer than usual. *Ran into a man with a missing fingertip*, she added, *from home query.* Cairo had to know about fingertip man:

he might jeopardise future operations. She explained how Stimmer had proved cooperative and had assisted her against the Ustaše. *Belgrade parcel promising*, she'd concluded.

The POWs stretched out aching backs and drank thirstily from their water bottles. Six of them would set out and light the paraffin lamps that were to mark the runway. For safety's sake, this would be done at the very last minute. Not that they had seen much German activity here, other than the distant sight of heavy Junkers, transporting officers north as the fighting swept up through the Balkans. From tonight, Stimmer would be gone, flown out by Lysander with one of the wounded POWs, a young man with a shattered left arm Ana feared had turned septic.

Amber chatted to the POWs, even exchanging a few cordial words with Stimmer, who had shown himself amenable to shifting boulders from the runway, desirous perhaps of putting miles of Mediterranean between himself and the Partisans as expeditiously as possible. 'I will talk to your friends in Cairo,' he told Amber, when she handed him a water bottle.

'What have you to lose?'

'Acting as a traitor to my country?'

'Think of it as escaping from a place where everyone wants you dead.'

'You have such a comforting way about you, Fräulein.' He gave her that half-smile of his. 'And yet I wonder whether you're as confident about everything as you seem.'

This prisoner ought not to be talking to her in this way.

'The Partisans I can understand, this is their country and we are invaders. But you, for you this operation is something else, and I cannot understand what. A chance to prove yourself?'

Amber turned her face away so he couldn't see how his words were affecting her. She couldn't entirely understand what the operation meant to her, either. Impressing Robert? Carrying out a duty to a country she'd loved as a child, a country she had a family link to? Serving the war needs of her own country in assisting an ally? All of these. But something else altogether, too. Coming here had served her own interests. It had enabled her to throw off the mundanity of her old life and show herself what she could do.

Would she have signed up if she'd known what it would mean? The militia officers pushing her down onto the ground and ripping her clothes away? That dark classroom on the Slovenian border, Naomi's body slumped in a chair, blood trickling from her mouth?

'Are you really so certain about what is happening here?' Stimmer went on.

'You talk too much.'

He bowed his head.

But there was something she still wanted to say to him. 'You stopped those two Ustaše militiamen.' She looked away from him.

'They were undisciplined and delaying my return with a prisoner,' he said coolly. 'Please don't imagine it was anything more chivalrous.'

'You took a while to tell them to stop.'

He looked up briefly. 'I told you before, Yugoslavia is a strange place.'

'What do you mean?'

'It does things to one's mind, to one's morals. But I should have intervened before I did.'

She took back the water bottle. He was honest, she'd give him that. If she'd met him at any other time or place, she might almost have liked him. 'Your break is over. There are still boulders to shift,' she told him.

'Cairo will come as a pleasant rest.' There was a slight edge to his voice now. She wanted to tell him that he would not be tortured, that falling into the hands of British intelligence was not like being taken for questioning by his side.

'I will tell them how you cooperated with me,' she said. 'And that you protected me, too. In your own good time.'

'You are too friendly with that German,' Ana told her, approaching with a rake. 'You forget he is an enemy.'

'Oh, I certainly know who is and who isn't an enemy.' Amber was tired and thirsty. For once she let herself snap at Ana. How dare she preach at her when she'd entertained her very own Chetnik son in the lodge that night? Ana's eyes widened.

'All right. I see you will not let me forget that night. Please remember that it was my son who told you where these men were.' She nodded at the labouring servicemen.

'And please remember that Stimmer protected me from the Ustaše and has information he will pass on to the Allies.'

'Let's hope the information is worth all the effort getting him out of here.' Ana sounded suddenly weary. Amber thought about the things she'd accused Miko of doing.

'Ana . . .'

'What?'

'I accused you and Miko of having had something to do with Naomi's death. He's on the enemy side, but he has helped us. I was wrong to blame him. I'm sorry.'

The other woman studied her, and then gave her a rare smile. 'I would have made the same accusation in your place.' She swung the rake over her shoulder. 'But you were wrong, yes. I'm going to clear the small rocks. Some of us work instead of chatting to Fascists.'

The pilot above shone his searchlight down towards them. Amber checked her watch. Right on time. The Lysander circled lower, almost dazzling the reception party with its lights, before bumping over the ground. The engines were still running as the co-pilot opened the doors, shouting at them to take hold of a container. Amber hoped it was medicine for Ana and Branko's group. Two further crates were quickly passed out to the waiting POWs, who in return handed over a small sack containing letters they'd written home. The POW who was to fly out with Stimmer carried a sack in his good arm. 'You'll have to stow that somewhere so you can handcuff yourself to the prisoner,' Amber warned him. 'I doubt he'll try anything in the plane, but just in case. What on earth is it?' The sack seemed to contain a small body, rippling and moving.

'Down. I helped the farmer's wife with the cows and she gave it to me so my mum can stuff an eiderdown for my little sister.' The co-pilot held out his arms for the sack and the POW followed it in, helped up by Amber and Ana.

Stimmer was halfway into the hatch after him when a small round object bounced along the strip towards them.

Ana shouted, dragging Amber back. In the light of the flare bursting above them, she could see Stimmer's eyes widen. The ball exploded. Ana and Amber dropped to the ground. Another round object was rolling towards the plane and now she could hear engines overhead: A Henschel ground-attack plane. Amber screamed at the POW and Stimmer to jump down from the Lysander. The co-pilot pushed the POW out onto the tarmac, he landed awkwardly but rolled clear. Now the co-pilot was shouting at the pilot to take off, but it was all taking too long and the Henschel was firing at them, at first apparently randomly but then picking out Ana, who rolled over and over to escape the bullets. Poised above the Lysander's wheel, Stimmer paused, looking up at the cockpit. The pilot writhed as flames crackled around him. Stimmer pulled off his jacket, climbing back into the plane, wrapping the pilot in the jacket, dragging him towards the opening. Everything was taking such a long time. Amber shouted at them to hurry. The pair had nearly made it through when the Henschel banked and flew back above the landing strip. Bullets pinged against the Lysander's casing. For a moment it seemed Stimmer would drag the pilot clear of the plane. Amber rose to her feet to help, running to the plane. Ana shouted a warning. The world shattered into fragments. Ana was pulling at her arms, telling her she had to get clear. She couldn't understand the hurry and couldn't rouse herself enough to stand. Ana was dragging her, the rough surface of the strip jolting her, scratching her exposed skin. The explosion came aeons later, bringing with it the crashing of metal shards to the ground. Then there was silence.

When she lifted her head Amber saw the remnants of the Lysander scattered over the landing strip. A small crater had formed just inches from her. Ana was rubbing her arms, talking to her in a low, urgent tone that Amber could register but not understand. She'd saved her. For the second time.

'Sit up slowly,' Ana was saying. 'Easy now. Can you move your legs?'

'Stimmer?'

Ana said something else she couldn't hear but her expression told Amber everything. Disaster.

The POW with the septic arm was shouting at them, but Amber couldn't hear what he was saying either. The stench of burning feathers filled Amber's senses. Some impulse made her check her watch. Three minutes had passed. Surely wrong? She shook the watch. The hands remained on the same numbers. Weeks, months, of work by so many people, gone in such a short time. She bent to the side and vomited.

A few pieces of scorched down floated gently to earth beside them.

13

'That was that,' I tell Dr Rosenstein. 'A costly mission to bring out an important enemy officer destroyed.'

And Ana had saved me for a second time, burning her left hand badly as she pulled me away from the flames.

'But the landing-strip tragedy wasn't the end of the operation?' Dr Rosenstein asks. 'Tragic and costly though it was? You managed to get the servicemen to safety? Which was your objective, wasn't it?'

'True.'

'And then what?'

'Once we'd escorted the men to the next courier, Ana and I returned to the farm. By then spring was well and truly there.' I'd still felt leaden, unable to even decipher the emotions inside me, but Ana was unexpectedly gentle and kind.

They were sitting outside the farmhouse in the spring sunshine. Almond and apple blossom flowered on the trees in the orchard. The valley in which the farm sat lacked the jagged limestone formations of the karst, softer and lusher in its vegetation.

Amber felt her muscles relax. This morning she had carried bucket after bucket of water from the well into the farmhouse for the farmer's wife. Water, always water, needing to be carried – having had so many extra people living with them, the family needed repaying in any way possible. Fetching water for cooking, or cleaning, or irrigating crops was the simplest way to do this. When Amber returned home she was never going to take taps and running water for granted again. 'What?' Ana asked.

'I was reminiscing about modern plumbing.' Amber examined the marks on her palms where the bucket handles had dug into her.

'Hundreds of thousands of Yugoslavs don't have running water. Millions, perhaps,' Ana said almost automatically. 'Our revolution will bring about vast improvements in living conditions and sanitation for the proletariat.' She caught Amber's eye. 'Yes?'

'Is absolutely everything ideological to you?' Just weeks ago she wouldn't have dared to talk to Ana like this. The raid on the landing strip had released something inside Amber and she no longer feared what the Partisan woman thought of her.

Ana's face darkened. Then she smiled briefly. 'All right, I'll admit it: the bathroom in our apartment in Zagreb was possibly my favourite room. And we had soft towels and bath oils, too. I liked coming back from the hospital after a long shift and lying in the bath.'

'Glad you approve of some decadent bourgeois comforts.'

Ana scowled and then softened her expression into a smile. 'It is good to see you looking a bit more cheerful.' She pulled out a tin from her pocket. 'Make yourself useful, you child of the bourgeoisie.' Amber extracted and lit a cigarette for her.

'Can't wait to get this bandage off me.' Ana took the cigarette from her.

'At least it's not your right hand. If you were your own patient, you'd be urging patience.'

Ana sniffed.

Though who was Amber to counsel this woman on the virtues of patience and acceptance? She remembered her own silence over the last few days, her inability to communicate, even with the POWs for whom she'd been responsible. Ana didn't say anything, but her question was clear.

'I can't stop thinking about how much has been wasted,' Amber said. 'Time, resources, people.'

'You can't brood on setbacks. It makes no operational sense. Learn from them and move on, Amber.'

'Someone must have betrayed us.'

'A German reconnaissance plane may have seen what we were doing on the landing strip.'

'We kept a watch on the skies all the time. There was no plane.'

Ana said nothing, drawing on the cigarette.

'I never thanked you properly for dragging me away.'

'Just carrying out my duty.'

'And there was I thinking you actually thought I was worth saving as a human being, as a friend.' Amber said it lightly, but their eyes met. Something passed between them. Ana took another puff on the cigarette. 'Your hand, there'll be scar damage.'

'As long as I can carry out my role as Partisan and medic.' Ana traced a circle in the soil with a boot tip; no, not a circle, a spiral, growing wider with each loop.

'What about as a mother?' Ana glared at her, but Amber did not look away. 'You would do anything for your sons, wouldn't you?'

Ana grunted. 'You try and instil some sense into them when they are young, but you can only hope they do what's best.'

'You pretend to be harder on them than you actually are.'

Ana smiled. 'Their father was always telling me that I was too severe. But I was the one who sat up with them all night when they were little children and were ill. I was the one who read stories to them at bedtime and who taught them to swim and ride. Once, we were up in the mountains and Branko disturbed a rabid dog. It went for him and I chased it away by throwing sticks and rocks at it.' She glared at Amber. 'Why are you smirking?'

'I almost feel sorry for the dog.'

'My Branko is a fighter now.' Ana stubbed out her cigarette. 'Lots of young men will shed their blood in this war, or be taken prisoner. You and I have returned six servicemen to the Allies. They will go back to fight, to smash the oil fields in Romania so German fuel runs out. Or to bomb their cities into submission. Or to march on Germany, when you British and the Americans finally get around to it. And there are more Allied servicemen out there we can help. Branko will know where they are.'

Some of her enthusiasm leached into Amber.

'Be strong, Amber,' Ana told her. 'Act like a Partisan, not a pampered middle-class girl. Do not let this setback prevent you from striking again and again at the enemy.'

'It wasn't just one setback, though. It was Naomi, too.'

Ana nodded, looking softer than Amber had seen her before. 'And when that Ustaše tried to . . . hurt you.' Ana was blunt about most matters, but on the subject of the rape she had been guarded.

Amber looked at the ground.

'You are more than I thought at first.' Ana touched Amber on the shoulder, looking more serious. 'What happened to you was dreadful.'

'If Stimmer hadn't saved me . . .' She swallowed.

'That German had his uses. Some men have their limits, some sense of decency. I suppose that should give us hope. But most of them find . . . these things hard to discuss. Easy to carry out, perhaps, but when it's their own wife or daughter, that's different.' Ana shrugged. 'When you go back to England, I would not tell any man you are fond of what the Ustaše tried to do to you.'

Amber looked at her enquiringly.

'I can tell there is a man.' Ana nodded at her pocket. 'You barely smoke, but you carry that lighter everywhere, and you take it out of your pocket and stare at it sometimes with this dreamy look on your face.' Amber blushed. 'Someone you care for gave it to you, didn't they?'

She nodded.

'It will be hard for you to tell him what happened. The history of the Balkans has been centuries of occupation and rape by invading armies. In the twentieth century you'd hope that would change. But this war stirred up old barbarities.' Her voice had dropped to a near murmur.

Rape was something Amber had only rarely heard discussed at home. Occasionally, there would be a newspaper article about a man arrested or brought to court, but couched in vague terms. Amber could not remember ever discussing the subject with either of her parents and only very rarely with her friends.

'Of course it may be different in England, but . . .' Ana stopped, turning her head, listening to the sound of a horse approaching.

It was a boy of about eleven on a small, skinny pony. He dismounted and handed Ana a scrap of paper.

'Miko,' she said, peering at it. 'He must have guessed we'd still be here.' The scrawled letters on the scrap looked loose and badly formed. When she lifted her head, an expression Amber had never seen before, not even up in the mountains, had washed over her face. Fear.

Amber's mouth opened to ask the question. Ana cut her short with a shake of the head. 'Not dead. But a gunshot here.' She placed a hand on her own lower stomach. 'He seems in too much pain to write clearly, but says they can't remove the bullet. If it isn't done speedily . . .' she looked away but not before Amber could see her expression.

Miko would die. Amber pictured a Chetnik field hospital, dirty bandages, lack of anaesthetic. Ana was an experienced field surgeon. She had told Amber of the operations she had performed, of how the doctor who'd sheltered Naomi had trained her in surgery in Belgrade.

'They're taking him to a proper hospital in a town, but who knows whether there are still any decent doctors left.' She stood up, paper in hand, frowning. The boy was waiting for an answer, the pony grazing the grass. 'I was one of the best surgery students in my year. I could remove that bullet safely and meet you back at Branko's without anyone needing to know where I'd been.' There was a question, a plea, in her eyes. 'It's nearly two days' walk north, much less if I can borrow that pony. A day, perhaps two, to treat Miko. Then four days to get back to Branko's unit again. A week altogether, at the outside.'

'What would I tell Branko?'

'The truth.' She lifted her head and the worry in her eyes turned to cold pride. 'I have never lied to my sons.'

'But you're injured yourself, you can't even light your own cigarette—'

'I'd manage if you weren't here.'

'Well enough to operate? Can you really remove a bullet one-handed?'

'I'll rest the hand while I ride. And I can direct others if I can't use both of my hands by the time I've got there.'

Ana would be saving the life of her son, but healing an enemy soldier, enabling him to return to the fight. And if Amber let her go she would be assisting her in this deed. Amber dropped her head. 'I can't stop you.'

'No. But you can say you understand, Amber.'

'Do you mind whether I do or not?'

'When you first arrived I wouldn't have cared. I do now.'

Amber lifted her head, looked the older woman in the eye. 'You know what they'll call you? A traitor.'

Ana nodded.

'If you can deal with that, then go. Miko helped us find the servicemen. He warned us about that man prowling around on the border.' She swallowed. 'And he is your son.'

For a moment longer they maintained eye contact. Ana called the boy back and told him that there would be food and money for him in return for the pony, an exchange accepted with enthusiasm. 'What if you come across Ustaše?' Amber asked.

'I will travel quietly by tracks they do not know well.'

Amber remembered the near-confrontation with Miko's group, how she, Ana and Stimmer had jumped behind the bushes to hide. But they hadn't fooled Miko. 'But if you do run into them, how will you defend yourself?' In her mind's eye she could see Ana dropping the reins from her good hand, struggling to extract the Walther from her holster. 'Take a rifle.' Even more cumbersome to use in a hurry, but it would give Ana the ability to defend herself from a distance. 'So how exactly do I present this to Branko?' Amber was already dreading the conversation.

'Tell him I swore I would come to him or his brother if they needed me. I will return to the unit as quickly as I can. If Branko wants to punish me by firing a bullet into my head, he must do so then.' She strode off towards the farmhouse, presumably to grab her rucksack. 'I will be back to help you find airmen and get them safely out of this country. I am a Partisan, Amber. I know my duty. Expect me at Branko's.' She waved the bandaged hand at Amber.

Expect me at Branko's. No more of a farewell than that.

'But a week passed and she never turned up,' I tell Dr Rosenstein. 'I returned to her Partisan son's group and gave him the message from his mother.' I'm still choosing my words with care so that I don't give away the details. 'He was furious, calling her a traitor. The camp had a new member: a commissar, a political leader who kept an eye on the Partisans and made sure they towed the Communist line. Everyone feared the commissar might report back on them for any perceived lapses in ideology.'

'I hear a weariness in your tone,' Dr Rosenstein says.

'Even in the height of war they squabbled about what was or wasn't doctrinally correct. I couldn't understand why it mattered so much. I could see Robert's point when he said . . .'

'Said what?'

'I'm trying to remember. Something about how the Chetnik cause was probably closer to ultimate British interests. That was later on, though.' I was standing next to Branko, facing the men and women of his unit, feeling sympathy for him as, shoulders back, chin jutting forward, he explained to them what had happened to Ana. He used the form of words he and I had agreed, one we hoped would be not entirely untruthful if anyone decided to look into it, but which left out the salient details of exactly whom Ana was treating.

'My mother was treating a wounded POW and now finds herself the wrong side of the lines.' Branko stood facing the commissar and others, not a hint of his anger showing. Clearly one member of Ana's family didn't share her belief in always telling the truth. 'She will return soon.'

'What about the wounded here, waiting for treatment?' the commissar asked.

'My mother trained others in her work. They are skilled and will continue to provide treatment.'

In private with Amber, however, Branko's anger had surged out. 'My mother has brought shame upon herself,' he told her. 'Conspiring with that traitor brother of mine. Obviously I couldn't tell the others what she's been doing. Perhaps I should.'

'Before you do, bear in mind Miko helped us find those POWs and airmen. He showed us where the old landing strip was, he—'

'Don't try and convince me that I should be proud of him.' Amber had not seen Branko like this before. 'He has led our mother to abandon her duty here.'

'She's going to come back.'

'How could she consort with that despicable Miko?'

'Branko, your brother wants the Germans gone, too.'

'The consequences of the Chetniks' actions will not be limited to the length of this war.' There was a coldness in his tone. 'They will not be forgotten or forgiven. Tito himself promises a reckoning.'

'He's your brother,' she hissed.

'He's your enemy as well as mine, as your Mr Churchill would agree. Anyone who opposes the Partisans is a traitor. The correct way to deal with traitors is death.'

The commissar, a thin man in his early thirties with pince-nez spectacles, was walking back towards them. Branko opened a map. 'We should discuss other matters. Drop sites for more supplies. You're signalling Cairo?'

'The transmission's scheduled for tonight.'

Amber continued with her work, sending signals that enabled two further drops of supplies. Samuel and Daniel returned from an expedition east to the Bosnian border, bringing with them four downed American airmen. Amber shared with them the news of Naomi and sat with them while they lowered their heads in silence.

'She was young,' Samuel said. 'Just a girl, really, living in safety in Palestine, in the countryside.'

'She liked looking after the poultry,' Daniel said. 'Checking on the hens and collecting the eggs. I remember her coming inside with the baskets, smiling like a child. She chose to come out here of her own free will. But for what?' Daniel scuffed at the dirt with the toe of his boot. 'Her death was a waste.'

'It was more than that.' Samuel sounded furious. 'It was a murder, a betrayal.' He turned to Amber. 'You say there was a foreigner in the hills near the village, and you think he was involved with this?'

She nodded.

'When you are debriefed in England you must tell them everything, Amber. You must make sure they find out more about this man. If he is involved, he must be punished. Do you promise?'

'I've already told them. But I will tell them again.' A man of heavy build. A man who'd made her feel somehow queasy. How to explain that sensation? 'I promise.'

Amber escorted the four Americans to the coast, returning to Branko for a final few days, by which time Daniel and Samuel had disappeared into the interior for another expedition.

Ana was still absent. 'We have heard nothing from my mother.' Branko frowned as they sat by a stream, talking in low voices for fear of the commissar's long ears. 'I fear that she may not be able to leave the Chetniks now.' His anger seemed to have transformed into concern. 'They may have conscripted her.'

Experienced medics were always at a premium. Presumably Ana had spun some story about being a non-combatant civilian so that they wouldn't shoot her on arrival, but they'd be suspicious, perhaps keeping her under guard while demanding that she treated their wounded. Assuming she hadn't fallen into the hands of the Ustaše before she'd even reached Miko.

It was approaching midsummer now. Wildflowers bloomed in the fields and the mountains to the north and west had softened their outlines to a bluey-green. Branko and his group had pushed north, beyond the drop site where Amber had landed in March. He had regained territory and more. Something in his attitude towards her was softening now, too. The arrival of more weapons and medicine in the two drops had probably helped with that. The commissar himself had not scowled at Amber when she'd returned and something almost approaching approval had registered in his spectacled gaze. Word had come of a great landing of men on the Normandy coast, which also lightened the atmosphere.

'We Partisans are tough, Amber.' Branko adopted what she thought of as his poster-Partisan pose: chin out, chest up. 'We will do anything for our comrades. It doesn't matter whether you are a Croat, Serb or Bosnian, you can be a Partisan. This war will end. We will be one nation together.' He spoke with such passion that the poster-Partisan mask slipped for a moment and she saw him as a young man only a little older than she was.

'So much blood has been spilled,' she said.

'It hasn't been in vain. These terrible years can never be repeated.'

For his sake, for Ana's, she prayed he would be proved right.

Finally, another Lysander landed to pick up both Amber and a POW who'd escaped from Slovenia. She stood with Branko on the landing strip and watched the Partisans light the oil lamps, listening out queasily for the sounds of approaching Stukas. 'We didn't do so badly,' Branko said. 'You flew out your airmen and you arranged the drops for us. Those Brens and bullets, the boots and the food, they've helped us fight.' There was something approaching approval in his voice. 'Your operation was a success, Amber.' He put out his hand to shake hers, despite the presence of the commissar, who seemed to frown on conventional signs of politeness.

The roar of the approaching Lysander seemed to further embolden Branko. 'I'm going to send someone north to look for my mother,' he said. 'You're right. If she's been sucked into my brother's little world of chocolate soldiers-turned-Fascists, she's in danger.'

For a second their eyes met. He glanced over his shoulder to make sure the commissar was out of earshot. 'We were close as boys. When the war ends I must find him, make sure he is safe. In time he will see I chose the right side and he the wrong.'

By Branko's standards this was forgiveness of a high order.

'Together we will inspire the workers of Italy and Hungary and Bulgaria with our example. Perhaps even the workers in Germany.' His eyes shone with the fervour they took on whenever the revolution to come was discussed. 'There'll be no more war because brother will not fight brother.'

The plane bumped towards them, interrupting Branko before he could continue with one of his set-piece addresses. Amber scooped up a handful of Croatian soil. She removed her beret and placed the soil inside it, carefully folding the beret and placing it in her jacket pocket. 'Goodbye, Branko,' she said. 'Thank you for looking after me. And for agreeing to take Stimmer prisoner. I'm sorry we couldn't get him to Cairo.'

'You didn't have to come here, Amber. You and Naomi could have stayed out of this fight. It is so dangerous – deadly, sometimes.'

Did he just mean Naomi, or had rumours of her own ordeal been passed on to him? She couldn't imagine how; she'd told him about her brief capture by the Ustaše officers but omitted the details. Perhaps there was something different in her face. Their eyes locked. Branko resembled his mother and brother more than she had realised. She wondered if the three of them would ever be reunited.

And then he was gone, vanishing into the shadows.

'You came to like Branko by the end?' Dr Rosenstein asks.

I nod. 'I always respected him: he was a good leader and honest. He could bore on about Communism, but he sincerely thought that the country would be better off if Tito took power.'

'Maybe it was more than that? You perhaps admired him for not being able to wash his hands of his mother and even his brother, despite his fervent beliefs?'

It's true. Branko's more human side had moved me. Perhaps Robert's training hadn't entirely taken, after all, and I was still responding as one human being to another, without a filter, just as I had to Miko earlier on. Very dangerous in wartime.

'And so you said farewell to your operation with some sense of having made a difference?'

I think about it for a moment. And then I nod.

They flew Amber to Bari. Allied advances in the southern Mediterranean meant that SOE operations had relocated north to Italy. Had Stimmer survived he would have been one of the last to be interrogated in Cairo.

When the plane landed, a colleague of Robert's, a man Amber did not recognise, was standing at the edge of the runway to offer hot food, a warm shower and a bed for the night, and then a morning flight to England. 'You'll be debriefed in Blighty,' the SOE man told her. 'We have your parents' address and telephone number in Shropshire. Expect a call.'

14

'I was back in England before my mind caught up with the rest of me,' I tell Dr Rosenstein. 'The plane from Bari landed to the south of London; for what they termed operational reasons, nobody seemed able to tell me quite where we were flying.' Probably because resources were stretched as a result of the Normandy landings.

'It was cloudy and grey. Nobody was expecting me, and no transport was laid on. I had to find a mechanic to tell me exactly where I was and borrow some money from the aerodrome petty-cash box to catch a bus into London and then a train on to Shropshire.'

'A cold welcome,' Dr Rosenstein says.

'Well, I was safe. On home territory. Nobody was going to shoot or . . . assault me.' I pause. 'I couldn't help thinking that the Partisans would have managed a reception committee and some slivovitz. I had to make do with waiting an hour and a half in the rain for the bus and then sitting in a smelly third-class train carriage with a reconstituted egg sandwich.' I smile. 'Grumpy and ungrateful, I know.'

'Interesting that you can see yourself objectively and with humour.'

Is humour a bad thing to deploy in examining one's history? Perhaps Dr Rosenstein thinks I'm using it to distract or deceive myself, that I'm not taking myself seriously because I'm scared of what I'll find.

She leans forward. 'How did it feel, re-entering civilian life?'

I felt as though I was slipping down a fissure between two personae. 'Everyone expected me to be Maud again. I couldn't tell them, my parents, friends, anyone that I had been someone called Amber who had done . . . those things. In those places. They thought I'd been out in Cairo, doing Signals work, in the sunshine. While they'd all been struggling on with more air-raids and rationing.'

Of course, many other people had been expected to fall back into peacetime existence. I think of Jim, expected, he'd once told me, to return to his father's insurance syndicate in the City while the fingers of drowning children clawed at him each night. I'm not sure whether I can bear to relate my own early days at home. 'I had to get on with my life. And I have to do that again now.' I can hear something that sounds like impatience in my voice. I like Dr Rosenstein, I have found this process of untangling my past satisfying and illuminating. But I'm growing weary of it all now.

'Were you debriefed?'

'No. At least, not formally.' It had puzzled me. 'At first I thought it was because everyone was tied up with the invasion of France and pushing up through Italy and Yugoslavia.'

'You lived with your parents in Shropshire? How was that?'

'It was fine when I could get out of doors. I worked on a local farm as an unofficial land girl. I could cycle there. Being outside was easier for me. The farmer was an obstreperous old so-and-so. That suited me. I helped with the harvest and then lambing in the new year.'

'The rhythms of the natural world were perhaps a help?' Dr Rosenstein scribbles something. Perhaps she's going to see if I can help out on a farm near Woodlands. I might actually like that.

'By late spring 1945 the farmer's son, who'd been invalided out of the army, was fit enough to help his father again. He didn't want me around. Even though – or probably because – his injured leg made farm work hard for him.'

My father found me a job in the bank in the local town, but it was clear that this wasn't ideal: either for me or for the unfortunate bank manager. 'I felt lost,' I tell Dr Rosenstein. 'Abandoned. I'd sit with my sandwich during my lunch break and feel as though I'd fallen down a rabbit hole.'

One evening, I took out the beret I'd worn in Croatia, removed the soil and placed it carefully in a paper bag and put the beret on my head. Had I ever worn this to carry out my wartime work? Why didn't anyone from SOE contact me? By 'anyone' I meant Robert. Had my failure to get Stimmer to Cairo counted against me? Or did the loss of Naomi rankle with them? Nobody needed to punish me for either failure. I could do quite enough of that myself every night when I lay sleepless in bed, missing the hard physical farm work, rerunning events in my head. If I'd stopped Naomi from leaving, fetched Samuel and Daniel to help me persuade her. If I'd posted better lookouts at the airfield . . .

'Your parents didn't return to London once the V2 rockets were put out of action?'

'Our flat had been damaged in an air-raid. It needed repairs.'

'So by the time Robert made contact with you, you were in what kind of frame of mind?'

How to explain the cocktail of feelings? 'Angry. Frustrated. Confused.' I pull each ingredient out of my memory. 'It sounds so pathetic when so many people had lost lives, families, homes and countries. But I felt as though I'd been dropped, as though I wasn't worth anyone's time.'

'And Robert?'

Much of my frustration and anger arose from feeling abandoned by him. I was barely smoking since I'd returned to Shropshire, but I'd take out Robert's lighter and roll it round in my hand. I had to be careful not to do this in front of my parents, because that would have meant explaining where I'd acquired it.

I look directly at Dr Rosenstein. 'It was *him* I was missing. The feelings I had for him had grown stronger since I'd returned. I . . . I suppose I loved him, really. Even though months had passed since I'd seen him. Every morning I'd check the letters in the post in case there was something from him.' I'd creep downstairs as soon as I'd heard the letterbox clatter and search through the mail before my parents came down.

I had wondered if Robert might actually be dead. The fear had taken seed inside me. It would explain the silence. I hadn't prayed for years, not even on the operation, but I found myself standing at the bus stop in the mornings repeating something that sounded very much like a prayer: *Please don't let him be dead. Even if he doesn't love me, don't let him be dead.*

Maud and her parents were sitting around the wireless listening to the announcement of Victory in Europe when the telephone rang. Nobody much telephoned her parents and the three of them had looked at one another, shocked, almost uncertain what the sound was. Her father's voice sounded uncertain and quavering when he picked up the receiver, agreeing after a pause that this was indeed the correct number for Miss Maud Knight.

'You're probably doing valiant work growing turnips,' the familiar male voice said when she took the receiver.

'I'm actually working in a bank.'

'Well, I'm sure it's fascinating,' Robert said, as she struggled to switch her brain up a gear. 'But I know you, Amber.'

Amber.

'Not out celebrating tonight?'

She mumbled something about not having petrol to drive down to the nearest village.

'You're a girl who'd give anything for a trip to the city and a slap-up dinner. Shall we put something in the diary?'

'I'll have to ask the bank manager for leave.'

'Tell them you have an end-of-service medical. In Harley Street. Say it's mandatory.'

'Is it?'

'Complete work of fiction. But it will impress your boss. Damn it, when I first met you, you had a job in a doctor's surgery yourself, and that sounded grim enough, but working in a small-town bank sounds entirely unlike the Amber I once knew.'

'There's a certain satisfaction in making sure the work's done properly.' Hearing his voice was thrilling but had the effect of making her defensive, justifying herself.

'I hate to think of you stuck indoors, counting grubby bank notes or reconciling accounts.'

'It won't be forever. Once I'm back in London, I can find something better.' She hadn't the faintest idea how she would do this. Perhaps Robert would know people who might be interested in someone like her. 'I've picked up some new skills.'

'I remember what a whizz you were on the wireless transmitter. One of the smoothest touches on the keyboard your instructor had ever seen, he told me. Nimble little fingers you'd rather like to glide across your skin.'

She felt a blush spread over her cheeks. 'The pips will go in a moment. I'd better go. Tell me where I should meet you in London.'

'Eleven lives,' Robert told her, pouring her another glass of wine. She barely needed alcohol. Seeing him had made her feel inebriated. She studied the menu as though she had never seen anything so fascinating. 'Eleven men returned to combat, or to medical care. Four of them highly trained US airmen, gratefully received back by our allies. And the Partisans supplied with weapons that helped them fight the Germans.'

He smiled at her. 'Found something you'd like to eat? That menu promises much but the reality is probably whale.'

'I don't mind whale.' God, she sounded like a little girl trying hard to please. Why did he have to make her feel like this? She was trying hard not to stare at him, not to be a fool. She wished her heart would stop racing. Perhaps if she had another sip of wine . . .

This restaurant still wore the streamers put up to celebrate Victory in Europe. They had taken on a drunken air, some of the tacks having come undone. She wanted to compare Robert's real-life features with the memory of his face she'd carried to Yugoslavia. He looked a little more wrinkled around the eyes, perhaps a little thinner. But otherwise he was unchanged. Even if the menu was limited, the wine was good.

'All because of you, Amber.'

She looked down at the threadbare tablecloth. 'But I lost . . .'

'Every operation has its failures.' She'd forgotten how softly he could speak, that sudden gentleness in him.

'Stimmer—'

'Icing on the cake. He was never part of your original objective.'

Help the Partisans rescue POWs and airmen. Set up parachute drops. Report back on their organisation. She'd done these things, she supposed.

But Stimmer and what was in his head had been lost. She could still see the blackened-stains on the grass from the Lysander's burnt-out wreck. Singed white feathers had blown around the site for days afterwards, as though an angel had been set on fire, the farmer's wife had said. And then there was the loss of Naomi, too. The cost had surely been too great.

'You're thinking of Naomi, aren't you?' Robert reached across and squeezed her hand. 'I've known it go far worse: whole networks wiped out, agents executed, their families sent to camps, whole villages burnt down. We aren't still aren't sure how many of our agents ended up in German camps by the end.'

'I still don't know where Ana is. She went north to help her younger son.'

'A younger son?' He looked interested. She told him what she knew about Miko.

'Hmm,' he said when she'd finished. 'If she's still with him and got caught up in the retreat, she probably headed north into Austria to try and surrender to us there.'

'With the Chetniks, and the Slovene Home Guards, and the other pro-German forces? Ana was never one of them.'

He shrugged. 'She was treating one of their wounded.'

'Can't we do something? You must know someone in the area who can find them for us, who can explain who Ana is, and what she did for us?'

'She may well have been sent on to a displaced persons camp in Austria or Italy.' Robert frowned. 'Though she might be seen as a collaborator if she was caught with Chetniks.'

'I told you, she wasn't a collaborator.' He looked surprised at the vehemence in Amber's tone. She smiled, forcing herself to sound softer. 'She just went to operate on Miko.'

Robert ordered food for both of them. She couldn't even register what he'd selected.

'At least they're honest and not claiming it's chicken.' He filled her glass. 'It was pretty chaotic when the Chetniks and their allies surrendered. They were piling into this small Austrian town, tens of thousands of them, with the Partisans firing at them as they tried to surrender to the Allies. It was a mess.'

'What will happen to the Chetniks?'

'The decision may be taken to return them to Yugoslavia.'

Perhaps the restaurant's taped and grubby windows made the spring light look drab, as though it were still winter. Perhaps it was what was inside Amber herself that felt washed out and tired, incapable of responding to the blossom and tulips outdoors and the relieved faces of those still celebrating the peace; or to Robert, the one she'd been waiting for. In the days before she'd built up an image in her mind of how this evening would go, but it was shattering.

'The decision may be taken?' She repeated the words, which sounded so official, so impersonal.

'Yes.' He lit his cigar, studying it carefully. 'Something like that would be decided at a high level. Politicians are getting very nervous about offending the Partisans, or Tito's frightening big brother, Stalin.'

Amber thought of Ana, fierce, loyal Ana, trying to explain to some Partisan who didn't know her that she had fought the Germans and Chetniks in Croatia, that she had walked hundreds of miles with the wounded, caring for them, that she was not a traitor, and had only been with her Chetnik son because he had been injured. Would they listen?

'You're saying we sent people back to Tito, even though we knew they wouldn't be treated according to international law?'

'You know Yugoslavia, darling. It's a place like no other. Old hatreds. And now a new order running the country.' He puffed on the cigar, his eyes on her.

She thought of the Ustaše militiamen and camp guards on their knees in front of ditches, about to be shot, feeling the fear their victims had felt. A little part of her rejoiced.

Ana was a Partisan doctor who'd saved so many of the executioners' comrades' lives: she could give them names and locations, prove her credentials.

'We sent back thousands of Ustaše. Surely you're delighted to hear that those bastards got what they deserved?'

'I am glad that some of those evil men are being executed,' she said slowly. 'There was something that happened to me while I was briefly captured, something I haven't told anyone here about.'

An emotion that she could not interpret passed over his face. She remembered Ana warning her not to tell anyone about what had happened. She related the story of the rape briefly and as obliquely as she could. The colour seemed to leave his cheeks.

'That's appalling. We didn't really debrief you, did we? We should have made sure you were all right. I can only apologise.'

'I wondered when that was going to happen.'

'Regard this as the unofficial official debrief.' He smiled at her. 'More comfortable than going into some stuffy office.'

'It seems . . .'

'What?'

'A little delayed. And don't you need to make notes on what I say?'

'You're absolutely right. Unfortunately, I was tied up abroad. There was nobody else I could assign your debrief to. Nobody else I would want to do it.' He picked up his knife again, even though he'd finished the food on the plate. 'And don't worry, the details will be committed to paper. I will remember everything you've told me.'

She stared hard at her plate and the unfinished rabbit on it.

'For some men rape seems part of the armoury.' He was speaking very quietly now and he'd moved forward over the table so their heads were almost touching.

'Stimmer stopped them.'

'Did he now?' Robert put down his knife and looked at his empty glass. 'I think we need another bottle.' He put up a hand, summoning the waiter.

It seemed the conversation was over. She was half relieved, half surprised. Ana had been right to warn her not to try to have the conversation. Ana.

'Can you ask someone about Ana?' she said. 'Find out where she is? She saved my life, twice.' She told him how Ana had shot the Ustaše's car and later on pulled her clear of the burning Lysander when she'd lost consciousness. Robert seemed to sit up

'It will be looked into,' he said. 'But as I said, she's probably in a displaced persons camp, safe and sound.' He gave her that sudden warm smile of his. 'I can see why you made such a good operative, Amber. You care about the people you worked with. Some people claim it's all about being objective, dispassionate. But loyalty matters too. People feed off it.'

He understood. She felt a lump form in her throat. Oh God, she was going to blub. She'd held herself together so well at first, reminding herself that so long had passed since she'd last seen Robert. Perhaps he had another woman now. Perhaps he was even married again.

He put a hand out across the worn linen tablecloth and squeezed her hand. 'It's hard when there's nobody to talk to, isn't it?'

She nodded.

'If you were a man there'd be bars you could go to, people drinking there who'd know the kind of thing you'd done. But you're a woman. Stuck in the country,' he went on. 'Working with girls who spent the whole war in Shropshire, worrying about getting hold of nylons and wetting themselves about a dance in the village hall. How could they understand what it was like over *there?*'

She blinked. It was if he could see into her head. Two brandies appeared. They'd already drunk most of the second bottle of wine. Amber hadn't had as much alcohol since Cairo.

'You felt lonely out on the karst when Naomi left you. But you made friends with those Partisans; you worked closely with them. But now you find yourself back at what's supposed to be your home. And the people you should feel closest too, your family, have no idea what you did. And you can't tell them. That's loneliness, Amber, isn't it?' She felt as though a warm cloak had been swept around her, shielding her from the world. 'I know what it's like,' he said softly. 'I understand. You had that awful experience with the Ustaše. Then you saw that Lysander blown up on the runway. People killed. You nearly died yourself.'

'There were these feathers.' She swallowed. Silly, really, she'd barely thought about the down that the young POW had carried onto the plane. Except for once, when the farmer in Shropshire had killed a chicken and plucked it in the barn and the sight of the feathers had made her feel nauseous.

'Feathers?'

She told Robert about the down floating, singed, from the sky.

'Like angels burning,' he said. 'Strange how it's the small details that make the greatest impact on us. They're symbols, aren't they? We invest them with meaning.'

Darkness fell. The waiter pulled the blinds down, hiding the grubby windows. Soft lamplight bathed the restaurant and the diners. This was peacetime as it should be: knowing you were safe, and nobody was going to try to kill you. When they left the restaurant, the streetlights were on. She didn't even have to worry about toppling into the road and being knocked over by a vehicle lit only by feeble blackout lights. Robert took her arm. 'Let's stroll down to the river,' he said.

It was hard not to check a street for possible dangers; it was a habit she was trying to shed. The Shropshire town where she worked would not harbour snipers. Nor were there Ustaše patrols or Germans in London. She thought of asking Robert if other returning agents ever felt like this, but worried about sounding hysterical. He led her to Waterloo Bridge, now reconstructed. 'Did you know that women completed this bridge?' he said. 'It wasn't finished when the war started and then the Luftwaffe bombed it. There weren't enough male labourers because they'd all gone into uniform.'

She hadn't known this.

'So many things done by women that we would never have thought you could do. And now you can go back to your pre-war lives. Happy, knowing you served your country when it needed you. What now for you, Maud?'

She stiffened at the use of that name, which seemed to mark a step back from the intimacy of the restaurant. Was she now Maud again, for good? What was she supposed to do with Amber: discard that persona like a snake shedding a skin?

'I might go to university.' She'd given it a little thought. Her qualifications weren't wonderful but there might be more opportunities now.

'Why not?' They'd reached the midpoint of the bridge now. London lay around them: brown, slumbering like an old, exhausted beast. 'Remember Cairo?'

How could he imagine she wouldn't? 'This couldn't be more different.' She said the words with a passion that surprised her. 'I miss—' she turned to make sure nobody could overhear '—Egypt.' Being Amber, that more vital version of herself. 'And I miss . . .' She couldn't tell him she had pined for him.

'You miss all of it?' He held her arm more tightly. 'All the training?'

'Not the endless sessions in Rustum Buildings. Or the PT classes with the instructors shouting at us. But the sense of things mattering so much, of being part of something big and important. Nothing seems to matter as much any more.'

'Darling, you sound so sad. You need more fun in your life.'

His soft tone had become more brittle. She tried to smile; Robert mustn't think she had become a bore. 'I need to move back to London before I become a bumpkin, don't I?'

'I think that's a splendid plan.'

Presumably if she came to London she could see him. She waited for him to suggest this. The solid stone bridge, this bridge built by all those women, seemed to sway beneath her. Perhaps it was the brandy. Surely if it – the something that surely still existed between her and Robert –were going to happen, it would happen now? But he made no move towards her, leading her gently back to the north side of the bridge. 'Some of those women must have had calloused hands by the time they'd finished building this,' he said.

'My hands survived pretty well.' She stretched them out. 'My mother still complains about the state of my fingernails, she—' Fingers. Fingertips.

'What about your fingernails?'

'There's something we haven't talked about, something that had slipped my mind until now.' She flushed. 'That doesn't sound very professional.'

He tilted his head.

'We saw a man near the village where Naomi died,' she said. 'I mentioned him in that first signal I sent when I returned from the Slovenian border. A large man. I noticed that because it was so rare to see anyone who wasn't thin over there. He had a missing fingertip. A local said the Partisans had cut if off as a warning to him.'

'What about him?'

'There was something about him.' She shook her head. 'Perhaps it wasn't important, but you remember how you told me to trust my intuition? I mentioned him in my signal, do you remember? We thought he was possibly British or American.'

'There was so much going on at that time that I was hard pushed,' Robert said. 'Getting that Lysander over to you to collect Stimmer was the priority, but your signal would have been passed on to intelligence. Wonder what they did with it?' He didn't sound very interested.

He looked up and down the road.

'I'll find a taxi for you,' he said. 'It's late.' There was a weariness in his tone.

She opened her mouth but couldn't decide what it was she wanted to say. He'd already told her he was living in what he called a bachelor pad off Piccadilly. Could the same taxi not drop him off there and continue with her to North Kensington? A cab stopped and Robert gave it directions, opening the door for her.

'Thank you for dinner.' She sounded like a polite schoolgirl.

'Our pleasure. Oh, I nearly forgot.' He opened the briefcase and pulled out something round and red. 'I remember how much you used to like these.'

He passed her a pomegranate. She wondered where he'd been to get it, but knew he wouldn't tell her.

'The service owes you, Maud. You may need to forget about us now, but our gratitude to you remains.'

So that was all tonight had meant: a pat on the head from the organisation? She sat back in the taxi, pomegranate in lap, trying to work out what the feelings churning inside her meant. Anger? Yes, she was angry. How dare he switch into this kindly managerial role? Did he think she'd forgotten those nights in Cairo? She felt sorrow, too. She'd hoped Robert could resume where they'd left off. He'd given her that silver lighter before she'd flown out, more valuable and special than the one he'd given Naomi. He'd cared for her. But examining her feelings, she couldn't be sure there wasn't the slightest relief at being by herself again. Had she imagined a change of tone in Robert's parting words? Why had he felt it necessary to tell her to forget about the service?

The family flat was less musty than she had feared it would be. The workmen had made some progress: already repairing the sitting room ceiling and plastering the walls for painting. Her own bedroom was to be next. Mama was looking forward to choosing paint and wallpaper, if these could be obtained.

Maud switched on the lights. What a relief not to need to worry about blackouts. She found a bowl for the pomegranate, poured herself a glass of water and went to clean her teeth, cursing herself for having forgotten to bring down the cold cream for her face. The cistern shuddered and squealed into life as the water ran from the taps. She stared at it: water. At any hour. Sometimes during the Blitz the mains had blown, but you'd always been able to get water from somewhere. They drove round with emergency supplies, if necessary. You didn't have to take a bucket and find a spring.

She filled the tooth mug and rinsed her mouth. The water here didn't taste the same as the water of the karst. Her father would have liked a discussion on the subject of mineralisation, but she couldn't ever tell him that she'd been back to Yugoslavia; she'd signed the Official Secrets Act. She'd like to talk to him about trekking through the karst, to have told him about Naomi being murdered, and about the strange mixture of feelings Stimmer had aroused in her. Dad would listen quietly, nodding. He probably wouldn't have said much at all, but she would have felt his sympathy.

Her isolation seemed even greater following tonight's dinner. Seeing Robert, having those moments of open communication with him and feeling that he understood, underlined how she felt the rest of the time. In a city of millions, she might have been the last person left on the planet.

When she switched on the lights in her old bedroom, Robert was lying on her bed. Maud's hand went for the Ballester-Molina pistol she no longer carried. 'How did you do it?' She was proud of her ability to sound so cool.

'Told your taxi driver to take you the long way round. I already had a service driver booked. He knew a faster route.' He patted the candlewick quilt beside him. 'I can get into almost any building with the help of various bits of equipment. You'll remember the training.'

She perched on the edge of the bed. 'But why not just—?' She broke off. What was the point in arguing with Robert? He'd always have an answer. And her pulse was racing now, just at the sight of him on her old childhood bed. Could this be happening?

'So this was where little Maud spent her childhood nights.' He looked around the room, which had been stripped of pictures, ornaments and books when her family had moved to Shropshire at the start of the war.

'I wasn't that little when we lived here, I grew up in Serbia, remember?' She sounded harsh. Good. 'And there's not much of me left in this room.'

'But enough for me to imagine you lining up your books by size and colour on that bookcase. Laying out your shoes underneath the chest of drawers. Lining up your hairbrush perpendicular with the looking glass.'

How had he known all these things? She felt her cheeks burn.

'A somewhat eccentric girl, but gifted. Truly unique.' His tone was what it had been in the restaurant: low, confiding. 'Won't you lie down, Maud? You look so awkward, sweetheart.'

She lay down beside him, his arm round her shoulders. All the little hairs along the side of her body touching his seemed to stand on end. Her blood seemed to flow round her veins in surges of hot and cold. Why were things between them still so stilted? It was like it had been in Cairo at the beginning.

Minutes passed. Was it some kind of test? 'Oh, darling,' he whispered, 'you're making it so hard for me.'

Her eyes widened.

'Is it a test?' he said. 'This coolness? Are you angry with me for being out of touch? You know how our work goes.'

It was all her fault. Robert had found her standoffish this evening, although she'd worried that her feelings for him were emblazoned all over her features. She turned her face towards his so he could see her. He moved so quickly that for a second she imagined herself back in Yugoslavia, on her back in the dirt. Her muscles contracted. But he was stronger than she was. And he wasn't an Ustaše officer, he was Robert. Within a second her body had downgraded its response from repelling an attack to welcoming an advance. But a minute later when he pulled her dress up she froze again. Would her body let her down? If it hurt . . . ? She wouldn't be able to bear it if she flinched away from Robert, darling Robert.

He touched her softly between the legs, carefully, movements that were like someone stroking a small scared creature. 'Tell me if you want me to stop and I will.' With his other hand he tilted her chin so she was looking at him. 'You're in control.'

She murmured something in assent and he continued the stroking. It wasn't the same, the scents, the feel of him were different from that other man. He stopped stroking and looked at her. She nodded and waited for a stab of pain, like there had been before, but there was only a brief discomfort, gone before she could express it, and then she was somewhere else and Croatia was forgotten and he was murmuring words of affection, of love, into her ears.

'What a siren you are,' he said when they were lying together afterwards, clothes piled on the rug by the bed. 'Luring me back here.'

Her eyes widened.

He put a finger on her lips. 'I must go before your neighbours are up and about and spot me leaving.'

'Shall I see you again?' How could she possibly know what he wanted?

He was doing up his shirt buttons and blinked. 'I would hope so, Maud. Unless you make a habit of bringing men home for the night without plans for anything more serious?'

She flushed, remembering those years of the Blitz when she had done just that. Perhaps all the tenderness last night was a show. He might despise her now that she'd been tainted by the enemy. In France they'd shaved women's heads. She hadn't been a willing party in the encounter with the Ustaše, but he might still feel contempt.

He walked over to take her by the shoulders. 'Darling, I'm very serious about you, you must know that. I love you and I want to marry you.'

'What?' She propelled herself forward off the pillows and stared up at him. Never once had she imagined marriage to Robert as her destiny. If she'd had any hopes for the future, it had been as his mistress, carrying on an extension of their time together in Cairo.

'Isn't it the most natural conclusion to our time together?'

'It seems . . . sudden.'

She examined his face for clues as to his seriousness. It presented the same contours as it always did. His eyes twinkled but the mouth was set in a serious line. 'Darling?'

He released her and picked up his tie. 'Perhaps I misjudged things. You have me confused. I just never know how you're going to be, Maud.' He sounded so flat. Her heart would break.

'No, you didn't misjudge me.' He must have felt her longing for him on Waterloo Bridge. 'And I do want to marry you.' As she said the words she felt the truth of the statement. 'Of course I do. I just, I didn't expect . . .'

He straightened his tie. 'So we're official.' His eyes twinkled. 'But I don't even have a ring for you. I'll have to remedy that today. You're not going back until this evening, are you? Why don't I meet you at Euston?'

'I could come with you to choose the ring,' she suggested. 'We'd have more time together that way.'

'Darling, you'd be depriving me of the romance of presenting it to you on the platform. I'm thinking of *Anna Karenina*, or what's that film with Celia Johnson and Trevor Howard?'

Romantic encounters, passion and longing, something she'd barely dared imagine for herself. He told her where to meet him, seeming to know the time her train would leave Euston, even though she hadn't told him. When he let himself out of the flat she lay back on the pillows, staring up at the ceiling with its cracks and light-brown stains where water must have leaked in. She found her cigarettes and lit one with the silver lighter, lying back against the pillows, eyes half closed, letting the stains and the cracks form themselves into a relief map of an imaginary country. She traversed the landscape, picking the lee of the hills to shelter in, planning forays to streams to fetch water. *Robert loves me. I love Robert. We're going to be married.* This was what happened to people when they fell in love and the war was over and they could be together; it wasn't out of the ordinary.

She got up and went into the kitchen. The pomegranate sat in its bowl. She found a knife and sliced it in half, removing seeds one by one and letting the taste of them, so unlike anything grown in England, fill her mouth.

15

'I had a dream,' I tell Dr Rosenstein when I see her the following week. 'I mean, a dream I can actually remember. I wrote it down. It's not very interesting, though.' Her face expresses its usual gentle, yet keen, interest. 'It was about an apple. At least I think it's an apple.'

Dr Rosenstein's expression changes to one of mild puzzlement. 'Anyway, someone keeps trying to take it from me.'

'Robert?'

I shake my head. 'A woman.' I look Dr Rosenstein in the eye. 'Do you believe that dreams are so very important?' I've read some of the theories of Freud and Jung. Jim tells me that Dr Rosenstein is not supposed to be a particularly strong devotee of their schools, but she looks at me thoughtfully.

'Sometimes I think they're just bits and pieces of life that the brain hasn't stored away properly,' she says. 'Other times they appear more important. If an individual believes their dreams are worthy of examination, I am interested. That's why I ask you if you remember them.'

I'm thinking again about the woman in the dream who took my apple from me. I can almost name her. *Who is she?*

I must have said the name aloud. 'A friend?' she asks.

'No.' I put a hand to my brow. 'Am I regretting the fact that some-one stole my Eden from me? Or that I destroyed it myself?'

Her eyes twinkle. I'm taking this dream-business too seriously. She lets us sit for a moment in silence. During the war we were warned that there might sometimes be radio silences imposed to prevent the enemy knowing where we were. Dr Rosenstein's silence is working in the oppo-site way: allowing my recollections to float up into my consciousness.

Robert is not here in this room. He cannot intrude himself between Dr Rosenstein and me. I am safe.

'I never knew how he would be, day to day.' I tell Dr Rosenstein. 'But I loved him and he understood me. Nobody else did. Even before the war I wasn't an easy person, not as a child or a schoolgirl. Robert seemed able to peer into all the dark places inside me and tell me what was there.' Dr Rosenstein makes a note. 'Can you do that, too?'

'I don't know.' She puts down the pen.

'What's wrong with me?' I'm impatient now, with all of it. The polite lunches, the blunt knives at meals.

'I don't know yet. I don't think you're schizophrenic. Or psychotic. You've had a bad depression. And, of course, there was trauma from your wartime experiences. Those things put together can cause memory loss.'

'I want to remember. All of it.' I hear the anger in my voice.

She looks down. 'Let's continue. You had no idea what Robert had been doing in that last year of the war and just afterwards, before he made contact and took you out to dinner?'

'He was always vague. I didn't press him, I'd been trained not to ask questions.'

'When you say "trained", it's almost as though you're implying your husband had trained you for marriage as well as for your wartime work.'

My impatience grows. I would now like this session to end, for all the sessions to end. Dr Rosenstein fixes me with her half-serious, half-humorous brown-eyed stare. 'Come on. You were showing healthy impatience just a few minutes ago, Maud. You don't really want to run away now, do you?' I have never heard her talk so bluntly to me. 'To sit in that room of yours, gazing out of the window, whiling away another day. Wasting your prime. Day after day passing, year after year, until you're middle aged and your parents grow old and die. And then who'll be left to even remember you?'

A sound like a choke comes out of my mouth.

'Or would you like to keep going?'

I think of the solace of the syringe, how it brings sleep and forgetting. Would Dr Rosenstein give me an injection if I begged her? When we were being trained they'd keep us out on the Scottish hilltops in the cold and wet, struggling against ourselves. I am struggling against myself again now.

'I want to carry on,' someone says in a voice I can barely recognise as mine because it's so fragile.

'Tell me about the lead-up to your marriage and the wedding itself. What was the time of year?'

I give her a sharp look. She's obviously trying to catch me out. 'Autumn of 1945. We married in October, and in the six weeks or so beforehand, Mama kept taking me shopping. I tried to settle into being what they all wanted, but I kept jumping at things, seeing danger everywhere. That was new. I'd had occasional . . . episodes in Shropshire, feeling, I don't know, adrenaline flood me. But the farm work kept it at bay. In London, I saw menace in places there was none.'

London, August 1945

Maud picked up a roll of the fern-patterned fabric and tried to look as though she found it the most interesting object she had ever seen.

'There's not enough of that to make floor-length curtains, madam,' the shop assistant told her. 'If you want floor-length, in green, or a neutral, there's only the velvet.' The velvet was the colour of mulliga-tawny soup.

'We don't have enough coupons for floor-length. The patterned would look lovely and fresh,' Mama said. 'It would bring the garden into the sitting room.'

Robert and Maud were lucky to be having a garden in their new home. It had survived the last six or so years fairly unscathed, too.

'Lovely drape, though.' The assistant stroked the velvet. 'Even in a shorter length it would be insulating. Useful with fuel rationing.'

Coal shortages. Ration coupons. Maud would need to learn about these things. The knowledge of housewives would need to trickle into her as once the art of killing and deception had done. The roll of fabric she held was long and sturdy. In the case of a sudden attack, she could grab it and use it to knock opponents out of the way. There were cutting shears on the measuring table. Five paces away, and scoop them up with her left hand.

'I'll have the ferns.' She blinked, and looked again. 'Sorry, I meant the velvet.'

Or had she actually meant the ferns? Ferns, velvet. Velvet, ferns. Maud closed her eyes.

'Darling, you've barely looked at either roll.' Mama gave her another worried look. 'You may not be able to change the curtains for years.'

A bride was expected to show deep and exacting interest in each aspect of the marital home-to-be. Maud had managed quite well with the choice of saucepans. Probably because there weren't many to choose from. Large. Small. With lids. Without lids.

Someone behind them dropped a tin of pins onto the linoleum. Maud's hand clenched the fern fabric. She hoped Mama hadn't noticed.

'Change of plan, I'll take the ferns.' She made a supreme effort. 'Is there some way we could line the curtains to make them warmer? Some kind of . . . wadding perhaps?'

Was wadding the right word for something you stuffed between the curtain and its lining? Probably not, but the shop assistant looked relieved. 'We do have a fabric we could use to interline, madam. A wise idea.'

She liked the idea of being wise. The assistant rolled out something thick and spongy. She and Mama discussed it. Maud's part was over now; she could wait until they needed her coupons.

This basement furnishing fabric department was too small, too underground, too filled with rolls of material. Maud needed to be outside, even if it was drizzling and she didn't have an umbrella. She wanted a cigarette. Actually, she needed a drink. Maud looked at her watch. Half past eleven. If they walked slowly perhaps they would pass a respectable hotel and she could persuade Mama into entering for a sherry. But Mama would want sandwiches and cake, if the latter could be found. Her hand fiddled with the strap of her bag. Could you smoke down here, or would they worry about the material? Some of it might already be smoke-damaged.

'I'm ready for a break now,' she told Mama.

'We've barely started. Your clothes, darling. We need to head up to Bond Street now.'

'I won't need much,' Maud told her. 'I already have a wedding outfit and hat. And a few things to take on honeymoon.' *Darling, for what I have in mind, you won't need many clothes.* Her nightgown had been ordered. She hoped Robert would like it. More than like it; she wanted it to be the most alluring thing he had ever set eyes on. Had his first wife, Alice, been alluring on her wedding night? Maud tried to put thoughts of Alice out of her mind. Robert never talked about her.

'That won't do for the south coast in autumn. You'll need some fine woollens and a smart dress for dinner, if we've got enough coupons.' Mama's eyes focused on something distant. Maud knew she was thinking about the long-ago holidays on those Dalmatian islands and the clothes they'd packed: the sundresses and hats and swimsuits and sandals. She couldn't tell her mother that she'd flown over those very same islands, had trodden on Croatian soil again. 'And talking of hats,' Mama went on, 'you'll be wanting another one for when you leave the reception.'

Any change in circumstances seemed to require new hats. Maud still had the beret she'd worn in the mountains of northern Yugoslavia. It was squashed inside a drawer with her jumpers and cardigans, the handful of earth now wrapped in a paper bag inside it. Robert had suggested throwing out the beret when she'd told him she still had it. 'I'll buy you all the headwear you want when we're married, my darling.'

'Let's stop now,' she told her mother again. 'We could go back to the flat.' The renovations were complete, the cracks in the plaster filled in, the walls and ceilings painted, rugs brought down from Shropshire to cover marks on carpets and parquet.

Mama gave Maud a melancholy look. 'You don't seem to be very excited about buying all these things for your married life.' Mama had only one daughter, one wedding to plan for, and Maud was not rising to the occasion.

They'd reached the ground floor now. New stock must have arrived in the more glamorous household goods section: cocktail shakers and marble ashtrays were on display by the entrance to lure shoppers in.

How badly Maud needed that drink and cigarette. Mama was saying something about pillowcases. Was there a way she could distract her to such an extent when they got home that Maud could have *two* sherries?

In the street she noted a pillar box and a delivery van that would provide useful cover if anyone opened fire from above the street or from a moving vehicle.

Mama linked arms with her. 'So in just a week my daughter will be a married lady. We'll be able to go out for coffee and do some shopping.'

Why did you have to be married to do those things; wasn't it exactly what they were doing now? Maud ticked herself off. Hadn't she got what every woman wanted: a dashing husband, a lovely house to the north of Hyde Park (undamaged by the Blitz!), clothes? No need to carry out any kind of labour outside the house apart from, perhaps, a bit of charitable work. Or she could learn bridge, a skill that had eluded her so far. Possibly even think about university. Married women were allowed to study for degrees, weren't they? Amber was back to being Maud again, gauche, out of her depth. But Maud would learn. According to the books, women always did when they married the right men.

A gun pointed out of a shop door. She pulled Mama down. A cork popped out of the barrel. 'Bang bang,' the little boy said. Maud felt sweat bead between her eyebrows.

'Darling.' Mama was eyeing her, trying to release her arm. 'Whatever is wrong? Is it wedding nerves?'

'No. Yes.' For how else would she ever explain to her? Mama wasn't supposed to know anything about Amber and her war work, she was supposed to believe that Maud had spent it safely in the Signals section in Cairo. All this jumping at the slightest unexpected noise must seem utterly bizarre to her. Maud hadn't been so highly strung before she'd gone off to Egypt.

'Is it Robert?' Mama sounded truly sympathetic. 'Men can be . . . demanding even when they should be waiting for the marriage.'

Well, that was one thing she had no reason to feel twitchy about. But she couldn't tell her that without Mama finding out that Robert and Maud would not be jumping into the wedding night bed as strangers to its pleasure. 'No, Robert's very understanding.' And he was. Luckily, Maud was marrying the one person who understood what she had experienced. 'He's the only man I could ever imagine marrying,' she went on.

A smile spread across her mother's face. 'That is a truly wonderful thing to know. It was the same for your father and me.' And it must have been, the young girl from Croatia, formerly part of Austria-Hungary, and the one-time soldier from the other side who'd wed her and enabled her to enjoy married life in Kosovo Province, of all places, the sacred place of Serbdom.

Dad had made things right for Mama. Robert could make everything right for Maud, too. He'd turned Maud into Amber, and perhaps he could reverse the transformation and make her fit for the world of furnishing fabrics and hats.

Maud resolved to throw herself into the last of the planning for the nuptials: a service in the town hall in Holborn. A reception at Claridge's. A cake that had only one tier composed of real cake and the rest of cardboard, covered in royal icing. Champagne, because one of Robert's friends had liberated a German mess in France, and found a crate of Veuve Clicquot.

They found a taxi with its light on and drove back to West Kensington.

Maud sat with Mama in her pretty refurbished drawing room with the small glass of sherry she poured for her and nodded and smiled as Mama rang the florist to discuss flower arrangements for the town hall and hotel (very simple) and then the hotel to discuss the menu (very limited). 'You're drifting through this as though it's someone else's wedding we're planning, darling,' Mama told her, writing herself a note, probably about late roses or ribbons for the cake, in the notebook she had bought specially for the wedding preparations. 'Your mind is somewhere else.' She gave Maud a look suggesting there were many questions she would like to ask.

Poor Mama. She had probably always had plans for the wedding of her only daughter: a pretty church in the country, a grand reception, hundreds of guests. Instead she had a taciturn daughter who jumped at the slightest sound, a register-office marriage service and a small guest list. And a son-in-law she probably could not fathom, although on the few occasions they had met, Robert had been so good with her parents: open, quietly charming, interested in them. Robert was Maud's fiancé and she couldn't entirely fathom him either.

'You're happy with your wedding outfit?' Mama looked anxious. 'We've just got time if you wanted to change it?'

'I love it.' Maud really did like the pale-blue narrow-skirted silk suit with its dainty jacket. The slim fit was governed by the shortage of fabric, which was why she hadn't opted for a full-length wedding gown but something that she could possibly dye and wear again. People liked to claim that their clothes were made from parachute silk, which was certainly romantic, but the fabric for this suit had come from a business friend of her father's, who'd bought it in Belgium just before the war, and had swapped it for a cartload of Shropshire firewood.

Mama had known just the very woman in Knightsbridge to tailor a wedding outfit for her. The dressmaker had measured her up, looking puzzled at the measurements. 'Very slim round the bust and hips. Muscled arms and thighs. Have you done a lot of gymnastics, Miss Knight? Discus-throwing?' Such an unladylike figure for a bride. The crease on Mama's brow had deepened. She'd be wondering why her daughter had turned into someone so scrawny yet strong. Perhaps the long sleeves of the suit jacket were a blessing. In time, Maud's muscle would mellow into the pleasing softness required of a bride. And the rest of her would mellow as well.

'What are you wearing tonight?' Mama asked conspiratorially.

'Tonight? Oh, the dinner.' Maud mentally scanned the contents of her wardrobe. 'My black shantung.'

'Lovely. With the pearls?'

'Probably.'

'You'll do Robert proud.' But then she looked at Maud's nails. 'Oh, darling.'

'I'll buff them. They'll look better.'

'This will be your last night out with Robert before you're married.' Mama leaned back into the chair and smiled.

'Yes.'

'These final romantic nights out as a fiancée are such an important time for a young bride.'

Was she a young bride? Sometimes she felt centuries old. Tired. More exhausted than she had been when she'd come back from Yugoslavia, or during her months working on the farm, even though she did very little these days. During the day she could nod off anywhere almost immediately. And yet at night, when she longed for sleep, her brain almost buzzed with electricity.

'Tell me again who the hostess is?'

'Cecilia Holdern. Wife of James Holdern. I think he was at school with Robert, or something. Would have been the best man if we'd . . . gone for that kind of wedding.'

Mama sighed. Maud could see her making a big effort. 'And they live in Holland Park?' she asked.

Maud tried harder. 'They have two little girls.'

'No son yet? I expect she'll keep on trying.'

'I have no idea.' Maud fiddled with the lace tablecloth on the small side table.

'Don't get finger marks on that, darling. You wouldn't believe how hard it is to get things properly cleaned these days.'

'You'll have to tell me which laundry to use.' Maud knew little about this side of managing a house. She let Mama talk about delivery vans, starching, delicates, housemaids, nodding and smiling. Somehow she pulled herself out of her own body, viewing herself as she sat in the yellow-and-white upholstered chair: a bride-to-be imbibing her mother's knowledge. Was that what normality was like? When did it become your own reality? Could someone look at her now and tell that she was an impostor, a fake, just pretending to be this bride-creature?

'What does this friend of Robert's do?'

'He's a doctor.'

Mama served a lunch of soup and ham sandwiches and sent her to her room to rest afterwards. Maud couldn't concentrate on the book she was reading. She lay on top of the eiderdown, staring at the newly painted ceiling. She must have dozed off because it was five when she looked at her watch and Mama was knocking on the door with a cup of tea and a biscuit for her. 'Plenty of time to get ready. I'll take your dress and press it for you.'

Maud could run a bath. The hot water wasn't bad here and it need only be a shallow one. Mama would be delighted to think of Maud pampering herself, behaving like a proper bride-to-be. The steam would flatten her hair, but she could probably borrow some piece of evening headwear from her mother and plonk it on the top of her head. Mama owned a beaded silver toque, which might look dashing with her black dress.

She needed to get this evening right. There'd been something new in Robert's tone that had made her aware that this dinner mattered to him, that Maud playing a particular version of herself was important.

During their wild days and nights in Cairo secrecy had been important; they had been very far from an established couple. Since they'd become engaged he'd taken her out to dine in restaurants once or twice, always different ones, but she hadn't met his friends. He'd been too busy. The Russians' growing aggression meant that his section, or whatever it had evolved into – Robert was always a bit vague about the new department he worked for – was still very active. Maud might have used the free evenings to see her own friends, but making the effort to track them down seemed to require more energy than she could muster.

She lay in the bath and let out long breaths. What a luxury all this hot water would have been only eighteen months or so ago, water that she hadn't had to carry from a stream or well and heat up herself in a tin basin, huddled behind a sheet hung up for modesty.

As they reached the Holderns' front gate, a middle-aged woman in a long faun uniform coat and little peak-brimmed hat was coming out of the door. The nanny.

Robert and Maud stood back to let her pass. Cecilia Holdern, blonde, creamy-complexioned, in her late twenties, came to meet them, greeting Robert with a delighted squeal and pecking Maud on the cheek. She showed them into her drawing room, bright and warm to an almost pre-rationing degree. Cecilia introduced Maud to James.

'So you met Robert when he was working in Egypt,' she said. 'Doing his special work.' She almost dipped her head in reverence as she mentioned it.

Maud glanced at Robert.

'Cecilia's a very old friend, darling,' he told her. 'Trustworthy.'

The Holderns would understand. Maud felt her muscles relax.

'I thought my James had been brave enough.' Cecilia's husband had been an army medic, one of the first off the landing boats on D-Day, Robert told Maud; a terribly brave man who'd saved lots of lives in battlefield conditions.

'You landed on the Normandy Beaches, didn't you?' Maud said. James blushed slightly at the compliment.

'A bit sticky at times, but nothing like what Robert got up to in the wilds of Yugoslavia, dealing with those brigands.'

Robert made a little noise in his throat.

'Now don't be modest, darling.' Cecilia laid a hand on his arm.

Maud blinked.

'Your bride needs a drink,' James said, opening the drinks cabinet. 'Stop making me jealous while you heap praises on Robert the Balkan Hero.' Ice clinked in a glass. 'Pass the poor girl this nice stiff gin.'

They sipped their drinks and then a middle-aged woman in an apron appeared and whispered in Cecilia's ear.

'Let's be seated,' she said. 'Nice and cosy, just the four of us.'

'So did you have a lot of parties in Cairo?' James asked Maud as he pulled out her chair. 'I've heard about the Gezira Club and Shepheard's Hotel. Nice to know that some of you were living it up.'

Maud could almost smell it for a moment: the spices from the little street stalls, the reek of ordure, the blossoms on the trees in the gardens, the lemon in a gin and tonic.

'All a bit racy, I dare say.' His eyes crinkled.

'Egypt had its moments.'

Robert was watching her closely and seemed visibly to relax. Maud took a spoonful of Brown Windsor soup.

'What are you going to do now?' Cecilia asked Robert. 'Everyday life must seem a bit flat after all your adventures.'

'I'm hoping to carry on in the same line.' Robert rubbed his nose. 'But without needing to work with the commies. Better not say too much. Essentially, I suppose I'm a kind of civil servant now.'

'Bah, I know you're much more than one of those stuffy old things.' Cecilia leaned towards him, her tone confiding. 'I just know you'll be off doing something top-secret soon.'

'Now, don't scare Maud,' James told her. 'She'll want her husband home promptly at six each evening, not risking his neck.'

Cecilia gave her a kind smile. 'It'll be so much easier when you've got little ones.'

'That may not be immediately,' Maud said. 'I was actually thinking of finding another job for a while.'

Cecilia's eyebrows arched into polite surprise. 'You're going to be so much busier as a wife than you can possibly imagine.'

Maud wondered how organising laundry and planning meals could possibly last a whole day. But clearly they were expected to do so.

'And children come along more quickly than you think they will, and then life is just so full. Our two keep me so busy I barely have time to think.'

'All the same,' Maud continued. 'I would quite like to do something.' She picked up her wine glass and took a sip. At times, she wouldn't even have minded her old receptionist's job back. Could she do something more demanding? Did she have enough of a mind for science to try for medicine? She hadn't been bad at Biology and Chemistry at school. Imagine finding Ana some day and telling her she was a doctor, too.

'Thing is,' Cecilia said, 'once you're married, you'll find getting a decent job pretty hard. To work in the Civil Service or teaching you have to be single, don't you?' She paused as the housekeeper came in and removed the soup plates. 'And really, was work so very fascinating? I don't think you'd want to be doing your Signals job any more, would you?' she went on. Maud opened her mouth and closed it again.

'Certainly that kind of work might become tedious,' Robert said. 'Important, though.'

'Of course.' James laid his spoon down. 'Don't know how we chaps would have managed without you girls. But, speaking as a doctor, I'm sure it's a good thing to have a bit of a rest now, Maud. Good for your nerves.'

'You must admit, darling, you can be a bit jumpy,' Robert said.

'Let yourself go, Maud,' Cecilia said. 'Enjoy being released from the grind of work. Have fun.' Her eyes sparkled.

'She certainly will.' Robert said the words solemnly. Maud looked at her glass. The claret seemed to have gone down more quickly than she'd thought. James saw the glance and refilled her glass.

'Perhaps I could go to university,' she said.

'Would you have time?' Cecilia asked, after a moment.

'Maud's very bright,' Robert smiled at her. 'It's surprising what she can turn her hand to. But I must admit, I'd rather selfishly like her to lavish her time on me.'

'Look after that bridegroom of yours,' Cecilia told her. 'Those of us whose husbands actually came back from danger have so much to be grateful for.'

The housekeeper brought in the next course: a kind of stew, a *daube*, Cecilia told them. 'It's rabbit tonight, not beef, I'm afraid,' she added. 'Sometimes James's patients drop off a meat joint for us, but there was nothing this week.'

'I love rabbit.' Robert certainly ate with relish. Would she have to devise meals like this for him when they were married, Maud wondered. She could trap a rabbit and stick it onto a spit to roast over an open fire. Perhaps she could lay a fire in the back garden of their new home and cook meals out there. The thought made her lips twitch.

'You look happy.' James topped her glass up again. 'Must be the thought of approaching matrimony.'

'Yes.' She smiled at him. Of course she was happy about the approaching marriage. Happy wasn't quite the right word. Relieved, surprised, nervous? She struggled to place how she was feeling exactly. Cecilia observed her, her pink, smooth cheeks those of a woman who has never been trained to kill. 'Where were you during the war?' Maud asked, trying to be a good guest.

'The middle of Dorset,' she said. 'You wouldn't believe the racket just before D-Day, all those tanks moving towards the ports. American soldiers all over the place. Worried I'd be ravished in the lanes.' She gave a little chortle.

'Of course, you folk in Cairo can't have an idea of how dangerous it was in London, even after the Blitz ended. Alice— ' Cecilia broke off, looking at Robert. There were no photographs of Alice in his Kings Road flat because they'd all been in the house where Alice had lost her life to the bomb.

James was looking down at his plate. He swallowed and turned to Maud. 'The fear of Cairo falling to the Germans must have passed by the time you were in Egypt, Maud,' he said. 'Your parents must have been relieved you were somewhere safe.'

'They didn't really know much about my war work,' Maud said.

Nobody did, apart from Robert. The thought made her feel lonely.

'You let them think that I was just some kind of party girl,' she told Robert when they had thanked the Holderns and were walking towards the Bayswater Road in search of a taxi that would drop her back at her parents' flat. 'A popsy.'

'It's just simpler, really. Security is still so tight.'

'But not for you. They seemed to know all about your work.'

'James is such an old friend, I trust him entirely.' A mist, the first of the autumnal ones, had fallen.

She peered to look at his face. 'But not as far as my work is concerned?'

He tucked his arm into hers. 'I'm so proud of what you did. You must know that?'

'I do.' She squeezed his arm. 'But that wasn't what I meant.'

'What did you mean, Miss Sphinx?'

'I don't really know. It's just hard. Adapting. Pretending that everything I did was very routine, rather a bore. Apart from the parties.'

It would have been good occasionally to hear someone ask her if she was all right. She would have assured them that she was, of course. If only there'd been another former agent she could talk to. Men probably went to bars and met up and reminisced with people they could trust not to blab. But she was lucky to have her future husband as a confidant.

'At least I know I can talk to you.'

'Do you know what, darling? Some people say it's best not to talk about the war and churn up all those painful memories. You'd be better off distracting yourself. That's what James says, too. And he is a doctor.'

She thought about it. Distraction made sense in some ways. If you laid down new memories perhaps the old ones faded.

'And Cecilia will be a good friend for you. Not too far if you don't mind a walk.'

It couldn't be more than a mile or a mile and a half. She thought of her trek across northern Croatia and smiled. 'How did you come to know the Holderns?' she asked, feeling shy about putting the question.

'James is – was – Alice's brother.'

'What?' She stopped in the street. 'Alice? Your wife? You didn't tell me that.'

'What difference does it make?' He shook his head. 'Oh Lord, I'm sorry, darling, I thought I'd mentioned it before. Sorry.'

'I hope I didn't say anything to upset him. Or you either.' She rewound her mental tape of the night's conversation. Robert pulled her gently onwards. 'You never say much about Alice. Did she look like James?'

She could see him weighing up his answer. 'Perhaps a little around the eyes.' He nodded to himself. 'Yes, the almond shape. And that hazel.'

'It's good that you keep in touch with Alice's brother and family.'

'We all grew up together, James, Alice, Cecilia and I. Our families lived close to one another in Sussex.' It was the most he had told her about his upbringing.

She was about to ask more questions when he looked back along the road. 'There's a taxi.'

Something else about the dinner puzzled Maud. As she switched off her bedside lamp later that night she realised what it was. Having been so keen to agree that her wartime work had involved transcribing signals in Cairo at a time when the German threat was past, why did James, Dr James Holdern, brother of Alice, believe that Maud's nerves needed settling? Had James imagined that Cairo was such a dizzyingly oriental city that any Western woman would return in a state of over-stimulation? His sister, Alice, had not liked the Orient after all, she remembered Robert telling her on the bridge in Cairo. Perhaps James regarded this as the appropriate reaction to the place.

'A very unsettling night out,' Dr Rosenstein says. 'I can see why you felt as though your past was being somehow denied.'

'It felt like that, it made me even more uncertain about who I was. Things felt unreal.' I say the last word with reluctance – perhaps it will make me sound mad.

'Unreal?'

'As though I couldn't be sure what was really there.'

'Did you suffer from hallucinations?' Dr Rosenstein asks.

'No, but . . .' I tell her how sudden noises bothered me. And how I'd gone through a stage of not liking to look at my own reflection.

'Give me examples,' she says.

I close my eyes, remembering my wedding day. October of that same year.

On her wedding morning Maud worried that she wasn't actually the woman in the mirror at all. A stranger had appropriated her features. Or was the woman in the mirror the real Maud? Had Amber split from Maud at some point so that there were two versions of herself in existence? If this were the case, which one of them was actually marrying Robert?

To distract herself she placed her little ivory hat on her head, and set it at a slight angle, which suited her face. No veil because the fabric would have cost too much and, besides, a hat somehow felt more dignified, more adult. She had no intention of casting herself as a blushing bride, and Robert would probably have laughed had she done so. He'd probably already had one of those, anyway. Alice. Maud pictured Alice as a slight, classically beautiful English rose in a long white silk dress and veil. As the wedding photographs didn't seem to have survived the bomb that had killed Alice there was no way of knowing what her predecessor had looked like.

The sun was threatening to make an appearance, her father told her over breakfast. It looked as though it were going to be a golden autumn day, the city putting on its brightest aspect. Mama offered to help her dress, but Maud couldn't imagine what Mama could do that she couldn't manage for herself. She was about to say this when she caught sight of her mother's face and suggested she help with her hair. 'You are a sophisticated young woman now,' Mama said, hands resting on Maud's shoulders after she'd placed the last hairpin into her daughter's chignon. 'Not the mixture of vamp and tomboy you were before you went away to Egypt.'

'Vamp *and* tomboy?'

'You pulled it off very well. Too well, your father and I used to think.' She gave a wry smile. 'Whatever you did while you were away, it matured you, Maud. But I worry sometimes that it has changed you very deeply.'

'What do you mean?'

Her mother took a moment before continuing. 'It's as though you're, what's the saying? Watching your neck?'

'Watching my back. That's why I'm marrying just the right man, Mama. Robert worked with me. He understands. He'll help me back into the swing of things again.'

'If you're marrying someone who understands, you are very fortunate, my dearest.' She squeezed Maud's shoulders. 'But I like your plan of going to university, if you can find one that will take you. You are a clever girl. Being with other clever people and studying will help you.' Maud blinked, not wishing to show how touched she was by this unexpected support for her plans. Perhaps Mama could have a word with Robert, persuade him that a new bride could combine the role with being a student.

The taxi drive with her father to Holborn town hall went without her spotting snipers in alleyways. The ceremony ran equally smoothly, Robert and Maud reciting their vows without a slip, smiling at one another as they did so. *With practice, acting your assumed role will seem natural.* They were the only possible people for one another. They'd been through things together, or at least, had been connected by wireless transmitter. A team. Only Robert could really understand what she felt about Naomi. And Ana.

'Darling?' Robert smiled at her. 'Wakey, wakey.' He held out his regimental sword so that she could clasp the handle as they pretended to cut the wedding cake for the photographer. She glimpsed the side of her face in the reflective surface of the blade. Maud looked away quickly and managed to lose herself in the champagne-fuelled laughter.

Thank God for Robert's friend who'd liberated all the bottles of Veuve Clicquot. Robert didn't have many guests of his own here apart from the Holderns. Maud was glad for her parents' company and for that of the few school friends she'd invited. And for Peter, whom she'd invited in a fit of bonhomie, along with his fiancée. He gave her a warm smile and kissed her. She remembered how much she'd liked him, before she'd met Robert. How long ago their relationship now seemed, and how simple that life of dodging bombs and dancing in clubs. Peter belonged to the Maud who'd existed before Yugoslavia. How would her life have run if he hadn't introduced her to his friend Robert? But perhaps Robert would have found her one way or another. He'd needed her, hadn't he? Not exactly many girls hanging around London who spoke fluent Serbo-Croat and were prepared to go and live rough with the Partisans in occupied territory.

Robert had needed her then. He still needed her now. The sudden flash of realisation came to her as she sipped her champagne. He'd been so keen to marry her. It had been arranged so hastily – at his suggestion. Just six weeks to organise everything. He came up to her and put his arm around her waist. 'I want you by my side,' he whispered. 'Always. While you were away from me I worried about you. Now I know you're safe.'

After the reception bride and groom drove the short distance to the hotel, somewhere behind Jermyn Street. Someone had tied a few balloons to the back of the car and people smiled at them as they drove and a little girl waved. A shot rang out as they steered round Piccadilly Circus. Maud ducked. Robert placed a hand over hers.

'Just a car backfiring, darling.'

Maud sat up again, feeling foolish. When they pulled up she concentrated on entering the hotel lobby without letting herself down again. Robert went down to the bar to buy cigarettes.

Maud sat on the edge of the double bed. She couldn't avoid eye contact with her own reflection in the dressing-table mirror. She picked up one of the pillows. For all its fancy linen pillowcase, it had probably survived a few too many nearby dust-generating air-raids. Maud sneezed as she placed it over the mirror. It flopped obligingly over the glass, blocking her reflection.

Robert came back in with a packet of Senior Service in his hand. 'I've ordered us nightcaps.' He noticed the pillow over the mirror, of course he did, it was the kind of thing they had both been trained to notice. He frowned. 'Darling? Why didn't you just switch the lamp off by the bed if the reflection's giving you a headache?' He did this for her. 'See? The light doesn't bounce off the glass any more.'

Don't uncover the mirror. She'll see me. She bit her lip to avoid saying the words aloud.

Robert removed the pillow and replaced it carefully on the bed. Everything he did was always so measured, whether it was drawing on a map or dancing. It was only cutting that Groppi cake in Cairo that ever flummoxed him, the soft layers of sponge falling apart as he sliced them, the icing becoming messed up by the knife. Amber had wanted to laugh at him but had known, even then, that it would be dangerous.

Something was trying to push its way out of Maud. It would wriggle out of her mouth or eyes unless she picked up that pillow again and placed it over her face. Perhaps if she could induce ataxia in herself the worm would leave and Maud would die and Amber would be back. But which one was the real her? Robert answered the knock on the door announcing the arrival of the brandies. He passed her a glass. 'To us, sweetheart. To our survival.'

With her spare hand Maud touched her eyes: nothing coming out. She had survived. She was here, in London, on her wedding night with her new husband. Nobody was ever going to ask her to live rough on a mountainside, or help kill people. She would probably never have lice again. That last bit was surely worth celebrating.

'That's better. What are you smiling at?'

She couldn't tell her bridegroom that it was the thought of remaining parasite-free that had finally allowed her to express happiness. 'Just relieved it's all over.'

'You look all-in. Bit of a business, this getting married.'

'I might get changed.' If she took off the impostor's silk suit she might feel better, might feel like Amber again. She wished she had her Partisan outfit, or at least the flying jacket. Or her beret. Perhaps she could have worn the beret with this wedding outfit instead of the chic little hat. The image should have made her laugh but it didn't, not even now, on her wedding night, happiest day of a woman's life, everyone said. Why not? But she knew the answer. It was Ana preying on her mind, even today. Maud had half-hoped there might be some word of her by now. Robert was looking at her enquiringly. She put a hand to her brow. 'Seeing everyone, it made me think of old times.'

His eyes met hers, warm.

'I was thinking about Ana. Perhaps I could send her a small piece of wedding cake. If we know which DP camp she's in.' Would sending a small sliver of fruitcake be worth all the effort? Maud thought of herself on the mountains of Croatia, how she would have appreciated something sweet. Now was the time for Robert to tell her more about Ana. He'd promised to look into her disappearance. She waited. He said nothing.

'Perhaps she's moved out of the camp,' she said.

'Don't worry about Ana now.' He sat next to her on the bed and put an arm around her. 'You told me how tough and resourceful those Partisans were. Let's just enjoy this moment. Married at last.'

He sounded so happy. Two years ago Maud could never have dreamed that a man like Robert would have been interested in a girl like her. She'd seen the way other women peeped at him when they thought he wasn't looking, the way other men stood taller when he was around. He seemed to crackle with energy and yet at the same time there was a relaxed air about him. Mama's Women's Institute friends from the Shires had blushed when they'd been introduced at the reception line.

'I can't quite believe we're both here and not in some torrid night-club in Cairo or waiting for a tennis court to be free at the Gezira Club,' he went on.

Her nightgown was at the top of the suitcase, which the porter had placed on the rack. She opened the case and stroked its creamy silk folds. Robert would pull the dainty straps down her arms, roll the lacy skirt up her thighs. Perhaps it would rip, tear along the seams even though silk was strong enough for parachutes. But despite its strength a knife could cut through any fabric, even parachute silk, and reveal what was hidden underneath.

She had to stop these thoughts. This was the now, the reality, starting a new life with this man she loved. There were two parts of Maud: a scared, jumpy woman, and a bride who'd married the person she adored. She needed to push the first one away.

Maud stood up.

'Pass me my sponge bag, darling.' Her voice was steady. 'I'm going to freshen myself up.'

16

'Eisoptrophobia,' Dr Rosenstein says. 'Fear of mirrors, or of seeing oneself in them.'

'A sign of madness?'

'A phobia. Sometimes fears make people lose their grasp on reality, some are more debilitating than others. Some people don't like heights or spiders, but not to a pathological degree.' Dr Rosenstein makes a note. 'But telling me about your dislike of mirrors adds another piece to your story. It's helpful.' She gives me one of her long, searching looks. 'So you really did want to marry Robert? There was no sense of coercion?'

'No.' I'd felt desperate, almost. 'I loved him.'

'Where did you go for your honeymoon?'

I close my eyes, hearing the sea hiss on the shingle. 'The Dorset coast.' It was the last time I'd seen the sea. 'The weather was mild for England in early October, but foggy first thing.'

Robert and Maud didn't actually mind the fog and would have stayed in bed had the chambermaid not arrived each morning at nine. They'd sit in the hotel lounge drinking coffee and waiting for the sunlight to break through. Maud thought of the couple in *The Return of the Native* on honeymoon on Egdon Heath, not so far from here, of how they hadn't minded staying indoors, either. When they went out for a walk on the beach and she shared this observation with Robert he knew exactly what she meant. 'Though I have no intention of ending up in a Thomas Hardy tragedy, darling.'

They stopped at the shoreline, waves breaking gently in front of them. He held her in his arms. 'I can't believe we're really here.' When he released her she looked out to sea. A thin band of light lay to the south, towards France. It hadn't been so long ago that people had eyed the sea with fear, peering at it for signs of invasion. 'England is safe,' she said. People could go on honeymoon and make plans for the future.

'For now,' he said, very quietly. 'While we guard her.' His face had fallen into something set, almost sullen. He caught her looking at him. 'Sorry, darling, I mustn't bring work on honeymoon with me.'

Half of her was curious, wanting to ask more about his job, about the new team he was assembling in his office in St James's. But he was right, this was a honeymoon.

'Sergeant Troy drowned himself somewhere near here, didn't he?' he said musingly. 'When it all went wrong with his women. I read *Far from the Madding Crowd* a long time ago, though.'

She laughed. 'I think we should read some comic novels on honeymoon. P. G. Wodehouse, perhaps.'

'They say P. G. Wodehouse was a traitor, don't they? Broadcast for the enemy when he was interned.' Robert's face took on a closed-off expression. 'Sometimes it's hard to make the right choice.' He plucked a pebble from the shore and skimmed it across the waves. Five bounces.

'Very good,' she said. How strange it was that she was now the one praising him for a feat well mastered. He seemed to stand straighter.

'There are rumours of a local teashop baking fresh scones every afternoon,' he said. 'There might even be cream. And strawberry jam.'

'Both together?'

'I know, probably illegal. Funny how the thought of such fripperies can obsess you. I had a colleague in Cairo once who was obsessed with baked goods. Always seeking out pastry shops.'

They walked on. She thought of a cake from Groppi's, of a man coming into a training room and eyeing the ruined sponge with appetite, of how he'd brushed the crumbs from his moustache.

'And at first married life went smoothly?' Dr Rosenstein asks. 'You were content?'

Is content the right word? I remember how I used to pace the small house, looking at my watch. 'Yes. It was a change, becoming a housewife, making my husband and home the centre of my existence. But I liked turning the house into something I could be proud of.' I'd enjoyed painting the walls of the sitting room myself, to the horror of Mama. I'd even put up some bookcases. Constant movement had hushed the demons in my head.

'I felt as though I was joining the adult race.'

I place a hand on my stomach. 'But I was slowing down. I was walking miles every day, but moving around felt harder. Sometimes thinking did, too. And I annoyed Robert when I forgot things.'

'Did that often happen?'

'I didn't think so. But he was put out when I forgot to send things to the laundry.' I frown, remembering. 'Or didn't take his shoes to the cobbler's. Small things like that.'

'You were sick?' Dr Rosenstein is watching me very closely now. I want to run, run up to my room and get Ingrams to lock me in. But I am Amber, trained in making myself act bravely even if I don't feel it.

'Not sick.' Although hospitals were involved. 'Something else. Oh God.' A bolt of memory strikes me, searing my nerves, causing my body to jolt as though someone's applied electrodes to my temples. For a moment I think I might vomit with the shock of it. 'That silly dream I've been having, the apple . . .'

'What about the apple?'

'It wasn't an apple, it was a pomegranate. I used to buy them in Cairo. Robert brought one back for me when he met me in London for dinner.'

A pomegranate full of seeds, of potential, stolen from me. 'It was my future, but something more than that, it was life itself. And he let them take . . .'

I start talking. I'm there, back in 1946. The words come out all garbled. 'I've remembered what happened with that blade. Robert—'

'Slow down,' Dr Rosenstein says.

'But my dream—'

'Start from when you came back from honeymoon.'

The back garden of the house near Hyde Park was tiny, a little square with thin, dusty, soil, but when spring came Maud started a vegetable patch in its little flowerbed. Her parents drove down a trailer-load of topsoil from Shropshire, her father hinting at a favour carried out in return for petrol coupons.

'Do not ask your father what this favour was,' Mama said. 'But it got us to London without needing the train and for that I am grateful.' She fingered the new curtains in the sitting room. 'You chose the right fabric,' she said. Maud felt her parents' approval like sunshine. Robert welcomed them with enthusiasm and everyone seemed to enjoy their stay. Even when the little lapses Maud had made were related to her parents, it was done with affection and humour. It was strange how forgetful she had become since her marriage: leaving windows and doors open when she went out, mislaying her purse.

'It's nothing we can't manage,' Robert said, squeezing her hand across the tablecloth.

Mama gave her a sharp look across the table. 'You seemed organised enough when you lived with us in Shropshire at the end of the war,' she said.

'It's just a stage,' Robert said. 'You'll see.'

When her parents left, Maud missed them more than she thought she would, more than she had when she'd returned to boarding school as a child.

At least there was the garden. She never seemed to forget anything to do with that. The topsoil her parents had procured benefited the little plot. Each morning Maud went out to look for signs of vegetables shooting up.

Domesticity seemed to take up every hour at the moment, especially when she found herself in such a muddle with simple things. Surely organising a household ought to be straightforward? She'd made a list of things that needed doing, by day. She ticked them off as they were done: shirts and sheets sent to laundries. Books returned to the library. A suit of Robert's taken to a seamstress for alterations.

One afternoon Cecilia appeared with the remains of a cold roast for Maud. Maud was looking for her watch. 'I took it off at night as usual but it wasn't on my bedside table when I got up this morning.'

'Has it fallen off?'

'I looked all around. It'll show up.'

Cecilia placed the enamel plate on the kitchen table. 'You can mince this lamb and make a shepherd's pie,' she said.

'Thank you. How do I make the pie?'

'I'm not sure. Our cook does that for me. You could probably find a recipe.' She looked benevolently at Maud. 'It can't be that hard. Just don't go into a daydream and forget to take it out of the oven.' She looked at something over Maud's shoulder.

Maud turned to follow her gaze and saw her watch on top of the gas heater. 'I didn't put it there.'

'You probably did. When you were washing up or something?'

Maud blushed. When Cecilia had left she unwrapped the waxed paper and eyed the cold meat. A layer of fat, yellow and thick, had congealed around the bone. Maud made a dash for the lavatory.

She had to dash again, later on, when Robert was home and the minced-down roast was simmering in a frying pan with onion and stock. 'Sorry,' she called from the lavatory. 'I just don't think I can finish cooking it.'

'Potatoes,' he said. She heard him rattling pans. 'I'll boil and mash them. It'll be fine.'

When she emerged he'd poured her a glass of water. 'Sit down,' he told her. 'Don't move again this evening.' He put a hand on her forehead. 'Would you like to lie down?'

'No, I mustn't give in.'

'Stay there.' His voice was soft. He went upstairs and she heard him opening the airing cupboard and running the bathroom tap. He returned with a damp flannel and wiped her face very carefully. 'Don't you think, darling, that you might be expecting?'

'Oh.' She thought about it. 'I suppose, yes, I could be.' She did the calculations. It made sense.

He kissed her. 'I'm so thrilled.'

'So am I.' She said the words automatically but found they were true.

'You'll have to tell me what I can do to make it as easy for you as possible. I never had sisters, and Alice, well, she died before we could do any of this.' He sounded apologetic. 'Are there special things you need to eat or drink? Is it annoying if I fuss over you or will you let me pamper you?'

'I never mind being pampered.'

And he did pamper her, seldom returning from work without a small present: fruit from a stall near his office, a precious single piece of steak, a bottle of stout because the doorman at his office had told him that's what his wife always drank in her confinements, flowers, books he thought she might like. 'If I'm smothering you, I'll limit myself to one bunch of freesias a week and a juicy piece of cod a fortnight,' he told her.

'I like all the things you bring for me.' He looked like a small boy, relieved he'd found favour. The emotion this aroused in her surprised Maud. Robert was no longer her superior. They were equals, going into this big responsibility together. In the evenings he even read some of the books on pregnancy and childcare Cecilia had lent Maud.

'Not encroaching on your territory, am I?' he asked.

'Not at all. I'm just . . . surprised.'

'I surprise myself. I can't think of anything that's made me happier. I just . . .'

'What?'

'Oh, nothing.' He closed the book. 'Can I make you a hot drink? Is there something on the wireless you'd like to listen to?'

As the months passed, Cecilia appeared more often. Recommendations were made about perambulators, muslin cloths, doctors and midwives and the best place to have the baby. James Holdern had an old medical-school chum who ran a good maternity hospital near Marylebone, very handy.

Running this little house and garden and preparing for the next stage was all Maud did now. Cecilia's arrival two afternoons a week became a highlight, even though she was never sure if she actually liked Cecilia or not.

'How's Robert?' Cecilia would ask before she asked anything else. When Maud told her of Robert's presents, of his keenness to educate himself on babies, Cecilia shook her head. 'I've never known him like this. He's transformed.'

'He's been wonderful.' She told Cecilia how Robert insisted on bringing her tea and toast in bed before he left for work, how he rang every lunchtime to make sure she was all right.

But June turned to July and Maud found herself admitting that Robert had become more distracted, retreating to his small study after she'd served the supper.

'Work must be tough.'

'I think it is.'

Cecilia nodded at that morning's newspaper. 'Well, it's worrying, isn't it? The Russians wanting to build more nuclear weapons. The Communists in China.'

'There's always an enemy,' Maud said. Beneath the maternal outlines of her body something of Amber stirred inside her. *Keep your wits about you, don't lose concentration, don't be lulled into a false sense of security. Ask your husband about his work.* Sometimes when they were eating supper Maud would be conscious of Robert's eyes on her, watching her as she ate.

She would make more attempts to get him to talk to her about his work. Obviously there would be things that he couldn't tell her, but surely he could give her an idea of what he was doing?

'Darling, it's much of the same, keeping an eye on the Balkans, on how they're shaping up,' he said when she asked him questions. 'You know, it's so lovely to come back here in the evening and relax with you. Other wives would be blasting husbands with questions, but you know what the score is with sensitive work.'

It's not the war now, Maud told herself.

The days were passing quickly now. 'Pack a bag,' Cecilia Holdern told Maud. 'In case the baby comes early.'

'My due date isn't until October. It's only just September now.' Summer had vanished into a depression, bringing rain with it.

'Better to be prepared. You don't need that much.' Cecilia listed an alarmingly large number of items. Maud would need a small suitcase to take them all to the clinic. A good start would be to dig one out, leave it open to air in the spare room and then make it a daily goal to place necessary objects in it. Her own suitcase, the one she'd taken on honeymoon, was far too large; she'd need to be having triplets to fill it with maternity pads, nightdresses, nappies, matinée jackets and bootees. Her mother was well equipped with luggage of all shapes and sizes, but should a married woman need recourse to her parents for something like this?

Robert was still a little withdrawn, not as openly enthusiastic as he had been in the early months of her pregnancy, but the presents had continued. He would, she knew, be delighted to buy her a suitcase.

When they'd moved in to this house he'd stored his old suitcases and bags underneath the spare bed. The spare room was to become a nursery, the cot arriving in the following week, a present from her parents. She could usefully remove the suitcases and bags from underneath the bed and place them on the landing so that Robert could transfer them to the loft. At the same time she could choose a suitable case for herself.

Neither of them had brought much with them to this house, he because he'd been bombed out and she because much of her stuff was still in Shropshire. She pulled out a large leather case with his initials monogrammed on to it. Her own honeymoon suitcase. A Gladstone bag. Hatboxes. A vanity case Mama had given her for the honeymoon. And a small, old suitcase, a little battered, and singed slightly in one corner, but made of fine-quality leather, a label still attached to it. *ABH*.

Alice–something–Havers. The case must have been plucked from the ruins of the first home. It rattled when she shook it, but was locked.

Maud stood up, dizzy as she did, and perched on the spare bed. She could push the suitcase back underneath, or pile it with the others on the landing, leaving it without a comment for Robert to store in the loft. She couldn't take Alice's suitcase to the clinic with her. Even looking at it felt wrong, somehow. She knew Robert wouldn't like it.

A natural sense of curiosity is your best friend. Why shouldn't she look at something that'd been left in a bedroom in her own home?

Maud padded downstairs to the small room at the back of the house where Robert worked at night. She'd opened his desk before, looking for stamps and envelopes, but that had been when he'd been here to ask.

She found the suitcase key in a small drawer. Before she went upstairs, Maud sat at Robert's desk, staring at the blotter. *By the way, darling, I was looking for a suitcase and found that old one of Alice's under the spare room bed. Cecilia said something of that size would be perfect. But I don't know how you'd feel about my using it, as it was Alice's?* Using Cecilia's name would give her carte blanche.

Back in the spare room the suitcase opened easily. Inside was a brown-paper-wrapped package, about four inches deep and six by eight inches wide and tall, tied with string. *In for a penny. . .* There was no writing on the package, no indication as to what it might be.

She pulled out photographs in silver frames. Alice on honeymoon – somewhere with palm trees. Alice as a bride. Alice sitting beside what looked like a Scottish loch, easel in front of her, a paintbrush in her hand. Perhaps these photos had been safe in his office at the time of the bomb that had killed Alice in their home. He'd been discreet, tucking them away from Maud so she wouldn't have to look at her predecessor. Alice was beautiful: slender with what Maud imagined to be light-brown hair and almond-shaped eyes that did indeed resemble those of her brother, James. She'd doubtless been a fine artist. Jealousy, followed almost instantly by pity, flowed through Maud: pity for the dead girl who'd never lived to paint a peacetime loch again, pity for Robert, who'd suffered her loss.

She rewrapped the photographs and retied the string, replacing them in the suitcase and storing it back under the bed.

Mama could lend her a small suitcase – there was plenty of time to have it sent down from Shropshire.

The sun came out again at the end of September. You could hire deck-chairs in Hyde Park, though the man clearly thought that it was too late in the year and grumbled as he went to fetch them from his store. The flowerbeds weren't at their best at this stage of the year, but at least there was a sense that a park might yet become a recreation area again rather than somewhere to graze sheep and grow food. Robert and Maud were sitting reading the Sunday papers. Her deckchair was set too low for her. 'I'll never be able to pull myself up again.'

She waited for a moment to see if he'd help. When he returned to his newspaper she struggled to adjust the slats at the back. Robert watched her. He wore a light wool suit and one of the shirts he'd had made in Cairo and looked crisp and fresh. Young matrons bringing their children in to play in the park eyed him. One of his jacket buttons was coming loose.

'I'll have to sew that button for you. At least my war work taught me how to do that.' Basic repair work had been covered in training. If your breeches or rucksack ripped out on the karst there was no seam-stress to take them to.

He sat up straight. 'Never mention your war work.'

'I just meant that I can actually thread a needle.' He continued to look at her. She felt as she had in the classrooms in Cairo when he was training her. 'I wasn't going to say anything else.'

'You never know who might be listening.'

'To me talking about sewing on buttons?' She waited for him to grin and make a quip.

Robert sat back in the deckchair, opening the newspaper again. The very printed words on the front seemed to radiate anger. Had she been indiscreet? Nobody was anywhere near them. 'Did you remember to call the plumber about that pipe in the bathroom?' he asked.

'He's coming on Tuesday morning.'

'But don't you remember, darling, that I asked you to make an appointment for late afternoon so that I could leave the office a little early and be there too?'

'I don't remember you saying that, no.' She was certain he'd never mentioned anything about leaving work early.

He didn't seem angry, though, at the challenge. 'You need to relax more. I shouldn't nag you about silly things, should I?'

'I don't mind doing them.' It wasn't as though her days were exactly full.

He glanced at her abdomen. 'It's tiring for you. I should take over more of these things. I want you to concentrate on yourself. And the baby.'

A few days later he brought a large rectangular parcel back with him from work.

She unwrapped it. An easel and paints.

'Watercolours?'

'Poor darling, you must be feeling lonely.'

'There's the house,' she said. 'And the garden. All the vegetables to pick and preserve this time of year.' She was proud of the produce the little patch had yielded. 'Things to prepare for the baby.'

'Even so. Those things are a drain on you. Didn't you say you'd once enjoyed painting? I thought you could start again.'

'Me? I never had myself down as much of an artist.' She hadn't even picked up a paintbrush since about the upper fourth at boarding school. Robert was looking puzzled.

'I thought . . .' He put a hand to the side of his face.

But the idea of taking up watercolours enchanted her. She even went down to the library to see if there were evening classes she could sign up for. 'Painting will help keep you calm,' Robert told her.

Was she so obviously jittery? 'I could sit in the park and paint the Serpentine,' she said. 'The light from the water is so fascinating.'

'Yes.' He smiled at her with real warmth.

While he was at work she made some exploratory dabs. She liked the way the hard colour in the paint pallet became something fluid on the paper. But her brush strokes seemed only to produce spiky little trees. She tried to brighten up her attempt with some of the yellow paint and created what looked like a fire consuming the trees. Maud thought of the birds that might be nesting in the branches and felt nauseous. She tore up the sheet before Robert could see it. 'Perhaps I'll start with drawing,' she told him brightly that evening. 'Something simple, a wine bottle, maybe. To get my eye in.'

'A schoolgirl still-life?' He gave her a gentle smile. 'I thought you might want to stretch yourself.'

To paint to Alice's standard?

'You won't have much time soon. Cecilia always tells me how much there is to do when a baby arrives.'

'Yes.' She hadn't done much at all in the last week. It was so warm. Even bringing in the vegetables and washing them felt like serious labour. Yet by the time the clock hands had moved around to four, Maud felt restless. She'd taken to leaving the house, watching the men walking home and the children returning from the park. She walked across Hyde Park. Sometimes she skirted the northern fringe, emerging at the junction between Park Lane and Oxford Street.

Her father had once told her that the site of the old Tyburn gallows was somewhere here. If she half-closed her eyes she could almost hear the hurdle scraping across the rough road, the jeers of the crowd, the horse, skittish at the noise. She'd walk on before more impressions of the hanging and drawing and quartering could come to her. It was more direct to walk diagonally across, roughly southeast, to Hyde Park Corner, crossing into Green Park and sometimes onto St James's Park. But Tyburn drew her to itself. Some traitors were executed elsewhere, in the Tower, for instance, her father had told her, but so many must have come here to Tyburn to die: horribly tortured and maimed before they were killed. As a child, fascination had mingled with revulsion when he'd described the executions, until Mama intervened, telling Dad to stop his stories.

Maud would stare at the road where the gallows had stood, then walk on as quickly as she could, resisting the urge to turn around and ensure that nobody was following her. As she approached St James's her eyes would be peeled, wanting to see her husband before he spotted her. Each time she did, there'd be a sense of relief. He was always the most notable, the most vivid man in the crowds, his face tanned, his bearing athletic. Her husband, finishing a day at work, pleased to see his pregnant wife, but reprimanding her for walking too far.

Just like a loyal retriever, darling. They would stroll home together, arm in arm, past the worn-out, dusty buildings and the weed-choked bomb sites on the way to the park, Maud wondering if the city could ever be put back together again. Sometimes they found a public house Robert thought suitable for her and he would buy her a shandy.

One early afternoon, when nothing needed doing in the garden and the house was tidy, she left home although it was only half past two, Tyburn acting as a magnet. She stood gazing at the road, heedless of the cars, trucks, taxis and buses, wondering whether any of the German bombs that had landed near here had been powerful enough to blast away any lingering maleficence. One bad thing to kill another bad thing. Good coming from ill. Treachery could mean security. Death could mean safety. But, like a subversive imp, Amber whispered in her ear, telling her to pay attention.

Maud walked her usual route to St James's, but it was too early for Robert to be coming out of his office, so she continued on to Westminster then downstream as far as Waterloo Bridge. At this time of the year the evening came earlier and with it cooler air. She stood on the bridge above the Thames, thinking of those women who'd built it, wondering where they were now. Had they merged back into their pre-war lives with ease? Or had they found the transformation as baffling as she did? An elderly lady slowed as she approached Maud, frowning. Maud moved back from the parapet. 'Just looking at the river,' she muttered.

'You need to put your feet up,' the woman told her. 'Tiring stage you're at.'

Maud walked back over the bridge and along the Strand towards Trafalgar Square, where she found a Lyons Corner House and drank a cup of tea and a glass of water. She should eat something, but couldn't muster up the enthusiasm and continued on through Whitehall to St James's, her energy returning with each block she walked, her mind sharper again. She felt Amber in her once more.

In Victoria Street she crossed to the Army & Navy Stores. She would buy something for the baby, something less utilitarian than sheets and maternity jackets and muslin cloths. Maud found herself in the toy department. They hadn't bought any toys yet. What would such a small baby like? Her eyes made contact with the bright button-eyes of a small fluffy rabbit. 'No need to wrap it,' she told the assistant, 'he'll fit in my handbag.'

Maud left the store, checking her watch. Bang on time for Robert. The plump man in the tight suit seemed to materialise suddenly in the crowd without her having spotted him before. At first she thought he had accidentally bumped into Robert and was apologising. As she came closer she saw that they were talking: not just making conversation, but with intent, with emotion. Robert was shaking his head, trying to brush off the man, who put one hand on his shoulder to try and detain him.

Robert succeeded in freeing himself and moved on. Tight-suit man grabbed at him with his other hand, the left one. The skin was pale. Maud could clearly see the hand outlined against Robert's grey suit jacket. She looked at his little finger, at the stunted, stubby appearance of the digit. The man's face showed near despair as he failed to prevent Robert from walking on. On his upper lip a moustache had grown back. He looked better with the facial hair, she thought.

In the middle of a London street at half past five on an autumn afternoon, amidst the roar of buses and the shouts of newspaper ven-dors, Maud stood as Amber, out on the jagged Croatian limestone landscape, smelling its fresh air, an aroma which faded, replaced with that particular aroma of a schoolroom, old paper and chalk. And with the scent of blood. She felt something else, too, something that made her feel more alert than she had during the last heavy and flat-footed weeks. *Pay attention*, Amber said.

Maud shivered, knowing that she must not let Robert see that she had witnessed this exchange, that he must not notice she was fright-ened. She turned for home, walking quickly enough to draw curious glances from those she passed.

'A bit of a headache,' she told him from her armchair when he came into the house five minutes after her. 'I started to come to meet you but turned round.' He might have spotted her walking back across the park. 'Thought I should rest. Hope you didn't miss me.' She was impressed with her tone, how calm she sounded.

He kissed the top of her head. 'I did. I always do.'

'You were frightened of your husband, of his knowing you'd witnessed this exchange with someone you had met overseas during the war?' Dr Rosenstein asks.

I nod. 'I knew Robert would be angry. I had seen something, some-one, he didn't want me to see, found out something I wasn't supposed to know.'

'Which was?'

'I'd seen fingertip man . . . where I was carrying out my operation. But I'd also met him in Cairo before we were flown out. He ate some of that Yugoslavia-shaped cake I told you about. He hadn't lost the fingertip then.' The fat man bursting into the room at Rustum Buildings while we were looking at the slides. Robert's coolness with him. Had he – fingertip man – been a necessary but disliked ally? 'Robert sent him to kill someone I worked with.' I don't say Naomi's name.

Dr Rosenstein studies me without a word.

'And Robert did something else . . .' I think of the burning Lysander, of the feathers floating down. 'There was nobody else it could have been. Something that cost more lives. I really don't think I'm mad at all, you know.'

Dr Rosenstein leans forward over her desk. 'Go on with your story, Maud.'

'The next day I had another look in that suitcase under the spare bed,' I say.

Clever. Hide a key to a shallow desk drawer in a suitcase upstairs that itself could only be opened by finding a key in a different drawer of the same desk. Maud unlocked the suitcase, took out the photographs and desk key and packed it with her maternity clothes and those for the baby. She placed the case beside the front door, remembering that the toy rabbit was still inside her handbag, which sat on the console table by the door. It had taken her until this point in the afternoon, half past five, to make herself go through with it.

Bring the desk key down to his study and unlock the drawer. It was raining, so he wouldn't expect her to go and meet him. She unlocked the shallow drawer right underneath the desktop. Just big enough for a telegram to be stored.

Confirm Ana part of group shot Maribor. Maud read the telegram twice, before returning it to its drawer and locking the desk again.

The front door latch clicked. He was early – must have caught a bus to avoid the rain. Robert called out to her. He'd go into the garden, expecting her to be gathering the last of the beans, heedless of the weather, and then he'd look in the sitting room before going upstairs to their bedroom. He wouldn't expect her to be here in his office, but wouldn't be surprised: she sometimes came in to hunt for a stamp or envelope.

Robert went upstairs. She heard the light tread of his pre-war hand-made shoes on their bedroom carpet. He'd be removing his suit jacket, hanging it up. In another minute he'd come downstairs. Maud went to the bookcase and pulled out Robert's atlas, opening it on the Balkans. When he'd taken her out to dinner last May, he had mentioned a village in southern Austria, not far from the Slovene border. Ana must have been repatriated, trudging along the road by the river Drau with the traitors, the sadists, the Fascists to Maribor, or Marburg, as this atlas still called it, on the same river Drau or Drava in northeast Slovenia.

Robert came into the study. She knew she ought to have hidden the atlas but couldn't bring herself to move. He stood in the doorway, looking at her. 'Darling? I was worried that something had happened, that you'd gone into hospital.'

She nodded at the atlas open on the desk. 'You let me believe Ana was still alive. Why?'

He sat on the edge of the desk. 'You found the telegram?' He took his tin of tobacco and a pack of cigarette papers out of his inside jacket pocket. Robert still preferred to roll his own. He took his time, removing one of the white papers and laying it out on the desk. 'Why?' she asked again.

'When you went to Croatia in 1944, what you saw was just one piece of a puzzle.'

Maud waited.

'It wasn't just about driving out the Germans, winning what we called "the" war. There were other wars we couldn't lose.'

'Other wars?'

'Tito was pushing north. Was he going to keep on going through Slovenia into Austria? Grab some of the parts that had large Slovene populations for Yugoslavia? What territory might his friend Stalin claim next?'

Maud was thinking of the way the mission had been derailed from the very first moment. 'Your Chetnik contacts let you know they'd got Stimmer, an important military intelligence officer. You changed our drop site at the last minute so that I could pick him up. Stimmer knew you were secretly cooperating with the Chetniks. And thus the Germans.'

Dangerous stuff when Churchill had severed links with the Chetnik leader, Mihailović. Explosive information when Stalin was still being wooed and was essential to victory. Stimmer liaised with Chetniks as part of his job in German intelligence. So very dangerous for Robert to have this secret known if it came out in an intelligence interview.

'If Stimmer was sent to Cairo for interrogation, he might tell them that you were liaising with Chetniks, and thus the Germans. Fingertip man, your moustachioed plump colleague who likes cakes, was sent out just before us on some kind of secret operation. But the Partisans caught him and cut off his fingertip as a warning.' She thought of Naomi. 'Did he kill Naomi?'

'Not himself,' he said quietly.

'But he was involved?'

He bowed his head.

'Fingertip man told the Ustaše she was sheltering in the doctor's barn, didn't he?'

Silence.

'Why did you have her killed?' Her voice sounded tight, but controlled.

'Naomi didn't wait for new orders. She headed off towards Hungary by herself and stumbled into the wrong village at the wrong time and she saw the man you call fingertip man. Though he was still benefiting from an entire digit then.' There was a note of amusement in his tone. It made her hate him briefly.

'I saw fingertip man accosting you on the pavement near your office.'

Robert looked startled. 'You're still sharp, very sharp.' He couldn't seem to help a little pride creeping into his voice. Well, he'd trained Maud into Amber, hadn't he?

'Couldn't take the risk of Naomi surviving her mission to Hungary and telling someone that she'd seen a man who wasn't supposed to be there.' He lit his cigarette. 'It was regrettable. Naomi was a fine agent.'

'And Ana,' Maud said. 'Why couldn't you save her?' She thought of Ana's younger son. 'Did Miko know something?'

'Miko wasn't anyone who'd been involved in . . . my operation.' She noticed how he'd slipped back into that indirect, passive way of describing events, as though they related to someone else.

'But you couldn't risk Ana telling the British or Americans in Austria what had happened in that little village where Naomi died.'

'There was some uncertainty and some concern as to whom they might talk.'

She pictured Ana, fearing she was going to be marched back to Yugoslavia, talking to British officers in the Austrian village, begging them to liaise with Robert and prevent her from being sent back to certain execution. Did she beg for Miko too? She imagined Ana growing increasingly desperate as her pleas went unanswered, her explanations of her war work with the Partisans ignored, her insistence that she was no Chetnik, scoffed at.

'If it had been left up to me I would simply have had Ana imprisoned for a while until things were quieter, persuaded her to keep her mouth shut for her own sake,' Robert said. She noted that he was using the first person again now, as though finally letting himself admit his part in it all.

'She'd rescued Allied servicemen, after all. But the logistics of extricating her and placing her somewhere safe proved too complicated.'

Ana had trusted Maud so many times. When she'd begged the unit to take Stimmer into captivity. When she'd begged her to go after Naomi. Ana had risked the displeasure, perhaps even discipline of the Partisans. And above all, Ana had saved her from being burnt alive when the Lysander was blown up. Maud pictured her heading back in a line of broken combatants, elderly people and children towards the Slovene border, perhaps, expecting the shout, the tap on her shoulder, *Not you, you can stay.* Perhaps she had begged for Miko too.

'Who else knows this?' She spoke calmly, but the muscles tightened in her lower abdomen and she felt nauseous. 'Apart from your fingertip colleague, who's now back in London.'

Robert said nothing.

'Just you.' She nodded. Something that was more than a muscle tightening but less than a pain made her sit up straighter. She wanted to place a hand on her abdomen, but Robert was watching her.

'I didn't mean you to find that telegram, Amber.' She noted the use of that name.

'You made a mistake? That's not like you.'

'Work has been distracting.'

'Fingertip man has been harassing you, hasn't he? Oh.' She remembered something, something from a long time ago.

He looked at her.

'I was only fourteen or fifteen, but fingertip man came to the mine in Kosovo when we lived there, didn't he?' The memory sharpened. 'And so did you.'

Two men, but only one came inside. He ate three slice of Mama's plum cake. The other man, slimmer, more active, stayed outside with Dad.

Robert nodded.

'That's how you came to know about me.'

Robert closed his eyes. 'Maud's father tells me proudly that she is skilled at canoeing and can hike for days at a time. She speaks Serbo-Croat and has a highly retentive memory.' His face softened. 'We wrote notes on your family, but it was the mine that concerned us most then, what might happen to it if the Germans invaded, what your father might do. But your family moved on and it was only later that we thought of you in regard to Balkan operations.'

Maud breathed out slowly. 'You made a mistake,' she said, when the contraction had eased. 'You should have destroyed the telegram. I would never have known for sure.' Her voice sounded sad, but she was starting to find it hard to concentrate on her own words.

'I forgot there was a spare key to that drawer in that old suitcase of Alice's. It was her desk originally, you see, she lent it to me for my office in London because I didn't like the one they gave me.' He sounded distant. 'But it's reasonable to believe that you'll do what is right, that you'll understand that the future security of Europe was at stake.'

Once again he was switching back into that distancing of himself from everything he'd done. Some of her contempt must have shown. 'We couldn't let it leak back to London or Moscow or Washington that we were still working with the Chetniks,' he went on, sounding less detached.

'And ultimately the Germans, in fact? Plotting with them to keep back the Communists?'

He nodded.

Maud stood up. The hand in her abdomen squeezed her hard. She clenched the desk.

'Maud?'

She couldn't speak.

'I know what's happening. Your pains have started. And they're coming more frequently, aren't they?' Robert sounded concerned. 'It's too early.'

She forced herself to stand up straight, to ignore the pain. 'You don't get out of it that easily.'

'What will you do?'

'I don't know.' The words came out as gasps. She couldn't say more now, had to let her body take over.

Robert picked up the telephone receiver. 'I'm calling James Holdern.'

'He's not my doctor.'

'He'll take care of things.' Another pain grabbed Maud and she was unable to speak as Robert asked the operator for James's number. Maud listened as he asked James to come round immediately, by car. 'Surely you must see that we need to put this behind us now, Maud? For the sake of the child?'

The contraction eased off. 'You're a traitor, Robert.'

'I love my country,' he said. 'I love Europe. A free Europe. Look at what's happening in the eastern European countries the Soviets have moved into: executions, torture, property requisitions. Just as I feared.'

'You didn't mind killing friends and allies for it. I can't forget that.' Tears pricked in her eyes because he was looking at her with such tenderness. 'I wish I could, I really do.'

As she looked at him, at that face of his, she longed not to have read the telegram, not to have recognised fingertip man on the pavement in St James's. She walked towards the door. There was a telephone box down the road and her case was packed. 'I'm sorry, Robert.'

He looked at her very carefully. 'You're very dogged when you want to be, aren't you?'

'You always knew what I was like. You thought you were so good at manipulating me.' She thought of her lapses of concentration in the early months of their marriage, of all the things she'd mislaid. Or had she?

'You hid my things and cancelled appointments to make me doubt myself and feel insecure. Just in case I—' Another contraction grabbed her. When it passed she saw that he had the tin of tobacco in his hand. He tipped out the tobacco onto the desk and pulled off the lid, which he threw onto the parquet floor. In a single swift and graceful move he bent and held the lid with one hand while he stamped it into a triangular shaped blade.

She would have panicked if the contractions hadn't started again. Surely the pains shouldn't be coming this quickly so early? When it had passed she looked at the blade. Her horror must have shown in her face.

'No, darling. You can't think I'd harm you like that.' Robert looked at his watch. 'James will be here in five minutes. You won't have to wait long. I hate to leave you in this condition.' He sounded truly worried about her.

Perhaps Robert had already made an emergency escape plan. Perhaps there were rail or aeroplane tickets. Or a car to drive him away.

'I'm not running away.' He could always read her mind. 'There's nowhere for me to go, that's my problem.'

He turned the blade so that it was pointing towards his own abdomen.

'No.' She hated him, what he'd done, but she couldn't lose him, not now. Maud lumbered towards him, her labouring body seeming to lighten momentarily as she grabbed at his hand to stop him. The tobacco tin blade flashed as it cut through his shirt, instantly producing a crimson line. They fell together, landing on the rug. Robert landed on top of her. She felt his warm blood soaking into her dress. The blade had fallen, lying just a few inches from her hand. She picked it up. With her other hand she pushed her husband's limp body off her.

'I love you,' he gasped.

The next contraction took her. She rolled over onto all fours. James was standing over her. He must have had a front door key. Amber was noting the details as Maud struggled. He placed a hand on her back and said something.

As the contraction passed she became aware of James running his hands over Robert, pulling up his shirt to examine the wounds, saying nothing to her. He picked up the receiver and asked the operator for a number. Another contraction rocked Maud. Liquid passed between her thighs, slightly bloodied: her waters.

James asked for two ambulances. He opened up the brown leather bag he had brought with him and took out a syringe. 'This will sting a bit but you won't feel anything else afterwards, Maud. There's a bed in a clinic a few minutes' drive from here. It will all be over soon.'

'Robert . . .'

'We need to be quick so he doesn't bleed to death.' He took her hand gently. 'You'll be fine, the baby's coming early but not dangerously so. I'll put pressure on Robert's wounds. The police will understand, Maud. Your bag's by the front door, I'll make sure it goes with you.'

The prick of a syringe in her upper arm.

Then nothing.

'I remember nothing after the injection,' I tell Dr Rosenstein.

'They must have used something called the twilight sleep on you, I believe it's a mixture of morphine and amnesiac. You gave birth to your child without regaining full consciousness and without the event imprinting itself on your memory, though I suspect that it is still there, somewhere. When you woke up—'

I take over. 'I was in that first mental hospital.' Drugged. Unable to remember anything, even that I had just become a mother. I was leaking milk and blood. I'd thought it was sweat and urine, but they'd bound me up so tightly I couldn't feel much. They were kind, I recall now, and spoke to me gently. Perhaps even they had scruples about taking a newly delivered mother away from her infant. James Holdern had been there once or twice, too. I remember him sitting beside a policeman, shaking his head. *Some kind of labour-induced psychosis . . . hormonal . . . Delusional. Dangerous to herself and others. Terribly sad about the baby, but we'll look after him.*

17

My memory has returned completely. My solicitor has been summoned. I've told him what I can of my wartime work and my suspicions of my husband's treachery and his attempts to cover it up.

Why did you never tell me about the baby? I asked my mother when I wrote to her.

> Dr Holdern told us it would upset you and precipitate another psychotic incident. Kinder to let you forget; at least until you were more stable and you could talk to Dr Rosenstein about it. But we obtained a copy of the birth certificate for your son, our grandson. His name is David.

I burn at the loss of my son. I am surprised I do not sear through objects when I look at them. But the anger seems to ignite my memory. Dr Rosenstein cuts my drug doses again, but warns me that she will keep me on some of the tranquillising medicine until we know that the anger will not overwhelm me.

'You are firing on all cylinders, old girl.' Jim shakes his head admiringly when we're out in the garden by the dovecot later and I tell him. 'You'll be out of this gaff before you know it. Your redemption is close.'

'What about you?' I ask, feeling a pang. I will miss Jim, my companion. 'How's it going with Dr Manners?'

He sighs and shrugs. 'Apparently I still say strange things. I know I think them. And dream them. They don't like that . . . outside. Even though I'm not a threat to anyone, I'll probably be a loon for the rest of my life.'

'You're not a loon, that's a hateful word. You just don't remember. That's why you say things people don't understand. Your memory's still tied up in knots. When you unravel it properly, you'll feel differently.'

'You may be right.' He looks doubtful, though. 'But sometimes I wonder if we aren't the only sane ones. You'd be insane to want to remember some of the things you and I saw.'

I've never told Jim much about Yugoslavia. I know without telling him that he would understand the girl with a bloodied mouth slumping slowly over in her chair in front of a blackboard. A Lysander plane on fire, the men inside turned to shrieking live skeletons inside it. Downed pack ponies gazing puzzled at their own splaying innards. My back pushed down onto the rocky track and the sickly scent of a man's hair oil in my face. But now these images remain in the past and will not bother me again.

'What about those men who came to see you?'

Jim looks at me as though he doesn't know what I'm talking about. 'Didn't you have visitors?' I put up the stepladder.

He frowns. 'Oh, them. They were nothing . . . just administrative.'

'So you're staying on here at Woodlands?'

'So it seems.'

Perhaps Jim will look after my doves when I have left? I will visit, of course. Or perhaps I could take them with me? I worry about the buzzard. I know, rationally, that my presence at Woodlands doesn't mean that the doves are any safer from the buzzard, but my heart is telling me the opposite. I peer inside the dovecot and see what I was hoping I'd see.

'They've hatched,' I call softly to Jim. 'Two chicks. Squabs, they're called.' I stand still, looking at them for a moment, and then climb quietly down.

'You love those doves, don't you?' he says sorrowfully. 'They're the one thing about Woodlands you really do like.'

'I like Ingrams and Dr Rosenstein,' I tell him. 'And I don't know how I would have managed without you, Jim.'

'Don't say that.' He looks emotional. Perhaps I have been insensitive talking about my release. 'I hope your doves will be safe, Maud. I hope the buzzard doesn't get them.' He wheels away, leaving me alone. Jim is still in limbo, knowing that remaining at Woodlands is the best he can expect for himself; fearing that the funds may not be available for him to stay and that he will be sent to somewhere less compassionate. I want to call him back. But something in the stiff set of his back tells me this is not the moment, that he needs to be alone.

Dr Rosenstein and I have a further session a few days later.

'Where is David now?' I ask.

'I am still finding out. Not with your husband, it would seem.'

The baby would be about nine months old now. Still too difficult for a single father to bring up. Even with a nanny.

'Did Robert have any family?'

'No.' He had told me that he was a single child, both parents dead. Then I have a revelation. 'I think James Holdern's wife has David.' My dream about the woman stealing my pomegranate? That was Cecilia. Or possibly Alice, James's sister who died in the Blitz before she could have a child herself. I tell Dr Rosenstein this. She raises her eyebrows. Perhaps it's too fanciful. 'Your solicitor will find out all the details about your son.'

'David's with the Holderns, I know it. Cecilia has a nanny for her own children – we met her coming out of the house just before we were married.' *Of course I will help, dearest Robert,* I hear Cecilia say. *What a tragedy. Poor little David. Poor Maud. Some women are too highly strung for childbirth.*

And having my boy would complete her family of girls and provide her husband with some kind of convoluted link to his dead sister. I muse on all this as I walk around the garden again. Another missile has landed on the grass by the wall. This time it's a large stone, almost a rock in size. The boys have been in the lane again. Jim approaches.

'Sorry about yesterday.' He sounds calmer. 'Don't know what got into me. Must do more juggling: it helps me.' He looks at the stone. 'The local lads again? They seem to be stepping up their antics, don't they?' His expression is almost calculating, unlike his usual self. Perhaps there was once a more ruthless side to Jim, before it was stamped out of him by those days and nights in the lifeboat watching the children die. 'Do you think they know where the doves are and are trying to hit them?'

The dovecot is set up away from the wall, but not so far that a missile couldn't strike it. Of course, the boys don't even know it's here so it would only be by pure fluke that they might manage to hit it. But even so.

'Have you thought about how much you'll miss the doves when you leave, Maud? Really?' Jim sounds sad for me. 'I mean, you can leave, of course, and try and get hold of your son, but there's no guarantee, is there? At least here you have the doves. And Ingrams and Dr Rosenstein. And me.' He comes closer and I see his face is like a mask trying to restrain the emotion inside him. 'We care about you. You know you're safe here, don't you?'

I step back. 'Of course.' His visitors have upset him; I've never seen him so unsettled. I'm surprised Dr Manners let them trouble him like this. 'It's all right, Jim,' I tell him. 'I'll be safe outside Woodlands. And I'll come and visit you. You'll be juggling at least five balls by then.'

'Oh Maud, old thing.' He shakes his head, looking more like the old Jim. 'Don't listen to me. Of course you want to get out of here. Why shouldn't you fly away like your precious birds? They shouldn't . . .' He breaks off, looking confused.

'Who shouldn't do what?'

'They shouldn't make it so hard on us,' he says, sounding almost tearful. 'That's what I meant.' He looks at his watch, which is probably showing the wrong time as he doesn't always remember to wind it up. 'I need to go, Maud.' He walks over to one of the nurses who are always around when we're outside and asks her to take him inside.

I wonder what this thing is he needs to do. Ten minutes later, when I come inside with Ingrams, I see him emerge from the ground floor cubicle that houses the telephone. Although it's for patient use, I have never made a call: it's a complicated business involving forms signed by our doctors and by the director himself. Perhaps Jim's financial problems are so serious that permission has been granted for him to call his solicitor or bank manager or whoever acts as his de facto guardian. His parents? Or maybe his recent visitors have requested he call them.

I'm wearing rubber-soled shoes and Jim doesn't hear me. I watch him shuffle towards the staircase, where another nurse waits for him. His shoulders are slumped, defeated.

'Come along,' Ingrams says. 'Let's sort out that dose for you, Maud.' They're reducing my medication every other day now and it won't be long before I don't take anything at all. I'm impatient, wanting to stop the drugs immediately, but Dr Rosenstein, though sympathetic and encouraging, is still keen to do it more gradually, in case the process proves difficult.

I don't think it will be difficult.

'How much longer will it be?' I ask Dr Rosenstein next morning. 'Until I can see my son?'

'I've written to your solicitor. He has written back to me and confirmed that he is delighted to hear of your recovered memory and is investigating the best way to return you to normal life and give you access to your son.'

'Access? I don't want access. David should live with me.'

'I know. On the positive side, I would imagine we are talking days, a week at most until you leave us. When you're off the drugs completely.' Dr Rosenstein scribbles notes on her pad. 'I don't want you to be struggling when you leave, Maud, I want you to walk out of here ready for resuming normal life, for regaining your child, for finding some work you can enjoy.' There's a note of something that sounds like a warning in her voice. She lays down the pen. 'I should tell you that there has been some interest in you.'

'Interest?'

'I have been reminded that you are bound by the Official Secrets Act.'

'Who reminded you?'

'The director.'

I've only met the director once, a week or so after I was first admitted, and such was my state I can barely remember the encounter. The director sees some patients himself, eminent ones, Jim has told me: judges, politicians and generals, those types. Not that we've had any of those for a while.

'I've been careful in what I said.' But I probably wasn't careful enough. The pieces could be put back together.

Dr Rosenstein looks down at her hands. 'I have never written down anything that might cause problems for you.'

'So why's the director so anxious?'

'I'm not sure.'

A tiny curl of suspicion loops around my guts. 'It's him.'

She looks up at me.

'Robert. Somehow he's found out that I'm starting to remember.'

'But how?' She gives me her most reassuring smile. 'Nobody here talks to your husband.'

'Not even the director?'

'He hasn't been involved in your case. Your solicitor arranged for your transfer from the original . . . hospital where you were placed by your husband.' Her lips curl slightly at the mention of that institution. 'Your husband signed the paperwork, but never came here himself. We need to proceed with caution so that . . . people aren't anxious about what you might say. For that reason, I'm going to be vague about the true state of your recovered memory. I can't lie, of course. But I may not write everything in my notes.'

When we've finished she opens the door for me. Ingrams isn't there. 'I don't think you need escorting any more, Maud,' she says, smiling. So I'm free to go out to the gardens alone to check on the doves. There are more empty beer bottles by the wall. More worryingly, someone has knocked over the bird bath. The plinth is broken. I go back into the house to find Ingrams, who will know how we can report this. He brings a tray and watering can out, so we can set up a temporary water station for the birds. 'This won't take much to fix,' he says. 'A bit of mortar. I'll speak to the gardener. Don't you worry about it, Maud.'

'It's those boys,' I say. 'How did they get in, though?'

He shakes his head and I see that he's worried. 'The gates are secure and they couldn't climb the walls. They're too high.'

'But it must be someone from outside?' The green-baize-door people are never in this part of the garden. Poor souls, most of them wouldn't possess the energy necessary for vandalism.

Ingrams is eyeing the wall. As far as I remember from the few occasions I've been driven out of Woodlands, the lane behind it has a ditch, so that the climb up to the wall is even more difficult than it would be this side. Difficult, but not impossible. The wall is supposed to keep us in, though, not others out.

> We are working hard with your solicitor, darling [Mama writes]. We do not know about your wartime work – you only ever told us you'd been working in Signals in Cairo, and we had no idea that you and Robert had been involved in something more active. I know you can't say more about it and we won't ask for details. We are having trouble tracking him down and his solicitor does not seem able to provide us with the information we need. Of course, we can apply to the courts if necessary. Just a few more days and you'll be out of Woodlands yourself. We cannot wait to have you home. Robert sent us your things at the time of the divorce and your father took them out of storage. I found the sweetest toy rabbit in your handbag. Your baby will love it, I know.

'I took my last medication yesterday,' I tell Dr Rosenstein.

'How do you feel now?'

'Fine. Perhaps a little more on edge, a little more aware of what's around me. But that's natural, isn't it?'

I know I will have a battle on my hands with Robert and I want to be prepared. *Adrenaline is your friend – use it.* He taught me to be courageous in mind and body and I'm going to turn those attributes against him now.

Dr Rosenstein is pulling paperwork out of files. 'We thought Friday after lunch for your parents to come and collect you. They have quite a drive, don't they?' She peers at me. 'What is it?'

'Nothing.'

She waits.

'My doves. Well, not really *my* doves. I'm just wondering who will look after them.'

She puts down her pen. 'I remember the patient who looked after them before you did, Maud. She went home. She worried too that the birds would be neglected after her departure, but we have gardeners and they'll look after them. And I am sure that another patient will be happy to take on their care. They are such beautiful birds.' She stops, sniffing.

I've been noticing the smell, too, for the last five minutes, but it hasn't bothered me until now. Something's burning in the garden. A bonfire? But the scent reaching us isn't that of dead leaves. It's wood. And something else.

All the hair on the back of my neck stands on end. Dr Rosenstein stands up and goes to the door, calling for Ingrams.

She opens the door to the garden. Ingrams is running across from the house. I see where they're looking. The dovecot is on fire. Doves fly, wings in flames, trying to free themselves, only to crash to the grass. Some of them scream. I haven't heard sounds like that before. There's a smell of burning feathers. A plane's on fire, men writhing inside it. I'm trying to reach them, running across the lawn. Ingrams and Dr Rosenstein are calling. They can't catch me. Nobody ever could at school, either. Another dove tumbles to the ground, flapping burning wings. I stop and turn, scooping up the bird. Its feathers feel hot in my hands. It trembles and emits a sound I can't describe. The hen dove who hatched the eggs.

'I'm sorry.' I wring her neck and feel something break inside me.

The youth is still standing, matches and an old newspaper in his hands by the dovecot. He says something to me.

'What did you say?'

He watches Ingrams as he runs towards us, making sure there's still time for him to climb up the stepladder and over the wall. 'Does it remind you of your friends in Croatia?'

I freeze.

'It was your fault they all died, Amber.' The youth recites the words rapidly, as though he has learnt a complex script by heart and wants to get it over and done with. 'The militia men pulled out Naomi's teeth,' he tells me in the same stilted way, reaching for the stepladder. 'And your friend Ana and her younger son – not all those shot by the Partisans died immediately. Some were buried alive.'

I spy an unattended spade and barely break stride to pick it up. I have the pleasure of seeing the youth's face as I approach.

Ingrams has reached us, holding up his hands, calling to me.

'Who told you those things?'

'Nobody, I didn't mean . . . I just . . . I'm sorry about the doves, miss.' He's backing away, stumbling over the stepladder, back to the wall. He can't understand the Serbo-Croat words I use as I raise the spade above my head and bring it down on him. But he knows he's being punished and deserves it. He drops the ladder. His hands go to his head and he cowers as I tell him he deserves to die for what he has done. He shouts that it's only fucking birds, I'm a loony, deserve to be locked up here with the others.

The youth has a gash on his shoulder. He puts his hand to the blood and looks from it to me. Ingrams is here now. 'Put down the spade, Amber.' He says it gently. I'm about to do what he wants when yet another dove flutters down from the dovecot. Its wings have been singed and it will never fly again. Prey for a fox. I strike off its head with one stroke.

'I'm going to kill you,' I tell the youth. 'I'm going to find a knife and stick it into your cowardly belly.'

'Amber,' Ingrams says again. 'Think, Amber.'

'He deserves to die.'

'Nobody deserves that, Amber.'

I close my eyes.

'Drop the spade.'

I throw it down beside the dead bird. 'That's it,' I tell Ingrams. 'It's all over now for me.'

'It's not, it needn't be, Maud.'

'The pack. The electrodes.'

'No.' Dr Rosenstein runs up, breathless, not used to running. 'We were just at the point where you had faced up to it all. You needn't go back to the beginning, Maud.'

'There's no point. Look what I've done. Another attack.' The court, this time. A trial. Prison.

'Think of your child,' she urges me.

David, lumbered with a mad mother. 'Too much damage,' I tell her. 'Don't you see?'

The youth must have thrown another bottle onto the lawn before he climbed over. I pick it up and smash it against the wall so that I am holding a jagged glass weapon. I slash my right wrist before they can reach me. Some of my blood trickles over the dead white dove on the grass.

Jim is there, his face drained of colour. He mumbles something. I only hear the last words, '. . . not like this.'

Dr Rosenstein and Ingrams bind my bleeding wrists and someone drives me into the local hospital for stitches. A doctor injects me with something. Mama and my father come to visit, but by then I'm drugged and can't talk to them. Some strange men come in and look at me and talk to Dr Rosenstein. Voices are raised. I hear all they say, but the individual words are like pearls that have fallen from a string: lacking order or pattern. Later, just before I'm due another dose, I see Dr Rosenstein sign something. She almost throws the piece of paper back at them. Her face is black as she tells them to get out of the ward, but when she turns back to me her eyes are gentle. I hear her remonstrate with the nurse who comes to give me the drugs but the nurse obviously wins the argument because a strap is applied to my upper arm and the syringe plunged into me.

A private ambulance takes me back to Woodlands a couple of days later. Ingrams meets me at the door. He looks at me wordlessly, but I know what he is telling me. When we get to the top of the stairs we will turn left. It's always been the Woodlands way: suicides and those who are dangerous to others are always roomed to the left, behind the green baize door, because it is easier to keep an eye on them in that part of the house that has been fitted out for the truly mad. Patients are not alone in their rooms, which are tiled and easy to hose down and have been fitted with all kinds of equipment not deemed necessary in my old room with its soft rugs and writing desk.

We walk up the stairs, past the family portraits. When the green door is opened to receive me, I see its reverse is reinforced with steel panels and four rows of locks. Ingrams has the keys but once the door is open he does not follow me through because he belongs to the other side. 'Take care of yourself, Maud,' he says softly. 'Maybe I'll see you again soon.' I know he's only saying it to be kind. I won't return to the other side of the green baize door. Attacking that youth with the spade, attempting to kill myself: I have become the person Robert tried to make me out to be last year. He let everyone think I was psychotic. He has done it again now. It must be him, still plotting against me.

Someone else will now be living in my old room with its window seat: Woodlands always has a waiting list; there's no shortage of people who don't know who they are and what they've done. None of the rooms this side of the house face the drive, so I won't be able to sit and look out at those coming and going. I try to express these thoughts but the drugs they've given me have dulled my powers of speech and I can't say what I feel quickly enough.

I make a final effort as the nurse closes the door behind us. 'I know I had a baby,' I shout. 'His name is David. I made it to the end, Ingrams. I remembered everything.'

There's a snatched glimpse of Ingrams's face: half sorrowful, half joyful, before the door closes on him and the nurse takes me by the arm.

18

'We won't give up on you, Maud,' my mother tells me when she's allowed to visit me at Woodlands. We aren't alone in the visitors' room, of course. Mama looks furtively at the other patients, at their mismatched clothes and their faces that don't express anything. Do I look like that too? There's no mirror in the room I share with three others, but I steeled myself to glance at my reflection in the bathroom glass before the nurse brought me down here. I would have liked to have worn lipstick, but I don't know where mine is. I think my eyes still look like my eyes, but how can I tell how they appear to other people?

'What are they going to do with me?' I ask her. Mama's lowered eyes tell me that it isn't anything I would like. 'Can I talk to Dr Rosenstein?'

'You're not her patient any more, *draga*.' She hasn't used the old Croatian endearment for years, so I know things look bad for me. Mama explains that my removal to this wing means I am no longer under the care of Dr Rosenstein but that of Dr Manners, who treats all the patients behind the green baize door, along with certain of the more severe cases who are on the other side, such as Jim.

'Can I write to her?' I want to tell Dr Rosenstein that it was my own fault, not hers, that I did what I did.

'Give me the letter and I'll see if I can get it to her.'

'Are they going to charge me for what I did to that boy?'

Mama nods.

'I didn't mean—' But I had meant it. I had wanted to punish him.

A policeman comes to talk to me. I had thought they'd take me down to the police station to be charged, but apparently it's different when you're really mad. My solicitor sits beside me. I haven't met him before. I sign the statement.

'It will probably be all right,' my solicitor tells me when the policeman has gone. 'You weren't brought to trial last time so you don't have a criminal record to complicate things.'

'Will I have to go to court?'

'To answer the plea. If you plead guilty there won't be a trial. And your psychological state, the mitigating circumstances—'

'What were those?'

'The intruder climbing in here and damaging asylum property.'

'Burning the doves,' I say.

'We will say that you were acting as an agent of Woodlands as you had cared for the doves in the past. You were protecting Woodlands property.'

Calling the doves property makes them sound something other than creatures of feather and blood. I want to enter a plea that the boy taunted me by talking about terrible things that had happened, things I had witnessed in Yugoslavia, but my solicitor urges me not to.

'Why not?'

He has a kind old face and now he looks almost distraught. 'Thing is, Maud, my dear,' we have agreed he should call me this, as I hate being referred to as Mrs Havers, 'there is no proof at all that those things you refer to having done in Yugoslavia actually happened. And if they did happen, they are covered by the Official Secrets Act.'

I stare at him. 'Of course they happened. They parachuted me into Croatia. I operated there for nearly four months. I helped rescue prisoners of war and downed airmen.'

'There is no record,' he says. 'We have files relating to your job in Cairo, but nothing proving that you left Egypt for anywhere else. And the boy denies saying anything at all to you.'

No witnesses. Ingrams reached me after the boy had thrown those words at me. Did he actually say them at all? My drugs had been recently stopped. I was probably in a heightened emotional state, anticipating my release, seeing my baby. Could I have imagined what I thought he'd said to me? I'm back on a variety of medicines now, of course, and my memory is already growing treacly. Jim said something to me, too, didn't he? Something strange? I can't remember what it was.

The case comes to court. I attend on the first day to say I am indeed I, whoever I am, and to hear the charges against me. I plead guilty, as instructed.

The boy I attacked isn't there, but a middle-aged man and woman in plain, worn clothes sit at the back and eye me. They must be his parents. Is the boy still badly hurt? Perhaps they need his wages to support the household. But then I remember the doves and I hate that boy and despise him and I am not sorry for what I did.

I'm guilty, but as I'm already under lock and key there is little else the judge feels he has to do, my solicitor reports back the following afternoon.

'You won't be going back to your old wing,' the nurse tells me later that day, finding me standing at the green door as though I could look through it and see Ingrams standing there on the landing, waiting to take me up to my old room or out to the garden. 'Forget about it, Maud. This is your life for the foreseeable.'

Life on the wrong side. Forever.

But in a way it is easier being behind the baize door. Very few expectations are placed upon me. The drugs keep me bobbing along beneath the surface of complete awareness. I try hard to keep myself looking as I used to. They let me keep the face cream and lipstick Mama sends me. A hairdresser comes out from the town to set my hair once a week. Sometimes they let me walk in the gardens outside our wing. They aren't extensive like those on the other side where I once played badminton. No gardening for me, either, and certainly no visits to the doves, if any are still left. I wonder if the survivors flew away. Their home is destroyed. Can they find another safe place to roost? I crane my neck as I stand by the barred window of the room I share with three others and scan the cloudy sky. I don't see the birds, but I see the buzzard, floating on an air current.

I read the novels Mama sends, though they are screened and anything deemed too likely to excite me isn't allowed. An elderly major improves my chess on afternoons when the Kaiser's artillery isn't shelling him in a Somme trench.

There's someone at Woodlands I would like to see, someone who can explain what happened to me. The drugs have made my memory sluggish and I can't pull his name out of my mind at first. Tim. No, Jim. My friend Jim who was so worried about the doves. I found his concern touching but why had he really wanted to remind me of their vulnerability?

I force the coarsened threads of my memory to write this question on a scrap of greaseproof paper I find stuck to the bottom of a cake when I stack the enamel tea mugs and plates on the tea trolley. You have to try and please the staff. My survival instinct is muted, but I still remember that. When nobody's looking I carefully remove the greaseproof paper from the cake and take it to the room I share. One of the women has a stub of pencil and lets me borrow it so I can write out my thought. I can't remember how my normal cursive handwriting goes so I carefully form the capitals: WAS J BLACKMAILED BY R?

I fold the greaseproof paper and stick it under the inner sole of my shoe. I might remember to take it out when a visitor next comes to see me. It's been a long time since anyone's done this, though. Probably, my parents have been told I'm too volatile, and this may be true, even though most days it's only at the end of the afternoon that the monsters rouse, curling their tails around me, flexing their claws, showing their fangs. And now the beasts have my son to taunt me with. I know Robert will never let me see David. All I have is the name, David.

In one of her letters my mother tells me she paid a surprise visit on Cecilia Holdern's house early one afternoon when she imagined the good doctor's wife might be out shopping or visiting friends. As my mother suspected, David is being looked after in the house by the same nanny I met just before Robert and I married.

> The nanny came to the door. She seems kind. I think she felt sorry for me, but she wouldn't let me look at my own grandchild, told me Dr Holdern had given her strict instructions not to let anyone connected with Maud Havers, or Maud Knight as was, into the house.

I also have a divorce, it seems, applied for without my knowledge and without my consent being necessary, on grounds of my insanity. Does he think he can persuade me, too, that I never parachuted into the hills and worked with Branko and Ana? That I never headed north in pursuit of Naomi and found her mutilated body?

But I can't bring up the subject of my wartime work with my parents in a letter. They've probably been told I am imagining the whole thing. It would just make me sound deluded. Could I commit my suspicions about Jim's role in my undoing to a letter, or would that just prove to the people who matter that I am truly paranoid?

These questions ripple through my mind during the sweet spot of the day, when I'm not so heavily drugged I can't think straight, but not yet so assaulted by the monsters that I can't concentrate.

If Amber is still around she's so cowed and beaten these days that I can't find her. To be honest, it's almost easier to let her stay away. She doesn't belong here.

ENTR'ACTE

19

Mandalay Care Home, Sussex

Maud will nod her thanks for a cup of tea, occasionally managing to mutter the words. It's pretty well all she says. But she never wets herself and doesn't attack anyone or wander off.

She just won't join in. Apparently she hasn't communicated much, not since some time in the late forties.

Dissociative, says one of the nurses who fancies herself a bit of an expert on mental disturbances. *Some part of Maud is stuck somewhere. A place that's a long time ago and a long way away, I'd say. A bad place.*

Maud plays patience and solitaire. Sometimes you'll see her pick up a newspaper and fill in some of the crossword as she puffs on a Senior Service. Recently she has been seen reading the international news. Occasionally, when some of the sharper residents play bridge, she listens in to the bidding with a look on her face that suggests she knows how the game works.

Knowing Maud has her marbles is aggravating because it suggests she would be able to converse if she could make an effort.

She ignores the television for most of the time – can you blame her when it's only drivel such as game shows and soaps? But her gaze flickers towards the evening news, increasingly so in the last few months.

Tonight it's Sarajevo, capital of poor old Bosnia. Kate Adie talking about the siege. Maud's back straightens. One of the old boys starts gibbering on about something he wants to watch on the other channel.

'Be quiet.'

And everyone does, because Maud speaks so little. Her voice is clipped, almost patrician, that of Celia Johnson or the youthful Queen Elizabeth when she first took the throne. The lounge falls silent but for the reporter on the TV screen, showing burning buildings, women screaming in the streets, children clutching their skirts. The TV watershed means it's too early for them to show all the details. Thank God.

Maud isn't adhering to the watershed. She stands up and starts talking: fast and accusingly, swearing, blaspheming, crying. Her newspaper has fallen to the carpet. Her eyes are filled with fury and pity. She's switching in and out of a language nobody can understand, one full of Zs and Ks. Yugoslavian? Is that what they call it? Bosnian? Does Maud know this place of death and terror on the television? Has she been there herself? She's standing now, almost as upright as a young girl. An assistant tries to persuade her to sit down and Maud shakes her off. 'I remember now,' she shouts. 'Hearing this language has brought it back to me. He needs to go to prison. He's wicked. A traitor.'

'Who?'

'My husband, of course.'

Maud doesn't have a husband. She's been divorced for decades. Nobody has visited her for years. Around the lounge a ripple of half-fear, half-fascination laps the residents. They haven't been as animated since this year's Grand National, when a pool of those who can still tell a horse from a donkey put fifty pounds on Party Politics at 14-to-1 and watched him win.

It's fascinating to see the place erupt, but probably best if nurse can come and give Maud a sedative before she harms herself or things get out of hand.

PART TWO

20

The Bays sheltered housing complex, southwest London

I'm mostly Maud these days. Amber had a bit of a burst into my life three years ago, when she started shouting as I watched the news about the siege of Sarajevo. Came as a shock to me. They'd stopped drugging me as much, which probably meant that my response to the events was more acute. I'd forgotten how deeply one could feel things. It hurt, seeing that city pulverised, seeing Serbs, Croats and Bosnian Muslims turn against one another, seeing the dream of Branko and Ana implode.

Yet, awful as it sounds, that appalling Balkan war on the television screen each night was my cure. I feel ashamed of how it worked on the dead parts of my memory, binding fragments together that had been split from one another for decades. Watching the Balkans on fire de-balkanised my mind.

'Trauma cures trauma, perhaps?' I asked Dr Ahmed, the psychiatrist, when he next saw me and explained that I no longer needed to be living in an institution; that I could avail myself of care in the community.

'Perhaps it can.' He shuffled his papers around, as though looking for something in my notes he could use to answer.

'What do you think is wrong with me?' I corrected myself. 'Was wrong with me?'

'There's the thing, Maud – over the last half-century a lot of diagnoses have been suggested where you're concerned, ranging from schizophrenia to shell shock.'

Shell shock made me laugh. If the official line is that I worked in Cairo in Signals at a time when there was no risk of invasion, how was I supposed to have experienced anything leading to shell shock?

'There have also been mentions of a particular psychosis affecting women who've given birth. And some of the drugs you were prescribed may have muddied the waters. None of the people who've treated you have come to a definitive conclusion, but your first psychiatrist, Dr Rosenstein, was certainly very thorough.'

'Attacking that hoodlum with the spade was what did for me,' I told him. 'I was close to release when I did that. Dr Rosenstein thought I was sane.'

'So her notes say. Your family and friends probably thought that it would be better for you not to go to prison.' Dr Ahmed had soft brown eyes. He reminded me of Dr Rosenstein a little. 'They must have expected that you would recover and could be discharged.' The wound I inflicted on that youth was perhaps more superficial than we'd thought. How long a prison sentence would I actually have served if I'd pleaded guilty without any mitigation on the grounds of insanity?

I could have killed that boy as easily as I could apply a lipstick to my mouth. Did something stop me from striking the dove-killer in a more deadly way: my reason? My conscience?

My parents always vowed they'd have me released – that, rather than discharged, is the word they used – from mental institutions, but my father died suddenly of a stroke in the early fifties and Mama of cancer a year later. Then there was nobody left other than my elderly solicitor. I drifted from Woodlands when it closed down to Stoke Park, an asylum or psychiatric hospital, whatever you want to call it, on the

Kent coast, and then to The Mandalay in Sussex in 1972. And now here I am in The Bays in a southwest suburb of London, a complex of ten bungalows set around a patch of green, with a warden. My house is tiny, just one living room with a small kitchen area off one end, one bedroom and a bathroom.

My parents left me all their furniture and possessions and some remain in storage. I unpacked some of my own clothes and books, some of the things I'd owned before the war. The clothes were fit only for secondhand shops now. In an old handbag I found a small furry toy rabbit, in remarkably good condition. Never used. Presumably the other baby things went with David to Cecilia's. I discarded the bag but put the rabbit in the display cabinet I remember from our time at Trpca mines. He could guard the minerals. The rabbit appeared very soft against their angular, crystalline outlines. I knew how he felt.

No psychiatrists now. Nor any of the other therapists: psychologists, counsellors, analysts, I have seen over the years. I miss them. Most of them were interesting people and I enjoyed charting the fashions in psychiatric medicine over the decades. We've had some intriguing sessions as they tried to pin the diagnosis *du jour* on me. After my parents died I stopped asking about being released because I hadn't a clue where else I could go.

Sometimes I thought of writing to Robert, reminding him that I was still around, hopefully worrying him that I clearly remembered my wartime work and what had happened on the evening I went into labour with our son. That I suspected his role in my downfall at Woodlands, knew he had worked with someone within the institution to find out my weak spot and exploited it. I have often thought about those mysterious men from the ministry who came to see Jim and possibly threatened him in some way. Jim must have told them about my love for the doves and mentioned the yobs throwing things over the wall. Easy enough to bribe one of the boys into carrying out more serious damage, or to blackmail Jim into doing some of it. It would make sense of that muttered comment of Jim's that I didn't quite hear. Jim had betrayed me, but he was horrified at the reality.

But Robert would just ignore me or claim I was deluded. And finding his address proved difficult when I had to rely on mental hospital telephone directories that often had pages ripped out of them or had suffered other, indescribable, assaults. Perhaps my solicitor, or his successor, could have helped more. I probably didn't know the correct way to phrase my letter asking for help in finding my son.

From the mid-seventies they would probably have given me day release to go and see David, if he'd agreed. I had enough money in my trust fund to pay for the necessary chaperone. But before I could manage this, Robert, too, died. In 1976, in Greece, my solicitor told me. I felt the most extraordinary mixture of relief and grief when I found out.

I thought of approaching James and Cecilia Holdern and asking them to put me in touch with David. I even found an unsullied London telephone directory which told me that they were still resident in their house in Holland Park, the house where Robert and I dined on Brown Windsor soup and daub of rabbit just before we married. The house where my son was taken after his birth. I hoarded coins and made the call from the telephone box in The Mandalay. A woman answered. She sounded foreign. A maid? She told me that Dr and Mrs Holdern were on holiday. I couldn't think of a message to leave so I hung up. I was a coward. I was not Amber; I'd lost that part of myself. Amber would have fought harder for her son.

My solicitor told me he understood that Robert Havers told his son that I was dead. We would think of a way of contacting David and telling him that this is not true. It would be done with delicacy, because knowing his father lied to him in such a way would come as a shock.

Then my solicitor died. He was well past retirement age. Another solicitor was assigned to me. *How would you like me to proceed, Mrs Havers?* he wrote.

Mrs Havers. Just seeing that surname made me shudder. I should change it by deed poll. Knowing I am still alive might be equally repugnant to my son. He'd managed without me for decades, after all; probably has a job, a family of his own. Why would he want to be saddled with an institutionalised elderly mother he has never known? I would be a shame or an embarrassment to him.

I have no instructions, I replied to the solicitor.

I think of David every single day, marking his birthday each year silently and telling myself that my longing for him is not one he can possibly reciprocate as he thinks I'm dead. In a way, that's what I am.

Amber hasn't made her presence felt again. I can manage, just about, if I'm Maud, eccentric, quiet Maud, with her limited but intense interests: the cryptic crosswords. I still like gardening and help maintain a local park, for instance. These days I'm even trusted with garden implements.

The money left to me by my parents enabled my move to The Bays. My own space. I can eat when I want. When I knew I was going to be released into the community I asked if I could take cookery lessons. My trust fund authorised a taxi to take me to evening classes for six months. I have extended my repertoire of dishes and can cook pretty well anything I like.

It's lunchtime now. I switch on the Radio Four news. A Serb paramilitary group has killed dozens of civilians in a town in northeast Bosnia.

If Branko is still alive he must be appalled. Branko's – and, at times, his mother's – ideology sometimes made me roll my eyes, but his heartfelt desire for a Yugoslav state that didn't allow for violence on grounds of religion or ethnicity was something I admired.

Thursday is my day for helping in the community, as it is called. A minibus picks up half a dozen of us from the borough and drives us to a local park. As always, I find the noise of the streets a shock after a week in my little enclave. At least the park is peaceful.

I pick up rubbish, prune rosebushes and scrub bird muck off benches. It isn't mentally demanding, but the exercise is welcome.

We volunteer gardeners are a strange bunch. Definitely green-baize-door people. But we have had our little triumphs. We have protected the ducklings from prowling cats. There was once a young girl weeping on the bench. We offered her a can of Coca-Cola and coaxed her into a smile.

Maureen, who manages our small team, asks for a word with me. I light a cigarette and sit down on a bench with her. Although in every way different from Ingrams, not least in the fact that she is black and female, there's something in the gentle yet firm way she talks to us that reminds me of him. I never had more than a distant glimpse of Ingrams again after they shut me up behind the green baize door.

A light breeze blows the cherry trees. Some of the pink blossom drifts down. I remember sitting in the orchards of a farmhouse in northern Croatia where I was holed up with the POWs and airmen. It was almond blossom: paler, almost bridal.

'That language you can speak,' Maureen says. 'Romanian? Bosnian?'

'Serbo-Croat.'

'Is that what they speak in Bosnia?'

'A form of it. There are differences, but the language is essentially the same. Why?'

'A colleague of mine in another borough has these women from Bosnia. They've been given visas because of . . . well, the things we saw on the television.'

Ethnic cleansing. Rape.

'My colleague wants to help them, but finding interpreters is hard and money's an issue.'

'You want me to talk to the women?'

Maureen nods. 'They're learning English quickly but there are some things that you can only describe in your own language.'

'I don't talk much,' I say. 'Even in English.'

She laughs. 'You're known for your silences. But I hear you talking when you're working here, Maud.'

'It's easier outdoors.'

'Perhaps talking in a different language would help you?'

I look at her, wondering if she knows just how profound what she has said is. If I spoke in the language of my childhood, would it connect me with a deeper part of myself, a part less troubled by all that has happened to me?

'Where would I have to go?'

'Paddington.'

'How would I get there?' I half hope it might be too difficult.

'My colleague said she'd book a taxi for you. If there's budget.'

I feel my cheeks go red. I really don't need public money spent on me, but don't want to flaunt my prosperity. 'I could go on the train up to Waterloo and jump on the Tube.' The idea of me just jumping onto a Tube as though there hasn't been an almost fifty-year gap since I last used public transport makes me laugh at myself.

'Perhaps someone could go with you the first time.'

I trekked across wartime Yugoslavia with a map and compass. But now the London Underground is hostile territory.

'You'd need briefing, too,' Maureen says. 'About what the women have experienced. It's horrific stuff, Maud. Multiple rape. Loved ones murdered. Burnt-out homes. Concentration camps. You wouldn't believe it.'

Oh, but I would. I doubt that Balkan warlords have changed much in fifty years. My knuckles clench as I look around this little park, where mothers push buggies knowing they won't be gang-raped and boys kick footballs in back gardens knowing they won't be taken into the woods and shot.

'Sometimes I feel . . .' Maureen starts and then stops.

'Feel what?'

She looks the nearest Maureen could ever look to embarrassed. I keep looking at her until she continues. 'I'm a social worker, not a psychologist or counsellor. I'm probably talking out of turn.'

I mumble something.

'I didn't mean to upset you, Maud.'

'You didn't.' Although the conversation is certainly shifting something inside me, something that's felt immovable and solid for decades.

I want to tell her about David, about my son. I want to ask for her help, but the longing for him has been unspoken for so long that I don't know how to express it.

I stand up. 'I'd better get putting those bark chippings round the saplings by the pond.'

I feel her eyes on me as I go to the shed. The chippings have been delivered in large canvas bags. When my efforts to untie the strings at the top fail, I pull my penknife out of my gardening belt and cut the thick canvas, producing a slit of about an inch long. I strike more forcibly, ripping into the bag. *Large incision on the victim's right side.* Mama once told me the details of my husband's wounds. I clasp my knife hard and stab across the bag. I catch the canvas, but produce only a tear.

I transfer the knife to my left hand and stab again at the canvas bag. The cut is cleaner but small. Why on earth would I have made such a feeble attempt at knifing my husband when my wartime training would have taught me to attack in the most efficient manner? I would have been vulnerable to a counter-swipe from him as my right arm swung across his body.

Why didn't anyone ever challenge Robert's account of how it was he came to be stabbed? Dr Rosenstein helped me recall the events of that evening and see clearly that I hadn't stabbed him. Others must have known that, too. Cutting open the bag of chippings has just reminded me of his lies. Lies uttered to save his skin, even if they meant depriving me of my freedom. And my child.

I manage the train up to Waterloo by myself, after Maureen, on her day off, takes me to our nearest station and shows me how to buy a ticket and which platform to stand on and how to be sure that I'm on the right train. 'You'll know that it's Waterloo because it's the very end of the line,' she told me. I am hoping this visit to the Bosnian women does not prove to be my Waterloo, too.

The train is ninety-six seconds late when it reaches its end point. Nobody seems surprised. Although Maureen has told me how to get a bus or Tube from Waterloo on to the meeting place, on my arrival I feel too flustered to attempt this and stand in the taxi rank instead. I can remember how to do taxis, how to add on the ten per cent if the driver is obliging or amusing.

We drive over Waterloo Bridge and I think of my husband telling me, years ago, how women finished off its construction because all the men had gone off to war. Down the Embankment we travel, passing buildings I remember, and many I don't think I have ever seen before. London was still wearing a cloak of decrepitude when I was last out and about. Big Ben looks cleaner than I recall. All the smog has gone now. On down to Birdcage Walk and right past Buckingham Palace, which also looks more sparkling than I remember it just after the war. I wasn't in London for Victory in Europe Day but watched the King, Queen and princesses on the balcony with Winston Churchill on a news film.

Constitution Hill now and the Wellington Arch. Then we're shooting north along Park Lane, the traffic suddenly moving more speedily and carrying me almost faster than I can bear towards Marble Arch and the junction with Oxford Street where Tyburn gallows once stood. Where they once hanged the traitors: drawing and quartering them too, if they really wanted to make a point. The driver pushes a button and the window beside me opens. 'Thought you looked a bit hot,' he says. I mutter a thanks.

I can't remember the name of the mews in which our marital home stood. As it isn't a through road we won't pass the house. I'm not sure I would even recall its number now. Perspiration beads my brow. 'The city looks pretty this time of year,' the driver remarks. I mumble agreement. 'Much cleaner nowadays. I remember what it was like when I was a boy. All those coal fires.'

'It was so grubby just after the war,' I tell him, feeling proud that I am carrying on a conversation with a stranger.

'You don't look old enough to remember that.'

It is a strange effect of my years inside institutions that I look, in some ways, younger than my seventy-one years. I've heard people remark the same thing of nuns and prisoners in certain Russian penal institutions. Lack of rich food? Limited alcohol? My teeth are not wonderful but are better since I've started going twice a year to the dentist, and they're still my own, which is remarkable for anyone who has been through British psychiatric institutions for most of their adult life.

'Were you here in the Blitz?'

I tell the driver how I went dancing in nightclubs on heavy nights and this tickles his sense of humour.

'Did you stay in London all through the war?'

'I was a special agent.' I can see his eyes studying me in the rear-view mirror. He nods, mouth turning up slightly. He thinks I'm nuts, a dotty old biddy who's making it all up. Can I be sure that what I have told him is actually true? Robert's long dead. There's nobody left who can corroborate the facts.

The taxi pulls into the kerb outside the hall where the meeting is to take place and the driver opens the door for me. I collect myself and am glad I mentally rehearsed the paying of the fare, rounded up with a tip. 'I hope your day goes well.' The gentleness in the driver's voice touches me.

I stand at the door, unseen, for a moment before going in, inhaling the institutional smell of wooden floors and tables and chairs that spend too long stacked up in an unaired room. The smell reminds me of arts-and-crafts therapy in a hut in the grounds of Stoke Park where they taught us green-baize-door people basket-making and pottery.

A handful of small children riffle through boxes of toy cars and building bricks. The women are quiet, as quiet as newcomers usually were when they first showed up at Woodlands. But I don't think sedatives are causing the quietness: these women have the stillness that results from deep trauma. They're like trapped animals that have been released but can't quite reconcile themselves to their freedom, waiting for the hunter to return and deliver the fatal blow.

I look at their faces and see the features of some of the people I grew up among, with their sculpted cheekbones and long smooth chestnut hair. I recall the daughters and wives of the workers at the Trpca mine. And, of course, Ana. Ana was older than these girls when I knew her, already the mother of two young men, but she was still a beautiful woman and her brown hair had hardly any grey among it.

The group eyes me warily as I approach, looking for Pam, the outreach team leader who has set up this meeting. She's a short woman with a London accent. 'Thanks for coming.' She touches my lower arm gently, as though to acknowledge that it was a hell of a thing for me to get myself from the suburbs to the other side of the city.

Pam introduces me to the women, and to as many of their children as she can identify, laughing as they scamper away. 'We're pleased with how the little ones are coping. And the older kids at school. But these ladies have complicated needs and I need someone who can speak to them in their own language.'

'How should I . . . ?' I don't know how to begin.

'I thought I'd set you up in a corner there with a cup of tea and they can come up to you one or two at a time. But first perhaps introduce yourself to them in their language?'

I pull old words and phrases out of my memory. 'My name is Amber.' I pause, seeing the confusion on Pam's face. 'That's what I was called when I lived in . . . Yugoslavia.' Too complicated to give more details. 'But, I'm known as Maud, too. I don't know Bosnia myself but my mother was born in Sarajevo.' My voice isn't loud enough; I'm not used to talking to so many people. I raise it. 'So you see, I have a little connection with you. Even if the way I talk doesn't sound exactly like the way you speak.'

One or two of the women seem to lose some of their stiffness. They are all looking at me now. I want to run out of the hall. *You will feel intimidated, scared, too, sometimes. But you have it within you to do what is asked.*

'I want to help you with any language issues you have. Again, you must forgive me if I sound stilted and old-fashioned. I hope we can understand one another.' I put a hand to my throat, which feels the strain of so much talking.

Nobody says anything.

'Tell our visitor your names.' Pam points at the first lady.

One by one they provide the information, but as though they were handing it to a concentration camp guard. I smile and nod as the introductions are made.

'If you tell me more about yourselves and any particular problems with . . .' I look at Pam.

'Housing. Accessing medical services. Schooling.'

I translate. 'I'll be over there,' I say.

I sit down at the table Pam has set up. 'I am not doing this very well,' I tell her as she brings me my tea. 'They're not exactly rushing over.'

'They're wary. Some of them have had dreadful experiences.' A small boy pushes a toy car towards us. Pam picks it up with a smile. 'Try playing with the children. If they see the kids like you, it will help.'

I'm a woman in her early seventies who has barely had contact with small children. I never built brick towers with my son, never lined up toy cars and lorries for him to race. I pick up the car and push it back at the little boy. My push is a bit over-enthusiastic and the toy crashes into the wall. His eyes widen. I think he's going to cry but he roars with laughter. Did Cecilia play with David like this? Or did she leave such frivolity to the nanny? Perhaps Robert was kind to David. He was cruel to me but his son was his own flesh and blood. I push a fire engine towards the little boy, who laughs again. A small girl turns to look. Before I know it I am surrounded with toddlers carrying toy vehicles for me to crash into the wall. The women remain where they are. I have travelled all this way to play cars. But I'm actually enjoying myself now. Let the women sit there in silence.

I sit down on the ground because it's easier on my gardening-stiffened back and am surrounded with babbling small children holding toys. A girl of about three sits beside me, looking up at me solemnly. When I smile at her, she puts her hands over her eyes. Do I frighten children with strangeness of the insane upon me, even though I was never really insane? Living with people who had lost their minds must have passed on to me something of their otherness, even though I have been so careful with my appearance today, standing in front of the mirror and pulling out eyebrow hairs according to the instructions in a women's magazine I bought. I even applied lipstick, a heather-rose that the warden at home approved for me. I filed my nails. I dressed in the new clothes I ordered from a catalogue. But still I scare infants.

Her shoulders move up and down. She's laughing, not crying. She glances at me from between her fingers and grins. I smile back. 'Peepo.' Even useless old Maud can play this game.

A pair of arms swoop the girl up. I look up and see her mother, a woman with a burnt face, standing with her child in her arms. 'I would like to talk to you,' she says in her own language.

I stand up, feeling the joints in my knees creak. The woman places her daughter on the floor and tells her to look at the books.

When we sit down she explains that she would like to write a letter to the teacher to explain that her older daughter is scared of getting undressed for PE in front of the boys. Her eyes glance away from mine and her voice tightens. Pam has already provided a writing pad and pen for me. 'Shall I ask if your daughter can get changed in the lavatories?'

The woman nods. When I've finished she signs her name at the bottom and addresses the envelope very carefully. 'Thank you.' There is the ghost of a smile. Apparently emboldened by their friend's success, two other women approach me, sisters from a village in Bosnia that was abandoned to the Serbs. They introduce themselves as Esma and her younger sister, Naida. They would like me to translate a letter they have received from a consultant gynaecologist treating Esma. I do not know the words for all the medical terms and have to draw diagrams on the pad, feeling my cheeks burn. I explain that the woman must make another appointment in six months and offer to make the call. There is a telephone box across the road. When I've spoken to the consultant's secretary, Pam suggests that we sit inside in a circle and have a chat.

The women look at their hands. Eventually one of them, silent until now, asks me about my mother, where she lived in Sarajevo, nodding silently when I say that I can't remember and my mother is now dead. 'I never visited the city,' I say. 'I wish I had. Perhaps one day it will be possible again.'

We sit in silence for a moment.

'Did you ever go back to Yugoslavia as an adult?' one of the sisters asks.

'In 1944 I was in the north, near the Croatian–Slovenian border.'

Puzzled looks. They're too wary to ask me why.

'I was working with the Allied forces,' I say.

Pam looks at her watch. 'We can continue next week, if Maud can come back?'

'I'd like that.' The words come out before I'm aware I've spoken them, but it's true.

My mind feels as though it's been flushed out; I feel dazzled by the contact with the women. Vocabulary I haven't used for half a century floods my mind, even as I leave the hall. And just speaking the old language seems to have woken up part of my brain that's been long dormant. Amber stirs within me. She's been lost for so long I almost feel shy in front of her. Amber is trying to tell me something and I'm not sure I want to hear it.

I can't face another taxi drive so decide to walk back to Waterloo across Hyde Park. I remember those evenings in my early married life when I would walk to meet my husband coming from St James's. I move briskly among the joggers and dog walkers. I have kept my fitness. I remember how hot it was that summer, how my lower legs ached when I did this walk. I was pregnant, expecting that child I never met because he was pulled out of me and taken away while I was still in that twilight sleep they'd induced in me.

My son David, the boy I never saw when he was the enchanting age of those toddlers back in the hall. I have allowed cowardice and torpor to overcome my longing for him. Kinder to keep myself away from David, who has probably grown up viewing Cecilia as his mother. And he has never attempted to find me, either.

But all those years ago as I walked across this park I had felt him move inside me for the first time. A pang of excitement had shot through me. I think now of Ana, whose love for her younger son, the boy fighting on the wrong side, was so strong that she crossed the lines to be with him. My love for my child had been a lukewarm force in comparison.

A young woman walking a West Highland terrier peers at me with concern on her face. I realise my cheeks feel cool. I have been weeping as I walk. I haven't wept for decades – the drugs they gave me seemed to suppress the impulse. Something barbed and relentless is ripping my heart out like a fish hook. I turn off the track and head towards a clump of trees where I can wipe my eyes.

For the first time in years I crave a cigarette and a drink. I've had a sherry or an occasional glass of wine over the years, but now I want a whisky. It's lunchtime, so something must be open.

I have drifted away from the route I meant to take. I'm heading almost due south and will come out of Hyde Park at Knightsbridge. I walk down Sloane Street, looking for a pub. There used to be a place I came to with Peter around the time of the Blitz, in towards Belgravia. I can't remember where to turn off to the left and walk too far, coming to Sloane Square, finding myself staring up at Peter Jones, the store where I came with Mama to look at furnishing fabrics. Its glass curtain wall seems the same as it had in 1946. A sandwich and a cup of tea in its café will do as well as a Johnnie Walker and cigarette.

Inside the store the displays dazzle me. A woman sprays my wrist with scent and I jump as though she's opened fire on me. She apologises, looking aghast. I wander on through racks of scarves and bags, looking for cover. There is simply so much stuff. Did anyone own all these things when I was young?

I take escalators and lifts up and down, dazed, until I find somewhere that can serve me an egg and cress sandwich and cup of tea. This is surely what a woman my age should be doing. A grandmother, perhaps. That thought makes me clutch my cup tightly. Could David now have a family of his own? How would I find out? Birth certificates can be obtained, I know that much. But if I don't know when any possible grandchildren were born, or who their mother was, how can I take things a step further?

I need to find my son.

21

Esma and Naida are becoming more confident with me. 'Yes, yes,' they say, in English, when I gently urge them to extend their vocabulary. 'But now, with you, we want to talk in our own language.'

And talk they do, about their home in Bosnia. We sit out in the small paved area behind the hall and smoke. They tell me about the neighbours who were Serbian Orthodox but worked alongside them at harvest time, whose christenings and weddings they attended. 'All gone.' Esma says it softly. 'We were one village, but not now.'

'And our cousins elsewhere in Bosnia had Croatian friends too,' her sister adds. She looks at me directly. 'You fought with the Partisans. Your comrades were from all over Yugoslavia?'

'Croats, Serbs, some mixtures.' I remember Ana with a pang. 'I even had a friend with one Chetnik and one Partisan son.'

The women's eyes narrow at the mention of the Chetniks. 'Some of the Serb militias shout about being descendants of Chetniks,' Naida tells me. 'Boasting that they do what they do to honour their Chetnik fathers and grandfathers, for the glory of Serbia.'

'Then they're fools.'

'Dangerous fools,' Esma says very quietly. I think of the gynaecological operation she has been booked in for. I haven't asked questions but they have told me that they and their children were locked in a house that a Bosnian Serb unit set on fire. The sisters tried to shield the children, receiving serious burns to various parts of their own bodies. Eventually they managed to break out of a downstairs window. I do not know whether Esma and Naida were raped before or after the fire, but have gathered that a group of men was involved. The sisters tell me that the doctors treating them here in London are kind.

Thinking about doctors makes me think of Ana again.

'My friend's Chetnik son risked his life for us,' I say. 'And they were both shot at the end of the war, even though she had saved many Partisan lives during the fighting.'

The two of them say nothing, they don't need to.

'We really should carry on with your English.' I force myself to put away the past and concentrate on the modern vocabulary that might help two young women with children find work in London. I have to do some research myself, as fax machines and word processors are not part of my everyday vocabulary, though I have hopes of acquainting myself with the latter.

'You have children, Maud?' Esma asks me as we are packing up the chairs and tables when the session is over.

'I . . . There's a son.' I realise it's a strange way of putting it. 'I, err, haven't seen him for a while.'

They nod without commenting but their faces are studies in incomprehension. There is no civil war in England, no imprisonment of males. Why would a mother not be in regular contact with her son, her only child?

'I would like to see him again,' I go on. 'In fact, I'm trying to find him.'

Am I? Have I actually decided this? What exactly have I done to further this intention? For the last half-century I have let myself remain the passive victim of my former husband. *While at times the agent must drift, unremarked on the waves around him or her, lethargy must be avoided. Watchfulness, alertness, rather than passivity, are essential . . .*

When I'm back in my bungalow I look again at the copy of David's birth certificate, which is all the information I have. I barely know where to begin my search. My solicitor now is a young woman who inherited me. Most of my knowledge of the law as applied to families, missing children, wills and trusts is drawn from Dickens and may not be much help.

The firm's telephone number is on top of the headed paper they use each time they write to me. I haven't used the telephone much. Maureen rings me once a week or so, as a friend, rather than as a professional. I'd probably feel more comfortable setting up a wireless set and sending a signal. The thought of doing this in the bungalow makes me smile briefly. But using Morse code, making the signal so tight and concise, would be very much easier than telephoning. I'll write to my lawyer – Claire Erskine, her name is – instead.

> I know we haven't met personally, but I have handled your affairs for a few years now and am delighted to help you with this matter. We usually refer our clients to a firm of private investigators [her answer comes]. We have found them reliable and trustworthy. Would you like me to pass on details of what we know of your son to them?

The reply is far less lawyerly than I anticipated. I could make a trip up to Miss Erskine's firm. If I can manage a journey to Paddington, Lincoln's Inn Fields should be within my capabilities.

Esma and Naida nod approvingly when I tell them. 'And when you meet your son we will help you buy new clothes and do your hair,' they tell me.

I put a hand to my bob.

'You want to look your best for your son, no?'

I remember reading how the women of Sarajevo would risk snipers to visit a hairdresser, would somehow procure cosmetics even in the worst days of the siege. Looking your best is a way of showing the world that you cannot be defeated.

I nod. 'We'll go to Bond Street.' My mother always rated Bond Street for new outfits.

Esma looks startled. 'Bond Street cost a lot.'

'That's all right.' We spend an afternoon the following week in what seems like every clothes retailer between Oxford Circus and Selfridge's. I'm glad we don't go any farther west of that, towards Tyburn.

We buy what my mother would call a 'Best': a summer suit in silk and linen for meeting David and a Nearly-the-Best for the solicitor in a heavier fabric, plus long-sleeved shirts in silk, linen and cotton variously, and a pair of jeans, which I imagined would be too young for me but am told firmly are fine. They insist on adding a silk scarf to my purchase that would probably cost the same as a week's family shop for them all.

I want to buy the two women something for themselves to thank them. After a cup of tea and further arguments they allow me to buy clothes for their children and a few saucepans for their kitchen in John Lewis. Then Naida steers me into a beauty salon not far from the office where I was once interviewed for my wartime job. It's run by a Bosnian woman. She says something quick-fire in a low voice that I can't pick up. I spend an hour being plucked and manicured. When the bill is run up at the till it seems less than I expected.

'We took off a discount. For them.' She nods towards my two minders, who smile slightly. 'They say you have helped them.'

'I wrote a few letters and made a few calls, that's all.'

'And you have rewritten their CVs so they can apply for jobs. And now they speak better English.'

'They're not bad.'

She hands back my credit card. 'You are a nice lady, very honest and polite. But you should not go offering to pay more than you need.'

Esma hails a taxi for me. 'Don't go on the train with all those bags; they will surely rob you.' It's as though I'm planning to take a night train through mountains frequented by brigands.

The drive back takes a long time because of the traffic, but it's the first time I've seen some of these parts of south London in years and I like staring at the new tower blocks and road junctions, trying to recall what was here before the war.

Claire Erskine, my solicitor, is younger than I anticipated. In my day there weren't many female lawyers. Not that I knew many solicitors at all.

She shows me into a meeting room, walls decorated with watercolours of places that could be anywhere. The offices are a bit of a disappointment compared with their old stone exteriors. I suppose I was hoping for something more Dickensian. Perhaps there was war damage.

She opens a faded grey cardboard file. 'Your legal story with us, if you don't mind me calling it that, starts at the time of your wedding to Robert Havers, when your father redrafted his will. When you were sectioned, or as they called it then . . .' She swallows, obviously not liking the old typed words on the paper in front of her.

'Certified mad,' I interject.

'. . . your father took advice about the legal situation. He'd given you some money on your marriage, you may remember, obviously intending you to benefit from their estate when they'd both died. My predecessors advised another redraft of the will and the setting up of a trust, with your parents as trustees, plus a lawyer at this firm.'

'What happened when both my parents died?'

'The trust was set up so it could continue, with this firm appointing successor trustees. You'll recall us writing to you from time to time, enclosing a valuation of the assets?'

I blush. I didn't respond to these letters once I was considered capable of receiving my own post and they arrived at the various institutions

I inhabited. I start to explain the lethargy besetting me, but Claire smiles. 'It wasn't a problem for us. But I am so glad you want to show more of an interest in what's yours.' A pause. 'Everything that's yours.' Another pause. 'You've bought your bungalow, of course, giving you security. But there's enough money left for you to do whatever you'd like.' She looks at my suit.

'I was encouraged to invest in my appearance.'

She smiles. Claire herself is dressed impeccably. She takes out some pages from the file. 'I'll make copies of these latest quotations. And you might like to think about whether you need your trust to continue. You're an adult of fit mind. Just as your parents anticipated you would be again.'

I feel a warm glow. They knew me, that I was not mad.

'Before we move on to the main reason for your visit, I must just hand over this.' She pulls an envelope out of a file. It's brown, official-looking. From this she extracts a smaller envelope. Pale blue. The address on it is written in a woman's hand, I think. It reminds me of my mother's.

'It arrived here just this week.' She hands it to me.

The intended recipient is simply 'Miss Amber'. It is addressed to the War Office, Whitehall, London, England. It has been stamped with a foreign office mark and various other franks that I can't read.

I turn the envelope over and, sure enough, there's a return name and address on it.

It can't be. I blink and look again. Ana. 'She never came back. I thought she'd died.'

'Not only is she alive, but very tenacious to have thought of a way of getting in touch with you.' Claire looks at her watch. 'I have a three-o'clock, unfortunately.' Her voice is down to earth. 'You'll be wanting your son's address?'

'He has made contact with you?'

Claire shakes her head. 'But your private investigator reported back to me last week.'

'They found him?'

'Yes.' A simple, short monosyllable.

'Did the investigator talk to him?'

'No. That's not within their brief. But I have a full name and an address in Durham. You can write to him.'

'Will he——?' There's something in my throat.

'I can't answer that question for you,' Claire says gently. 'But as one person, one mother, actually, to another,' she glances at a small photograph on her bookcase of a toddler I missed before, 'what do you have to lose? If David doesn't want to see you, you're in the same position as you are now. And if he does . . .'

If David doesn't want to see me I'm actually in a worse position. At the moment I inhabit a misty borderland where hope mingles with longing, unilluminated by that harsh little word, no. My son has not shown any interest in seeing me for all these years; why should that situation change?

Claire has a taxi called for me. Perhaps I look shaken.

But I compose myself enough to insist on stopping at Waterloo. I sit on the train with my letter in my hand. I've never seen Ana's writing before. Between Vauxhall and Clapham Junction I gaze out at the concrete buildings and remaining redbrick terraces, factories and shops, but I'm seeing a landscape of mountains and rocks, waterfalls, harsh in the early spring light, but softening by the day.

I start to read.

22

April 1990

My dear friend Amber,
I do not even know your real name, or where you live. When I left you, you were sitting among the blossom. I had to rush north to treat my boy, Miko.

I thought I would see you again before you left for England. I wonder if you have thought of me since then?

Miko's Chetniks never knew I'd been a Partisan, I kept that to myself, telling them only I was a doctor. I treated Miko. But then they insisted I stay with them. The Ustaše were sniffing around and I didn't want to do anything that would draw attention to me. Despite all my efforts to slip away once Miko was better, I found myself on the march north to Bleiburg in southern Austria at the end of the war, armed Allied soldiers ahead of me, and vengeful supporters of Tito behind me. In Austria I pleaded with the British to allow us to surrender to them.

I explained who I was, whom I'd fought with. Miko told them he had helped Allied combatants escape. He even showed them a note that an American airman wrote, confirming that Miko had assisted him. The officers left the room and we heard them talking. The younger one wanted to hold us in Bleiburg while they checked our details, but his companion overruled him.

So back we went, trudging east over the Slovenian border along the road to Maribor, or Marburg, as the Germans called it, guns to our backs, spat at by the very people I had fought for. To the south of Maribor there were tank traps. Convenient. They tied our hands behind us and made us kneel at the edge of these huge ditches. Miko pleaded for me one last time. He gave them names of battles where I had treated wounded comrades. We did not mention Branko because we had already agreed that it would be dangerous for him. Miko and Branko had chosen different paths, but they still loved one another.

I overheard the guards talking about the war and discovered that one of them had a cousin who'd been wounded two years earlier, when our Partisan unit had retreated for a hundred miles, bearing our casualties on stretchers while under fire. I called out to him and persuaded him to listen to my story. This guard cut the wire from my hands and told me to run for my life. I pleaded for Miko to be spared in my place. For a second or so I thought I had succeeded. But his officer shook his head and told me to say goodbye to my boy. Our eyes met and I turned my head before they could fire the bullet. I heard the thump as my son's body toppled into the ditch.

I do not know where I spent that night or the next. I found myself heading south-southeast, towards my old log cabin. I spent six months there, at first living off the tins stored behind the fireplace, and when these ran out I bought food from that old woman who'd sold us provisions in the March of 1944. I'd hidden money in the cabin just before the Germans invaded and checked it was still there when you and I spent the night there. When it ran out I treated the locals in return for food. But the local commissariat found out about me and I knew I would not be safe there.

I headed east to Zagreb, where I had lived with my family before the war. Our apartment had been taken over, but our former maid took me in. I shared her room for four months before Branko found me. He had believed me executed, but rumours of a female doctor who'd survived Maribor had reached him. Even his passion for Tito and the party was not great enough to dampen my elder son's wish to look after me.

Branko did as well in the peace as he had in the war. Tito thought highly of him, and rightly too, he is a diligent and clever man. By the early 1950s Branko managed to rehabilitate me and I worked again as a doctor. He came to London on government business more than once, each time asking British ministers about you. You seemed to have vanished.

I retired to our holiday home on the Dalmatian coast in the late sixties. Tito died in 1980 and after that things were not the same for Branko. He saw the resurrection of a militant Serbian faction that would resist any signs of the federation breaking up. He smelled war, in short. He resigned his government job and started a small business near me.

And as you'll know, war came again to Yugoslavia, Amber. I will not waste time and energy writing about these terrible years. They are rebuilding Dubrovnik now and I certainly hope I never have to see another bombed city.

On a happier note, I am a grandmother four times over. Branko's eldest boy bears his uncle Miko's name.

I hope my letter will reach you and that you will be able to write back to me at this address. Are you married? Do you have children and grandchildren?

Do not leave it too long, my friend. I am old.

Ana

23

I retreat into myself after I read Ana's letter. For days I don't leave the bungalow. I tell Naida and Esma I'm ill.

A week after I ring them, they knock on my door, carrying a bottle of slivovitz and some flowers. Naida is through the door before I can open my mouth, followed by Esma and the smallest of her children in a small pushchair. Esma plonks the toddler outside in my little garden, telling him fiercely that if he touches anything apart from the grass he will suffer terrible consequences.

'Sit down.' Naida points at the kitchen table. She and Esma tidy my kitchen and make a pot of strong coffee before I can protest.

'You're not ill, Maud. Only in here.' Esma points at her heart. 'What is it?'

I can't think of how to explain, so I pass them Ana's letter. They read in silence. When they finish, they nod. 'Bad times for Yugoslavia,' Naida says. 'And for your friend's son. But at least she has lived a long life with her other son and she has had her work.'

'That's true,' I say. 'But all those wasted years when I could have seen her.' If I hadn't been locked up, I could have flown to the Dalmatian coast to spend time with Ana in her holiday house. Perhaps I could even have visited our own family house, long abandoned, on Šipan Island near Dubrovnik.

Ana's letter has reassured me that I haven't imagined my time in Yugoslavia during the war, something that has sometimes worried me. It was real. The months we spent working to return Allied servicemen really happened. Stimmer, Miko, the murder of Naomi, all these things were facts. The burning plane was real, too, not just an image a damaged mind had thrown up at me.

'You must visit Ana,' Esma tells me. 'Women in the Balkans can live a long time if men don't kill them in wars.' She adopts a brisker note. 'I think she makes you sad when she asks about your family. How you get on with letter to your son, your David?'

'How have I been getting on?' I repeat. 'I've been drafting it.'

She looks at me.

'I've made a good start.' One paragraph.

Naida gets up. She brings my writing pad and envelopes from my desk and places them in front of me on the kitchen table. 'We take him out for a walk,' she nods towards the toddler crouching down outside to examine my terracotta pots. 'When we come back, we post letter.'

'We post *the* letter,' I correct her. She gives me the smile that is always so sudden and sweet it makes my heart ache.

'You have one hour.' Esma's tone reminds me of the one used by Ana long ago, when she thought I needed shaking up.

It's obviously the approach I need. I write.

I have never stopped thinking about you, David. For years – decades – I wanted to write to you, but I thought having a mother in a mental institute would be an impossible burden for you, that it would be better for me to keep in the background. I thought that if you wished to see me, to get to know me, you would come to me. I realise now that I was wrong, a coward, why should you seek out the parent who hadn't bothered to make any contact with you? My only excuse is that the years of living in institutions has perhaps robbed me of the confidence to behave as a normal mother would. Please forgive me.

There is so much to tell you, but it's not for a letter. If you could find it in you to meet me, I would love to see you.

Your loving mother
Maud

As I write the address in Durham on the envelope, I wonder what David does up there. I don't know the north of England well. In 1943 a train carried me to the Highlands for training, but it travelled up the other side of the Pennines to cross the Scottish border at Carlisle.

When Esma and Naida knock on my door, I show them the stamped and addressed letter. 'We post for you,' Esma says, taking it, a glint in her eye.

Just in case I change my mind.

When they've gone I go outside to smoke. A snail is leaving a trail on the patio tiles, a series of curls that look like question marks, preceded by a long and almost perfectly straight line. I should pick it up and throw it over the fence, but I can't bring myself to do this, convinced the snail is writing out my fate for me.

I wait. Weeks pass and it's autumn again, days before my son's birthday, before the anniversary of my finding the telegram in Robert's desk drawer and the last encounter that ended with him lying bloodied on the floor. I write to Ana, not saying much but telling her how thrilled I am to hear from her. *I would love to visit you*, I write. *I will come soon.*

Summer isn't relinquishing its hold without a struggle. I still sit out in my sheltered little garden some lunchtimes. When I go to visit

Esma and Naida in the flat in Vauxhall that their two families share, Esma serves me coffee on the balcony. Sometimes only one of them is there, looking after the children while the other works. 'Naida's working now, but she goes to Liverpool this weekend,' Esma tells me. 'Visiting a cousin of ours.'

I have struggled to grasp their family relationships. Esma tells me of the young woman from a village a few kilometres away from theirs who has apparently found her way to the Mersey.

'A long trip for Naida,' I say.

'Not too bad. Goran will drive her.'

Goran is another cousin of theirs, a young man who has lived in London for three years now.

'M1 a lot of the way. Fast road, if you leave very early. You have been on M1, Maud?'

'No.' But I remember watching a television documentary when it opened. The closing of railway stations and the opening of all these fast highways passed me by. When transferring me from one institution to another, the social worker driving me was supposed to take us on a motorway. I don't know the number, but it was somewhere to the south of London. I was excited, but the motorway was closed owing to a lorry having shed its load, a not-uncommon occurrence, the social worker told me.

I held a driving licence in my youth. Perhaps it can be renewed if I take some lessons. There's a tunnel under the Channel now: I could drive to Paris. The thought makes me smile. I answer Esma's unspoken question by telling her I would like to travel before I am any older.

'You're only seventy-one. The world is your mussel,' she tells me in English. I laugh for the first time in days. My world is a muscle I can strengthen.

'Naida seemed to go on her trip on a whim,' I say. 'She didn't mention this cousin before.' I explain what a whim is.

'Oh, my sister, that's how she is.' Esma makes a face that combines irritation, amusement and something else: a deep knowledge of her sibling, born of growing up and sticking together as adults.

It strikes me as I leave the flat that nobody has ever really known me very well for long. My parents did until I left for my war work. Those most vital, most important years of my life were lost to them, so they didn't really know me again when I returned. Naomi had an insight into me – not always a flattering one – born of a short but intense spell together in Cairo. And Ana, following a similarly brief period in Yugoslavia.

Robert knew me best of all, looked deep into me, found the person who'd respond to a call to arms such as the one he offered me. But then he had me thrown into an asylum, took my child away and divorced me.

Yet he knew me.

And now nobody exists who can see the whole of my life as a single line. Even if I find him, my son will know so little about me. But I need to try to see him. Until he appears, my world lacks its sun, my son.

The post has arrived when I return home. I pick it up, heart pounding. There is no letter from David.

I'm thinking of making a last cup of tea the following Sunday. In my kitchenette I pick up a cloth to dry a mug that doesn't need drying because it's sat on the draining board for a whole day. I stare at the linen fabric. I'm wearing my reading glasses and can see the tiny gaps in the weave, holes that are vast enough to swallow me up because I am nothing, nobody, someone whom my own child does not wish to acknowledge.

I give myself a pep talk: *very self-indulgent: staring at an inanimate object and coming over all metaphysical.* What would Ana say? It isn't so much what she'd say as how she'd look: those fierce eyes. I put the cloth back on the hook.

There's a knock on my door. Peering through the spyhole I see Naida. I open up. 'What's wrong? Is there news from Bosnia?' Fear rushes in to replace my lethargy. 'Is one of the children ill?'

'Nothing bad.' She takes my hand. 'May I come in, Maud?'

She sits me at the table.

'He's outside in the car.'

I stare at her.

'Your David.'

I stand up, not understanding.

'Goran drive me to Durham. Not Liverpool. We lied. Sorry.'

'*Drove* me.' Even now, I have to be pedantic.

'He take me to the address of your son. I knock on door and ask him why he doesn't answer your letter.'

My lips are moving, asking silent questions.

'David was in hospital. Just back.'

'He's sick?' I've left it too late. I will lose my child, too.

She nods, pointing at her head. 'Brain problem.'

I freeze. Does he have some kind of mental illness? Is there a hereditary disorder I have passed on, despite the doctors' assurances?

'Is better now. I bring him in?'

'What?'

'I told you, he in the car.'

'David?'

'Who do you think, John Major?'

'No. I can't—' I sit down again, my stomach in my mouth. I'm not even wearing the outfit I bought for this meeting. My scarred wrist is exposed in the three-quarter-sleeved jumper I'm wearing. 'I mean, yes, bring him in.'

'It's been a long journey. He is a man. He has been ill, not allowed to drive down here in his own car. He needs to eat and drink.' I almost smile at her insistence that a male could not be expected to last a car journey without sustenance. She waves me down. 'Here.' She pushes my handbag over to me. 'Brush your hair and put on lipstick. Where's that scarf you bought?' Her quick glance finds it folded on the table by the front door. In two or three folds it is tied around my neck. 'That's better. Like the Queen but more fashionable. He will like.'

Meekly I tidy myself up and sit, clutching the base of my chair as though the wood will anchor me to the world. A car door opens and closes. They walk inside.

'I wait in car with Goran,' Naida says.

'Hello.' The man has a deep voice, a little like his father's perhaps, with that near-purr in it. He is a bit taller than Robert. I think his face has something of my own father's in it. I blink repeatedly, like a fast-action camera, trying to fill my mind with his image. My hands lift, I want to touch him, but I don't know how. I think of my mother, how she would greet me after a long school term, and go to him, pulling him into a hug. He is tight in my arms to start with, and then he softens. I want to rest my head on his chest, which is broad like his father's was. *Don't overdo it.*

I release him and gesture towards a chair. 'Would you like something to eat and drink?'

'It seems a bit mundane,' he admits, 'on first meeting you, but I would give anything for a coffee.'

I try to read his tone. Wary at the moment, I think. Can you blame him, dragged hundreds of miles south by two Bosnians to meet a mother he doesn't know? I remember Goran and Naida, still in the car outside, and go out to apologise and tell them to go home; David can sleep on my sofa tonight or in a local hotel if that is too much, too soon. Naida gives me a wink and instructs Goran to drive her home.

'I hadn't a chance to reply to your letter,' David says when I return. 'I was admitted. Bit of a nuisance.'

'What is . . . ?' It seems impertinent to ask my own child what the problem was.

'I sometimes have seizures.'

Relief and then anxiety flood me.

'I've had them all my life, but the medication sometimes needs tweaking.'

'All your life?'

'Yes.'

I think of David's birth, not that I can remember any of it. But could a baby born so suddenly, with an unconscious mother who couldn't assist in any way, suffer some kind of injury that might cause seizures? Perhaps they used forceps on him, damaged his head, while I was unable to protect him. 'I'm sorry.'

'Oh, most of the time I'm fine. Doesn't stop me doing anything.'

I go into the open-plan kitchen to prepare the food and drink, and hear the chair creak behind me. He's going towards the display cabinet. 'Those minerals are from the mine where your grandfather was engineering director.' How can it be that I am talking so normally? Inside I am like a cold jelly, shaking and sliding.

'Interesting. It's my line, too. I'm a geologist by training.'

So he's not just Robert's son: something from my side has been inherited, too.

'Tell me about yourself. Do you have . . . ?' The words can't pass my lips. I'm being greedy, asking for too much.

'A family? Yes. Paula, my wife. Two children, Sophie and Michael. Both at university now.'

Sophie and Michael. And *Paula,* my daughter-in-law. I repeat the names silently to myself.

'Your father, Robert, what did he say about me?' My shoulders stiffen as I ask the question.

'Not much. Dad told me you were very ill, in hospital, when I was old enough to ask about you.'

How often did you ask? I want to know.

'Then later, at about the time I was starting school, he said you were dead.' The words have a flatness to them. I try to imagine what it must be like to believe someone dead and decades later receive a letter from them.

'Did you know what was wrong with me?'

'When I was old enough to ask questions he said it was a serious mental illness. It sounded like some kind of psychosis.'

'It wasn't.' I sound so defensive. 'I mean . . . the psychiatrists tell me it was probably a series of traumas or something triggered by childbirth.'

His eyes widen. 'After she had Sophie, Paula had something the doctors called postnatal depression. I'd never heard of it before. She was lucky, they treated her quickly and she didn't suffer again the second time round.'

'Did she find it hard to remember things?'

He nods. 'Usually it was things that didn't matter, but she panicked that she'd forget she had a baby.'

The silence between us feels easier. 'It must have been a huge shock to find out I was alive. I'm amazed you agreed to leave your house with Naida and Goran at all.'

'Paula is convinced that I'm part of a Balkan kidnap plan aimed at subverting the peace process in Bosnia.'

I hear my own laugh. The cold, sliding feeling starts to disappear. 'People from that part of the world can have a certain persuasiveness to them.' I think of Ana persuading me that her son Miko was not going to harm me or my operation. Then I think of the persuasiveness of my ex-husband, how well he could spin a line. Deceiving his own son? Not a problem. But then perhaps Robert hadn't intended to be cruel.

'Robert might have thought that it was kinder to let you think I wasn't . . . around.' I'm going to try hard to be reasonable. The mad woman will be rational.

'Who knows what my father thought.'

I turn and squint at him, to see what his expression is.

'I tried to find out about you,' David says. 'About five years ago now, I made quite an effort. Of course, I didn't realise you were still alive or I'd have searched the telephone directories.'

He reads the unasked question in my face. 'I tracked you to Stoke Park in Kent. I wrote to the regional health board, but it seems there was a fire and all the patient records were destroyed. So I decided to go back to your time at Woodlands and see if your psychiatrist there knew anything more about you.'

For a second I see a boy's vulnerability in my middle-aged son's features. I tell him how I'd relocated from Stoke Park to The Mandalay in Sussex and then on to here.

'I did find your first psychiatrist, though,' he says. 'I wrote to her.'

'Dr Rosenstein?' Dr Rosenstein of the slender, expressive fingers with the photograph of her little girl in her office.

'She was very old, dying in fact, so she couldn't write back to me. But she asked her daughter to reply, saying she remembered treating you. She said she was sorry and shocked to hear you'd died young. She also said she had no doubt about the truth of what you told her. Of course, I didn't understand what she meant by that then. She said something about a senior civil servant telling her that she was not to treat you or talk to you again.'

A senior civil servant. Could it have been another of Robert's cronies? I'll never really know for sure. I doubt there are any surviving records I could use to prove it. Robert probably never put down on paper how he researched exactly who was at Woodlands with me. All the same, I'm still certain he sent that mysterious visitor to threaten Jim and force him to help with the plan to keep me locked up. Robert knew that the sight of the flames that burned when the Lysander was blown up had haunted me, and he was clever enough to work out how he could use an assault on the dovecot to arouse that trauma.

I never stood a chance against him.

'What did my father really do in the war?' David looks directly at me with Robert's hooded eyes. 'Because this is what it was all about, isn't it? Covering something up? Before he died, when he was starting to lose his mind a bit, James Holdern let something slip.'

Not for the first time.

'Robert was a very effective operator in the Balkans, opposing the Germans,' I tell him. 'He aided the Partisans, but felt anxious about growing Communist influence in that part of the world as the war ended. He started helping the Partisans' rivals in an attempt to keep Tito from heading north into Slovenia and then possibly into parts of southern Austria. He prevented the exfiltration of a German intelligence officer who would have exposed him.' Years of mulling it over have given me the ability to précis Robert's activities fairly neatly.

'I'm imagining he went against express orders to offer no assistance to the anti-Partisans, the Chetniks?'

I nod. 'If anyone found out, he would have been in trouble.' A traitor. I don't use that word.

'Would you have . . . ?' David shifts in the chair.

I think about it. 'I'm not sure. I did care for him. But bad things had happened to other people I was fond of.' I tell him briefly about Naomi and what had almost happened to Ana. 'Even then, who knows what I would have done. I was about to give birth.'

There's a silence while I consider all this as I serve coffee, bread, cheese and fruit. I remember that I have a bottle of slivovitz given to me by the sisters. I pour us small shots. 'To us.'

'To us.' We drink and help ourselves to bread and cheese.

'So Dad had you committed. No doubt with James Holdern's help. That man could pull a lot of strings.'

'Was he unkind to you?' My fingers tighten on the cheese knife.

'James? No. He treated me like a rather distant nephew, but he was kind enough and had my seizures treated by a specialist.' He butters a slice of bread. 'So you confided in your psychiatrist?'

'Not all of it. Not exact locations and names. I'd signed the Official Secrets Act. But enough to make Robert and whoever else he was working with worried.'

'But he managed to keep you locked away?'

'I think he leaned on someone I was close to inside Woodlands to push me into a kind of nervous breakdown.' I explain my theory about Jim.

'I don't know what to say,' David says. 'My father sounds like a monster.' He puts a hand to his head. I picture the wires of his brain that have been firing the wrong kind of electricity. Are they still causing him problems?

'He was . . . my husband.' I cooked his meals and walked to meet him from work in the evenings, and I did those things because I wanted to. 'He could be, oh, so kind, so perceptive. He could make me feel he was the only person who could understand me. I don't think you can fake that kind of thing, not completely.'

David puts his hand down. 'Once we were in the pool, in Greece with the Holderns. I was about six. He was keen for me to swim. I was scared, couldn't let go of the side. James told Dad just to throw me in: quickest way to get over a funk.'

Again my hand clenches the cheese knife.

'Dad ignored him. He pulled me out of the water and sat me on his lap. He described all the feelings I had, what I thought would happen when I let go of the side, how my head would go under and I wouldn't be able to breathe. It was as if he could see inside me. He told me I didn't have to swim, but also to think of going back to London and telling my friends I'd done a whole length by myself. He described how I'd have this warm glow inside me, how the other kids would look at me. How good that would feel. I got off his lap and jumped in, to the shallow end, mind you, and swam three strokes unaided.' He peels an orange, seeming reflective. I feel the need to pull him back to me.

'Do you have photos of the family?' I ask. David pulls a wallet out of his jacket pocket. 'I didn't have much time to pack, my Balkan drivers were . . . insistent, but there should be a picture in here. A bit out of date. They were still at school when we took this. We were skiing in France.' A woman with bobbed blonde hair. Two blond children who must have been in their mid-teens when the picture was taken. I devour them, find bits of my parents in their features. And something of Robert, too, particularly in Sophie, whose stance on her skis is panther-like. Her eyes are slightly narrowed in concentration as she smiles for the camera. I sense purposefulness. Michael is perhaps a little like my mother: nonchalant, amused. I express these observations to David. He laughs.

'I wish Michael had been more purposeful in his A-levels, but he's worked hard since he's been at university. Sophie is quite driven. She's in the sixth form.'

David tells me more about my grandchildren as we eat and drink. I tell him more about Mama and Dad. David outlines his own work in the Geology department. I wish my father could have heard him talk; they share a love of minerals and rocks. They should have spent time together, years back, before my father died. Anger floods me. I take a breath, trying to hide how I feel from my son. Robert was his father, after all.

'It was so wrong,' David says, perhaps seeing this struggle play on my features. 'All of it, but perhaps the worst bit was telling me you were dead. But . . .' He stops. On his face I can see a mixture of pain and something else: a question, perhaps even an accusation. And a fair one, too.

'You're wondering why I didn't make contact myself years ago?'

'I do understand that you thought you were sparing me some kind of stigma,' he adds.

I explain the places where I have lived, how the life there, even when you're not medicated, becomes so contained, so removed, that the thought of doing anything other than the quotidian is impossible.

'There's something else,' David says. 'I don't know if it helps or not. Dad let me think you'd been mad. That you'd died. But he also told me you had been a very brave young woman, had carried out a secret mission he couldn't describe. "Heroine" was the word he used. He said I could be proud of you.'

I bow my head to the table. For minutes I can't speak. I have to acknowledge something I have struggled with all these years: despite all he did to me, a small part of me has retained love for Robert. And I still believe he loved me. He deprived me of my child and my freedom in order to protect himself, but Robert was a man who could split himself into parts. He taught me to be someone else during my operation and it was a lesson he himself had learnt well.

'Dad also showed me some photos of you, on your wedding day. He told me you were beautiful. I see you still are.'

Our fingers touch briefly, just the tips, over the table.

'I didn't stab him, you know.' We haven't yet talked about the particular incident that had me locked up.

'What?' David stares at me. 'Stab him? That was the reason they sent you to the mental hospital?' He sounds shocked. Robert spared our son this detail. David pushes the plate aside and stares at the table.

'That scar on your father's abdomen?' He won't believe it wasn't me. 'It was on his right side, wasn't it?' I continue.

'Yes.'

'I'm right-handed.' I show him the cheese knife in my hand. 'And I was trained in combat. If I'd wanted to inflict a serious or fatal wound, I would have done it properly.' David frowns but then nods.

'James started to say something about the scar once but Cecilia shut him up.'

I lean forward. I have long wondered whether James knew the truth about what had happened in that scuffle in Robert's study. At least Robert didn't tell our son the lie about me stabbing him. Perhaps he had enough decency not to claim I'd done that to him.

We sit in silence for a moment.

David puts a hand to his head again. 'I'm still finding this a lot to make sense of. That he would do something like that to himself.'

My son is a child of the peace. He cannot think of cut flesh without being shocked. I am pleased that this is so.

'Would you mind if I rang Paula?'

'Help yourself.' I point to the receiver. 'I'll step outside for a cigarette.' I stand in my garden, shaking, looking at the last of the asters, waiting. David doesn't believe me about the stabbing. Why did I mention it?

Perhaps Paula will tell him to come home straight away, if there's a train he can catch at this time on a Sunday night. Everything has unfolded so abruptly. He must need time to think, to reflect. And perhaps it's been enough. What have I been hoping for? Why would he want to bring an elderly woman like me into his family?

I look for my snail. I want to see what words its slow trail is forming. But the snail does not show itself.

David opens the back door. 'I didn't mean to banish you. Sorry. The conversation lasted longer than I thought it would.'

Paula definitely told him to come straight home and leave the mad mother. David looks pale. 'I think we need another slivovitz,' I say.

He puts a hand to his throat. 'I don't suppose you have any wine or beer?'

He reminds me of myself when Branko offered me a flask of some fiery Balkan spirit on my first night with the Partisans.

'May I look at the crystals?' he asks when we've each drunk a glass of claret.

It's a good plan. Gives us time to absorb what's been said, to process it. I unlock the little mahogany cabinet, which came from the cottage in Trpca, stored on my parents' deaths and restored to me when I moved here.

'Who's this little fellow?' He points at the rabbit.

'He's yours.'

David's eyebrows rise.

'I bought him for you before you were born. Then I put him in my handbag and forgot all about him. Somehow he never went with you . . . when you went to the Holderns.'

David picks up the rabbit. 'I like his expression.'

'Take him,' I say. I bite my lip. Why would a middle-aged man want a soft toy?

'I'd love to.' His fingers tighten on the rabbit. 'But won't you miss him?'

'No.' The word starts as a lie because, in fact, the toy has become something of a silent companion since I moved here. But as I say it, I realise that I am delighted that it might finally be united with my son, even so many years too late.

David puts the rabbit on the table beside his empty wine glass and returns to the cabinet, picking up crystals and minerals, looking at them. Something in his eyes reminds me of my father again. It gives me confidence. I can make this easier: show David that he doesn't have to have split loyalties.

'Robert was under a huge strain just before you were born,' I say. 'He might have wanted to confide in me.' I can still remember my husband's expression at times when he looked at me. 'I found out about what he'd done. He had to think quickly. He got me locked away, but he chose Woodlands for me, knowing that Dr Rosenstein was regarded as enlightened.'

Robert wanted me on the right side of the green baize door, treated gently. Perhaps the couple of years he estimated I would be locked away would give him time to cover his tracks. Perhaps he could persuade me to say nothing when I came out. I might forget key parts of what I'd seen or be nudged into interpreting them in a different light. But I recovered more rapidly than he had anticipated. He wasn't ready. His dealings with the Chetniks might still get out.

'You mentioned Greece?' I say. A country where the British authorities couldn't touch him.

'He spent a lot of his time in Athens or on an island where he owned a small house.'

While I sat in grey day rooms Robert was out in the bright sunshine, free to come and go as he pleased. The mellower feelings I have been experiencing towards my former husband fall away. He didn't deserve his freedom. He was the criminal, not I. If he was here in this room I might take the cheese knife and stab him, for real this time.

Ana comes suddenly into my mind. Fierce, passionate Ana, who wouldn't think twice about killing an enemy; and yet she's speaking to me now and her words are words of reason. She tells me that rage destroys the good with the bad. Anger now will drive my son away from me. Ana was furious with Miko for joining the Chetniks, but when it came to it, the desire to heal him was stronger than her rage.

This is no time for anger.

David is still holding a silvery grey rock in his hand. Galena: a lead sulphide. He twists it so that its little speckles glint in the light. I remember my mother dusting these same minerals in the display case when we lived in Kosovo. They'd catch the sunlight and reflect it around the sitting room of our cottage in beams of white, silver, gold and violet. Mama would have spent part of the afternoon in the kitchen, letting the Serbian cook put her feet up, stoning plums or cherries for one of the cakes she loved to bake for my father and me. She would have let me beat the eggs, or scrape out the mixture into the baking tray. My father would come in, sniffing at the fragrant aroma. I should tell David about these scenes.

It's late now on an autumn night in London, but some of the Balkan sunlight seems to enter the small bungalow. 'I should find the photographs of our house in Kosovo,' I tell David. 'Those were happy days. And our holidays on the Dalmatian coast were good ones, too.' Somewhere there's a photo of my father and me in a canoe, paddling on a sunny Adriatic.

My own child and I have only known one another for a few hours in our entire lifetimes. Much between us remains wary, uncertain. But now I sense something else between my son and me: a willingness to try to know one another, to push beyond the past.

It's late, but David and I have time.

AUTHOR'S NOTE

As far as I know, the only female agent operating in Yugoslavia during the Second World War who could possibly be classed as British is Hannah Szenes (sometimes written as Senesh), a young Jewish woman in her early twenties, originally from Budapest, whose family had sent her to safety in Mandate Palestine. Hannah, a poet, volunteered to train as a British paratrooper and landed in Yugoslavia in 1944, on an operation very similar to that of my fictional character, Naomi. Hannah made it (just) into Hungary, but was almost immediately arrested and eventually executed. Amber and her operation are entirely fictional, but loosely based on the work carried out by a number of British and Allied operatives in Yugoslavia during the middle and latter stages of the war in Europe. Because the war in Yugoslavia is so complicated (even Robert's cake is a simplification), keen military historians will probably notice some details have been simplified, although I sincerely hope that the main thrust of the story of the Partisans and Chetniks remains true to life.

ACKNOWLEDGMENTS

As has been the case with pretty well every book of the nine I have written, special thanks go to Kristina Riggle and Johnnie Graham for reading and providing me with sensitive and probing comments on various drafts of this book. A big thank you to Sammia Hamer, Victoria Pepe, Celine Kelly, Emilie Marneur, Bekah Graham, Hatty Stiles, Sana Chebaro, Emma Coode and Trevor Horwood. Thanks also to my children for bearing with me cluttering up the kitchen table with my laptop and research books. A pat to Isla for providing entertainment and exercise.

ABOUT THE AUTHOR

 Eliza Graham spent biology lessons reading Jean Plaidy novels behind the textbooks, sitting at the back of the classroom. In English and history lessons, by contrast, she sat right at the front, hanging on to every word. At home she read books while getting dressed and cleaning her teeth. During school holidays she visited the public library multiple times a day.

At Oxford University she read English literature on a course that regarded anything post 1930 as too modern to be included. Despite this, she retains a love of Victorian novels. Eliza lives in an ancient village in the Oxfordshire countryside with her family. Her interests (still) mainly revolve around reading, but she also enjoys walking in the downland country around her home.

Find out more about Eliza on her website: www.elizagrahamauthor. com or on Facebook: @ElizaGrahamUK.